D0095743

The Hound of Justice

ALSO BY CLAIRE O'DELL

A Study in Honor

The Hound
of Justice

A NOVEL

Claire
O'Dell

Fitchburg Public Library
5530 Lacy Road
Fitchburg, WI 53711

HARPER Voyager
An Imprint of HarperCollins*Publishers*

This is a work of fiction. Names, characters, places, and incidents are products of the author's imagination or are used fictitiously and are not to be construed as real. Any resemblance to actual events, locales, organizations, or persons, living or dead, is entirely coincidental.

P.S.™ is a trademark of HarperCollins Publishers.

THE HOUND OF JUSTICE. Copyright © 2019 by Claire O'Dell. Excerpt from A STUDY IN HONOR © 2018 by Claire O'Dell. All rights reserved. Printed in the United States of America. No part of this book may be used or reproduced in any manner whatsoever without written permission except in the case of brief quotations embodied in critical articles and reviews. For information, address HarperCollins Publishers, 195 Broadway, New York, NY 10007.

HarperCollins books may be purchased for educational, business, or sales promotional use. For information, please email the Special Markets Department at SPsales@harpercollins.com.

Harper Voyager and design are trademarks of HarperCollins Publishers LLC.

FIRST EDITION

Designed by Paula Russell Szafranski

Frontispiece © Brandon Bourdages/Shutterstock

Library of Congress Cataloging-in-Publication Data has been applied for.

ISBN 978-0-06-269933-6

19 20 21 22 23   LSC   10 9 8 7 6 5 4 3 2 1

To the women of the resistance—
For taking names and getting it done

1

JANUARY 20. *Tuesday, for those who need to know. The day we get ourselves a shiny new president and . . .*

Well, at least we get that. I might not be so thrilled with a President Donnovan, but I'm glad as hell Jeb Foley didn't win the election. Foley would have done his best to drive the country backward into some mythical glorious past that only he and the old white men think of as better times. So, there is that. Maybe by the next election, the Democratic Progressives can stop bickering long enough to find a candidate who is democratic and progressive enough to fit the party name.

But enough about politics, let's talk about me. Because today I prove I'm ready to take up regular duties as a surgeon and leave behind this purgatory of in-between. Or at least, that's the plan.

My occupational therapist and I sat on opposite sides of her worktable. The air carried the faint scent of roses and the metallic smell of electronics. Afropunk music played softly in the background. This was Sydney's domain, as different from the rest of Georgetown University Hospital as Sydney herself.

Today she wore a sleeveless tunic of dark purple silk, embroidered with silver along the edges. Her hair was braided in narrow cornrows. No jewelry except a single silver spider-shaped earring.

"Thank you for skipping the party today," I said.

Sydney Okora regarded me with narrowed eyes. Her family had immigrated to the U.S. in the early 2000s, but when 2017 came around, her parents returned to Nigeria. Sydney had remained behind to finish her university studies. She was considered the best occupational therapist throughout the Eastern states.

"How could I resist?" she replied. "Your bright and cheerful self means more to me than any parade."

She spoke lightly, but I knew she understood how much I needed to prove I was capable of performing surgery with my new prosthetic device.

"I'm ready," I said. "More than ready. You said so last time—"

"I said nothing of the kind." Sydney's voice was soft, almost gentle. She reached across the worktable and laid a hand over my right arm. "My dear Dr. Watson, I realize that arrogance is a prerequisite for surgeons, but we are concerned with more than your ego. Consider, if you will, your patients."

I sucked my teeth. She was right.

"You think I should wait."

Sydney shrugged. "If you ask for my professional opinion, yes. You will need at least another month, most likely two, before you can attempt the most basic surgical operations. However . . . I believe an unofficial evaluation today might prove useful."

Useful for whom?

But I was not about to argue this concession. If I could prove to Sydney that I had mastered not only basic manual dexterity, but the complex programming of my new and very expensive prosthetic device, she might support me when I applied to the CMO to change my status.

"So," I said. "What kind of test would you recommend?"

She offered a brilliant smile. "The best, of course. But no, to give you an honest answer, there are three tests I would recommend. Play a melody on our practice keyboard. Knit me a dozen rows. Or . . . you might try braiding your hair. Since we are not conducting a formal evaluation, I shall leave the choice to you."

The keyboard exercise involved opposing action of flesh and electronic hands, with a necessary control for tempo and precision. I had practiced several different melodies daily, here and at home. Sara Holmes, who shared the apartment at 2809 Q with me, played the piano with skill and passion, and my clumsiness drove her to distraction.

Knitting. Another item in Sydney's playbook. Definitely not my favorite, though I had often wished I had the skill or inclination.

Oh, but braiding my hair.

When I first met with Sydney, she had asked what I had missed the most when I lost my arm.

Braiding my hair, I had said almost at once. *I miss braiding my hair.*

The most difficult test, the one I was most likely to fail. Even so . . .

"Door number three," I said.

Sydney nodded, as though she had expected this answer. "Very well. We shall start from the beginning."

The beginning meant *Prepare my stump and attach the device.* Though I wore my device everywhere during the day, Sydney insisted we start each session by removing it. Only then could she observe me as I went through the drill of prep, examine, attach. Every movement, she insisted, must become as instinct.

My new metal friend, aka the AIM 4675 programmable prosthetic arm, represented the most recent advances in target muscle re-innervations. A lightweight steel alloy mesh covered the arm and protected the very expensive electronics inside. The device itself had been custom-built to match the stump of my left arm, which was all that remained after an enemy bullet shattered bone and flesh. In the bright lights of Sydney's lab, the mesh seemed to wink at me. A mischievous device.

No, dammit. It's a device, not a living sentient thing.

But it would allow *me*, alive and possibly sentient, to reclaim my life.

"Are you timing me?" I asked Sydney.

"Not today. Unofficial, remember?"

Right. Let's get on with this.

Sydney kept her lab on the warmer side, unlike a hospital operating theater. Sydney's cat, Onomatopoeia, an ancient and irascible Persian the color of an overripe peach, sprawled on the floor, taking a long and deliberate bath. I glanced toward Ono, who paused just long enough to glare at me, tongue tip sticking out from her mouth.

I love you too, kitty-cat.

I surveyed the table and its supplies. Antiseptic wipes, check. Gel sleeve, check. Electronics test unit, check. Talcum powder measured out onto a sterilized cloth. Check.

"Supplies ready," I said.

Sydney made a note on her tablet with her stylus.

Next step. I rested my device on the worktable, flipped the control panel open, and pressed the sequence of buttons that would release the vacuum. With an almost too human exhalation, the arm dropped away from my stump and landed on the worktable.

I doubled over and clutched the edge of the table, suddenly dizzy. No matter how many times I had executed this procedure, there was a moment when my blood seemed to drop to my toes.

It never gets easy, the techs in the army had warned me. *Just easier.*

I inhaled slowly, let the breath trickle out from my lips. Not the most convincing display for someone who wanted to prove her competence. I kept my gaze on my device, as if contemplating the next step. I couldn't help comparing this sleek modern arm to the one it had replaced, an ancient ugly thing, its mesh tarnished and battered long before Saúl Martínez had amputated my arm, then argued with the military bureaucracy for even that inadequate device. And yet, that old and inadequate thing had served me—not well, but well enough, throughout a difficult time.

But Sydney was watching, and whether or not she timed me, she might decide that any hesitation meant I wasn't ready.

I shut down memories of Old Device and picked up New Device.

All these weeks and months of drill made the next few steps automatic. I examined New Device, from the socket and its electrical connectors, to the mesh covering, down to the tapered fingertips. The arm was as shiny and perfect as it had been this morning when I went through this same drill. But the rules said no shortcuts, and I had to agree. Do the drill right today, in the nice clean lab, and you won't make mistakes next month, when you're in the middle of an emergency.

As I made my examination, I reported my findings out

loud. No tears or dents in the metal mesh. No sign of corrosion where the electronic leads would connect to the contacts implanted in my stump. The programming panel opened and shut to my thumbprint. No dents. No scratches. The device looked nearly untouched, which you would expect since the arm had left manufacturing only six weeks ago. Even though I wore it daily, I never did anything more exciting than travel between my apartment and Georgetown hospital, with occasional side trips to the VA.

(NB: Sydney tells me the device is rated battle hardened. Its electronics can withstand acid, extreme temperatures in both directions, and even being submersed in liquids for weeks at a time. Maybe we should go to the beach together.)

"Device ready and operational."

Another notation made. I tried not to worry about the slight frown Sydney made, but I was sweating, and not just from the warm air.

I wiped my stump with antiseptic and dried the skin with a clean cloth. Next the talcum powder. After eight months of practice, I could maneuver the cloth onto my palm without much trouble. Once I was sure, I clapped the cloth over my stump.

A pang shot up my arm, and my stomach did a flip-flop. I pressed my lips together and breathed through my nose until the nausea faded. Somewhere in front of me, Sydney Okora was making notes about my competence, but I forced myself to ignore her. This was only a first test, I told myself, a progress report.

The gel sleeve was easier. I'd practiced this maneuver at home constantly, and it only took me a moment to slide the sleeve over my stump.

Now for you, my friend.

My hand closed over New Device, midway between its

wrist and elbow. Sydney had advised me to give the thing a name. *You will never be friends,* she told me. *But you might become allies. And allies have names.*

I had not yet reached the point where names made sense. Maybe next week.

The cap of the device fitted easily over my stump—the first and most obvious difference between Old and New Device. I had to twitch the gel sleeve with my teeth to undo a crease. Next time I would remember to check that, I told myself. If Sydney was recording all this, I no longer cared. I had a goal. Prove myself. Prove I was ready to take my place once more as a true surgeon.

A few taps on the control panel and the device clamped onto my stump. I felt the slight adjustments it made, the upper ring holding tight while the lower part eased a few millimeters in circumference, rotated, then clicked onto the electronic connections. After that, the adjustments rippled through the cuff, until my skin no longer felt twisted or pinched, and the device itself felt like a natural extension of my body. If I closed my eyes, I could almost believe I had never lost my arm.

Almost. Not quite.

I flexed my left hand. The fingers obeyed my thought, nearly as fast as my ghost hand, that invisible hand that lingered long after its amputation. "Obeyed my thought" was incorrect, of course. Electrical impulses from the brain activated the connectors implanted in my stump, which in turn triggered the device's numerous nanoprocessors. But Sydney encouraged me to use the phrase as yet another mental trick to integrate this metal arm as part of my body.

One by one, I curled the fingers into a loose fist, then pinched the air between my thumb and forefinger, then all the others in turn. Sydney had given me this exercise on our first day together. I'd made a great deal of progress, but I could still sense a brief delay between thought and movement.

That brief delay was why I had suggested today for this evaluation, and likely why Sydney had agreed. With the inaugural parade, anyone who could had taken a day's leave, and this wing of the hospital was emptier than usual. Emptier and quieter. Nothing to distract me.

So. Next step.

I had last braided my hair in April the previous year. Then came the attack on Alton, Illinois, when I lost my arm and nearly lost my life. Since then, I had kept my hair cut in a short Afro, but at the beginning of December, when Georgetown first offered me this fabulous position, I had started to let my hair grow. It was almost five inches long—definitely long enough to prove I had mastered the first stages of my new device.

Lazarus? Might I call it Lazarus, the arm risen from the dead?

I pressed a square button on the cuff. A small panel slid open to reveal an LED screen and two rows of touch-sensitive dots. I ran my fingers over the dots in the pattern for diagnostics. The LED status panel flickered, then glowed green for clear and ready to go. Now I carefully tapped in the sequence for small motor control.

A ping from arm to brain confirmed the programming.

I took a deep breath. "Ready, both of us."

Sydney laid out the necessary supplies: comb, clips, a small jar of cream, and a spray bottle of water. I dampened my hair and combed it out. The water Sydney provided me smelled faintly of roses. *Tiny steps*, I told myself. *I do not need to conquer the world today. Only one braid.*

I parted my hair and clipped back all but one small section, then scooped up a dab of the hair cream. The cream was expensive stuff, rich and buttery, possibly from Sydney's own stock. Then I tilted my head down and pictured my new hand grasping a thick strand of hair.

My metal fingers closed over a strand and gently parted the section in two. Using both metal and flesh fingers, I parted the two sections into three. What ought to have been an automatic gesture required all my attention.

Strand over strand. Do that two times. Add a bit more to the middle. That's right. That's my Janet.

My grandmother's voice came back to me, so strong I almost fumbled my hold. Ivy June Watson. Almost ninety years old. I had built up a picture of her as an imperious, implacable old woman, but there were older, fainter memories, from long before my parents announced their decision to leave Georgia for Southern Maryland and what might as well have been the North.

My fingers trembled, both metal and flesh. I sucked down a deep breath. Found the center of my concentration again. And really, there were worse memories than my grandmother teaching a four-year-old how to braid her hair.

Strand over strand, little girl. Add a bit more of that fancy cream your father done bought you.

I added a dab more cream and continued the braid. Half an inch, two inches. Nearly to the end. Time to finish off the braid. But as I reached for the clip, my prosthetic fingers gave a nervous twitch. My hair sprang loose, and the braid unraveled.

Dammit.

I smacked the worktable with my fist. Ono hissed at me from her corner, her fur ruffled, her ears flat.

I had it. Almost.

My left arm ached, flesh and ghost alike. My head throbbed with barely suppressed rage. A distant part of me observed that rage, almost dispassionately. The benefit of six months' therapy? Or was I simply tired?

"You did well." Sydney's tone was impossible to read.

"You mean I did better than you expected."

"We had different expectations, you and I. That doesn't mean you failed. Would you like to make another try?"

Yes, I would. But a headache lurked behind my skull, and my stomach felt mildly queasy. Caution overruled passion. "No. Thank you. Perhaps next week."

One day, I would not be able to refuse. One day, I would have to charge into surgery as though I were God. After all, a surgeon cannot expect the best of conditions. She must be ready to serve her patients anytime, anywhere. When the ER overflows. When a code blue sounds or the enemy overruns the border.

"You were right," I said. "I was wrong. I need another month at least."

Sydney said nothing. An answer all by itself.

"We can talk," I continued. "Tomorrow. About different drills. Whatever you think necessary. But please, not now."

I carefully undid the braid and combed out the hair. My right hand trembled. My device moved in awkward clicks, like an echo of my thoughts and emotions. Sydney remained silent, no sign of her thoughts on that blank face. Only when I moved toward the door did she round the worktable and lay a hand on my arm.

"You did not give up," she said softly. "You made a good try. You'll make a better one tomorrow. Remember, this is just one small obstacle, one small rock in your climb up and over the mountain."

A lovely platitude. Perhaps I would have it framed and hung on my wall. I thanked her anyway and hurried from the room before I said anything I might regret.

Georgetown University Hospital had changed very little since I interviewed there, almost four years ago. The halls were just as wide and lit by enormous windows. Dark blue tiles lined the floor, and the walls were painted a soothing green. My office was located on the third floor, one level down from the executive suites. Yet another signal of favor undeserved.

My workstation blinked awake as I sat down. I swiped my fingers over the bio-security pad. A holographic keyboard appeared on the desktop. The workstation connected me to the hospital network, dozens of medical research sites, and the public internet.

My Georgetown messaging app launched automatically in one window. A second, smaller window for my private apps appeared in the lower right corner. When I tapped the notifications icon, my private email opened up with a message from my old friend Jacob Bell.

Dear Janet,

Been a while since I wrote. Things are going about what you might expect, what with Donnovan promising peace and the GOP telling us we have to give in order to get. Which is, we ain't gonna get a peace that leaves us alive, unless we fight for our rights. I said that much in my latest, but a couple donors to the news squirt didn't like that, so I might need to dial back the honesty or find another job. I'll let you know. Leastways the college side of things is doing okay. Tell Sara I love her.

Dear Jacob, I thought. *I love Sara too.* Sara had done her best to help Jacob find a job to pay his bills while he studied for a degree in therapy, but not all loose ends stayed tied up neatly.

I started to type a reply, but I got no further than Hey, hello. I couldn't fake cheerful right now. Maybe tomorrow.

Next up were two spam messages, asking if I was interested in DIY shed projects. Um, no. Delete, delete. Onward through the junk my filters had not sorted out. I was zipping through the messages on autopilot when I had to backtrack with a curse. From address: Grace King. My sister.

Janet,

Aunt Jemele wrote to me last week. Gramma has taken a turn for the worse. Jemele says her mind wanders. It might be Alzheimer's, or something more profound, if anything could be more profound than that. We need to talk, you and me, about what we can do for her. I know you aren't much for family, but this is Gramma, after all. Jemele's getting older. Most of our cousins have left the farm. Call me when you can.

Love, Grace

I closed my eyes, more distressed than I had thought possible. Alzheimer's. Dear God in heaven. I had always thought of my grandmother as invincible. Strong. Stubborn. Smart.

Braid two stitches. That's right, girl. That's my Janet.

Oh, Gramma. How can I make this right?

Next week, I would call my sister and we could arrange proper care for our grandmother. At least my new job was good for that.

A job that required nothing more of me today. Our weekly staff meeting had been canceled, courtesy of the inauguration. One-on-ones with my two interns had been postponed until tomorrow as well. The blinking digits on the screen showed three P.M. Five o'clock rounds had not been canceled of course. And Dr. Hillaire had that surgery scheduled for four P.M. She had an older model of my AIM 4675. I could observe her techniques . . .

Abruptly I shut down my workstation and stared at the blank silver frame, which seemed so much like a portal into nothing.

Right. I know where that kind of thinking gets me. Nowhere good.

Well I was of no use here today. I wasn't even required to go to rounds. I collected my coat from behind the door, slung my bag over one shoulder, and headed out.

P

Cabs and buses were out of the question today, what with all the tourists, and the Metro wasn't much better. I set off on foot along Reservoir Road toward Wisconsin, then turned down a side street to avoid the crowds near the parade route. Even so, I came across more than one group of angry protesters. Most of them young white men with red baseball caps that had become—to me—a symbol of the old bad days when the U.S. slipped over the edge into fascism. Lots more were waving Donnovan/Webber signs, and one young woman had shinnied up a telephone phone and was fiddling with an electronic ad board. The board went dark a moment, then the lights flickered back on, spelling out VICTORY in the Democratic Progressives' party colors.

As I approached Volta Park, the crowds grew bigger and noisier. Uglier. A mob of red caps had started a fight with a group of young black men. Police were already moving in, Tasers in hand. One of the young black men crumpled to his knees. He threw his hands up in surrender, but not before a cop struck him again.

Dammit.

I started to run toward the man. Before I'd taken a few steps, one of the red caps staggered free of the brawl. He stared around wildly, his lips curled back in a snarl and a gun in one hand. That stopped me. Guns were illegal as hell, but I wasn't about to debate the Second Amendment with him.

I ducked into the nearest alley and crouched behind a dumpster, my pulse skipping. A gunshot rang out. Immediately after, a cop shouted orders through a bullhorn for everyone to stand down. The noise from the brawl had turned into a roar. This was going nowhere good, fast. I slid my cell from my pocket and tapped the contact number for Georgetown's emergency room.

A woman answered right away. "Georgetown Emergency."

"Dr. Janet Watson," I said. "There's a fight going on. Near Volta Park. You might want to get ready for incoming casualties."

The barest pause. "What kind of casualties? Did you call the police?"

I gulped down a laugh. "The police are already there. That's part of the problem." I wanted to say more, about the red cap with the gun, the police with their Tasers, when I heard the crackle of an automatic weapon. "Listen," I said. "I can't talk. It's going to blow up fast."

I shoved the cell into my pocket and raced down the alley to Thirty-Fourth Street. Some of the commotion had spilled over here, too. Mostly shouting, but it wouldn't be long until shouting turned to shoving. Then to something worse. Maybe I should call the ER again, give them an update.

Just then another gang of red caps came into view.

Right. Not out here.

Grocery stores and other small shops lined the block. With a glance over my shoulder, I ducked into the nearest one. The door swung shut, leaving me in a sea of quiet. I peeked through the tinted glass of the door. The gang had already passed by, and I released the breath I'd been holding.

"Welcome to Rainbow Books," said a voice.

I spun around, startled.

My refuge was a tiny bookstore, barely wide enough for two rows of shelves and the narrow aisle in between. What little I could see of the walls looked old-fashioned—the plaster painted cream above and rich indigo below, with a chair rail in between. The bookshelves were packed tight with paperbacks, sorted neatly by category. The air smelled deliciously of paper and ink, and a faint cinnamon scent that seemed to beckon me deeper inside.

Books. What a lovely surprise.

The woman at the checkout register smiled at me. "Looking for anything special?"

Her name was Adanna Jones, according to the nameplate next to the register. She was a black woman in her late forties, dark like me, with faint lines beside her eyes and her mouth. Her glasses were round, with dark red rims. Her hair was tinted a dark gold, and it puffed out like a cloud of sunrise behind a patterned head wrap.

"I don't know yet," I said. "To be honest, I came inside to get away from the crowds."

"As good a reason as any," she said, clearly amused. "But now that you're here, take a look around. We have new books, used books, poetry, novels . . ."

I was afraid she would try to hover over me, but Jones merely gestured toward the shelves and went back to tapping at the register's keyboard, leaving me to explore.

The latest bestsellers occupied a display at the front of the store. Farther on, the shelves alternated by category. Literary. Romance. Travel guides. Dictionaries. I came across a used books section stocked with early de Bodard and Kuang, even earlier Jemisin, but I already had copies of those. I drifted back to the newer SF section. The latest literary-SF crossover novel, from a brilliant new writer. An anthology of translations from Japanese authors. I picked out a book at random and frowned at the cover. Two men, both in drab overcoats, with a city skyline in the background. It looked . . . generic.

Maybe I should call the ER again.

"Having trouble finding the right book?"

I jerked away from the voice with a cry, and my arm swung

up to ward off the attack. The owner of the bookstore stood a few feet away, her eyes wide and wary.

"Sorry," I muttered. "You startled me."

"I see that," she said. "I'm sorry. Would you rather I left you to browse? Or would you like any help? I have a new shipment of books."

She was being kind, deliberately so. I wanted to growl, but I felt too raw with my own self-pity. If only I'd been brave enough to confront those police, to tend to the wounded. Except I knew what happened to black women who argued with the authorities, even in these enlightened days.

Besides, it wasn't her fault.

I managed a rueful smile. "You don't need to apologize. I—"

A dull boom rattled the building. I dropped to the ground without thinking. It was Alton, Illinois. It was the enemy overrunning our medical unit. Throwing grenades. Launching rockets at the radio tower. For a moment my vision went dark and I couldn't breathe.

(The radio towers squeal. Warning, warning, warning. This is not a drill.)

Dimly, I was aware of Adanna Jones scrabbling toward the wall. The next moment, I had snapped out of my flashback and was running out the door. This wasn't Alton, but there were people who needed me.

Outside, hundreds of people streamed past. A whistle shrilled overhead. I dropped to the pavement and rolled close to the building. A heartbeat later, the explosion came—loud—as though God had clapped her hands together and deafened us all.

My ears echoed from the explosion. My heart was beating far too hard, far too fast. My right hand was scraped raw by the pavement. My left arm, my shiny new left arm, had taken a few scratches, but I was alive.

Breathlessly, I waited for a third explosion.

None came.

All around me, others had fallen or dropped to the ground. A kid was sobbing. From farther away came a steady wail, punctuated by screams and curses. I staggered to my feet. Broken glass littered the sidewalk. At the next intersection, the traffic light had fallen into the street, and the corner building had taken damage. That way then.

I pushed my way through the panicked crowds. "Let me through. I'm a doctor."

The magic words. I would have laughed if I hadn't been so frightened.

One of the bombs had exploded on P Street, just two blocks away. I made my way through the tangle of metal and blood and lacerated bodies. Smoke from the explosion drifted through the street, and I nearly choked from the scent of burning flesh.

(*Memories of Alton flood my brain. One, two dozen patients from the medical unit sprawl over the ground, left in a bloody mess from the confederates' bombs.*)

I swallowed back my memories and pressed on. The first casualty I came across was dead. Bled out. His skin almost gray, except where his throat gaped from a wound. Two, three, a dozen more dead were tumbled about. Most of them adults, but more than a few children. I was sweating and swearing as I checked each one for a pulse.

At last I came to a woman, alive. She was panting hard, the way wounded soldiers did when the pain had gone from terrible to impossible. I checked her over as swiftly and gently as I could. There was nothing obviously wrong. Just a few scrapes and bruises . . .

"Can you wiggle your toes?" I said.

She stared at me, uncomprehending. Then her mouth

twitched open. She gasped for air, and the light faded from her eyes. Dead? But how?

I rocked back on my heels and stared at the body. Only then did I see the blood pooled underneath her.

Goddammit.

She'd died before I had a chance to save her.

I swallowed my grief, which did no one any good, and went on to the next.

Three more adults, all beyond help. Another one twitched in the last throes. There wasn't much I could do without a medical kit. I stopped the bleeding with tourniquets. I helped dig out those buried under rubble. By the time the first ambulance arrived, my throat was raw from the smoke, but I could give my credentials to the EMTs and deliver a summary of the victims' injuries.

Jennie was an EMT I'd met back when I was a resident. "You coming along?" she asked.

"Damn straight I am."

These were my patients, after all.

But as I jogged after my patients into the ER, one of the senior attending surgeons stepped into my path. Dr. Allison Carter. Tall and lanky, pale blond hair with a hint of silver, and more than the usual arrogance, if that were possible. Rumors said she might be our next chief medical officer.

"Where are you going?" she demanded.

"To change into scrubs. You'll want as many surgeons as you can get. It was a bloody mess out there—"

"You can't. You aren't cleared."

"What?" I lurched to a halt, confused. "What are you talking about? I'm a surgeon, the last time I checked."

"Not here." Her voice was cool, almost indifferent. "Hernandez wants you properly trained with that device before she lets you inside a surgical theater."

"But I could—"

"No. No, you can't. Look, Watson. I don't give a flying fuck if you were the biggest goddamned hero at Alton, Illinois. Here, you're just an equal-opportunity gimp, with one hand and a bad attitude. If you really want to be useful, go help the ER with triage. I have work to do."

Midnight. Eight hours later.

Surgeons and nurses of the night shift had joined with day shift to deal with the influx of patients. I'd done my own part to help triage the wounded.

Even if I was an equal-opportunity gimp with an attitude. Did that still rankle? Yeah, damn straight it did.

I paid off the cab driver and stared up at 2809 Q. All the windows were dark at this hour. A lamp outside illuminated the front door and cast a circle of light over the two sets of steps winding through the narrow front lawn. Come spring, ivy would cover the lawn, and wildflowers would grow from planters under all the windows, but right now, the ground was bare, and the air carried the raw wet scent of winter. A few snowflakes drifted down from the skies.

I climbed the steps wearily and pressed my right thumb to the biometric lock. The door clicked open, complaining softly on its hinges, as if it too had had a long and exhausting day. Outside our apartment, I paused. Light leaked around the edges of the door, and I heard several voices. Men's voices. Sara Holmes was awake then. And she had visitors.

I braced myself to face strangers and opened the door.

All the lights in our apartment were turned up high. The sweet stale odor of clove cigarettes filled the air, which was hazy from the smoke. Holmes herself was sprawled on the couch in our living room, her feet propped on the table and a bottle of whiskey in her lap. A small hand-built radio sputtered and squawked in one corner—one of the underground stations that broadcast over the dark net. A small video box rested between her feet. She was alone.

I plopped myself into one of the chairs. The ashtray overflowed with ashes. One lit cigarette was propped against the edge. On the vid-box, a square pale face shouted incoherently. A chyron streamed past, labeling the man as Richard Speiker, a leader of the Brotherhood of Redemption.

Sara tilted the bottle and took a swallow. "You idiot."

Her voice came out as a growl.

Ah, that would be directed to me.

I cleared my throat. "I'm sorry. I should have called."

"Goddamned right you should have called." Her speech didn't slur, but I noted that the bottle was half-empty.

"I'm sorry. I thought you would—"

I thought you would know already.

A thought better left unsaid.

When I first met Sara Holmes, she was a freelance operative for one of the government's alphabet agencies. FBI. CIA. That kind of spy. She had special implants that connected her to the great ocean of data courtesy of the web and other, less public sources. With those implants, Sara would have heard every detail, official and not so official, about today's events.

But the agency had disabled Sara's implants—just one consequence of our unauthorized investigation into Adler Industries and the shame of Alton, Illinois. That we'd succeeded in our investigation, and that it had proved useful to the government, meant we'd avoided prison. It had even led to my job at Georgetown University Hospital. However, as Sara put it, her chief could not overlook Sara's sins, so Sara had been put on an extended leave of absence.

Sara clicked off the radio and vid-box. Silence dropped over the apartment.

"You frightened me," she said softly.

That got my attention. Nothing frightened Sara.

"I took a cab home," I said. "I've learned that much."

She laughed, a strange wheezing laugh. "I thought you had blundered into the wrong place at the wrong time. And—" Here she gestured at the silvery discs behind her ears. "These are no longer quite so informative as I would like."

Did I happen to mention that Sara was not taking this enforced leave very well? Right. A bit redundant, that piece of information.

"The only place I blundered was into a bookstore," I said. "Two streets away, and safe enough. I've been at the hospital since then. Doing triage."

"Good for you. Want a drink?" She lifted the bottle.

I shook my head. "I have an early start tomorrow. My session with Faith."

"Ah. Her."

Sara's tone was impossible to read, but I was used to that.

"What *did* you hear about the bombing?" I asked.

"Terrorists. Obviously. A fringe group from across the border called the Brotherhood of Redemption, according to my sources. You saw their leader there." She indicated the radio and video box. "Though why they are considered *fringe* is an interesting question. Very incompetent terrorists. That much is obvious."

A swift and vivid memory of the blood, the tangle of bodies, the cries of the wounded, the silence of the dead overwhelmed me, and I needed a moment to recover. "They did a pretty good job, from what I saw."

She made a dismissive gesture. "They were amateurs. Otherwise we'd have a different president by now."

Oh, dear god. Those explosions over by Thirty-Fourth Street could have taken out Donnovan, his VP, and any number of others in the line of succession.

"I suppose we should be grateful," I muttered.

"Never regret the enemy's stupidity," Sara replied. "What puzzles me is why the New Confederacy would wish to assassinate the man who offered them peace, even at the price of compromise."

"What does your chief say?"

"I don't know. I'll find out next week."

Next week marked the end of Sara's leave of absence. Good. Holmes with a mission had proved impossible, incorrigible. Holmes cut off from her usual information sources and left adrift? Well, I hadn't murdered her yet, but the odds were shifting in that direction.

She offered the bottle again. This time, I took a swig of the whiskey, then stood up. "Time for bed," I told her.

Sara grunted and lit another cigarette.

I headed to my bedroom and shrugged off my coat onto the bed. It landed with a thump, which surprised me. When I searched through its pockets, I discovered a small paperback. Something something classic SF in the vein of some author whose name I didn't recognize. The cover was as generic as the title. It took me a moment before I remembered the bookstore—Rainbow Books. I must have stuffed the book into my coat pocket before I plunged into the chaos. God. I'd have to make time tomorrow to return it.

I dropped the book onto my desk, and myself onto the bed. My bones ached. My muscles ached. And my shiny new device, though it fit my stump so perfectly, felt like a heavy useless weight.

Practice, Sydney Okora told me every week. *Practice until your new device becomes an extension of your own body.*

I raised my left arm and curled each finger one by one until I had a fist. The faint light from the corridor seemed to catch fire along the mesh covering.

Next week, Sara would resume active duty with the FBI, or whatever shadowy subsection of the agency she belonged to. Next week, she would get her implants activated. She might even gain that much-needed assignment.

But what happens to us? What happens to this apartment? How much longer will we have this refuge of beauty?

I ran through the usual exercises Sydney had assigned me. Finger curls. Stretches. Slowly at first, then faster. My metal hand lagged only a moment, if that, behind the ghost hand of memories. Was I truly making progress? I couldn't tell, not today, not after Allison Carter had shamed me in the ER.

Even so, I persisted.

By the time I finished, Sara had turned off the radio, but Richard Speiker's voice droned on from the vid-box about the dangers of white annihilation. Once, I had believed his kind was an anomaly. Once, in spite of all the evidence against me, I had believed our country had escaped the fascism of the late 2010s. Apparently not.

Speiker's voice faded away. The apartment was dark and quiet. I undressed for the night and removed my device. Lazarus. Maybe I would ask Faith what she thought about the name.

2

Ten thirty A.M., Wednesday. I had twenty more minutes to fill with Faith Bellaume, and I was damned close to saying, *Let's stop pretending. We aren't neither of us feeling it today.* Oh sure, Faith had started off with a pointed question about yesterday's bombing and whether it had called up the old bad panic courtesy of Alton, Illinois.

Of course it did. Created a whole new set of nightmares, too, thank you very much.

But I wasn't up to talking about my nightmares, so I offered an answer straight out of the Good Patient Handbook. Yes, I'd panicked. (*The patient admits to a natural reaction.*) But I'd managed to get my panic under control. The drills, you know. They helped a great deal. (*Patient acknowledges the value of medical advice.*) From there I babbled on about the everyday stress that came with a surgeon's job, carefully skirting any mention of my confrontation with Dr. Allison Carter.

I'd about run out of invention when Faith held up a hand.

"You are angry."

Statement, not a question.

Okay, then.

"I'm always angry," I said. "Ask me something new."

She nodded, as though she'd expected this push-back. "Very well. You are angry. Why, then? Why, when you have that expensive new prosthetic, and a job beyond anything you hoped for?"

All the words I had flayed myself with for the past six weeks.

I sucked in a breath and hunkered down onto the padded bench, metal hand clasped in flesh. The air in the room seemed unnaturally thin, as though I had climbed a mountain. More dangerous were the sparks, like lightning, that signaled a storm of rage.

Safe space, safe space. Remember your safe and happy space.

I reached out for that small and vivid memory, of the moment when the acceptance message from Howard University showed up in my inbox. My parents—both my parents, alive and enveloping me in hugs. My sister, Grace, standing off to one side, rolling her eyes, but with her mouth tilting into a smile. And me thinking, *I did it. I will do it. Yes, I can.*

Of all the moments in my life, this one remained strong. Faith had worked with me for weeks, first choosing a memory, then teaching me how to immerse myself in all its details whenever despair sucked me into the dark hole of rage and terror.

With an effort, I untangled my fingers and forced out a breath.

"I want to be a surgeon," I said.

"You've mentioned this from time to time. How goes the occupational therapy?"

"It goes," I said. "Not as fast as I would like."

"Hmmmm."

"I understand this will take some time. I just . . ."

I just want to deserve my very expensive new device and that high-paying new job, which, by the way, came courtesy of the U.S. government, or at least of Sara Holmes. All to keep me quiet about the events of last October.

"I'm not sure I can explain," I said. "It's complicated."

That was our code word for "subjects of a sensitive nature related to national security," or what I called "things we were not allowed to discuss in any detail."

Faith nodded. "We are constrained, you and I."

What a pretty way to put that. Sara's people had offered me a choice. Choose another therapist, one cleared to discuss any issues related to Adler Industries and the events in Alton, Illinois, and Jonestown. Or, continue to meet with Faith Bellaume, but with certain restrictions.

I chose Faith. I could tell when a representative from the agency had visited her to explain these restrictions, because throughout our next session, she had studied me with an air of open curiosity. She'd said nothing, of course. Nor had I.

I tried again. "It's a matter of whether I deserve these gifts. Yes, yes, that's all the baggage of memories. I know. But . . . I would be happier if I were making faster progress. Georgetown isn't a charity. They'll want good value for their money."

Another *hmmm.*

"And," I went on, "I want good value for that money too. I have my pride. I trained hard to be a surgeon. I thought I'd lost everything after Alton. Turns out life gave me a second chance. I don't want to screw this up."

"Which frightens you."

"Of course it does."

I took another deep breath, remembered how my father had gripped me by both shoulders and said, laughing and crying, *Goddammit, girl. Goddamn, I knew you'd do it.*

"I'm frightened," I whispered. "Frightened and tired and fresh out of epiphanies. Check back next week for a new delivery. I need you to help me out today."

"All right," she said softly. "Let's start with our list of guilty words."

Meaning, words that poked at my guilt.

"*Deserve*," she said. "*Charity. Value.*"

I shuddered. Words that my parents had used all the time. Not against me or my sister. But still. Words soak into our brains, Faith told me early on in our sessions. Good and bad ones, both. Her job was to teach me how to recognize them first, then how to cope.

The coping part was going slowly.

"My value is not the same thing as my job," I recited. "It's not a marker of what I deserve."

"You don't sound convinced."

"I'm not. I— It's complicated."

"Ah, that word again. Necessary, I understand. But you must not use that word to avoid difficult topics. Well, let's talk about charity today. You're a surgeon. How long does it take for your patients to recover?"

An all-too-obvious question, but at least I was more annoyed than angry.

"It depends on the injury," I replied.

She laughed, a low musical laugh that reminded me of my mother and the South. Faith had been born in Mississippi, as her parents moved state by state toward the East Coast after Hurricane Katrina. Yet another tenuous bond between us, and another reason I chose to keep her as my therapist.

"Very well," she said. "We won't argue the matter. But consider . . ." Here she leaned forward over the table. "Consider what you lost at Alton. You lost your arm. You lost your confidence. Your sense of self, or at least the one you depended on for so many years. You need time, Janet. Time to learn this new definition of your body. Time to *heal*."

I'd never heard her speak so passionately before. I caught my breath, unable at first to reply, or look away.

She smiled—a bit ruefully, I thought.

"So," she said. "Let us discuss a few techniques."

In our remaining time, we talked about trigger words, about coping, about the necessity for kindness. Faith and I both knew that talking was the easy part. She could not teach me kindness; she could not magically erase the arguments I heard between my grandmother and my parents, or the belief that if I only gained this one success, then all the anger between them would disappear.

But talking did help, at least for a time. It was like steam escaping from the boiling kettle. Better to talk than explode.

Our session came to another predictable end. I drank a last cup of lemon-flavored water, while Faith regarded me with those calm brown eyes. Any moment now she would launch into the usual windup—a summary of what we'd discussed, the reminder to practice my one-minute meditation, a comment that she would see to refilling my scripts for antianxiety meds . . .

"We are making progress," Faith said. "*You* are. I can see it."

"Except?" I prompted.

"Except that you have these moments, where you lose yourself to the world." When I started to speak, she held up a hand. "Mind, I'm not saying you don't have cause to be angry. You do. But there's a difference between acknowledging your anger and letting it harm you, and while our talks, and your medication, can help, I'd like to explore another technique. One we can use in addition to talk therapy. I'll tell you more about it next time. It will be your choice, naturally."

Naturally. Faith had proved remarkably persuasive these

past six months. But no, I was being unfair. Every single decision about my therapy had truly been mine alone.

I nodded. "Thank you. Until next time."

Afterward, as usual, I met with the assistant to schedule my next appointment. Every two weeks, these days, when once I had come two or three times in a single week. Perhaps I was making progress after all.

Even so, I felt queasy as I made my way to the exit of the VA hospital.

Outside, the day was raw and cool. Late January, with clouds scudding overhead and the scent of snow in the air. My back ached, where Nadine Adler had shot me.

A taxi came around the corner—one of those auto-drive cabs with the fancy new technology designed to recognize a human flagging them down. Its medallion signaled it was available, but when I waved a hand toward the camera sensor, it never slowed.

A second cab coasted along, another auto-drive. It, too, passed me by.

I blew out a frosted breath. *Damn. I should just walk.*

A third cab zipped by, only to stop halfway down the block for a young white couple. One wore military fatigues; the other was heavily pregnant. The servicewoman glanced in my direction, clearly embarrassed. She spoke to her partner, and they both gestured for me to take the cab. I shook my head and smiled to show I was okay.

A few more taxis drove by, some with drivers, some not. Six months ago, when I had an old, battered device, when I dressed in patched fatigues, no one had stopped for me, not without a lot of arguing. Seems that nice clothes and a shiny new device didn't make much difference.

Another cab, with an actual human at the wheel, pulled over to the curb.

"Taxi, ma'am?"

He was black, like me. And he reminded me of Jacob, with his close-cut Afro, speckled with silver.

I climbed into the cab. "Georgetown hospital, please."

"You got it, sister. How fast you wanna go?"

"As fast as the speed limit, my brother. That fast and no more."

He grinned, and the taxi jolted into traffic.

I leaned back and closed my eyes. Therapy always left me drained and off-balance. Afternoon rounds would cure me of that. I could watch from outside the circle of doctors and interns, an interested observer without any need to truly involve myself in the patient's fate.

What about your own fate, my friend?

I heard those words in Saúl Martínez's voice. Back in the service, on one of those days where we'd lost too many patients, and I was ranting in despair, Saúl had served up shots of whiskey and advice. He'd warned me about the danger when a surgeon crossed the line between caring for their patient and seeing every setback, every death, as a judgment from God.

Saúl, dead last October . . .

I pressed both hands against my eyes. Drew a steady breath, then another, and focused on this moment. Saúl's death was not my fault. Nadine Adler had ordered his murder simply to make certain he and I could not discuss all those mysterious deaths. I knew that. At the same time, I wished I had never emailed him about Belinda Díaz. He might have lived. He might have—

My cell buzzed for an incoming message. I dug the phone out of my pocket and swiped the screen.

EHernandez, read the display.

Chief Medical Officer Dr. Esma Hernandez, that was.

I pressed my thumb to the identi-pad and tabbed the *Accept* icon, but the call had already switched over to voice mail. *Shit.* Had Carter complained about me then? I wouldn't have been all that surprised. Carter had a reputation for trampling roughshod over people she considered competitors. I hadn't thought of myself as one, but who could tell?

The voice mail icon blinked. Reluctantly I pressed the button to hear the message.

"Dr. Watson. I have a few issues to discuss with you. It's nothing but politics, but I want to get your input. Come see me ASAP once you report in."

My stomach folded into a cold knot. *Issues. Politics.* Those were all code words for *We regret offering you this position.*

Girl, you are letting your imagination run away with you.

Maybe so, but sadly, I couldn't order my imagination around. The twenty minutes to GUH seemed more like a hundred and twenty. When the driver pulled over to the curb, I tipped him an extra ten and jogged up the steps to the front door.

♀

Dr. Esma Hernandez leaned over her desk and fixed me with a pleasant smile.

"It's a matter of politics," she said. "Personal as well as hospital politics, this time. I warned you at the beginning that there would always be someone who resents you. For your title, your salary. Never mind your qualifications. It's the same for everyone."

I fixed an equally pleasant smile on my face and waited for the rest.

"In your own case," she went on, "we have the extra matter of your new device and occupational therapy. Some see this as special treatment."

Those were a *reward*, I thought. Not to mention, a bribe for my silence. But of course, those who granted such rewards would expect more. They always did.

"What's your advice, then?" I asked.

She paused a long moment, and I braced myself.

"A delay," she said at last. "A short one. We originally planned for you to transition to full-time surgeon in June. Now . . . I believe we should wait until later in the year. Meanwhile . . ."

Meanwhile, she wanted me to submit an abstract to the fifth annual International Conference for Critical Care, sponsored by Georgetown University, with additional funding from the federal government. I vaguely recalled noise about the event its first year. Saúl had made several caustic remarks about buying a good reputation with a couple open bars and a spotlight on ambitious doctors.

Still. Conferences had their good points. And Georgetown liked their senior medical staff to give talks and write papers.

"You could present a paper on treating patients under wartime conditions," Hernandez went on. "Write up a few proposals and we can review them together. Depending on the reception, you could submit a fleshed-out version of the paper to medical journals."

And it would quash any rumors of special treatment.

I accepted the paperwork from Hernandez. Something in my expression must have showed because she quickly said, "It's political, nothing more. It's the game we play at this level. You must understand."

"Of course," I said.

We exchanged perfunctory smiles. Perhaps that was all Hernandez required—a reassurance that I would play the game of politics. But when I stood up to leave, she gestured for me to stay.

"I've been remiss with our one-on-ones," she said. "Tell me . . . how does your training go? Sydney forwards me regular reports, of course, but I like to hear things from the patient's perspective."

Oh, you do, do you?

"It goes," I said slowly. "We've scheduled an official evaluation next month."

"That's excellent," she said, with far too much enthusiasm. "I know we told you that you would have six months of training, but if you need more, you shall have it."

More code words, this time for *Are you worth the time?* And *Is this occupational therapy worth the money?*

Both of them dangerous questions.

I could only nod, however, and murmur something about researching an appropriate topic for the conference. Hernandez didn't mention my confrontation with Carter the day before. I didn't mention any doubts about my progress with my device.

"Do you think you can have that abstract to me by the end of April?" Hernandez said. "Deadline is May fifteenth."

"At least one," I replied. "We don't want to limit our options, after all."

Hernandez eyed me with faint suspicion—perhaps I'd overdone the bland and cooperative—but all she said was, "I have every confidence in you, Dr. Watson."

♀

I took my leave and retreated to my luxurious—my undeservedly luxurious—office. *Undeserved* was another trigger word, which I could recognize, but which I had not yet learned to ignore. Later, I told myself. Later I would review all the lessons Faith Bellaume had taught me. Later I would practice my drills with fingers and hands, which might not translate directly to surgery, but which were nonetheless necessary.

I spread the sheaf of papers from Hernandez across my desk. This conference—this conference launched and supported by Georgetown University—had collected all kinds of prominent speakers over the past four years. Surgeons from all over the Federal U.S. and the rest of the world would scrabble for even ten minutes on the schedule. It was only when I read the list of attendees that my heart took a sudden and uncomfortable leap.

Angela Gray, MD, PhD. Specialty: Orthopedic surgery. Proposed topic: Research into physical therapy for children younger than six.

My stomach twisted into a knot. Oh god, no. It was bad enough to face the rest of my peers with my uncertain status here at Georgetown. I could not, just could not, face Angela again.

My workstation pinged softly. I rubbed my forehead and sighed. When it pinged a second time, I tapped the ID pad to unlock the workstation.

My schedule for the day materialized in the center of my screen. Morning rounds, and the block of time I marked "Private" for Faith Bellaume, had already passed into the grayed-out zone of recent history. My OT session was outlined in yellow, meaning tentative. For that, I clicked *Confirm*.

The OT appointment scrolled up, to be replaced by my weekly one-on-one with Anna Chong, one of the two surgical interns I now mentored. Or at least, mentoring her was my goal. Chong liked to argue—my god, she loved to argue. It must have been part of her DNA. Whatever advice I gave, she challenged me, and our sessions left me exhausted. Had I been that arrogant? Likely, yes. Make that definitely yes.

Saúl Martínez would have known how to handle this brilliant young woman. He'd have challenged her right back, then listened hard to what she had to say, until the argument turned into a conversation.

As if on cue, my workstation chimed with an incoming message. From Chong? I tapped the virtual mouse and a new pop-up appeared center screen. Dr. Watson, could we move our one-on-one to tomorrow? I would like to observe Dr. Carter's surgery this afternoon.

I slapped the keyboard. The message winked out.

Dammit. Such a reasonable request, and yet I felt betrayed. By Carter, who had shamed me the day before. And by Chong, who clearly wanted a genuine working surgeon as her mentor.

Welcome to the pity party, I thought. *Why don't we all eat some worms?*

Right. Enough of that. It was eleven thirty A.M. Time enough to get started on that abstract. I tapped Chong's message again and told her that tomorrow would be fine, and we could discuss Carter's techniques, if she liked. Then I turned my attention to possible topics for that conference.

♀

Five topics considered; all five discarded by noon. I toyed with the idea that Hernandez intended to break my spirit with this task, but that was too egotistical, even for me.

I broke for a late lunch with residents Letova and Pascal. Someone had left the cafeteria video monitors tuned into a newscast channel. Images of earnest pundits alternated with video clips showing Richard Speiker and other leaders of the Brotherhood.

. . . We will not be silenced. We will not surrender. The fate of our culture is at stake . . .

Words that recalled the terrible years under Trump and

his enablers. When the news pundits told us to give hate a platform or else we would endanger free speech. Finally, Pascal marched over to the video controls, and in spite of protests from a group of orderlies, she switched the box off.

"Damn them all to hell," she muttered when she returned to our table. "And by 'them,' I mean those bastards in the Confederacy."

She picked at her salad, scowling at the croutons. She and Letova worked the day shift this week, but both had been summoned to emergency duty last night. Nina Letova in particular had that exhausted grieving look of someone who had lost a patient.

"I hate them," she said in a low voice. "Bloody murderers. There were children yesterday . . ."

She rubbed the back of her hand over her eyes. "Sorry. Sorry. I'm fine. Or I will be. You know how it goes."

"That I do," I said softly.

Fifty people dead. Two hundred more injured, most of them still in critical condition. Sara Holmes had said the terrorists failed, but for once, the official newsfeeds and underground squirts agreed. Terror was terror, whether you hit your original target or not.

One P.M., with Sydney. She gave me a new exercise involving a touch-sensitive board, which measured the pressure of my fingertips against its surface. My goal, she told me, was to aim for the lightest touch the surface could measure. I managed it just once.

Three P.M., I spent the time for Anna Chong's one-on-one reviewing more topics, with intervals dedicated to hating Allison Carter.

Four P.M., Veterans Advisory Committee. One of the duties I had where I felt truly useful, what with my experience in the service. Maybe all that time in the VA Medical Center counted for something.

Five P.M., afternoon rounds.

Seven P.M., done for the day. I shut down my workstation and keyed the lock for privacy. I'd made little progress toward a suitable topic for that damned medical conference. Pascal had promised to help me brainstorm later in the week.

Outside the day was cool and raw. In less than three months, we'd see cherry blossoms over the Mall. Right now, I was grateful for my down coat and insulated gloves, both of them gifts from Sara Holmes.

I was getting better at accepting gifts these days. Maybe that counted as progress too.

A cab slowed down as I approached the curb. I waved it on. A walk would do me good. It came back to me that I still needed to return that damned book.

Quite a bit had changed on Thirty-Fourth Street since the day before. Most of the windows were boarded over. The traffic lights around here blinked yellow, and the street itself was cratered and cracked. They had cleared away the broken glass, at least, and I didn't see any signs of blood.

No, that would be the next street over. Where you saw the dead and dying.

Rainbow Books was warm and quiet. A few customers browsed the shelves. Adanna Jones sat behind the register, counting out change to an elderly black man. I waited until he had exited the store before I approached the counter.

She glanced up and smiled. "May I help you?"

"I came to return a book," I said awkwardly, holding out the novel. "I didn't mean to take this without paying—"

Now she recognized me.

"Oh, I remember you. You went charging straight into danger."

She accepted the book and glanced at its cover. Her gaze flicked up to mine as she assessed me, this reader in her shop. "Not a book you would care for," she said. She hesitated, then went on, "I saw you tending to the wounded. You're a doctor?"

I hesitated, not sure what to call myself these days.

Trigger words, whispered Faith's voice in my memory.

"I'm a surgeon," I said. "Or I will be again." I lifted my left arm and twisted my hand around so that the mesh glittered in the bright lights of the shop. Adanna Jones did not even flinch at the sight of Lazarus, nor did she offer me any obvious pity.

"You were in the war," she said.

I nodded. "Alton, Illinois. Though I didn't expect to see combat."

"Neither did my brother," Adanna said. "He was a company clerk, behind the lines at Jonesboro. He died when the enemy overran their post."

Another death I could blame on Nadine Adler, whose drugs had turned ordinary soldiers into killing machines, for both the Confederacy and the Federal States.

"I'm sorry," I said.

She shrugged. "So am I. I miss him every day. You've lost a few friends yourself, I can tell."

I wanted to tell her about Saúl, about my parents, but I was all too aware of the presence of other customers. Besides, this woman was not my therapist.

"I should go," I said. "I promised my chief medical officer I would write a paper, only I seem to have run out of ideas."

"Ah, what you need is inspiration. I believe I have the book for you."

She disappeared into the back of the store. Moments later, she returned with a small slim book in hand. "Try this one," she said. "No, I don't want your money. Consider this a gift, in honor of your service."

Poetry, by Rumi, said the cover.

Well, there were worse sources of inspiration.

I tucked the book into my pocket and headed back out.

Apartment 2B at 2809 Q Street NW was empty, which surprised me. Sara had texted me earlier, saying she would be home for dinner, and please to let her know if I planned any further adventures.

A slow cooker with a bubbling stew of chicken and peppers and beans waited on the kitchen counter. Next to it was a plate holding a freshly baked loaf of bread. No note, but Sara's absence and this dinner told me everything I needed to know. Sara had cooked, then had been called away unexpectedly. Perhaps her exile had ended early.

I spooned out a bowl of stew and carried it and my new book into the living room, with its grand view of DC. Twilight had fallen. The skies were a murky starless gray. The Washington and Lincoln Monuments were like two strokes of light amidst the gathering dark, but even as I watched, the lights of the city winked into life.

I propped my feet on the table and balanced the bowl in my lap. Savored the first bite of stew, then opened the book of poetry Adanna Jones had given me. *A Call for Seekers of Truth,* said the dedication page. Hmmm. That could prove interesting . . .

3

Ten days had passed since "The Bloody Inauguration," as the newsfeeds dubbed it. The squirts had even blunter, bloodier names. Melodramatic, both of them, but this time I agreed. I'd been right in the middle of things. I'd seen the bodies like shredded rag dolls.

One of the victims of the bombing lay in a hospital bed, connected to an IV and at least two different monitors. Athena Washington, fifty-four years old. Her husband and grandson had been killed immediately. Her daughter had survived the bombing, only to die before the ambulance reached the hospital.

Morning surgical rounds had begun half an hour ago. Dr. Teresa Navarette was the chief resident in charge. The intern making the presentation was fumbling with her notes, and generally making a hash of things. Any moment now, I expected Navarette to intervene with a question guaranteed to set this poor young woman at ease. She was good that way.

"Yassin."

Allison Carter shouldered her way through the crowd of

interns and residents. She cast a brief glance at me in my shiny clean scrubs, an even briefer glance at my shiny new device.

"What is your analysis?" she said to the intern.

Yassin stuttered. I can't say I blamed her. An impatient Carter could be intimidating.

"Dr. Carter."

That was Navarette, attempting to rescue her intern.

She and Carter exchanged smiles. Two sharks circling about their prey. Carter outranked her, but I suspected Navarette could match her point for point.

"My apologies," Carter said. "However, I didn't want a good lesson to get lost in protocol."

Oh snap. Snap and cut.

Navarette pressed her lips together. She hardly ever got angry, but today was a close one. I tamped down the urge to intervene. That would only make things worse. Two attending surgeons arguing in front of the interns, even if one was a senior member of the staff, and one not yet cleared for duty.

Carter favored me with a brief glance—a dare? A check to see what I thought?—then smiled. "If you don't mind, I'd like to make the presentation."

Navarette nodded stiffly. Yassin vanished into the background. Grateful? Unhappy? I couldn't tell.

"Athena Washington," Carter rapped out. "Her immediate family all died in the explosion or shortly thereafter. Ms. Washington herself nearly bled out from secondary injuries from the blast. She owes her rescue to those on the scene who kept pressure on the wound until our emergency crews arrived. Her condition has stabilized, but we are monitoring her closely in case of any sudden changes in blood pressure or possible infection."

She paused to survey the interns and residents. Her gaze passed over me as though I were a ghost.

"It's something we need to watch out for," Carter went on. "Factors outside the purely medical condition. Dr. Watson over there will confirm what I say. She's seen more than any of us in the war. And this was an act of war."

Twenty gazes swiveled around to me.

"It's true," I said. "My old friend Saúl Martínez always said that surgery was just the beginning. If we weren't careful, we lost our patients to despair."

Or to drink, or drugs, but let us not mention those here in Georgetown's pristine corridors.

But Carter was watching me, her expression encouraging. "I agree with your old friend," she said. "Do you have any other observations you'd like to share?"

Oh, so we're no longer a gimp with an attitude?

I put my irritation in my pocket, however. All the interns were watching me expectantly, and quite a few of the residents.

"Dr. Carter is right to say we should monitor this patient closely," I said carefully. "I'd also recommend grief counseling, as soon as possible. Emotional distress is as tricky as infection. It might only become obvious days or weeks later. Especially with someone who has lost all her family."

"Which is the course you chose for yourself," Carter said. "Or you might have succumbed to despair any time this past year, Dr. Watson. Am I right?"

A direct hit, that. Had she aimed it with malice? No, simply a pointed lesson. Whatever her motive, I was down with pointed lessons.

"Correct," I said. "Although, if I might quote my friend Saúl again, I'm too damned stubborn to give up."

The interns laughed quietly. The residents needed another moment before they did the same.

Carter went on to give the vital statistics for Athena Washington. Higher-than-usual blood pressure, but nothing outside the normal range, and typical for her age and weight. A nail propelled by the blast had penetrated her liver, but the injuries were not life-threatening, and the organ was regenerating at the expected rate.

And what about her family? I thought. *Has she been left alone, the one survivor?*

As if she had read my thoughts, Carter immediately turned toward me. "You have a question, Dr. Watson?"

Protocol dictated that the chief resident ask the questions, but we'd already abandoned protocol when Carter wrested the surgical rounds away from Navarette.

I shook my head. "Not at this time, Dr. Carter."

Carter's gaze lingered on me a moment longer before she nodded toward Navarette. "My apologies for disrupting your rounds, Dr. Navarette. Dr. Watson, thank you for your suggestions. Please, carry on."

Anna Chong sat opposite me in my tiny sleek office. We'd had our one-on-one the day before, but Anna had texted me in the middle of the night, asking for a second meeting—at my convenience, of course. An exquisitely worded text that nevertheless implied an undercurrent of panic.

I'd read her records, back in December, after I accepted Georgetown's offer. Her parents had emigrated to the U.S. during Barack Obama's first term. Her brothers had studied at an exclusive private high school, where only the best were admitted. Her sister had graduated from Cornell last year, and Anna herself had entered medical school a year earlier than usual, where she outperformed all her classmates. She spoke English, French, Mandarin, and Cantonese fluently. She would have an offer of residency wherever she liked.

And yet, here we were.

"You aren't happy," I said.

She shrugged. "Happy doesn't matter."

That was not the answer I expected.

"I owe fifty thousand dollars in student loans," I began.

Chong regarded me with disdain. Her mother was a senior diplomat. Her father was a managing partner at one of Wall Street's top investment firms. She had no money worries.

"But money isn't the only debt we carry," I went on.

She flinched. That was a hit. A palpable hit.

"We have other obligations," I said.

The mask slipped back into place and she adjusted herself in the chair. *No problems here,* said her attitude. I wasn't fooled any longer. Anna Chong might have come from a far different background than mine, but I could read the clues.

"You have obligations to your family," I said flatly. "We all do. None of them outweigh our debt to our patients. So, tell me. What has distracted you this past week that you asked no questions today during surgical rounds?"

Another flinch. "I didn't have any questions."

Right. And dogs don't howl at the moon.

"So, no questions," I said. "What about Dr. Carter's analysis of Athena Washington?"

Anna shrugged. "It was a good one. I agree with your recommendation about counseling."

She had listened to that much at least. Good.

"As your adviser, I have an assignment for you," I said. "Write a ten-page paper about a surgeon's obligations to their patients, and how that outweighs any obligations to their parents."

That produced a startled reaction. "I—what do you mean?"

"Exactly what I said, future doctor Chong. If your parents are yammering at you to finish your studies, and your residency, as quickly as you completed your undergraduate program, then they might be valuing their expectations over the good of your patients. Think about it, Chong. We can talk next week."

Anna shot me an unreadable expression. But instinct said I had made the right guess.

♀

My session with Christo Bekker proved to be a much simpler affair. Bekker had come to the U.S. from South Africa on a scholarship. We'd talked five or six times since I joined Georgetown. I'd also observed him twice a day during rounds. He answered all the chief resident's questions. When he presented for his cases, he was painfully thorough. And yet, and yet . . .

I made a note to myself about empathy as a necessary attribute for doctors and gave Bekker the same assignment I'd given Chong. He accepted it as he had accepted any other suggestion I had made to him these past two months. Polite. Always respecting those who outranked him. He had never questioned me the way Anna Chong did.

A few phrases from Rumi's poetry came back to me. Something about betrayal and trust. Was that truth speaking in those verses? Angela Gray had betrayed me, or so I thought at the time. But perhaps I had betrayed her first, when I turned down all my offers and went off to the war.

Thoughts about Angela, about Chong and Bekker, cycled through my brain as I met my obligations to Georgetown University Hospital. Five more topics considered and discarded for that medical conference. Another OT session, during which Sydney's cat and I growled at each other. Afternoon rounds.

By six thirty, I only wanted to drag my sorry self to the nearest cabstand, which would drop me off at 2809 Q. Why, oh goddamned why, had I insisted on taking back my career as a surgeon? I could only look forward to longer days, to weekends on call, to those dark moments when I knew a patient would die.

Why?

Because you care, my love, said a voice very much like Sara Holmes's.

♀

Seven P.M. I was in a cab—an elderly car with an even more elderly driver, Lilly Black, who had picked me up without any of the usual difficulties. She and her husband owned their own cab company, and she still liked to drive the streets. Said it kept her sassy.

The cab's leather seats were thick and comfortable, and crisscrossed by scratches. The scent of cloves filled the air. Afropop, turned down low, came out of the radio speakers, interspersed with crackling news from the cab company dispatcher. If I were lucky, I'd make Q Street by eight P.M., what with the Friday night traffic.

Better than a goddamned dirt farm.

And far better than last year, that oh-my-god miserable year. The terror of Alton. My entire world smashed into bits. Working as a med tech at the VA Medical Center. Scratch that last one. The job had been tedious as hell, but I'd made . . . not friends, exactly, but a sort of temporary found family.

A buzz from my cell interrupted my thoughts. Or so I first thought, but the screen was blank, and there weren't any notifications showing.

Huh? Oh. Right. Sara.

Long ago, Sara Holmes had slipped a texting device into the pocket of my cargo pants. I had tried more than once to return the device. Each time, Sara had refused. Lately, I'd taken to burying the damned thing underneath my laundry or in the far corner of my closet. No matter where I stowed it, the device always ended up in my bag or my coat pocket.

The thing buzzed again, louder. It was in my bag, then. Swearing softly, I pulled out the device, which immediately went silent, as if waiting for my next move.

I swiped a thumb over the surface. Nothing happened.

"Damn you, Sara Holmes," I whispered to the screen.

The screen flickered. A stream of LOL emojis scrolled past. Laughing at me, was it?

"Fine," I said. "If that's how you feel, then see you tomorrow."

NO!

The word flashed on the screen in giant yellow letters, then vanished, replaced by the words Let's get trashed. —S

"What the hell?"

Oops. That came out louder than I meant. Lilly Black had glanced up to the rearview mirror, obviously startled. I smiled and waved the texting device, as though that were an explanation. She sucked her teeth in disapproval.

I pressed the device against my mouth and whispered, "What's wrong?"

No, no, no. Nothing wrong. Opposite news. Good news.

The screen blanked for a moment, then . . .

Back in the saddle at the Old Farm. I want to celebrate. Meet me at the Quarter Glory Bar. 14th & U.

I knew the place. Quarter Glory was your typical upscale, gentrified bar, in what used to be a neighborhood where prostitutes hooked up with customers, back before the war. The prostitutes had drifted east and south, toward southern Prince George's County. The customers had either followed or had paid higher fees to the ones who remained.

Lilly Black delivered me to my destination within half an hour. I offered her a double tip, which she first rejected, then took with an air that said I was not her favorite customer.

Once inside, I scanned the crowded room.

"Janet! Janet, my love!"

Sara waved at me from a booth in the corner.

I waved back uncertainly. The Sara of these past two, three months had been moody at best, dangerous at worst. I wasn't sure if bright and cheerful was an improvement. As I slid into the booth opposite her, she hailed a waitress and ordered two whiskeys, and an extra-large portion of calamari. "Eat," she told me, "for tomorrow we die."

"How jolly you are."

"My love, I would not wish to disappoint you."

Her voice was low and rough, as always, but her eyes were unnaturally bright, and her whole being seemed contained. If I had not known Sara, I would have guessed she was already tipsy.

The waitress, with the name tag TIFFANY, arrived with our whiskeys. Our order of calamari would be ready within twenty minutes, she told us. Sara offered her a giddy smile. "That is perfect. And may I say that you are a credit to your profession?"

Tiffany made a hasty exit. I regarded Sara with some tolerance, and a great deal of dismay.

"You frightened her."

"Not always a bad thing. Drink your whiskey, my love. We are celebrating my return into the fold."

We drank. The bar was noisier than I had expected, even for a Friday night. One of the loudspeakers blared out grinding blues, so loud my blood seemed to thump in time with the music. Dozens of white women crowded around the bar, all of them dressed in crisp navy suits, hair pulled back into sleek French braids. Politicos, lobbyists, lawyers, and suchlike. They were matched by an equal number of men, dressed in dark gray pinstripes.

I leaned over the table. "So, what's the news? This can't be about your leave of absence. It's about those terrorists, isn't it?"

"Tsk, tsk. You are impatient. No, I have nothing to report. Not yet."

She downed her whiskey and signaled to our waitress for another round. I settled back into my chair and resigned myself to a long circuitous conversation.

Two more whiskeys arrived, followed shortly by our calamari.

"You are a goddess of service," Sara told the waitress.

Tiffany laughed, somewhat nervously. "Is there is anything else you need, ladies?"

Before Sara could speak, I hurriedly said, "Nothing right now. Thank you."

"Spoilsport," Sara said, after Tiffany had gone.

"Be nice. I know you can."

Sara simply smirked.

We dropped into silence, concentrating on the calamari. I was hungrier than I had realized, and whatever else had changed in this neighborhood, or with this bar, the food was excellent. Maybe Sara couldn't, or wouldn't, tell me any details about her new assignment, and maybe we wouldn't have our lovely apartment much longer, but one thing—one of the many things—I had learned from Faith Bellaume was to treasure the good moments as they happened, and to store them away in memory for later.

Meanwhile, Sara's mood had turned quieter, less manic. She picked at her calamari with an absent air. Once or twice, she tilted her head. Listening to that constant stream of data that came through her implants, the stream she had so obviously missed these past two months.

"Listen," she said.

It was as though she had echoed my thoughts.

"What did you say?"

Sara took a delicate sip of whiskey. Then she reached across the table and clasped my right hand in both of hers. "Listen," she said softly.

I started to pull back, but she gripped my hand tightly. A hard, round object pressed against my palm. Oh. I had the sudden image of spies passing secrets to one another.

Sara's mouth tilted in a lazy smile and her gaze seemed unfocused. A stranger would have believed her drunk. The waitress would have confirmed that impression. But I knew this was yet another performance by the peerless Sara Holmes.

She released my hand and leaned back. I glanced down to see a single earbud in my hand. No wires, no plugs, just a smooth ivory disc with mesh on one side. As I studied it, the ivory color darkened until it matched the pale brown of my palm.

My fingers closed over the earbud, and I rubbed my forehead with my knuckles. Sara was scanning the bar through half-lidded eyes. Keeping watch, no doubt. Well, then. Let's give this spy business a go.

I rested my head in both hands. Lazarus was cool and slick. My other hand was damp with nervousness. Then as casually as I could, I slid the bud into my ear.

At first, I couldn't make out anything except a faint crackling. Then, abruptly, the channel cleared, and I heard the familiar voice of a reporter for a popular mainstream newsfeed, repeating the latest news from the capital. One voice replaced another and another in a continuous stream of bits and bites.

". . . the actions of one extremist group are creating a speed bump for President Donnovan's promised negotiations with the Oklahoma and Missouri government . . ."

". . . senior representatives from the New Confederacy

have distanced themselves from Richard Speiker and his associates, but others in the newly formed Confederate Council voiced support . . ."

". . . perhaps the first crack in what until today was a unified front for the rebel states . . ."

". . . more evidence that our nation cannot heal . . ."

The voices abruptly stopped. Once more the noise from the bar washed over me. Was this a taste of Sara's implants? How could she track so many voices, feeds, yammering at her without pause?

The earbud buzzed and crackled in my ear. Then, a voice, barely audible, all too familiar, spoke. "We are the martyrs of civil rights," said Richard Speiker. "Your dead, your blood will pay for ours. This is just the beginning."

This time the bud went silent and stayed that way.

I opened my eyes to see Sara's bright gaze across the table.

Oh. Now I knew what her new assignment was.

"That's against the rules," I said. "Even your rules."

Not a question.

"My rules are subject to revision," Sara said. "Besides, you deserved to know."

She picked up her glass, which was empty, and signaled our waitress for another round.

4

By ten P.M. I'd had enough, and I said so. Sara grinned, unre-
pentant. Her eyes were glazed, her hand unsteady, but I knew
it was all a performance.

"I'm tired," I muttered.

"And I'm hungry," Sara replied.

She called for a second plate of calamari, along with
deep-fried zucchini chips, and two shots of ouzo. I wanted
to protest, but the manic gleam in Sara's eyes warned me off.
If I argued, she'd only make more trouble. So I nibbled the
calamari and zucchini, and sipped my whiskey. The ouzo I
ignored.

Let's get trashed, Sara's message had read, but I noticed she
wasn't any more trashed than I was. Less, maybe. Still, you
wouldn't have believed it from the way she acted. Oh, she
didn't do or say anything really outrageous. Definitely nothing that would have had the management kick us out. But the
Sara of tonight was a bright and giddy Sara, who laughed a bit
too loud, and who chattered a bit too fast.

A pretend Sara. A lying Sara. What else was new?

I scowled, which only made her laugh louder. She tossed off that third—or was it fourth?—whiskey and launched into a series of dirty jokes. When she got to the one about the GOP senator, the lobbyist, and the Russian diplomat, I finally snorted a laugh.

Funny Sara. Drunk Sara. Sara who observed me through slitted eyes.

Devious Sara. This was all part of a play she'd written. *So happy to be your supporting actress.*

Around midnight, she called for the bill. Her treat, she told me. Well, I wasn't going to argue. And I definitely wasn't going to argue when she tipped Tiffany with a fifty-dollar bill. Poor woman probably felt as though a tractor-trailer had run over her.

If only you knew, I thought as Tiffany gathered up the bills and hurried away before Sara could change her mind.

We squeezed through the crowds and popped out the doors, onto the sidewalk. A cold wind blew down U Street. Crumpled sheets from newsfeed prints danced over the concrete pavement. In the alley next to the Quarter Glory, garbage piled up between the overflowing trash bins. DC's trendy young rich might have reclaimed bits and pieces of this neighborhood, but the old nastiness still lurked in the corners.

"We are never going to find a cab," I said. "Not at this hour."

"Nemmermind," Sara mumbled. "I wanna walk. Fresh air, yanno."

She slung an arm around me. I staggered back into the ironwork fence outside the bar, caught the railing, and hauled us both upright.

"Damn you," I whispered. "I should let you gut yourself. Didn't you scold me once about walking around late at night?"

Sara pretended to nuzzle my ear. "Don't worry. We have backup. But watch out for the watchers, my love."

I managed not to react. Much.

Apparently, Sara had read my emotions far too well. She laughed and drew me into a close embrace. "My apologies," she whispered. "I have a dreadful sense of humor, as you know all too well. Come, let us make tracks for home."

Then she swung away from me, holding on to one hand.

Right, I thought. *And when we get home, I'm going to ask you for some answers.*

I linked my arm through hers and we set off for Q Street, somewhat unsteadily. A few bars on the block were still open, and their light spilled out into the winter night, but once past Waverly Place, we entered the old neighborhood.

This part of U Street hadn't changed since the seventies. Tattered billboards decorated the buildings with ads for spiced rum, cheap auto insurance. The upscale bars were replaced by kitchens that doubled as blues joints, and the air stank of garbage and weed.

I tried to steer us down Sixteenth. Sara resisted and pointed ahead.

"Let's take the long way home," she said, and giggled.

I sighed. "You have a reason for this, of course."

"Of course. An entire collection of them."

"Such as . . . ?"

"Is this one of our questions?"

Months ago, after we signed the lease to our apartment, Sara had cajoled me into having dinner with her. The lure she used was a promise to answer three questions honestly. I had used up two questions that night but kept the third for another day. The habit of frugality learned in childhood? A doctor's natural caution?

"It's not," I said, "but you'll answer me anyway. Because I deserve to know."

"So you do." We walked in silence a few moments. Overhead the skies were like a burnished arc of steel, pricked with stars. Our breath, frosted with cold, escaped in wisps and curls. I had the sense that Sara was sifting through all the details for those reasons, choosing the least dangerous of them.

Too late. Anything you tell me is dangerous.

"It comes from our adventure of last year," she said finally. "An issue of trust, my chief tells me. I am on probation. I have my implants back. Mostly. But I cannot romp freely through the data streams as I once did. Also, I—we—no longer control the privacy of our apartment."

I digested the implications of this.

"So, your people have us under surveillance. What about those other watchers? Do they have a name?"

"Names are *so* dangerous, my love. Even here, away from all ears, electronic or otherwise, I would not speak of them, lest they vanish like brownies when you thank them."

I snorted.

Sara's smile gleamed bright in the lamplight. "Very like my own reaction. But to continue. I am no longer resting. At the same time, I am. One case overlaps the other. One set of friends might include several from the other. So, we act our parts for whoever watches, to confirm what you are to me, and what I am to the world. However . . ."

Her voice dropped even lower, but softer.

"I have another month or two in DC while I investigate how the Brotherhood of Redemption smuggled those drones into the city and past all our security. Such an operation required any number of traitors—people on the inside, people at the border. This so-called fringe group spent a great deal of money, only to fail. Donnovan lives. The negotiations, whatever the newsfeeds say, will take place by summer."

"But . . ."

We were whispering, heads close together, like lovers. Or spies.

"But they didn't fail," I said. "People are afraid."

Sara was silent awhile. The only sound was the ring of our boots over the pavement.

"It's possible," she said slowly. "One of the many permutations of possibilities on my list. The bombing arranged by extremists from our own—yes, they exist—to prevent any compromise with the Confederacy. The Brotherhood, used as pawns on the chessboard of politics, to make our president even more eager for peace. In fact . . ."

Her voice died away. Her head tilted, as though an invisible someone had addressed her. Listening to her news streams, I suspected. Those news streams she had missed so badly these past two months.

I still wore the earbud—and only now did it occur to me to ask how or where she had acquired such a device if her chief no longer trusted her completely—but it had told me nothing since the one burst of news. Just as Sara told me nothing now.

Remembering the watchers, I hooked my arm through Sara's and drew her close. We continued on in silence.

SATURDAY. *Ten A.M. For once I was glad I had no regular duties at the hospital. Sara had vanished before I woke up, leaving me with a carafe of cold coffee and some stale bagels. I grumbled and cursed, then realized I was acting like a spoiled child. What my mama would say to me now. Maybe today I would treat myself to Hudson Realty's concierge service. Or maybe I could toast some bread myself.*

Time to settle down, drink some coffee, and write a damned abstract.

SUNDAY. *One* A.M. *Where the hell did the time go?*
Around two P.M. *yesterday, I remember thinking to myself,*
Hmmmm, recovery rates for traumatic injures . . .
Before I knew it, I'd jumped down that rabbit hole and into
the glory land of statistics. Twenty gigabytes of search data
downloaded. Several false starts jotted down. I think I ordered
takeout for dinner, but I can't swear to that.
   Time for a glass of wine and sleep.
   No sign of Sara.

Tuesday morning, Georgetown discharged Athena Washington into the care of her cousin and an ambulatory home care service. Ain't single-payer insurance a beautiful thing? My father told me about the old, old days, when only the rich could afford decent health care and the politicians gave lectures about how the lazy poor deserved whatever happened to them.

Then along came Alida Sanches and the Democratic Progressives. Will anyone remember her bloody fight to make single payer happen?

Sorry. My bitterness must be leaking through.

The mainstream media feeds were all lit up this morning about Donnovan's latest speech. The GOP called single payer a burden to society. They claimed we couldn't afford such fancy extras as home health care and uncapped benefits. Donnovan said the GOP had a point. He said we all needed to make sacrifices in these difficult economic times.

I wondered what kind of sacrifice Mr. President had in mind for himself.

But at least for now, Athena Washington had her medication, and her grief counseling, and her cousin from New

Jersey. I made a note to myself to contact my federal representatives about Mr. Donnovan's remarks, then turned my attention to the next medical day.

Morning rounds. Uneventful.

OT with Sydney Okora, an extended session where I
made my first attempt with Lazarus's custom programming. Sydney had provided me with a flank steak, thawed,
and ordered me to cut ten-millimeter slices. My results . . .
were not as good as I had hoped. Not as embarrassing as I
had feared.

Late-morning therapy with Faith Bellaume was canceled
because her daughter had gone into labor six days before her
due date. I thumbed back a message that expressed concern
and hope but paused before I pressed *Send*. Why had I not
bothered to learn Faith had a daughter? Maybe I should write
my own paper about doctors and empathy.

By five P.M., I was ready for afternoon rounds.

First patient, a ten-year-old named Javier Arroyo. Teresa
Navarette, the chief resident, was in charge. Anna Chong was
presenting the case. Javier himself was drowsy with sedatives. He looked like a tangle of wires and limbs.

"Patient Arroyo," Chong said. "Admitted January twenty-
ninth with symptoms of appendicitis. Surgeons Carter and
Letova were on duty. Letova removed the appendix within
the hour. Patient was discharged two days ago with a recommendation for follow-up visits to his primary care physician.
He was readmitted this A.M. with high fever and a swollen
abdomen."

"What scripts were given to him on discharge?" Navarette said.

"Standard antibiotics and painkillers."

"Anything outside the ordinary with his surgery or recovery?"

"Nothing," Chong said.

"Then why the relapse?"

Yassin had one explanation, Bekker another. Others chimed in with answers straight from the medical textbook. Only Chong wore a dissatisfied frown, as though she wanted to say more but felt it wasn't right. Maybe I was reading too much into that frown, but I made a note to talk to her about groupthink and taking the easy explanation as the truth.

Then again, example made the best lesson.

"Why should we assume it's a relapse?" I said.

That cut the chatter. Even Chong, who loved to challenge me, had nothing to say.

Once again, Allison Carter had joined the afternoon rounds. "Why *not* assume it's a relapse?" she said. "Infection isn't unusual after surgery."

I glanced toward the chief resident. These were her rounds, after all. But Navarette had subsided with a tight little smile. Oh yes, let the attending surgeons provide a show for her students. I couldn't really blame her.

I folded my arms and faced Allison Carter straight on.

"It's *not* unusual," I said, "but we can't assume anything. At the very least, we need an MRI to make sure we aren't looking at blood clots. We should run as many tests as we can, so we don't overlook anything. Confidence makes carelessness, as my old friend Saúl Martínez would say. However, there's a bigger question here, in my experience."

I turned away from Carter to the interns. "What is the usual rate of readmission for Georgetown? Anyone?"

Anna Chong had the stats, of course. "The average readmission rate within thirty days for hospitals through the Federal States is just under fifteen percent, but seventeen percent for terrorist-related injuries. Georgetown's average rate is thirteen and fifteen percent."

"And for our patients from January twentieth?"

Yassin provided the answer for that. "Nineteen percent."

Higher than I had expected, but not outside the range of probability.

I nodded, as though I had memorized the stats myself. "Very good. Now, let's take our results a step farther. What about statistics for the length of hospital stay versus the severity of the injury versus the patient's personal circumstances?"

Carter shrugged. "Apples and oranges, Watson."

"Goats and monkeys," I snapped back. "Or don't you know your Shakespeare?"

Carter's lips thinned, and we regarded each other warily. Everything about this confrontation was wrong. Wrong for hospital etiquette. Wrong for how I'd come to expect my fellow surgeons to talk to me. Or I to them.

It's the war. Even here behind the lines, we're not immune.

Then Carter blew out a breath. "Fair enough. Time for the next patient, Dr. Navarette?"

Time and past time, Navarette's expression said, but she politely indicated that the interns and residents should precede her down the row of beds. I fell in behind, only to find Allison Carter at my side.

"Do you have a few moments?" she said quietly.

"Rounds aren't over. Can it wait?"

"I'd rather not. I have surgery scheduled shortly." Then she added, "It's not as though you are required to attend."

Ow. Was this a jab at my in-between status?

But I was curious enough to decide I didn't care. "Lead on, Dr. Carter."

We took the elevator to the fourth floor, then crossed over the walkway to the administrative wing. Carter's office was next to Hernandez's, another sign of her rank in the hospital hierarchy. She tapped the ID plate with her thumb and motioned me inside.

Her office was not the luxurious suite that Hernandez commanded, but close enough. A bright airy space, with floor-to-ceiling windows. The Potomac was a wide gray ribbon in the distance. Beyond lay Northern Virginia and its government buildings, which had overrun the earlier suburbs. Between Georgetown and the river, DC made a patchwork of gray concrete and parks glittering with frost, outlined by Lafayette's squares.

Carter indicated a small table next to the window.

"I'm sorry," she said as we took our seats. "We began wrong, and it's my fault."

Oh. Not what I'd expected.

"We were both at fault," I said carefully. "And for that, I'm sorry too."

Her smile was more a grimace. "Perhaps we were. But I'd like to mend that if I can."

By now I was wary. Oh, she used all the right words—though she'd been mighty damn quick to share the blame—and her offer to make amends was everything the employee manual and Ms. Professional Etiquette would recommend. Even so, I could not rid myself of the memory of Carter shouting at me that I was a gimp with an attitude.

My expression must have shown something of my thoughts because Carter gave me an uneasy smile.

"Yes, I was wrong," she said. "I used words that . . . that I regret. I should have expressed my concerns better. We're alike in many ways. We both get angry. We both care about our patients—all the patients here. We don't want them dying because of mistakes we could avoid."

Because you wanted to prove yourself.

That was like a punch to the gut. Because it was true.

I let a breath trickle out.

"You're right. We don't want them to die. For any reason."

"I'm glad to hear that." Carter stood and held out a hand. "I'm also glad we had this talk. We might never be friends, Watson, but we can certainly be allies."

I made a quick retreat from that exercise in hospital politics and headed immediately to my office. My face felt stiff from the effort to be calm, polite, and friendly. Inside, my gut roiled from suppressed anger. Good thing I wasn't really a surgeon these days, because I had the freedom to hide from the world until I ironed out my emotions.

I locked the door and keyed the "Private Meeting" indicator.

Private Meeting is right. Time for a little talk with yourself, Dr. Watson.

All right. Let's start. Therapy style. How are we feeling? Angry? Furious.

Goddamned furious.

Give me a name, a face. Who's the lucky soul this time?

Me. Carter. Both of us.

My hands curled into tight fists. I eyed the door, wondering how much damage I would do to myself if I punched as hard as I wanted to.

Not a productive line of thought. I unclenched my hands and started pacing. One of the tricks Faith Bellaume taught me. Walk and think. Talk out loud if you need to. Yell at the world.

Yelling out loud would not be a good idea, what with the thin walls and curious neighbors. So I walked, walked from one side of my office to the other, and yelled inside my head.

Stupid, stupid, stupid. Carter was right. I was stupid and selfish, thinking I could march right into that operating theater just on my say-so. If I can't manage to braid my own hair, I can't take a scalpel to someone else's body.

I bumped up against the opposite wall. Kicked it for good measure and spun around.

She didn't need to be so goddamned uppity herself though. Dr. Goddamned Allison Carter. Dr. I'm In Charge. She didn't need to take over rounds the way she did. She just likes to make sure everyone knows she's the alpha doctor.

Back to the other side of my office. I aimed another kick at the wall but stopped myself in time. *Not productive, Dr. Watson,* I told myself. Faith would have had a few words about trigger points. She would have calmly reminded me to practice my breathing drills, and had I skipped a few days this week?

I was still standing there, staring at the wall, when a knock sounded at the door. Oh god. I didn't want to talk to anyone just yet.

"Janet? Are you all right?"

Christ. Letova. For once I wished my friends didn't care so much.

I sucked in a breath, wiped a hand over my face, and opened the door.

"Hi," I said. "What's up?"

Nina Letova folded her arms and regarded me with deep suspicion.

Oh. Hell. She'd probably heard me kick the wall.

"I'm fine," I said.

"Huh. Could've fooled me." She glanced up and down the corridor, then stepped inside my office and eased the door shut. "Something happened, I can tell. Or is it more like *someone* happened? Was it Carter?"

Double Christ. The grapevine had already started to chatter about our little argument during rounds.

"Nothing all that dramatic," I said. "Carter pointed out a couple flaws in my integrity, is all. I didn't like what she said, but she was right."

"Oh, that," Letova said. "Been there myself, my friend. It's not so much *what* she says, it's *how* she says it." Her mouth twisted into a smile. "She's not all that bad, you know. She'll make a grand CMO once she gets her ego under control."

"Heh. I thought ego was one of the job requirements."

We laughed. The tightness in my gut eased.

"So tell me," I said. "What kind of lecture has Carter delivered to you?"

Letova flinched. All the humor drained away from her face.

"Hey," I said softly. "You don't have to tell me."

She blinked. Managed a smile. "Sorry. It was . . . It was today, as a matter of fact. You remember that kid, Javier? A simple appendectomy. No complications. All the indicators were good. We discharged him early. Then this morning . . ."

I laid a hand on her shoulder. I didn't hug her—Letova didn't care for hugs. I definitely didn't tell her any such fool thing as *He'll be fine. Don't blame yourself.*

"Go see your patient," I told her. "You're a good surgeon. You care about your patients. There's nothing wrong with that." Then I went ahead and said it anyway. "Don't blame yourself, Nina. The boy will be fine."

♀

Letova did not stay long. She had patients to examine, charts to review, another surgery to prep for. I tried to drown my doubts in research for that damned medical abstract, but I was too jittery to concentrate. I finally gave up and shut down my workstation.

A brisk walk would do me good, I decided, so I set off on foot for my apartment. The cold, dank February night matched my mood. Guilt was such an insidious emotion. Letova, distressed over her patient. Me, distressed over my uncertain status at the hospital.

Letova would recover. She had to. But I knew why she blamed herself. A patient had nearly died, in spite of every-thing. Ergo, it had to be her fault. Hidden complications that tests had not uncovered. Or the follow-up care was not as me-ticulous as needed. Or God herself, and why not blame the surgeon, because they were next in line?

You are not God, Angela had said. *Neither am I.*

Angela Gray would be in attendance at the conference. Perhaps I could discuss the matter of blame with her then.

My breath caught between laughter and a sob. Terrible idea. We would, both of us, end up weeping or raging. Or evicted by the conference security guards.

The steady drizzle turned to sleet, tiny specks of ice that stung my face. *God's tears,* one of my old teachers, back in grade school, had called it. As if God ever cried over the dead. *I wish she had. I wish she did.*

The sleet came down harder and faster than before. I dug my hands deep into my pockets and cursed myself for being such an impetuous child. I could've—I should've—walked out my jitters at home, in the warm bright parlor that was 2809 Q Street. Privilege 101, Black Edition. Limited, you might say. Yes, I had a hard time flagging down that cab, but less than other folks. And however much I complained, I could and did have a refuge.

Survivor's syndrome, Faith called it. *Doesn't make your anger any less real.*

Doesn't make it any more useful.

The neighborhood around Thirty-Fourth Street didn't look quite as broken as the last time. Cracks in the street had been patched with asphalt, and the traffic lights blinked yellow, red, and green the way they should have. Most of the shops were closed, their metal shutters lowered and locked. Even the bookstore was dark, and a sign on the door said, CLOSED. EXTENDED HOURS TOMORROW.

The next block showed evidence of light and life. I remembered a coffee shop one of the nurses had recommended. I could sit at the counter and warm up, before hunting down a cab.

ALICE'S COFFEE BAR, read the sign on the frosted glass doors. BEST DAMNED COFFEE IN DC.

A blessed cloud of heat wrapped itself around me when I stepped inside. I breathed in the scents of strong coffee, of cinnamon and vanilla and almond, while bits of sleet and snow from my hair dripped onto the welcome mat. No one even seemed to notice me. I found an empty stool near the front and ordered a cup of their premium brew.

The coffee came in an oversize mug—strong and hot and smoky, just the way I liked it. The waitress left me a pint-size jug of cream and a bowl of sugar. I mixed in a generous helping of cream and drank slowly, letting the heat soak through my skin and deep into my bones. Voices hummed in low conversation all around, punctuated by the clatter of spoons and cups.

So. Are we all done with the jitters? All it takes is a long walk and some nasty cold weather to give some perspective?

Maybe. Could be. My mother always said a dose of hard work was enough to drive away her blues. Too busy to fret, she would tell me and Grace. Usually right before she gave us a list of chores.

Even so, I wasn't quite ready to face the cold. I was about to signal the waitress for a refill when I caught sight of a woman walking down the aisle. Her face looked vaguely familiar— the round glasses, the hair tinted dark gold and barely contained by a brightly colored head wrap.

Adanna Jones paused and stared back at me, frowning. Then she recognized me, and her expression cleared.

"Hello," she said with a smile. "Did you enjoy the book?"

"I did. Thank you."

She wore a dark red sweater, knitted in a complicated pattern, and sensible black trousers. The sweater's yarn was dense and fluffy at the same time. The word *luxurious* popped into my mind. I wanted to say something profound about the Rumi, but then I caught a whiff of Jones's perfume—a mix of jasmine and cedarwood that sent my brain blank with unexpected attraction.

Oh god. Not now. Not here.

The last time I'd felt so damned awkward was in high school, right after I discovered I liked girls, not boys. I sucked down a deep breath, but the flutter in my stomach only got worse.

My blithering state must have been obvious, but Jones was kind enough not to smile. "Rumi is one of my favorites," she said. "His words make sense for, oh, so many reasons. If you liked the book, I could recommend another. Stop by the store tomorrow. Or whenever you have time, of course."

I finally took control of my tongue.

"Tomorrow, yes," I said. "I have the time."

Her smile was kind and gentle, as if she could read my thoughts but didn't judge me for them.

"Then I shall see you tomorrow. Unless . . . Tonight is my six-month anniversary with the store. Would you like to help me celebrate?"

Oh.

"Yes," I said, my voice almost breathless. "Yes, I would like that."

5

Friday, February 6. *Early morning edition.*

Last night I had dinner with Adanna Jones.

Let us pause a moment to consider the implications.

Or not. The night we met in the coffee shop, we had our glass of wine to celebrate Adanna's store and its first six months. Before the second glass, we decided we ought to meet again. Thursday night was the most convenient, we agreed. Not Friday or Saturday—those were reserved for serious dates. Not Monday, because Monday said, I can't be bothered. *Thursday, then, was almost Friday. It was me saying,* I'm interested. *And her saying back,* Me too, but let's take it casual.

So here I am, Ms. Casual, awake an hour before the alarm goes off, drinking coffee in my bedroom and scribbling down a bunch of messy emotions.

(Messy emotions. Redundant, that.)

(I see I'm avoiding the point again.)

(Will parentheses be my downfall?)

Anyway. Back to last night.

*We met up at her bookstore at seven thirty. Nice and
neutral. Practical, too. I could walk there from the hospital,
and Adanna could keep the store open until I showed up.
We'd agreed to have a glass of wine at a wine bar around the
corner, then take a cab to a Caribbean hole-in-the-wall that
Adanna knew.*

*One glass each of overpriced white Bordeaux. Chitchat
about the weather and what the hell President Donnovan
meant about bringing the country together.*

I set my pen down and leaned against the enormous fluffy
pillows, one of the first things I treated myself with from my
new Georgetown paycheck. Outside, gray clouds muffled the
skies, and the baseboard heater ticked a monotonous rhythm,
while sleet tapped against the windows. Lucky thing I could
afford a taxi if I wanted. No more trudging from bus to Metro
stop, my body braced against the cold.

If I had never met Sara Holmes, if I had never followed her
into adventure, would I have met Adanna Jones?

Pointless speculation. I *had* met Sara, there in front of Dalí's
Last Supper. I *had* followed her to 2809 Q Street and into adventure. And one reward of that adventure had been a position
at Georgetown, which in turn had led indirectly to last night.

I sighed, picked up the pen. Considered what next to write.
What Sara's colleagues would later read.

That had been another consequence of our adventures last
year, which Sara had made very clear the other day. We could
not expect any privacy, she and I. Her chief would monitor
Sara through her own implants and the recording devices in
our apartment. I expected they would keep a watch on me as
well. They'd rifled through my life once already.

Finish the entry, I told myself. *Otherwise it looks suspicious.*

One glass led to two. Just enough for my stomach to
unknot. By this time, a tide of DC's wealthy lobbyists had
invaded the wine bar. Adanna rolled her eyes. I smothered a
laugh. Let's go, I said. I'm hungry. So am I, she said.

The hole-in-the-wall was a place called Jammin Kitchen,
between Jefferson and Ingraham. No reservations, but
Adanna knew the cook's sister, and we only had to wait
twenty minutes for our table by the kitchen doors. She
ordered pelau, I ordered callaloo. The waitress brought us two
bottles of Red Stripe without our asking. Good call, that.

Another pause. The skies were lighter now. My alarm
clock had flipped over to six A.M. Morning rounds didn't start
until seven thirty A.M., but I liked to show up early to review
the patients' charts. Best finish this one up soon.

She asked about my job. I told her the basics. Lost an arm
in the New Civil War. Came to DC to argue with the VA
for a new device. Got one, along with a job offer from
Georgetown.

A masterpiece of editing, I thought. No mention of the
dead veterans. No mention of Adler Industries, and how
they—how Nadine Adler—had used our soldiers for profit.
Sara's colleagues would have no complaint about what I told
Adanna Jones.

When it was her turn, Adanna talked about growing up in
Chicago and attending university to study literature. She'd
married young, to an equally young man, both of them
clearly not ready for commitment. After they divorced, she
moved from state to state along the East Coast until she
landed in DC. She'd worked in bookstores while she got

her MBA, then longer until she saved enough to open her
own store. She was making enough to get by, she said, but
there were times she wanted to chuck it all and go live on
a farm.

No, you don't, I told her right back, and talked about
growing up on a dirt farm in Georgia, and how my parents
had to save for years before we could move up north.

Our conversation had dried up for a while. Adanna finished off her pelau. I thought about ordering another Red Stripe. We were in that stage between ordinary talk strangers used and something that might tip over into the personal.

Then I brought up the subject of books. There, there was something we could both talk about all day and night long. SF. Romance. Literary. Political thrillers. Stories about men and women. About women and women. Stories about black women, in whatever genre you chose. I ordered that second Red Stripe; so did Adanna. The waitress cleared away our plates and brought us a dessert menu that we ignored.

"All books are political," Adanna said.

"Don't I know it."

Her gaze swept up. I had the sudden strong realization that her hand lay close to mine—the one of flesh, that is. But Adanna had never once flinched away from Lazarus. She had taken me in, all of me, without any sign of disgust or false sympathy.

Oh, oh, oh.

My chest went tight. My throat turned dry.

I had no idea how long we stared at each other. Eventually, I remembered to breathe.

"It's late," I said. "I should go."

Adanna smiled. Her fingers brushed mine. "I hope to see you again soon."

My nerves still buzzed with remembrance of that moment. But no, I refused to record those emotions for the FBI or anyone else. I dipped my pen into the ink pot, tapped away the excess, and finished off the entry.

Talk about Georgia led to talk about families. Brothers and sisters. Cousins and aunts. I told her about my grandmother and how she had argued against my parents' moving north. She told me about her stepmother in New York telling her how DC was a bad place for a black woman who wanted to run her own business. Bullshit, Adanna had said, and proved her wrong.

We both had a good time, I think. Maybe I'll see her again. I'd like that.

There, entry finished. It might also be plausible.

Sara had taught me well, after all. How to admit the facts, while hiding the truth.

I blew on the ink until it dried, then put away my journal and writing supplies. Six twenty A.M. Plenty of time to get ready for work. But my hands lingered over the journal, as I thought about how much I had not written.

Dear Journal, I thought. *Dear minions of the federal government. If you think this is another one of those true-love confessionals, think again, sunshine.*

No. And I wish.

Maybe.

6

Friday at last. The day had started off cold and dark and dreary, the sidewalks slick with frost. By the time I stopped in the cafeteria after morning rounds for a cup of coffee, the skies had cleared, and sunlight poured through the windows. I paused a moment to savor the view. The whole month of February had been one big pile of cold and sleet, a month of snarled traffic and more than the usual accidents, which had brought us more than the usual number of patients.

But at last the weather had broken. At last I could glimpse what might be the turn of seasons.

Because at last it was Friday.

Because tonight—*tonight*—I had a genuine Friday night date with Adanna Jones.

We'd made our cautious dance through the days of the weeks, from that first auspicious Thursday, to a meet-up the next Tuesday for a coffee, to tonight. A Friday, with all its implications.

"What has you all distracted today?"

Navarette stood next to me with her own cup of miserable coffee. Her mouth was tilted in a mischievous smile, as
though she'd been reading along with my thoughts and emotions.

"I am not distracted," I said with dignity. "I am merely
deep in thought."

"Yeah, right. How come you didn't school me during
rounds?"

Oh. Damn.

I went for the casual shrug, but Navarette was having
none of that. "Spill, my friend. You have that dazed and silly
look of a woman in love—"

"Not in love—"

She snapped her fingers. "Knew it! Letova and Pascal both
owe me ten dollars. They were all, *Oh, Watson is so damned
serious all the time. She's not flighty like you, Navarette.* As if I
were flighty, but that's another subject. Come on. Let's have a
sit-down and you can tell me all about this woman."

"I can't," I said. "I have OT with Sydney in fifteen minutes."

Navarette grinned. "And you need more than fifteen minutes. That tells me all I need to know."

I hurried away before she could say more. Part of me was
outraged that Navarette and the other surgeons were betting
on my love life. The rest was dismayed they had even *guessed*
I had a love life.

And dare I call it that yet?

My mood, my lovely hopeful mood, drifted down to reality. A dinner date was not a love life. But it was a possibility,
I argued back. One date could lead to another, to other, more
casual encounters in the park, with the cherry blossoms like
vivid stars against the bright green of the Mall. After that,
well, we'd see.

♀

The moment I entered Sydney's domain, I stopped in surprise.

Is that . . . ?

A portable operating table stood in the center of the room—a basic model, with a flat padded surface and divided into two sections that could be raised or lowered. Next to it was a shiny metal stand, complete with surgical gloves, mask and head covering, and an array of instruments. A sterile sheet draped a figure on the operating table.

And yes, it was a body lying there. I would recognize that special stillness of death anywhere.

Sydney grinned at me from behind her worktable.

"Surprise!" she said cheerfully. "It's official eval time."

My heart thumped hard against my chest. Sure, I'd been arguing for weeks for just this moment, but the second or third time Sydney refused, I'd given up, especially after my so-called conversation with Allison Carter.

Ono slithered into view from behind the worktable and shot me a yellow-eyed glare. I gave the cat my best glare in return. She sniffed, as near a smirk as any cat could manage. Now that we had our hellos over with, Ono retreated to her cushion in the corner.

Sydney had watched this with her own smirk. "Well? Where are the cries of joy? Girl, you've been angsting all over the place, telling me you ought to get an official eval, since I don't know when. What's wrong? Changed your mind?"

"No, but . . . Am I ready?"

"You damn well should be," Sydney replied. But her voice was gentler than her words. "Let's take things slowly, and we'll find out."

I blew out a breath, then nodded.

"Good." Her manner shifted from friendly to cool and

professional. "You will examine two bodies today, Dr. Watson. Two different procedures, which I will describe in detail before each one. Do *not* rush. I won't be timing you today. Right is better than fast, as you damn well know."

I did know that.

And at least no one dies if I happen to make a mistake.

"Who is the first patient?" I said. "What is the procedure?"

Sydney tapped on her virtual keyboard, then made a notation with her electronic pen. A luminous square appeared in the center of the table.

"May Tillerson," she said. "An eighty-seven-year-old diabetic with a history of ignoring her meds. Cause of death, diabetic ketoacidosis. Her daughter reported that Ms. Tillerson appeared to be in distress the previous day. She did show signs of improvement by nightfall, but the next morning, she began to vomit. The daughter immediately called for an ambulance. She was brought straight into the ICU, where the doctors put her on IV, but she died that same day."

I could read the data between the lines. Tillerson had ignored her meds one time too many. Shock, exhaustion, the body old and tired. Perhaps the daughter might have argued her mother into going to the hospital earlier . . . But no, second guesses were useless at best.

"Why is she here?" I asked. "And what is the procedure?"

Sydney's expression flickered, but only for a moment. Was that approval? I couldn't tell.

"She is here because she wished to donate her body to the medical school. Her granddaughter is a student at Georgetown. The procedure . . ." And here Sydney referred once more to her virtual screen. "You are to open the patient's abdomen. You will examine the organs and report your findings. Then you will close the body."

Simple enough, or it would have been, if I'd had two real hands.

Lazarus is my real hand. Sydney told me so often enough.

Telling was a helluva lot easier than believing. Ignoring Lazarus for now, I folded back the sheet from May Tillerson's body.

She was gaunt, her skin limp and folded around her bones, as though her muscles had evaporated. Her flesh, when I touched it, was cold but pliable.

"I'm not exactly a medical student," I said.

"Don't worry. We have a signed release from her daughter."

"Her organs are not suitable for transplant."

No answer given, none needed.

"Her pathology might be useful, however."

"It might," Sydney replied. "However, today's procedure will not undo that."

Meaning, *Get on with it, Doctor, and don't screw up the procedure.*

I tapped the sequence on my device for extra-sensitive feedback. Though I'd run through a dozen or more drills at this setting, I was still not immune to the strange sensations that crawled up the length of my prosthesis. After a count of ten, the sensation registered as pressure and the cold touch of a metal instrument.

(Is that possible? It must be, because the chill flows up my metal arm and into my flesh.)

Next, I pulled on the mask and head covering, then opened the sterile pack for the scrub brush and scrubbed my right hand and arm thoroughly in the sink. After that came the electron-beam sterilizer unit for Lazarus. Once I'd satisfied protocol, I drew on the pair of surgical gloves.

My right hand found the permanent marker on the tray. I

drew a line below the rib cage and around the right side of the abdomen. Sydney had not dictated which organs to extract, or what observations to make. No doubt she only wanted to see if I could cut a straight line.

—even if that flesh was cold and stiff and—

I set the marker off to one side and was about to start the incision when Sydney interrupted me.

"Left hand, please," she said.

Of course. I had to prove I could operate with either hand.

I shifted the scalpel to my left hand and pressed down into the doughy flesh. I'd not dissected a body since medical school, and I'd forgotten how the skin and body resisted the knife's edge. I pressed harder. The skin split and divided.

By now, the training from medical school and my residency took control. I cut a second and third slice through Tillerson's abdomen and lifted away the flap of flesh. Lazarus performed as expected, with crisp precise motions.

The organs had the appearance I expected from an elderly woman with numerous medical complications. However, I took no shortcuts. I examined the intestines, the kidneys, the condition of her liver. I gave a running commentary as I worked, which Sydney recorded on her workstation.

Then, my examination complete, I replaced the organs and closed the body. While Sydney tapped on her keyboard, I stripped off my gloves and laid them on the tray with the instruments. If I'd been in an operating theater, the nurses would have taken away the instruments and gloves, while I added my own final observations about the patient into the nearby audio recording device.

Sydney tapped a combination off to one side. The virtual keyboard and display went dim but did not vanish completely. Her expression was difficult to read. Deliberately so, I decided.

"Ready for patient number two?" she asked finally.

"Ready," I replied.

Sydney wheeled the operating table through the side door and returned with a second table and a second body, draped and covered as before. Another trip and she brought another stand with a fresh set of instruments and gloves.

Once again, I scrubbed and sterilized and pulled on fresh gloves. Before I removed the sheet, I studied the blank figure before me. My second patient was a much smaller person. Not a child, but not yet an adult.

"Her name was Tyonna Clarke," Sydney said. "Fourteen years old. She came to us originally on January twentieth."

My gut pinched in recognition of that date. "A victim of the bombing?"

Sydney nodded. "Her injuries weren't life-threatening, but damned painful all the same. A mild concussion, bruised ribs. Oblique fracture of the left tibia. The decision was made to immobilize the bone with wires and a brace. We kept the patient thirty-six hours to monitor the concussion and her recovery from surgery. Her prognosis was good, so we discharged her into her family's care, with home service visits for three days."

"That was a month ago."

What killed her? was my unspoken question.

"Her father brought her back to GUH two days ago. Clarke exhibited all the signs of organ failure. Vomiting. Elevated temperature. Abdomen distended and tender. The girl died within an hour of being admitted."

"Any history of drug or alcohol abuse?"

"Her father says no."

And fathers didn't always know—or want to know—what trouble their kids got into. Fourteen was damned young, but I'd had friends in middle school who had already started down Trouble Street.

"Her father has asked for an autopsy."

My attention snapped up to Sydney. "I'm no pathologist."

"No. Your task is to open the abdomen and record your observations. Gentner will take over from there."

That was a relief. Gentner was the senior pathologist at Georgetown. Meticulous to the point of fussiness, but that was part of the job, wasn't it? I pulled back the sheet.

Too damned young was right. Tyonna Clarke was a skinny brown girl just bumping into puberty. Hair braided into tight cornrows. Knobby knees and elbows. The dark smudges under her eyes spoke of those last agonizing hours.

I made the necessary marks on her abdomen, noting a line of sutures not yet dissolved near the upper right quadrant, then took up the scalpel with my left hand. The movements came automatically this time, as though my body and memory had locked together, with Lazarus along for the ride.

All that lasted until I had the abdomen open and I stared down into the cavity of this young girl's body.

I'd seen any number of mangled bodies in war, and many more riddled with cancer, or wasted and twisted by drugs. But never any organ damage to compare with what I saw today.

"Multiple thrombi throughout all the major blood vessels," I said to the recorder. "Signs of hemorrhaging . . ." I felt a flutter in my gut, which I'd not since my earliest days in medical school.

"Go on, Doctor," Sydney said softly.

"Necrosis of the liver," I said at last. "Signs of incipient necrosis in the large intestines, which accounts for the tenderness and swelling of the patient's abdomen."

With an official autopsy ordered, I could not shift the organs to make a more extensive examination, but then, that wasn't the real point of this eval. I continued to list as many symptoms as I could from visuals alone. When I had finished my observations, I closed the body and stepped back. My right hand was trembling. Lazarus held steady, but the point where flesh met the device's contacts shivered with a hint of electricity. The electronic version of nerves?

"Any further observations?" Sydney asked.

"Severe organ failure, sudden and painful. I've not seen anything like this before. The father was right to request an autopsy." I hesitated. "I noticed sutures. Was that part of her visit back in January?"

"A medical implant for time-release antibiotics."

I nodded. A common enough procedure.

"No allergy noted?"

"None."

So, and so. A mystery for Dr. Gentner to solve. That would make his day.

"How did I do?" I asked as casually as I could manage. The pinpricks of electricity had died off, replaced with a lovely sense of accomplishment. However, it would not do to make any assumptions.

Sydney tilted her head and gave me that wicked smile of hers. "You did well. Very well. I think we can move on to the advanced drills next week."

Friday, lovely Friday, was also the day for our once-a-month M & M conference. Morbidity and mortality, just one of a woman's monthly joys, Navarette liked to say.

By two thirty, the residents and attendings had collected around the conference table. We had three cases to review today, with Nina Letova as the first resident to present. She had both printed records and her laptop in front of her, which she fussed over until Hernandez gave her the order to begin.

Letova called up the stats on her screen, then tapped the keys to show her display on the conference wall.

"Patient Javier Arroyo," she said. "Ten years, three months old. Original diagnosis, acute appendicitis."

Her voice was cool, precise. Standard doctor presentation. But I'd heard Letova weeping the night the code blue sounded. *Don't blame yourself for anything outside your control,* our teachers always said. Hell, they were right. But when you lost a patient, it could be damned hard not to.

Letova went on with an overview of Javier's first visit to GUH. She recited the patient stats for the operation, what she and Carter had discussed for follow-up care, the scripts prescribed, the lack of complications, and the mandatory visits by medical technicians for any early discharge.

"What did the medical technicians report?" Carter asked.

The two women exchanged the briefest of glances.

"Recovery progressing as expected," Letova replied. "Temperature normal, blood analytics normal, appetite normal. Surgical site showed no signs of infection."

"Except the boy died." That was Hernandez, looking aged and grim. "Review the second visit, please."

We all knew the details. Letova had ranted about them enough this past week. But we were all professionals. We knew the value of the postmortem, the examination for any flaw. This wasn't a matter of placing blame. This was how to identify what went wrong so we could do better for the next crisis, the next patient.

"Patient readmitted by their father, exhibiting all signs of sudden-onset infection. After a consultation with the senior attending surgeon, I put the patient on IV with intermittent infusion, twice every hour. Blood tests indicated a bacterial infection. Patient was kept under observation, with the fall-back to increase the dosage if their condition changed. Unfortunately, Javier—the patient— The patient went code blue during the night."

He died. Let's call out what happened, no dithering. The child died, and his parents are suing the hospital for gross medical negligence.

But we didn't mention words like *negligence* or *lawsuits*. Not in M & M.

I decided to start with a few roundabout questions. "What could we do differently? How can we know a patient is ready for discharge?"

Armstrong, one of the older attendings, swiveled around to stare at me. "It's not guesswork, Watson. We have any number of procedures that are standard hospital policy—"

"Procedures that predicted nothing about this boy." That was Pascal. A good point, but everyone knew that Pascal and Letova were close friends.

Arguments broke out between Pascal, Armstrong, and Carter. Letova remained silent and blank. No sign of emotion, unless you counted her pale face, the sudden patches of red when Armstrong and Carter went into full angry attending mode, each one claiming greater experience with complications than the other.

At last Hernandez called a stop to the argument. "Next case, please," she said. "I have a few things to say after we're done."

That lit a fire under the other two residents. They hurried through their presentations, one hit-and-run victim, one alcoholic coma. Nothing unusual about either patient, and we were almost relieved to dismiss any possibility the surgeon could have done better.

We ran through the usual analysis, however. Checked against the usual warning signs. All was good, for all three cases. Really, how much could a surgeon do about the demon infection, or just plain damned bad luck?

Hernandez cleared her throat. "Before we go our merry way, I want to speak about a related topic."

She tapped the conference tabletop. A panel slid open, exposing a touch-sensitive control pad. Hernandez tapped again. Immediately the lights dimmed, and the screen grew bright. Now a square appeared on the wall behind Hernandez.

Navarette expelled a whispery sigh. "I was expecting this."

A colorful chart filled the screen—a scatter graph with each dot representing patients who died over the past six months. A red line traced the average of the stats. December showed a spike around Christmas, another spike at New Year's. Typical stats.

"Look at February," Hernandez said.

She tapped a few keys. That luminous red line seemed to twitch, like a worm, then reversed and angled upward. Not a spike, like December's, but clearly higher than usual.

"That's not all," Hernandez said. She tapped the virtual keyboard, and a new worm, an ugly greenish yellow, overlaid the red one. "Readmission rates. Those have held relatively steady over the past three months, but we had a jump this past month."

All of us stared at the graph. The statistics were clear enough, but I had the sense Hernandez was fishing for a particular answer.

"I am not happy," Hernandez said. "We need to find the cause for these readmits. More important, we need to find out why these patients come back to us only to die. Find out why and fix the problem."

"What if there is no cause?"

Hernandez shot Pascal a chilly stare. "That sounds like an excuse."

To her credit, Pascal did not defend her question. She

wilted into her chair and made a pretense of studying her tablet.

"Let me state the situation bluntly," Hernandez said. "If this trend continues, the hospital must rethink our policy of discharge. We'll need to implement more checks—more thorough checks—and procedures to ensure our patients don't return. *Especially* only to die."

Everyone went quiet as they absorbed this.

After a moment, Carter cleared her throat. "Perhaps we could institute a higher level of outpatient care, especially during the first week or two at home."

A higher level of outpatient care came at a higher cost, I thought. Our lovely single-payer health care only covered a day or two at the most. Anything beyond that was charged to the patient.

Hernandez herself was shaking her head. "That's one approach, but we need a plan to cover *all* our patients, the poor included."

Carter had a faintly surprised look, as though she'd forgotten the world included such creatures as the poor. Navarette covered her mouth with one hand. Several others smiled nervously. Only Letova appeared distracted, as though she were still working through Javier's case.

"Very well," Hernandez said when no one spoke. "Here is what I want. I want suggestions. I want well-reasoned suggestions that account for our entire patient population, not just a few. Treat this as a diagnosis, with different levels and different angles of attack. I won't set any deadlines, but I would like to see input from everyone as soon as possible."

Dismissed at last, Navarette, Pascal, and I headed toward the elevators as quickly as we could without seeming to, with Letova close behind. Navarette and Pascal were discussing the M & M in low tones. I walked quietly beside them. Would these new procedures—whatever they turned out to be— save more patients? Would they have saved Tyonna Clarke or Javier Arroyo?

Maybe. Could be. I had no idea. Death came at you however Death pleased. All we could do was fight the war one day, one patient, at a time.

Nina Letova punched the up and down buttons at the elevator. Her jaw was set. Her eyes narrowed. Was kind and gentle Letova *angry*?

"I don't like it," she said.

"I don't either," Navarette replied. "But we both know the probabilities. Patients die. Patients survive but forget to take their meds. Or they go back to old bad habits."

The doors hushed open and we got into the empty elevator. I swiped the security pad with my ID, then tapped the number for my office floor. Navarette swiped her own ID and punched the number for the outpatient surgery wing. Just as the door closed, she murmured, "I bet I know what has Hernandez all stirred up though."

Pascal and I stared at her. She shrugged but waited until the elevator hummed into motion before she spoke again.

"It's not just the patients themselves," she said quietly. "We have a reputation. We don't want to lose that, or we might lose the business of people like Senator Blake." She named the head of the Joint Committee on Health Care, a committee that had only grown in size and influence since the U.S. shifted to a single-payer system. "He was scheduled for a stent implant this June, the new combo type with the timed-release drugs and a remote monitoring component. I hear tell he's making noises about finding a different hospital. We lose his business, then word gets out why, and we might lose some of that lovely funding."

"Goddamned politics," I said.

It was everywhere. Even in death.

At last I was free of the hospital and my duties. Not a right and proper attitude for a surgeon, but I had an excuse. It was Friday night. My first *Friday* night with Adanna Jones.

(Memo to self: Goddammit, girl, you are not a teenager. Get your raging hormones under some kinda control. Friday don't mean nothing except dinner and some talk. Or were you thinking this woman might offer you some sweet dessert? Settle down.)

I left the hospital early; dropped by the apartment, which was blessedly empty; and changed into what I hoped passed for casual and nice. Black wool trousers. A purple sweater, bought new this past week from a local boutique. Those silver bracelets that Sara had given me last September. A necklace my mother once owned. I spent the last ten minutes fretting over my hair and polishing Lazarus before I dragged on my wine-colored coat and my black gloves, then set out for the restaurant.

The restaurant—Adanna's choice—was an old, established Vietnamese restaurant in the SW quarter. For all my years at Howard and then Georgetown, I'd never come across this place.

I was twenty minutes early. I settled into the booth the waiter showed me and spent a few minutes glancing over the menu. This was no trendy uptown spot, the kind Sara Holmes liked for our occasional nights out. Inexpensive, with only half a dozen main dishes. I turned over the menu to the wine and liquor selection, which was even shorter. Three white wines, one red, a couple fashionable martinis, and a list of draft beer.

"You got here early."

Adanna Jones slid into the seat opposite me. She wore her usual black wool coat, a voluminous sweater knitted from jewel tones, and two enormous silver discs suspended from her ears.

"I like to plan ahead," I told her.

Her mouth tilted into a smile. "Do you, now?"

My mood lifted even higher, if that were possible, at her teasing. "When I can," I said. "When it's right." Then, because I feared I had overstepped some invisible line, I quickly added, "So. How was your day?"

Her face took on that smooth expression I had come to classify as *Too damned bad to talk about*. But all she did was shrug and smile. "Worse than I liked, better than I feared. Mostly boring shit about accounts and shipping charges. How about you?"

We talked about death and disease. And politics.

Not the best topic for a Friday night date.

"Oh," I said lightly. "The usual, nothing more. My interns. My committee meetings. Pretty boring stuff."

Her expression didn't change, but I caught the flash of her gaze, the almost inaudible sigh as she leafed through the three-page menu. She looked weary, distracted, as if she wanted to be elsewhere.

Come on, Watson. You are not making a good impression here.

"However, I did have my first official evaluation today."

That caught her attention.

"I told you about my arm." I lifted Lazarus and twisted my arm around so that lamplight ran in silver rivulets along the mesh. "I'm going through the usual physical and occupational therapy. Plus, I need to learn how to use all the special features Lazarus has for surgery."

Her mouth quirked in a half smile. "Lazarus?"

"Ah. Yes." My face heated up with embarrassment. "That's what I call my friend here."

"I like that." Her voice was no longer weary, her expression no longer distracted. "So, tell me. What happens when you pass all your evaluations?"

She said *when*, not *if.*

"It means . . . everything. It means I can be a real surgeon again. It means I'm not stuck with a meaningless title, doing meaningless work, for far too much money—"

I stopped myself. My pulse was jumping, and I realized I was babbling. *Trigger words,* I told myself. *Damned poor time for them to show their ugly faces.*

I gulped down a breath and offered Adanna a shaky smile. "I'm sorry. It means so much to me. My therapist—my other therapist—says it's because I feel I've lost a part of myself. And more than just my arm."

There, I'd said it. I waited for her to reply.

"You are a brave woman," she said simply, no trace of pity in her voice or her expression. I felt a release of tension I hadn't realized was there.

Our waiter appeared in this moment, with an electronic pad and stylus in hand. I wanted to curse his timing. We both glanced over the menu and gave our orders, including a bottle of wine.

He returned within moments with the wine. Adanna and I touched our glasses together.

"To victory, however we define it," she said.

"To the best of all possible weeks," I replied.

We drank. I was about to mention how good the wine tasted, when the restaurant door swung open and Sara Holmes appeared in the doorway. She wore her rattiest brown leather jacket, tight worn jeans, and a knitted cap pulled low over her forehead. Her locs tumbled down her back, thick and wild, and she had that strange manic air I'd come to dread.

Her gaze locked on mine and she made a direct line toward our table. "Janet, my love. Do you have a moment?"

I glared at her. I had told her about Adanna Jones. Not all the particulars, but enough that she ought to have known how much this evening meant to me. I had not, however, told her the location for tonight's dinner, and part of me wondered how she had ferreted out that data point.

A question for later.

"I do not have a moment," I told Sara. "Not now. We can talk tomorrow."

Sara shrugged. "As you wish. I've had news that might interest you. But . . . as you said, we can talk tomorrow."

She made no move to leave, however. Instead she extracted a clove cigarette from her pocket and lit it with our candle. Everyone around us was staring, or frowning, or both, and the waiter was hurrying toward our table.

"Later," I repeated firmly.

Holmes finally seemed to notice Adanna. "Oh, hello. You must be Janet's new friend. So sorry to interrupt. Later, then."

She sauntered out of the restaurant, with a dozen pairs of eyes following her. Some looked scandalized, others sniffed in obvious disgust. The only person I cared about sat opposite me, her expression strangely blank.

"My roommate," I said awkwardly. "Sara. She's . . ."

". . . A free spirit?" Adanna said.

"Something like that."

"Hmmm."

To my relief, our first dishes arrived, hot and sizzling and aromatic. We spent a few moments sharing them out. Adanna asked for chopsticks. I chose to keep my knife and fork.

I stabbed the fork into my dumpling and dipped it into the chili oil. "Speaking of not-boring, I operated on a dead person today. That was part of my evaluation."

"Was it difficult?"

"Not as difficult as I expected. I've done this before . . ." Before Alton. Before I lost my arm. But I wasn't ready to talk about Alton with this woman, not yet. "It's part of our training," I said awkwardly.

I started to describe the procedure, then realized it was not the best topic for dinner conversation. From there I stumbled through a story about my interns and their very different personalities, but my every pause was answered by Adanna Jones with a noncommittal reply.

Goddamn you, Sara Holmes. You have a lot to answer for.

"So," I said brightly. "How about you?"

The rest of the evening went about as well as you might expect. We soon exhausted our supply of polite conversation. When our main dishes arrived, we concentrated on the food, with occasional comments on how delicious the meal was. When the waiter arrived with our check, we set down our utensils, and I couldn't miss the obvious relief on Adanna's face.

"My treat," I said.

She simply nodded. I thought she might flee at once, but she politely waited for me to pay the bill.

Outside, we paused on the sidewalk. The night was crisp and cold and clear, but clouds blurred the eastern sky, and a hint of sleet hung in the air. I had hoped to walk Adanna home, or at least to the nearest Metro stop, but obviously that wasn't about to happen.

"I'm sorry," I said.

"For what?"

"For Sara. She's . . . a difficult person. And I . . ."

But I could tell Adanna wanted to hear no excuses about Sara Holmes.

"Do you have a free evening next week?" I said.

She hesitated. Long enough that my throat went tight and dry.

"I'm a bit occupied next week," she said at last. "I need to write up my inventory before tax season hits."

A reasonable excuse, but I knew it was just an excuse.

I wanted to explain. I wanted to make an apology that mattered.

But doing that might bring her all kinds of extra trouble.

"I'd like to see you again," I said.

She nodded. "And I would like to see you but . . . One of the difficulties that Timothy and I had was honesty. I very much need my friends to be honest with me. Do you understand?"

I am being honest.

But I knew better. A person could lie with silence as well as words.

Adanna rested a hand lightly on my arm. "It's not the end of the world, Janet."

Oh, but it was an end of something.

♀

I walked back to 2809 Q Street through the cold and mist of this late February night. Punishing myself, Faith would call it. Damn straight. The weather decided to play along with my self-pity and delivered. Clouds moved in to block out the moon, the mist turned into a steady drizzle, and for the first time since December, my stump ached fiercely. By the time I reached the apartment, the drizzle had penetrated my coat and my face was stiff from the cold.

It took me two tries before I could fumble my right hand free from its glove. I pressed my thumb against the biometric keypad, praying to God, the God I told myself I no longer believed in, that the electronics and my own body wouldn't fail me.

The lock clicked open. I stumbled inside.

By the time the elevator reached the second floor, my face had begun to prickle with renewed sensation. A hot shower was my first goal, then a mug of scalding-hot tea. Then . . .

I paused outside the apartment door, dripping and shivering.

Voices, loud and distinct, leaked through the solid door.

Strangers. Damn it.

I nearly turned around to find a hotel for the night, but I was too weary, too cold. Muttering a string of curses, I unlocked the door and went inside. I could hurry through the crowd and take refuge in my bedroom. No tea, but at least the hot shower was still an option.

There were no strangers, no crowd at all. Just Sara Holmes, hunkered down in one of the parlor's overstuffed chairs. Sara had a lit cigarette dangling from her mouth. Her battery-operated radio sat in the middle of the table, tuned into an indie newsfeed about the upcoming peace negotiations. The porcelain bowl she liked to use as an ashtray was overflowing with ashes, and the air stank of cloves.

No whiskey, though. No drugs. She might even have been sober. Still, her strange, tense expression unnerved me. I made a quick scan for weapons. I didn't see any, but that meant nothing.

Holmes twitched. Her gaze swiveled around to mine.

She took in my waterlogged appearance, the puddle at my feet. Her expression did not change, but she took the cigarette from her mouth and clicked off the radio.

"Did you have a lovely time?"

"I did," I lied. "And you?"

Sara offered me a faint smile. "No. But I have certain options to support me."

Drugs, definitely.

"I'm tired," I said. "And cold. I'm going to bed."

"Good idea." Holmes leaned back and closed her eyes.

But just as I turned toward the bedrooms, she said, "By the way, I found a fabulous new diner uptown. Best damned omelets in DC, according to the reviews. We should go there tomorrow for breakfast."

I shuddered at the thought. "No."

"But I insist," Sara said softly. "Consider this my apology for tonight."

There was no apology good enough for what she had done.

"Goddamn you, Sara—"

She laughed. "To be sure, he or she will. But what about breakfast?"

Clearly, she would not stop hounding me until I agreed.

"Fine," I said evenly. "Your treat. What time?"

"Late. Very, very late." She took a drag on her cigarette and blew out a scented cloud.

I shambled off to my bedroom, trailing water as I went. Once I had closed and locked the door, I stripped off my coat and kicked off my boots. The rest of my clothes followed. There'd be hell to pay if all that water damaged the floors, but right now I didn't care.

I turned on the shower to its hottest setting. In a fit of caution, I locked both doors inside the bathroom, before I stepped under the needle-sharp spray. Points to Hudson Realty. They had advertised instant and unlimited hot water, and they had never failed to deliver.

Fifteen minutes later, the cold had melted away. I turned down the heat and scrubbed my skin with the fancy ginger-scented soap that Sara had given me for Christmas. By now a dull ache had centered itself just beneath my ribs, but at least I was warm again. I shut off the shower, dressed in my pajamas, and climbed into bed.

I should take care of Lazarus. I should swallow those pills Faith prescribed for me. I should . . .

Holmes had switched the radio on again. The newsfeed continued its endless yammering about Donnovan, the New Confederacy, and how Congress kept flip-flopping between hard-line opposition to the peace talks and how we had to compromise for the nation's good. Meanwhile, Richard Speiker and the Brotherhood of Redemption continued to threaten more attacks unless the Federal States met their demands.

Their demands were breathtaking and horrifying. Close all borders with Mexico. Hand over all named conspirators. (Though that list seemed more like a list of political dissidents and people of a certain color, if you get my drift.) I wanted to think Donnovan wouldn't concede anything to those terrorists, but these days I wasn't too sure about the man.

I pulled the cover over my head to shut out the radio. If only I could shut out the whole goddamned world for a few days.

Dangerous line of thought, Watson. Don't ignore those meds. Don't be neglecting that shiny new arm. Come on, girl. Get up and do what you have to.

I got up. Took my meds. Drank a full glass of water, then went through the proper drill to remove Lazarus and tend to my stump. By the time I retreated into bed once more, the radio had gone silent, but I could still hear Sara moving about the apartment. A restless Sara often took refuge in playing her piano, but not tonight. Come to think of it, not for the past three weeks. Perhaps what we had here was an obsessive Sara, not a restless one.

Another line of thought guaranteed to keep me awake. Luckily, tomorrow was Saturday. Luckily, I had no official position on the surgery roster. I was free to sleep late, as late as I wanted.

I want to be a surgeon again. I want two good hands. I want . . .

I wanted another chance with Adanna Jones.

But Adanna herself wanted complete honesty, and I couldn't give her that. She was right, too. If we couldn't be honest, then we had nothing at all.

Maybe Rumi had something to say about that.

February 28. _____

My dreams tonight are embarrassingly obvious—no need for Faith Bellaume to interpret.

We're in an upscale wine bar, Adanna Jones and I. I don't recognize the place, but it could be anywhere in DC. Anywhere at all, really. Glass-top tables. High stools. Too many mirrors. Lots of brass. The rumble of canned music with the bass amped up and the backbeat just a little off.

Adanna sits across from me, a bottle of expensive Bordeaux off to one side. Our glasses are full, the bottle close to empty.

She lifts her glass and mouths a toast I can't hear over the throbbing bass. I touch my glass to hers.

The moment I drink, the dream makes a jump to the left.

Our glasses are empty, the bottle full. A fat yellow candle burns inside its glass enclosure, and the bass has turned into a ripple of piano that reminds me of Sara Holmes at her most serene, however rare those moments have been. I reach for the bottle, but Adanna intercepts me with a light touch.

Janet, she says.

Her glance falls down to my device. For once I don't flinch when a stranger notices my missing arm. Perhaps because I don't think of Adanna as a stranger. Perhaps because her expression makes no judgment. She simply sees another part of me.

On impulse, I pull off my coat. I'm wearing a sleeveless tunic. (The outside observer, the part of me watching my dream, notes that I have no such tunic.)

I lay my bare arm on the table, palm up. The mesh glitters in the candlelight, all silver and bright.

Adanna glances at me, clearly asking permission.

I nod.

She rests her fingers on my arm, just above the wrist. I should not be able to feel her touch, but I do, and I draw a sharp breath.

Go on, I say.

She goes on. With a featherlight touch, she explores my arm, from the cuff where flesh meets metal, along the inner length to my elbow, and down to my wrist again. She notes the controls, hidden behind a discreet panel; the not-so-human joint at my elbow, even as it attempts to simulate the shape and bones of a human arm; the delicate wrist with the band shielding the complex electronics that allow me to twist and turn my hand.

Then she curls her hand around mine, and her fingertips touch my palm. Mine close around hers.

Lazarus, meet Adanna, I say. Adanna, this is Lazarus. This is part of me.

Her gaze lifts to mine. She smiles.

7

The moment I woke, the entirety of yesterday tumbled into my brain.

Christ.

I rolled over and squinted at the alarm clock. Only seven A.M.

I pulled the blankets over my head and tried to pretend the world didn't exist. Except my uncooperative brain kept handing me memories of the night before. Adanna, calling me brave. Adanna's expression wiped clean when Sara called me her love. We weren't lovers, she and I. Neither were Adanna and I. Hell, we were barely friends. But the air had sparked with potential, or so I thought.

Eventually, I gave up on sleep and pulled on fresh sweats and ambled into the kitchen. A loaf of banana bread sat under a glass dome, next to the coffeemaker, which had just finished brewing a fresh pot. And in case I had missed the point, *someone* had set out a clean mug and a note reminding me of the fresh pitcher of cream in the refrigerator.

Someone, I thought, *is just too damned clever for her own good.*

I collected a pot of coffee, the cream, and several slices of banana bread onto a tray and retreated to my bedroom. My latest acquisition from Rainbow Books was a complete set of Heather Rose Jones's Alpennia series in trade paperback. Women as scholars. Women as scientists. Women as friends. Just what the doctor called for, I decided, as I opened up *Daughter of Mystery*.

Around eleven A.M., Sara appeared in my doorway, dressed in loose faded jeans and a New York Yankees sweatshirt, and she'd gathered her locs at the nape of her neck with one of those high-tech ribbons that changed colors and patterns in reaction to sunlight and temperature.

"Let's go," she said. "Don't worry about your clothes. We're both fine."

We wrapped ourselves in our down jackets and set off through a bright crisp February morning. Any frost had vanished from the sidewalks, the skies were clear, and the sun poured down from above. Sara herself appeared subdued. She walked at a steady pace, her hands stuffed into her pockets, her face strangely taut.

"Another secret chat?" I ventured after a few blocks.

Sara nodded.

"Won't they notice?"

Her mouth twitched. "Hardly. No, let me expand upon that. My people might—scratch that, they *will* notice our walk and our breakfast. They will also notice I was an entitled shit last night, and that I am taking pains to make amends. I am sad to say my colleagues are so easily distracted by such maneuvers. Anyone else on my trail will likely reach the same conclusion—that ours is a personal and painful conversation."

So, you blundered into that restaurant and ruined—

I stumbled. Sara caught me by the arm. I hissed and wrenched myself free.

Damn you. Damn you, Sara Holmes.

Except . . . if I wanted to be honest, Sara had not ruined anything. At some point, Adanna Jones would have asked a question I could not answer. At some point, we would have had the same conversation about honesty.

I swiped my hand over my eyes, while Sara pretended not to notice.

"What about my friend?" I said.

"Safe."

I shook my head and burrowed deeper into my quilted coat, even if the weather didn't warrant it.

"You don't believe me," Sara said softly.

"How can I?" I replied. "You play so many goddamned games, Sara. Then you whistle me up like a pied piper. You might believe I am safe. And yeah, maybe last night's charade will keep Adanna safe. For now. But you aren't a goddamned god or superhero."

She opened and closed her mouth. A strangely uncertain response. Was Sara developing a sense of social awareness?

"You are right," she said at last.

"About what?"

"About everything, my love."

That casual endearment, which was anything but casual, no longer infuriated me. We were not lovers, Sara and I. We were friends, allies, companions in madness. We had offered each other trust, with certain limitations.

"What the hell does that mean?" I asked. "Are we in danger? Is *she*? And are these new enemies or old ones?"

Sara's gaze flicked toward me, and I caught the faintest wink. "Unknown. Except there is always an enemy. No, this isn't about the New Confederacy, at least not directly. It's about Nadine Adler. You remember her?"

Goddamn straight I did. The woman who had murdered my best friend, Saúl. The woman behind all those deaths in the New Civil War.

I realized I was shivering, and not because of the winter air. "You told me she was dead. The newsfeeds had vids and articles about how she was killed in a shoot-out with government agents."

Vids supposedly taken by witnesses with cell phones, showing a snow-dusted street that could have been New York or New Jersey, with a SWAT team rushing toward a single anonymous figure wielding an illegal rapid-fire gun. Falling back on excuses of "national security," the articles had danced around exactly when and where this shoot-out took place, but it had all been so very convincing.

"I did not lie to you," Sara said quietly. "I told you what the agency told me."

Which were lies, apparently. And the mainstream media had played along with those lies.

"How did she get away?" I said.

"She should not have. That much I can tell you." Her tone was light, almost fey. "I've learned a few interesting tidbits since the agency admitted me back into the fold. There was a curious delay, back in late October. You had your interrogation, I had mine. Five days. There was push-back from upper levels before they sought a court order for our friend Adler's arrest."

She tilted her face up to the winter sunlight, as if recalling that interrogation. I had always thought her ageless, but there were lines etched around her mouth, and the seemingly tireless Sara Holmes had shadows under her eyes.

"Adler returned to DC during that delay," she went on in a soft voice. "Apparently, she had installed a secret passage that allowed her to visit her office the following night, when she extracted a great deal of cash. She used the money to charter a private plane for parts unknown. A woman with a talent for foresight and planning out multiple outcomes. I could almost admire her."

I didn't give a rat's ass about Adler's talents and said so.

At that Sara laughed. "I agree. However. Back to the story. My chief believes Adler fled to Costa Rica. That is plausible. What I find less plausible is the apathy about having her extradited to face charges. Purely politics, my chief assures me, but I find it troubling."

"Do you think it's a conspiracy? That seems a bit . . ." I choked back the rest of my reply. *Stupid?* No, that would only provoke her. Ditto *obsessed* and *tunnel-visioned*. I went with the next-best word. "Um, far-fetched?"

Sara's mouth tilted in a smile as if she had guessed the track of my thoughts. "Perhaps I am a bit obsessed. Aren't you?"

Ouch. Point taken.

Luckily, I didn't need to answer. We had reached the diner with the best damned omelets in DC. Frederica's Finest was the name, displayed in blue neon script. Christmas lights bordered the windows and door, and the outside of the diner was covered in corrugated tin, polished to a bright silver.

"I have a few questions," I told Sara. "About what you told me."

She shrugged. "I have any number of questions myself. But the time for telling stories is over, my love. Let us eat, drink, and be merry."

She gestured toward the door and we went inside.

❦

We spent the next three hours in Frederica's, eating omelets and drinking coffee and pretending to have an ordinary conversation. Sara did ask me about my progress with Lazarus, and about the hospital in general. She listened and nodded in all the right places, but I had the impression she was listening to the newsfeeds from in her earbuds and was recording my words for later—TiVo for the high-tech world.

But I had not forgotten her comment about watchers, so I went along with her game. I described an amusing incident with Sydney's cat. I talked about hospital politics and how I needed to find a suitable subject for an abstract. Her attention perked up only briefly when I mentioned Hernandez and the M & M stats.

At four P.M., I'd had enough. "Thank you for breakfast. I should be going."

Sara's smile was brief and distracted. "Will you be home for dinner?"

"Maybe. I don't know."

She nodded, still distracted. I hesitated a moment, then left.

Outside, the sun was sinking toward the horizon and the light had dimmed to almost twilight. I didn't want to go home, not yet. I had an urge to walk past Adanna's bookstore, but I knew that was a terrible idea.

So, so, so. What about that abstract?

The air had taken on a raw damp edge. I flagged down a cab and was soon walking through the wide front doors of Georgetown University Hospital. Weekends were nothing but busy, and on this late Saturday afternoon, the front reception area was crowded. I threaded my way past to the employee-only region, where I swiped my badge.

The third floor was quiet. Any surgeons who had offices here would be with their patients, or in the theater or waiting on call in the cafeteria. I pressed my (one good) thumb to the bio-lock and retreated into my office.

My good intentions faded at the sight of my all-too-stark

office. No family photo cubes, no books, no decorations. Just my medical certificates.

I should go shopping, buy a few knickknacks. God knows, I have the time.

With a sigh, I adjusted the brightness of my overhead lights, then logged in to my workstation. My personal dashboard showed a dozen new messages, which I ignored. Instead I called up Georgetown's array of research portals, with connections to internal and public databases.

But those were all about someone else's ideas, someone else's research. If I wanted to impress Hernandez, I'd need an idea all my own. Something . . . compelling.

Death is pretty damned compelling, I'd say.

I extracted the data from Hernandez's workspace and called up the data analysis tool that Georgetown had acquired a couple months ago. A few taps on the keyboard, and the numbers sorted themselves by cause of death. I tapped the option to chart the data. That produced a scatter of data points all over the screen—not helpful. I tried sorting by date of admission. Now I got a chart that made more sense, though it didn't tell me anything new. We already knew these were deaths that had taken place within the last month.

So tell me something new.

My workstation waited, infinitely patient, for me to continue.

Almost patiently. Within ten minutes the screen saver would begin its graceful dance, and after another fifteen minutes, the workstation would shift over to its sleep mode.

Death. Death by discharge? Death by statistics?

More was at stake than my own medical career. The patients who trusted us for their care. The hospital itself, which depended on government funding for research and other expenses, such as this very data analysis tool. It was all about money and politics, as Navarette had said.

My attention wandered from death, to politics, then back to Sara Holmes. Her odd behavior—odd even for Sara— bothered me. Oh, sure, her explanation for barging into the restaurant last night made sense, but why say anything about Adler and her not-a-death? And when she did, why give me only part of the truth? Because it was obvious to me that she'd picked out which interesting bits to reveal. If we were friends, she'd tell me all the truth.

I very much need my friends to be honest with me.

Oh. Right. Thanks, memory, for the sucker punch.

My screen had shifted into sleep mode. I touched the virtual keyboard, and the screen came to life. Statistics, I told myself. There had to be a topic somewhere in all those numbers.

March 20. _____

Dear Jesus, black or white. Has it really been three weeks since my last journal entry? *checks dates* So it has. Damn. Next time I complain about not having enough to do, please smack me upside the head.

So what's been going on these last 2.87 weeks? Let's go with the ever-popular list style:

- Three official one-on-ones with my interns. Both of them full of spit and vinegar these days. Maybe I was wrong about Bekker. He turned in that essay I assigned, then went and started caring about his patients. Damn, I'm glad.

- One very long, very unofficial meeting with Anna Chong, where we talked about all the expectations life threw at us. Families. Culture. History, as dictated by the ruling gender. (And class, let's not forget that.) We both got a bit maudlin over our hospital cafeteria coffee. I talked about my time in the service. She talked about her patients and her girlfriend. I think Dr. Chong will do just fine.

- Six new impossibly complicated drills for my device.

- Three new epiphanies with Faith Bellaume. Collect $200 and pass go.

- Zero abstracts written, though I glimpsed the shadow of an idea. We'll see.

- Another long walk through NW DC with Sara. She didn't share any more secrets with me—not by spoken word, that is—but I've learned how to read Sara's moods these past seven months. Frustration bubbled and seethed just below that all-too-calm face. One of these days she'll tell me. Or not. She might regret that rash confession back in February. Me, I almost regret telling her she was obsessed with Nadine Adler. It might be true, but it will only encourage her.

- Three more evaluations with Sydney. Two official, one anything but.

Okay, that last needs more than just numbers and nouns. Time for a detailed entry. So. My next OT appointment, the one after I first opened up those bodies, came on Tuesday. Nothing special, just the usual drills. I showed Sydney that I could braid my hair, play the keyboard, and knit one, purl two. If you can manage the commonplace, she told me, you can manage the rest.

Same as she always said.

But.

Thursday, I walk into that ten-by-twelve workroom, with Ono the cat giving me the stank eye from her corner, and Sydney doing much the same behind her table. Go for it, Sydney tells me.

Go for what? I say.

Whatever you think you should.

Goddamn mysteries, I mutter.

But I settle down. I run through the finger exercises one by one. I demonstrate my control with the pressure-sensitive board. I've just taken up the comb to braid my hair when she stops me.

Let's try another test, she says.

She presses a button on her virtual keyboard. A moment later, an orderly wheels a body into the room.

Unannounced evaluation, Sydney says. You have to be ready all the time, not just when the world gives you a heads-up.

She's right, dammit.

To my relief, this evaluation is a replay of the first. I was to open the abdomen, extract the organs one by one, then replace them and close up the body. Lazarus and I do well, I think. There are only one or two moments when my ghost hand moves faster than my metal one.

Good thing, because Sydney springs another surprise at our next session. Our patient, the late Jonathon Benjamin

Franklin, has died from heart failure. An infarction undetected by the primary care physician and the admitting surgeon, both. My task is to examine the patient's heart with my micro-surgical implements. Simply a means to confirm what we already knew, she says.

A means to confirm my understanding with my device.

Use whatever micro-programming seems appropriate, Sydney tells me.

I do. From the micro-scanning device, which records everything to the hospital data storage, to the more general imaging that connects to Georgetown's image matching and analysis subsystem.

That third eval, though . . .

Another surprise, and this one harder than all the rest. No sooner do I sit down behind that worktable than Sydney announces I'm to run through all my drills, even the newest ones I've only learned the day before. Sydney times me with a stopwatch, while Ono the cat watches me, slit-eyed, from her corner. I have no idea how well I did. I just know I wanted to collapse into a corner after I was done.

She tells me I've won. I want to laugh, but I'm too wiped to care.

What else? Let's see. Hernandez assigned me to yet another committee. I assigned myself the task of observing a surgery at least once a week. And Carter—yes, Carter—suggested I shadow the night shift on the weekends. A good suggestion, both practical and political.

Speaking of practical and political, Hernandez announced a new policy the other day. From now on, all our higher-risk patients would be monitored after discharge, even those not discharged early. No more expensive home health care visits. Unless a patient objected—and that would lead to a longer hospital stay—we'd install medical implants that would transmit patient data to a wrist unit. Any sudden change for the worse, and the wrist unit would sound an alarm. Other cases might require implants with slow-release medications, such as antibiotics or blood pressure medicine. In both cases, the implant would dissolve within a few weeks.

Ain't modern medicine grand?

~~And that's all for now.~~

Okay, that's not all for now. Three more items for my list:

- One text written but not sent to Adanna Jones.

- Three times I stopped myself from walking past her bookstore. Stalking is not my style. (Does thinking about her count?)

- Six more nights without any sleep. Something is happening, I just don't know what.

8

April 4. Saturday afternoon. Back in the olden days, before my sister and I were born, today would have been a genuine spring afternoon, the air warm as fresh toast, the Mall ripe with cherry blossoms. Even when Grace and I were kids, flying a kite in that pocket field between our house and the Mall, we could tell the difference between winter and almost spring.

Those were the olden days, for good or bad. Nowadays, March and April liked to shake things up weather-wise.

And they used to say climate change was a left-wing fantasy.

I shrugged on my fleece jacket, zipped up the front, and surveyed the skies from the sidewalk of GU Hospital. They were clear at least. The temps had climbed up from the subzero range of last week, and with the recent warm spell, all that damned snow had melted away. I closed my eyes for a moment, felt a breath of warmth against my cheeks. A hint of rain was in the air, soft and clean, with the barest trace of green growing things from the nearby parkway. Oh, yes.

Several cabs zipped past, most with drivers, a few more of

the new driverless kind. One of them actually slowed down—a first for me—but I waved it on. God knows, I wanted to ride home today, but I'd checked my bank account, and I wasn't happy with the answer. I'd gotten into a bad habit these past couple months, flinging cash around. I still had those student loans to pay off, never mind my parents had taught me better.

So I turned away from temptation and set off along Reservoir Road. Forty minutes would see me home, and the fresh air would do me good. Between my regular duties, such as they were, and a full night shadowing the on-call residents, I hadn't seen the outside of the hospital for almost thirty hours.

At the corner of Reservoir and Thirty-Fourth, I paused to catch my breath. Adanna Jones and her bookstore were a few blocks south. I felt a tug deep inside me, as though I were being called home. But just as I had discarded those emails unsent, I simply shook my head.

It's not the end of the world, she'd said.

A breeze kicked up, sharp and cold. Time to get home. I could make me a pot of that expensive new tisane Sara had acquired. Blood orange and lemongrass, according to the label. After I drank the whole pot, I would wrap myself in blankets and sleep until Sunday afternoon.

I crossed over Wisconsin and angled through the side streets to Q. Several of my neighbors were out, walking their dogs. One of them even smiled and mentioned the weather. I smiled back, and she didn't flinch. Progress, of a sort. Or maybe they just needed to get used to me.

The apartment lobby was blessedly warm and quiet. It was always quiet, always private here. Residents kept to themselves. Part of the charm, according to Hudson Realty.

I ran up the stairs and unlocked the door to 2B.

"Sara," I said. "I'm home. Did you miss me?"

No answer, but I hadn't really expected one. I stripped off

my gloves and hung up my coat, thinking about that tisane. But as I turned the corner around the parlor, I stopped.

That parlor had been a mess Friday morning. Sara had left behind a heap of newsfeed prints all over the table, along with two empty wine bottles and a full ashtray. Sara herself had left a note that said, DO NOT TOUCH, PLEASE.

All the mess had vanished—the printouts, the bottles, even the note itself. The bare table gleamed bright with polish, and the faint scent of wood soap lingered, as though the air itself had been scrubbed clean. The cleaning service, I told myself, but still my nerves hummed with sudden apprehension. It was too clean, too quiet in this apartment.

"Sara?" I called out.

No answer. Again, nothing to be alarmed about. Sara popped in and out like a genie these days. Even so, I had a strong impression that something was wrong. A glance toward the kitchen showed everything neat and ordered. A second glance told me that Sara's herb garden was missing.

I remembered once, back in Suitland, my parents and Grace and I walked into our tiny house to find the television missing. I was twelve, Grace was eight going on nine. We both stared at the empty, dusty hole our cheap thirteen-inch TV had once occupied. My first thought had been, *Why did Mom and Dad move the TV?*

And like then, I stared stupidly at the empty counters a moment before I stopped running through reasonable explanations.

Thieves? No, not with the government spies keeping watch. Besides, what kind of thief stole an herb garden and left behind that fancy microwave, the even fancier coffeemaker?

I walked slowly down the hallway to our bedrooms.

All the doors were wide open—linen closets, bathroom, and both bedrooms.

My breath stopped in my throat. It took me a moment before I could speak.

"Hello?"

No answer.

I swallowed hard and walked into Sara's bedroom. That was when I understood that I wasn't dealing with a simple robbery.

The piano and bed remained. But all of Sara's expensive paintings, the ones that hid electronic screens in plain sight, had vanished. The floor gleamed bright in the late-morning sun, with no sign that anyone had occupied this room, and the walls themselves retained no screw holes or patches of brighter paint, to show where the paintings once hung.

Moving very slowly, I checked each closet one by one.

Empty. All of them.

When I came to the last and largest closet, I ran my fingers over the back wall. Once, this had housed a secret passageway. Now? I stared hard at the smooth plaster wall. Perhaps the stairway and underground passageway still existed, but you would never have known it.

I sniffed. No trace of fresh plaster or paint. Another sniff, directed at the room at large. Just a whiff of wood polish and cinnamon. Sara Holmes had simply vanished, as completely as her possessions.

A loud clanging broke the silence. I dropped to the floor, heart pounding. It was Alton, Illinois, all over again. The blare of the siren. The thunder of an airplane swooping low as its guns rattled . . .

I gulped down a breath. Realized the siren was the landline telephone. I was safe in Washington, DC.

The phone kept ringing, a loud insistent jangling guaranteed to rattle my nerves. Still shivering, I stood up and hurried into the parlor. Jenna Hudson had explained the presence of the landline to us when Sara and I signed our lease. She had described it as "as a favor to our more traditional clients." Until today, it had never rung.

"Hello?" I said.

"Dr. Watson? Dr. Janet Watson? This is Jenna Hudson."

Jenna Hudson, the senior partner for Hudson Realty. Also, if I guessed correctly, a member of the same agency that employed Sara Holmes. I sat down with a thump and leaned against the cabinet, suddenly emptied out with relief.

"Yes, yes. It's me. What's wrong? What happened?"

"This is a courtesy call. We need to put 2B on the market."

My intestinal tract gave a mighty leap. "What? Why?"

Jenna paused, and I heard a world of calculation in that brief silence. "A matter of security."

Even that much information was a concession. I could tell.

"Where is Sara?" I demanded.

No reply.

I sucked my teeth and considered several different curses. Not that cursing would make any difference to Jenna Hudson and the FBI. "Fine," I snapped. "You don't have clearance to tell me, or I don't have clearance to get any answers. What about our lease?"

"As you might recall, the lease includes an emergency clause . . ."

Of course, it would, I thought bitterly. Not that it had done me any good last September when I'd pored over every single page, looking for an out.

"Page ten," Hudson said. "Clause eleven, paragraph two—"

The damnable text sprang up sharp and clear in memory— something about acts of God and war. What did that have to do with Sara and her new mission?

"You need to give me proper notice," I said. "I can't just find another set of rooms tomorrow."

"Of course," Hudson replied. "The clause states that you have thirty days to relocate. In recognition of the short notification, we are prepared to offer you a twenty percent rebate on your last month of rent."

The phone clicked, a loud mechanical click, and the line went dead. Completely dead, without even a whisper of a dial tone.

9

I dropped the receiver into my lap and closed my eyes.

The timing of that phone call was no coincidence. The FBI had set a watch on our apartment—Sara had warned me weeks ago. Watchers outside saw me walk through the front door. The cameras and audio pickup had recorded the moment when I discovered Sara's empty bedroom.

I blew out a breath. Considered shouting out a string of curses for my invisible audience.

Let's not test their sense of humor.

All my fantasies of hot tisane and twenty-four hours of deep sleep faded away. I levered myself to my feet and stumbled back down the hall to my own bedroom. No doubt they were still monitoring me, but right now I didn't care.

A quick scan showed nothing obviously out of place. None of my clothes or books had been tossed around. Neither was the room unnaturally tidy. With a sigh, I set about making a thorough examination of my belongings. Books, none taken, none added. Same with my medications. Closets . . . well, I didn't rifle through all the pockets of all my clothes, but the contents seemed untouched, including that one jacket that was always falling off its hanger.

Next up, the subtler clues. I did a quick inventory of my cell and tablet. No obvious signs of tampering, but then, these were experts. I stuffed both items back in my bag and sat down heavily on the bed.

Sara had left on a mission. That was clear. And now Hudson and the federal government wanted their expensive apartment back.

I scanned the room again. I remembered how my breath caught that day Jenna Hudson first showed me 2B at 2809 Q. How I'd come to see this apartment, this room, as a refuge, both quiet and lovely. A gift, however temporary.

Perhaps that was the nature of beauty—that it was meant to be brief. Perhaps I was right about gifts, after all.

♀

I skipped the tisane and went straight for the bottle of Macallan single malt, a Christmas present from Jacob Bell, who must have spent a week's salary on it. *Oh, Jacob, Jacob. I wish you were here right now. We could trade stories about Sara. Stories about coming home and finding you didn't quite fit where you once belonged.*

Whining didn't help, but it sure felt good if you had someone to share with. The recording devices all over 2B didn't count unless the FBI came to take me away for a more personal discussion. So, I drank a long slow glass of the single malt, then went through the usual drill with Lazarus and my medications and took myself to bed.

♀

The moment I woke up, late Sunday morning, all of yesterday's madness flooded back into my brain.

Sara had vanished into a new mission.

I had twenty-nine days to find a different apartment.

Other duties could wait. I spent the rest of the morning taking stock of what remained from Sara's abrupt departure—the answer being, not much, other than the fancy appliances and my own clothes and books. I found a loaf of bread in the refrigerator, a few scoops of coffee in a glass jar, and a single paper filter in one of the cabinets. Everything else—dishes, food, the knives and their knife block, the glassware—was gone. That alone convinced me more than anything else that Sara would not return.

By the afternoon, I'd ventured out, all grubby in my hoodie and sweats, to acquire groceries and a few utensils. None of my neighbors said hello, but at least they didn't report me to the police. Then I hunkered down with a mug of fresh coffee and my tablet to research apartments.

Not so bad. Not so good.

My share of the rent at 2B cost me $1,200 a month. For $1,100 a month, I could rent a cheap one-room affair in the SE quadrant, utilities included. The neighborhood would not be as quiet, or as safe, and I would have to spend more for a Metro card, but at least I would have privacy, and no one would twitch the rug from under my feet.

I created a new bookmark folder and added six possibilities. Then I made a fresh pot of strong coffee and played online games for the next six hours. It was almost enough to let me slip outside the problems and complications of this world and this reality. Almost, but not quite.

Monday morning, I reported for duty as required. Luckily, I'd had time to reassemble my armor against the world.

Or so I thought.

Pascal was leading morning rounds that day. She glanced at me with a smile when I joined the group, but then a faint crease appeared between her brows. I made a quick adjustment of my own features, which led to her smiling once more, but after the rounds, she glanced at me again, her expression curious.

That was the pattern for the rest of the day. Concern. Curiosity. Sometimes outright suspicion. My only respite was OT with Sydney, where I rolled through all the drills by rote. Apparently, that was the trick, because Lazarus and I now worked as partners, without debating every motion. No, more than partners. We were like a single organism, like the Father and Son. Now all we needed was to find our Holy Ghost.

By five P.M. and the afternoon rounds, I'd almost convinced myself that everything and everyone were back to normal, including me. I even managed to argue with Carter, who paused as if by coincidence while Chong gave her presentation. Our exchange was professional, if not exactly friendly.

"Busybody," Navarette muttered afterward as we headed toward the vending machines. "She's not CMO, not yet. Maybe never."

I shrugged. I didn't trust myself to be fair.

"Speaking of CMOs, I heard a rumor . . ." That was Pascal, who had drifted up behind us. "Something about a certain CMO on a certain president's short list."

Navarette's eyes went wide. "A cabinet position?"

"I thought Donnovan nominated someone to HHS already," I said. "Unless . . ."

"Withdrew," Pascal said briefly. "Family reasons."

Oh.

"That explains why she's so frantic about the M & M rate these days," Navarette said. "I thought it was just the funding issue."

We reached the vending machines, and I slid my debit card into the slot. "Could be both, you know. Could be she doesn't want our patients to die. Not everything is about politics."

Navarette smirked. "You're such a goddamned idealist, Watson."

"Maybe." I punched in the code for a Diet Coke, and the can slid into the dispenser. My comment about politics had reminded me about Sara's vanishing act. Who was I kidding? Goddamned politics had run my life for the past four years. Politics had robbed me of my best friend.

Breathe. Breathe. You lost a friend, but you always knew she was temporary. Remember the ones standing right here with you.

Both Pascal and Navarette were staring at me with obvious concern. Oh god, what kind of expression did I have? I took that deep breath and smiled, however unconvincingly. Flipped open the tab and lifted the can in a mock toast. "To our CMOs, past and present and future."

Before I could take a sip, my cell buzzed with a text message. **Please report to CMO ASAP** scrolled across the screen. The same moment, the loudspeaker crackled. "Paging Dr. Watson. Dr. Janet Watson. Please report to the CMO's office."

Oh shit. This could be either very good or very, very bad.

Navarette punched me in the arm. "What the hell did you do, girl? Did you forget to laugh at one of her jokes?"

I gave Navarette an answering love tap. "Nothing like. Bet she wants my advice on hair."

Pascal laughed. "Ten dollars says you're right."

"Goddamned white girls," I said with a smile, and headed toward the nearest elevator.

My first warning came when I arrived on the fourth floor, to find the reception area outside Hernandez's office completely empty. No executive assistant. No clerks or other minions.

Warning number two: Hernandez and two men in dark gray suits waiting just inside her office suite. Hernandez had a particularly pained expression, which made the almost invisible lines on her face stand out. The men, however, were utter blanks. Gray suits, gray hair. I suspected gray eyes as well, but those were hidden behind tinted glasses.

What the hell—?

"Dr. Watson," Hernandez said. "These gentlemen have a few questions. I hope you don't mind."

"Questions about what?" I asked cautiously. "And who are you?"

"We're investigating any unusual communications that took place on Inauguration Day," said Mr. Gray #1. "Our records show you placed a cellular call to Georgetown hospital's emergency center to report an altercation in the streets. We noted a few anomalies about that communication, which placed you on our list."

A cell call? Oh, right. The mob of red caps attacking black men. Frantically I tried to recall exactly what I'd said, what I'd done, that hectic day. Judging from their expressions, these two men wouldn't take *I don't remember* for an answer.

I managed to swallow enough spit to clear my throat. "I remember making that phone call, but I don't recall any anomalies—"

I stopped, suddenly afraid. I wanted a lawyer, or at least a witness other than Esma Hernandez, who was doing her best to appear invisible. No, bad idea. These were clearly federal agents, from one alphabet organization or another. I'd not forgotten my interviews with Special Agent Davidsson last November. Quite likely these two gray men had all the necessary paperwork to justify a private interrogation in case I proved uncooperative.

"I don't remember any anomalies," I repeated.

Gray Man #2 nodded, as though he'd expected that answer. "You made a call to the emergency number for Georgetown University Hospital. Your exact words were, *There's a fight going on. Near Volta Park. You might want to get ready for incoming casualties.* Then you said, *It's going to blow up fast.*"

And not ten minutes later, bombs had exploded the next street over.

I breathed in through my nose, felt the nausea settle. These were the times I appreciated the drills my parents had put me through, me and Grace both. In a very calm and level voice, I recited the events of that day.

"On Thirty-Fourth Street, I saw several dozen men fighting."

No need to mention these were white men attacking blacks.

"The police had arrived on the scene."

With Tasers, which they used to attack the black men.

"A man . . ." Here I hesitated, then rushed ahead. "A man wearing a red cap drew a gun. I fled the scene but heard gunfire, so I called in to GUH for a heads-up. That would be at Thirty-Fourth near Volta Park. The crowds appeared restless in that area as well, which is when I took refuge in a bookstore."

"Until you exited a few moments later," said Gray Man #2.

How the hell did you know that?

But I continued to be polite, cooperative. "That is correct," I said. "I'd heard the explosions. Based on my experience in the war, I knew there would be casualties."

The other special agent tilted his head. Light glinted from the metal implants behind his ears. And just like Sara, he went still and silent, listening.

"We have confirmation from the DC police department," he said to his companion.

Thank you and goddamn you for not believing me.

Gray Man #1 stood up and offered me a hand. "I appreciate your cooperation, Dr. Watson. And thank you, Dr. Hernandez, for giving us this opportunity."

We went through the usual formula. Or at least I think we did. Truth be told, I couldn't remember a damned thing we said. The Gray Men exited through the doors. Hernandez settled back into a chair with a sigh.

"That was close," she said softly.

Close for you, or close for me?

"I don't need to tell you that we have a difficult road ahead of us," she went on. "Political matters. Matters of safety for our patients. You're one of the best surgeons on our staff, once you complete your training. I don't want to lose you. Our reputation . . . is a delicate matter these days."

I suppressed the urge to say she could take her reputation and stuff it somewhere dark and damp. "I understand completely," I said in that voice I'd practiced since elementary school. "You have nothing to worry about."

We smiled at each other, neither one entirely convinced. I took my leave and headed back to the vending machine to replace the soda I'd handed to Navarette. It was all very odd, I thought. The Bloody Inauguration had turned bloody over a month ago. Why the hell were people bothering me now?

10

"That woman likes to play favorites," Navarette said. "That's my one and only complaint about her."

That woman meant Hernandez.

"Liar," Pascal said easily. "Why, just this morning, I counted six complaints, five snarky remarks, and one very filthy rant. And that was before rounds. You, my dear, don't have just one complaint. You have a small zip code's worth."

We had gathered in the cafeteria over limp spaghetti and slices of what claimed to be garlic bread. It was a late lunch for all four of us. Half the tables were empty. A few nurses occupied a table at the opposite end of the room, while interns eyed the not-so-promising list of specials. Even so, Navarette and Pascal kept their voices low as they continued their argument.

"You know what I mean," Navarette said. "She picks a favorite. Heaps them with attention, special perks. Tells them they have a bright career ahead. Then she . . . changes her mind."

Her glance toward me was brief but expressive.

I shrugged and concentrated on winding spaghetti around my fork. Navarette had not asked about my summons to Hernandez's office three days ago, but she was obviously curious. Pascal, too. Only Letova, who had come off a very long shift, kept quiet and huddled over her cup of coffee.

"Take Carter, for example."

Pascal wrinkled her nose. "You take her."

"Oh hush. You know I'm right. We all believed Carter was the golden child," Navarette said to me. "First that surgery-and-transplant fellowship, then senior attending just a year later. Rumor said Hernandez was pushing for Carter to be named the next CMO. Way too soon, but maybe not, not if Hernandez gets that cabinet post."

By this point, our conversation had dropped into a whisper, and we all leaned close together.

"But then *you* came along," she went on. "Rumor said you were the new golden child, with all those perks and that shiny new device. You were not just a damned talented surgeon— you were a hero."

I twitched at the word *hero*. For a moment, I saw the muddy ditch in Alton, Illinois, where I hid with my patients from the enemy soldiers. Quickly I pushed the memory aside. "I'm hardly eligible for CMO."

"No, but—"

"Enough." Letova slammed her cup down, slopping coffee all over the table. "Can't you do anything else but gossip? And I thought you were too goddamned serious for these stupid games, Watson."

The three of us glanced at each other. Letova's voice was rough with anger. Her eyes were red rimmed from exhaustion. She'd been edgy all week, but not like this.

Letova pressed both hands against her eyes. "I'm . . . I'm sorry. I didn't get much sleep yesterday."

"David giving you trouble again?" Pascal asked.

David was Letova's brother, an angry young man who had frequent run-ins with the police. Drugs. Shoplifting. At least one arrest for arson, when he set fire to a local mosque. Nina never made excuses for him, but she never stopped taking his calls.

Today, she merely shrugged. "Something like that." She wiped up the spilled coffee and dropped the napkin into the cup. "I should get going. I need to stop by the grocery store, and I don't want to fall asleep in the frozen foods aisle."

Navarette laid a hand on her shoulder. "My medical advice is that you go straight home and go to sleep. Leave the shopping for tomorrow."

"But—"

"No buts, sunshine. You are wiped." Navarette snapped her fingers. "Better idea. Anyone on call this evening? No one? Why don't we head out to a bar or a movie? Pascal, call your wife and tell her you need to make a medical intervention and she's on kid duty. Letova, go home and take that nap. But after that, my friend, we are going to get you stinking drunk. Watson, are you with us?"

I was damned tempted. But . . .

"I want to," I said. "But I have an appointment."

"A date?" Pascal asked with glee in her voice.

I flinched, shook my head. "No, no date. Unless a real estate agent counts."

"Ah. Right."

Comprehension all around. I'd told them about finding a new apartment, though I hadn't mentioned the reasons. Navarette's eyes narrowed, and she gave me a speculative look, but she didn't ask any pointed questions.

Good thing, because I had no pointed answers.

By seven P.M., I had negotiated the Metro from Georgetown hospital to a redbrick apartment building in the SW quadrant. The advertisement had promised "the luxuries of modern comfort"—whatever that meant—at an affordable price.

Now the real estate agent, a woman with fluffy white hair whose name I'd forgotten the moment she told me, was giving me the official tour. As she led me through the narrow hallway, past the galley kitchen and into the combined living/dining room, she gave a running commentary that was an expanded version of that same advertisement.

". . . six hundred square feet for this apartment, which is the single-small-bedroom floor plan. Fully appointed kitchen, complimentary Wi-Fi, and miniblinds . . ."

God. Miniblinds.

". . . a business center on the ground floor, fitness club, and covered parking . . ."

I glanced into the bedroom with its full-length mirrors and its deep-pile carpeting. Whoever had selected the color scheme had done a masterful job with bland. Pale beige walls. Dark beige carpets. The minimal trim painted a shade exactly between the two. The absolutely odorless air, as though it too had been scrubbed clean and erased of life.

Very safe. Very dull. I couldn't help but remember Jenna Hudson showing me 2809 Q Street for the first time.

. . . A comfortable couch and two chairs occupied the space in front of the window. An old-fashioned telephone in one corner, a small cabinet equipped with electronic devices. The whole room had the air of something from the late nineteenth century, but with grace notes of the twenty-first.

". . . a very quiet neighborhood with easy access to . . ."

The agent's voice trailed off. It took me moment to realize she'd stopped talking. I plucked my thoughts away from the past and 2809 Q Street and turned around with a smile. "My apologies. My thoughts went wandering. You were saying about the terms?"

She'd said nothing about the terms, but she was a professional. "Two thousand for the rent, with all amenities included, except the fitness club, which requires a small monthly fee. If you prefer more space, we also have a floor plan for a larger single-bedroom."

I recalled the description from the advertisement. Seven hundred sixty square feet, five hundred dollars more per month.

"I don't really know," I said slowly.

"Of course. Take your time to think it over. The application fee is fifty dollars in case you decide to move forward."

She handed over a sheaf of brochures, which I accepted more out of politeness than any desire to live in the country of the beige. In turn, I promised to call her back within a week.

Outside, I breathed in the night air, laden with exhaust smoke and the promise of rain. The Metro station was the next intersection over, the shops and restaurants of Chinatown only a few blocks farther on, and I could hear the traffic on 395. Quiet, but not silent.

Better than a hostel, I thought. *Better than a dirt farm.*

My first impulse was to text Navarette and join the merry crew wherever they had ended up. But I was in no mood to be merry myself. Instead, I took the Metro to Wisconsin, then walked to a Turkish diner I knew, where I ordered a plate of falafel sandwiches and a pot of spiced tea.

Waiting for my food, I leafed through the brochure. I found no surprises there. The glossy photographs of the various apartments all looked alike to me. There were a few larger suites that seemed more appealing, but they cost nearly three times as much.

I am such a spoiled brat these days, I thought.

I had just flipped to the back of the brochure and was scanning the prices a second time when a faint buzz sounded from my bag. I dug out my cell, thinking it had to be Pascal or Navarette. But the cell was quiet, and the buzzing didn't stop.

Oh. Could it be . . .

I hurriedly sorted through the jumble of clothes and books and other oddments, to fetch out Sara's texting device. When it buzzed again, it was little more than a soft vibration. Before I could speak Sara's name, the screen flickered once, then a message scrolled by.

Continue to look confused, my love. But say nothing. Return this device to your bag, eat your meal, then read your book. Once you are truly private, you might consider the message embedded within.

Sara. She was somewhere nearby—she had to be.

My pulse beating faster, I followed her instructions: shrugged, rolled my eyes, tossed the device back into my bag. When my meal arrived, I concentrated on the falafel sandwiches as though nothing else existed.

So far, so good.

I pushed my plate away, then poured a second cup of tea and rummaged through my bag for the paperback I'd stowed there in the morning. S. A. Chakraborty's latest novel. *Epic fantasy at its finest,* read the cover.

But when I pulled the book from my bag, my pulse gave another jump. Someone had inserted a bookmark at the end of the first chapter—a thick piece of paper folded in half. I never used a bookmark. Angela had teased me endlessly about this habit, but I liked picking up a book and flipping through the pages to where I'd left off. If I couldn't remember, I told her, then maybe I needed to reread a chapter or two.

Reading was impossible. All I could do was pretend to scan each page. One page, one sip of tea. Once I finished the cup, I set the book aside, facedown, and poured a third cup while I contemplated the dessert menu. When the waitress returned, I sadly shook my head and said I had decided against having anything more, and could she please bring the check.

I replaced the bookmark where I had left off "reading" and returned the book to my bag. After I paid my bill, I stopped in the restroom and locked myself in the first open stall.

Now I was shivering. Sara had given me the texting device. I had always assumed she had one of her own. But what if the FBI had confiscated hers? What if they wanted a second, and more private, interview?

Well, there was only one way to find out.

I extracted the so-called bookmark. The paper was thick and textured. One side was blank. The other was covered with familiar handwriting that sprawled over the page.

> *Dearest Janet,*
>
> *I need a very great favor from you. Do you remember where we first met? Of course you do. So. If you are willing to accept the challenge, go there Saturday morning at ten A.M. Wait for a bald man wearing a white carnation . . .*
>
> *Just teasing, my love. What I really want you to do is contemplate the exquisite view for as long as seems plausible, then continue to #819 Seventh Street. If all goes well, and our mutual friends do not interfere, we shall have another of our private talks.*

No signature, but I recognized that exuberant handwriting, not to mention the equally exuberant and unpredictable mind behind the set of directions. Running my fingertips over the upper corner, I found the expected pattern of raised dots. I held the sheet over the toilet and pressed hard against the dots. A sharp prick against my thumb was all the warning I had before the paper exploded into a shower of ashes.

I dusted off my hands and flushed the toilet. Stared down at the whirlpool of ashes.

Oh, Sara, what have you done now?

❦

For the rest of Thursday, on through Friday night, I did my best to pretend I was nothing more than Janet Watson, a surgeon (of sorts) at Georgetown hospital, and not someone in secret communication with a covert government agent. I joked with Navarette about the young man who had flirted with her, and the hangover Pascal insisted she did not have. I even sent a message to the real estate agent with a request to view the larger one-bedroom apartment.

Ten A.M. the next morning saw me underfed and undercaffeinated in the basement of the National Gallery of Art. Sara called Dalí's *Last Supper* a moveable feast, since the museum liked to move its location every year or so. A typical Sara joke.

I hate you. I love you.

Complicated emotions for a complicated woman.

Twenty minutes passed while I contemplated Dalí's luminous painting. It was silent here. Like a church at midnight. Like the medical unit at dawn, when the enemy slept. I practiced the one-minute meditation Faith had taught me, attention focused on the air rushing into my lungs, the pressure against my chest, and the sensation of light filling my veins.

Breathe in, breathe out. Don't try to clear your mind. Let your thoughts hover.

Once, just once, I had the impression that someone stood

behind me. The skin between my shoulder blades itched. I resisted the urge to spin around and continued my study of Dalí's *Last Supper*. It was, after all, an excellent choice. I could make out the analogies embedded in the scene, the layers of meaning and images the painter had added to a straightforward depiction of this famous biblical story.

A few visitors came into the gallery, spending only a few moments before they continued to the next exhibit. I waited another five minutes before I'd had enough of Dalí myself and headed back toward the exit.

My cell charted my course from the museum, directly up Seventh Street, to the address Sara had given me. PHAN MINH TRADING COMPANY, read the sign. Dark red shades covered the windows from the inside, which were plastered over with signs in Vietnamese and English, advertising a sale. I pushed the door open and found myself in a crowded entryway, with an electronic cash register on one side and a narrow aisle winding toward the back.

A young woman behind the cash register nodded at me. "Welcome. Please let me know if you need assistance."

I need to find a certain secret agent.

But I simply smiled back and nodded. "Thank you."

Not sure what to expect, I continued along the aisle. Shelves on either side carried jars of spices, herbs, dried noodles, teas, and more. Overhead, a wingless paper dragon floated in the air. I skirted around an enormous stack of pottery, only to find myself in a small open space with two tables underneath a window

Once more, I sensed a presence behind me. *Sara.*

I spun around.

A short stocky woman stood behind me. She was the opposite of Sara—box braids tumbling over her shoulders, round sunglasses, and an oversize trench coat with too many pockets. I would have pegged her as one of the army of homeless in DC, except for the glittering diamond earring that dangled from one ear.

"Hello," she said. "Glad you could make it."

"Who are you?" I demanded. *And where is Sara?*

"We met once, last year," the woman said. Her voice was light and breathless. "My name is Micha."

Micha. Now I remembered. This woman was Sara's cousin, the one who had located a car for me and Sara last October, so we could flee DC and track down who was killing veterans from America's New Civil War. Her coloring was as dark as Holmes's, her skin was stretched tight over her cheeks and jaw, and in the light from the window, I caught a glint of gray in her braided hair. Odd. I had imagined her as a much younger woman.

Micha tilted her head and smiled, as though she could guess the trajectory of my thoughts. She gestured to the table under the window. "You do remember me. Good. The tea here is excellent. I invite you to share a pot with me. No one will bother us."

"Including you?"

She chuckled. "Sara was right about you. Sit. I'll order tea. You can always leave, after all."

I took a seat at the first empty table. Glanced around the narrow space. An orange cat, perched high on a shelf to my left, stared back at me with that same condescending expression as Sydney's cat, Ono. Another cat, this one a dark tabby so ancient that its spine showed through its thinning fur, dozed in a patch of sunlight. It blinked at me, sniffed, then dropped back to sleep.

Cats were so damned judgmental.

Moments later, Micha set down a tray with a pot, two cups of translucent porcelain, and a pile of napkins. She slid into the chair opposite me and poured out tea for us both.

"We have five minutes," she said, "possibly a few more, before anyone cares how much time you spend in this shop. So please listen while I explain."

The tea was scorching hot and fragrant, with a whiff of smoke and a lovely flavor I had never tasted before.

"Go ahead," I told her. "Start off with why you forged that letter."

Her mouth quirked in a smile. "A matter of national and personal security. You would not have agreed to this meeting unless you believed the note came from Sara. No, don't leave yet. Hear me out. The very short explanation is that Sara believes treason has been committed here and—"

"What does that have to do with me? She's a federal agent—"

"Not anymore."

That flat statement stopped me cold.

"What do you mean?"

"I mean that our beloved Sara has gone absent without leave from her service. She did submit the necessary paper-work somewhere after or during the fact, but naturally that does not absolve her from crossing borders and engaging in forbidden activities."

Oh, dear god. Those were a lot of words that boiled down to treason.

"What does she want with me?" I whispered.

Micha didn't answer right away. She drank her tea, her gaze turned inward. Her face was all strong lines, brush-strokes of ink and umber. Her slim hands held the cup lightly and surely. I waited, almost patiently. Five minutes, or less, before the watchers noticed.

"As I said, it's a question of national security," she said at last. "Sara has not shared all the details with me, but she tells me the plot involves Nadine Adler and a faction within the New Confederacy."

Oh, dear god. I was only joking when I told her she was obsessed.

Apparently not. My gut twisted over into knots at all the implications.

"Was it—is it the Brotherhood?"

"Them or another like them. Sara did not specify."

Christ. She'd done it. Tossed her career into a bonfire. And now she wanted to involve me.

"What . . . What does she believe is the plot?"

Micha's lips thinned. "Sara has not shared that detail either."

A hint of exasperation showed in her voice. Aha. I was not alone in wanting to smack Sara Holmes upside the head. "You cousin wants the impossible. You don't even know what she wants of me. You can't even tell me where she is—"

"She's in the New Confederacy. Oklahoma. I should not say even that much."

Fuck.

"What does she want with me?"

"She . . . she needs a surgeon," Micha said. "She told me you were the only surgeon she could trust. I'm to bring you to her, if you agree."

Across the border. In the middle of the New Confederacy.

No, no, no. Not after Alton, Illinois. Not after what happened last October.

Already I was trembling.

Micha laid a hand next to mine, not touching. "I told her she was wrong to ask this of you. I understand. I'll find someone else. Perhaps I can persuade Grandmamma to help."

Sara's grandmother, who granted favors but demanded

even more favors in return. Well, that was just a warm fuzzy reassurance.

"But just in case . . ."

I jerked my head up. "In case of what?"

Micha stood up and smiled. "In case you change your mind," she said. "Use the text device Sara gave you. Just say yes, nothing more. Let me know by midnight." She paused a moment, then added, "Just remember, they are watching you."

♀

I fumbled my way through the rest of the day, though I'm not sure I recall any details. I ordered takeout at one point, ate, and washed up my dishes, possibly in that order. By evening, I was sunk into the couch facing the grand bay window. The sun had vanished below the horizon and the DC skyline was edged in crimson.

By this this time, the haze in my mind had cleared and I was angry.

Goddamn you, Sara. You had no right to barge into my life. No right to offer safety and beauty, only to yank it all away. You goddamned didn't have a right to send your triple-damned cousin to lure me into a scheme that can only ruin both our lives.

Trouble with being angry, it made it hard to sit still. I grabbed my bag and headed out the door.

The walk to the Mall needed only twenty minutes or so. I skirted around the Reflecting Pool and fetched up by the Lincoln Memorial. There I stopped at the bottom step and braced myself, in military rest, as I stared up into Lincoln's blank white face, illuminated by the spotlights.

Hello, old friend. Nice to see you again. And what were you thinking? You who wanted all us black people gone from these United States. You who didn't go to war against slavery, as much as slavery went to war against you and the North.

Lincoln said nothing. He never did—one of his most irritating traits. If only we could haul the dead before a court of law, the heroes, the villains, the ones with good intent, the selfish narcissists. If only we could demand the truth from them, or better, if we could make them confront the truth. Trump, for instance . . .

But Trump was long dead now, and his ancestors in politics would never confront the truth. However much I wished it, Lincoln and others like him could not undo history.

The problem was today, with Nadine Adler and the New Confederacy.

I sighed. I could see exactly where this was going. A sensible Janet Watson would remain in DC. Take that very boring apartment with all its amenities and miniblinds. Hold fast to the new life Sara herself had gifted me.

Except that Sara had saved my life two or three times over. Never mind that she had drugged me, turned my life upside down, and wreaked havoc with all boundaries between us.

Goddamn you, I thought, but without any real anger.

I took the texting device from my bag and held it to my mouth.

"Yes," I said. "Yes, I will."

A single line of text scrolled over the device.

Will send you further instructions on Monday. Until then, be discreet.

11

Monday showed up like the ghost of Christmas past, humorless and with a faint foreboding. I put myself on automatic, as if I were prepping Lazarus and my stump. Morning rounds. A one-on-one with Anna Chong. A brief exchange with Carter about a patient who might qualify for early discharge.

Then I came to the one point in the day where I absolutely could not go by rote.

"How are you today?" Faith Bellaume said.

Not an idle question, that. I sifted through a dozen possible answers, wishing I'd had more specific instructions from Micha. The last time I'd lied to Faith—lied deliberately—Sara Holmes and I had worked out exactly what to hide, what to reveal. I wasn't sure I was up to solo work.

Then, it was as though Sara whispered in my ear.

Tell her the truth. Tell her you hurt.

I nearly flinched. But yes, I did hurt.

"Not . . . as well as I'd like," I said. "I hurt. Everything I expected from Georgetown . . ." I struggled to draw a breath.

"I had hoped too much. I've worked hard. I thought I would be rewarded. I need to recalibrate those expectations."

"Why does that hurt?"

Because I'm taking all those expectations and throwing them out the window. I have to. I need to. But I'm still afraid.

I took a sip of water as I considered how to answer her question convincingly. "Perhaps *hurt* was the wrong word. I'm afraid. Of failing. Of disappointing my mother and father, even though they aren't here to see me fail."

"Fair enough. But have you considered that you want to fail?"

I sucked in my breath. "You think—"

"I don't think anything," Faith said gently. "I'm only asking you to consider the possibility. Remember what we talked about. How children absorb the attitudes around them, even before they're conscious of those attitudes." As I opened my mouth to protest, she held up a hand. "I am not accusing your parents of doing that. Or your sister, Grace. But you told me how your grandmother fought with your father about moving up north."

Oh. That. Yes.

I rubbed my hands over my face, which felt curiously numb. My father and my grandmother had shouted at each other for days over my parents' decision to leave the dirt farm and Georgia for a better life up north. Even years later, their conversations by telephone had turned into bitter arguments.

Well, I couldn't tell Faith the truth, not all of it, but I could acknowledge the truth she told me.

"I think you might be right." My voice came out hoarse, and I had to take a deeper drink of water before I tried again. "Thank you for that insight."

Her mouth tilted into a wry smile. "Insight belongs to the patient, not the therapist. But you're welcome."

Our conversation continued—patient on her end, distracted and halting on mine—over the next twenty minutes. I talked about my grandmother and her Alzheimer's. We spoke about the burden of guilt, visited unto the second and third generations. All the time, I was aware of her watchful gaze. Eventually we came to the end of our session.

"So," Faith said. "Shall I see you again in two weeks?"

Now I hesitated. For all I knew, Micha meant for us to take off for the New Confederacy tonight.

Pretend nothing has changed, said that voice that could have been Sara's.

"Yes," I said. "Two weeks is fine."

Faith Bellaume frowned—I almost expected her to denounce me as a liar—but she said nothing more than, "Until two weeks, then."

Danger avoided. Discretion preserved.

The rest of my Monday afternoon faded back into the ordinary and mundane. Afternoon rounds proved to be a repeat of the morning. Nothing life-threatening or even faintly unusual. For the first time in a very long while, I felt competent, and not merely as if I were going through the motions.

Nevertheless, I didn't dare to breathe deeply until my so-called ordinary workday ended and I could shuck off my useless scrubs. My scalp itched. My skin felt sticky with invisible sweat. All I wanted was to disappear into apartment 2B with another cup of that delicious tea.

At seven P.M., the hospital locker room was empty, wrapped in the sharp scent of antiseptic, overlaid by sweat and latex. Most of the surgeons and other doctors either worked in the on-call room or had not yet begun their shift. I was glad. I couldn't bring myself to pretend much longer. Micha had told me to expect further instructions today. She had not shared when or where to expect them. Family resemblance, much?

A hot shower put me into a better mood. My face no longer felt numb. And if disappointment had a distinct smell, at least I'd rid myself of that. I scrubbed myself dry and reattached Lazarus before massaging my scalp with the new hair oil I'd bought the week before.

Back in the locker room, I dug out my street clothes.

And stopped when my hand encountered a book-shaped object. The outer surface was slick, the corners blunted, and when I ran my fingers around the edges, I could make out the rough-cut edges of pages. Definitely a book. A hardcover, no less.

I fished the book out of my bag and examined the cover. *Trail of Echoes,* read the title. *An Elouise Norton novel, by Rachel Howzell Hall.*

Oh my. One of my favorite books, from one of my favorite detective series. Talk about strong black women taking names and getting shit done. And this was not only a hardcover but a signed limited edition.

Every detail spoke of Micha and her ingenuity. I didn't usually buy hardcovers, but this was the kind of book I would treat myself to.

And today, I think, I will treat myself to a good dinner.

An hour later, I had a table to myself at Sally's Kitchen, near the back of the restaurant. The waitress set the plate of shrimp and grits in front of me, then refilled my glass of water. "You sure you don't want nothing else?" she said.

I took in the mound of grits and shrimp, with its clouds of sharp, spicy goodness, and considered that anything more might be fatal. "Nothing for now, thank you."

"Well, you just let me know if you change your mind, honey."

She winked at me and went on to her next customer.

I set to work on my meal—no hardship there. Sally's had been a favorite of mine since my days at Howard University. Back then, I'd hurried through eating so I could get back to my dorm and my studies. Tonight, I took my time, savoring each bite while I tried not to think about the book in my bag.

One thing hadn't changed—I'd be taking home at least half the shrimp and grits for dinner tomorrow. With a sigh, I leaned back and signaled to the waitress.

"Dessert?" she said.

"Oh, Lord, no. But a glass of wine would go down well."

The waitress delivered the wine and a carton for my leftovers. "You take your time, sweetheart. I can tell you had yourself a long day."

A day that would get even longer before I was done.

With the stage set, I retrieved Micha's book from my bag and casually leafed through the opening pages as I sipped my wine. Lou, her partner, the opening notes of the mystery, were all just as marvelous as I remembered. However, I was part of a new and different mystery myself, so I stopped reading and ran my fingers over the edges of the pages.

Nothing, nothing, nothing . . .

And then I found it—a sheet of paper inserted in the middle of chapter 3. Casually, I paused. The sheet was nearly empty, except for three short paragraphs in close-written script, in handwriting utterly unlike Sara Holmes's. (But very much like Micha's, I suspected.) In the upper right corner was a raised pattern of dots.

And I knew what that meant.

I settled back into my seat and read from the beginning of chapter 3. Every once in a while, I turned back a page or two, as if to double-check an earlier clue in the plot. At last I reached the page from Micha.

The following instructions are critical for proper care and handling. To wit, excessive exposure to heat proves fatal to certain fabrics. Use only the gentlest soaps and conditioners. Air-dry when possible. When you have committed these to memory, please dispose of your instructions according to government regulations.

I snorted. The handwriting might have been Micha's, but the style was pure Sara. Was this straight-up family resemblance or deliberate imitation? I read on.

Ignore the previous persiflage. Now for the true instructions. Keep this letter in the book and keep the book in your bag. There will come a time to destroy our evidence, but not yet. Here are the first steps into adventure . . .

 Step #1. Return that last phone call from your sister and ask about your grandmother. Do this tonight and no later, please. Your sister will tell you that your grandmother's health has not improved, and that she needs professional care.

I must have choked, because my waitress paused next to my table. "Is something the matter, honey?"

"No. Nothing," I said quickly. "Just swallowed the wrong way."

Nothing except that Micha *and* Sara's people had rifled through my life, apparently. Damn them both.

"Mmmm-hmmm. Lemme fetch you some more water, then."

I accepted the water, and on second thought, ordered a small carafe of wine, before I returned to my instructions.

Tell your sister you will make all the necessary arrangements in person. If she objects, or she wants a reason, tell her that you feel guilty for all your good fortune.

Oh god. She did know Grace.

Step #2. Request a month's personal leave from work. Do this tomorrow, as early as possible. If your CMO wants a reason, tell her you want to review home care facilities for your grandmother.

Right. How the hell was I supposed to do that, if I was faffing around the New Confederacy?

It was as though Micha had read my future thoughts, because the next line read:

Don't worry about the apparent contradictions. I'll take care of everything. Step by step is how we shall dance across the border, find my cousin, and save the world. When you are ready for the next set of instructions, press the dots in the margin next to these words.

I ran my fingertips over the margin—lightly, because I wasn't certain I wanted or needed to read those next instructions. The dots were faint, little more than a pattern of imperfection in the heavy paper. Not like the dots in the upper right corner, which would turn these pages into dust. Something . . . even more ingenious, I guessed.

I'll find out soon enough.

I refilled my glass and settled down to read the rest of chapter 3.

12

I splurged and took a cab back to 2809 Q Street and the apartment I no longer shared with Sara Holmes. Once the door to apartment 2B closed behind me, I dropped my bag in the entryway and tossed my jacket in the general direction of the closet.

They are watching you, Micha had told me, back in the tea shop.

A totally unnecessary warning. They'd been watching me and this apartment for several months, according to Sara. Still, the reminder was a good one. I continued into my bedroom, where I changed into sweats and a T-shirt. Even if no one monitored the apartment at this precise moment, the knowledge that cameras recorded my every movement left me queasy.

I glanced at the clock. Only nine P.M. Far too early to call Grace on the West Coast. So, dear reader, what would Janet Watson do, to fill in the hours?

Tea. Tea would be good.

I filled the kettle and set the water to boil, then fetched

my new/not new book from my bag. By the time the tea had brewed, I had read deep into the unfolding mystery of the present, which tied inexorably to Lou's past.

Girl, I know all about that. I poured a cup of tea and glanced once more at the clock. Too soon, yet. Grace and her family would be finishing up dinner right about now.

Around eleven P.M., I yawned and set the book aside, then wandered into my bedroom, where I made a pretense of checking my messages and email on my tablet. After a suitable delay, I called up a video-chat channel and dialed Grace's number.

Within a couple beeps, the screen illuminated to show a man's dark brown face. He glanced down at what had to be the caller ID display, then back at my face. "King family residence. May I ask who's calling?"

I recognized Grace's husband. Colin, that was his name. We'd met briefly at their wedding five years ago, each of us eyeing the other suspiciously. Less than a year later, I had vanished into the military, and two years after that, Grace and her husband had escaped to the West Coast.

"Colin, hello," I said. "It's Janet. Grace's sister—"

Shouting broke out in the background. "Papa! Papa! Is that Aunty Kayla?"

Two girls wrestled their way into the video pickup. Both of them were laughing and shrieking. In the background, Grace was demanding that her children stop acting like wild animals, but I could hear the laughter in her voice.

"Hush," Colin told his daughters. "Go back to your mama. Ain't you both supposed to be in bed by now?" Then he leaned closer to the screen and said softly, "Janet? Is something wrong?"

Everything, I thought. I had to quash the bubble of anxious laughter before I could go on with my charade.

"Nothing's wrong," I said. "May I speak with my sister?"

He hesitated a moment. "I guess that's okay."

Okay? Since when is talking to my sister not okay?

Before I could say anything I regretted, Grace replaced her husband in the video pickup. "Janet." Her voice was breathless. "What's wrong?"

What was wrong is that when I called my family, they could only think of disaster. My own damned fault, with me not calling them or answering their messages, except to make excuses. Not that Grace ever made it easy to talk or write—

I pinched the bridge of my nose and reached for that quiet deep inside, the one Faith had taught me about. "Listen," I said. "I'm sorry I didn't call you sooner. Nothing is wrong. I just wanted to talk about Gramma."

Grace frowned—the exact same way our mother had frowned whenever we disappointed her. Only now did I realize that faint lines fanned out from my sister's eyes, and her hair had taken on a silvery cast. Grace was three years younger than me, but she had aged faster and harder. How much of her life had I missed these past few years?

"Took you long enough," she said.

My baby sister was too damned good with delivering guilt. No doubt she got that from our father's side of the family. Except . . . except this time, she was right.

"I'm sorry," I said. "I know I haven't . . . I haven't done right these past few years. I'm sorry." My breath puffed out in a weak laugh. "Maybe I felt guilty."

"Girl, you should feel guilty."

But I heard a touch of humor in that statement.

"So tell me," I said. "How is she?"

"Not so great," Grace said. "The doctors say it's definitely Alzheimer's. Getting worse these past two months."

Oh. Christ, indeed. And where was his mercy now?

"Fucking Alzheimer's," I said.

My sister blew out a breath that was almost a laugh, but not quite. "That's what I said. Aunt Jemele still lives at the old home, but she's getting on. There's Uncle Jimmy, and Uncle Samuel, but they ain't so young themselves, and the older grandkids have been leaving as soon as they can."

"Can't say I blame them," I murmured.

Now she did laugh. "Damn you, Janet. You always did say too much. But yeah, can't say I miss that farm."

"So," I said. "Tell me about these home services."

Aunt Jemele had sent Grace a list of services in the county. We talked about the options available down in rural Georgia, and the ones that might prove best for our grandmother. The overlap between the two was slim, but better than I had expected.

After that, we talked another hour. About the dirt farm as we remembered it. About those first years in the DC area, how it all looked like a jumble of concrete, except those few pocket fields behind the house, and how we had to learn what seemed like a whole other kind of English. About East Coast, West Coast, and how white people were all alike but at the same time they were all different. But I noticed Grace never spoke about our parents, or about anything grand or tragic. Neither did I. Perhaps it was enough, for now.

"I was thinking," I said. "Maybe I should make a visit. See what those facilities are like. I am a doctor, after all."

Grace snorted. "As if you would let anyone forget."

"Damn, you, Grace. I was just trying to—"

She cut me off with a wave of her hand. "I know, I know. I shouldn't have said that. I'm sorry." She sighed and rubbed her eyes with her knuckles. In the background, I heard Colin ask a question, but she shook her head at him and mouthed a reply.

Seems Colin thought I was causing trouble. I almost told Grace to forget about it, and we could talk later, but then she turned back to me. "You're right," she said. "You being a doctor will help. Those home care places, maybe the government pays for everything these days, but *everything* means all kinds of different things, depending on who you talk to, never mind about how they treat their people."

She made it too easy, my sister did, to follow Micha's instructions.

"I need to ask for personal leave," I replied. "But I want to get down there by next week. Maybe sooner."

"Good." Her expression wavered. Then she said, "You always did what's right."

I wish that were true.

But those damned cameras were keeping watch, so I simply shrugged. Grace and I said our good-byes, and I promised to send her a report on my findings. Then I clicked off the chat line and powered down the tablet.

One A.M. Tomorrow would be a long and weary day. But then, I'd trained for days exactly like that, back in the service, and earlier, during my residency. So, I took my tired self off to the bathroom, where I followed every step of the drill to care for my stump and my device. And because Janet Watson would do such a thing, I poured a small glass of whiskey and settled back into my pillows to read one more chapter about Elouise Norton and her search for justice.

🔎

I set my alarm for five thirty. By six thirty, I had collected a croissant and a cup of extra-strong coffee from a neighborhood shop and was sitting in the hospital cafeteria with Letova and Pascal.

"Snob," Pascal said as she eyed my breakfast.

"I wish," I replied. "But today, just today, I could not face the coffee here. Perhaps I should petition the hospital to change their menu? Think management would go for that?"

Pascal snorted. Letova smiled and shook her head. Then her cell blinked with a notification. She frowned at the screen. "Gotta go, Doctors. Duty calls."

"Same here," Pascal said, as she drank the last of her coffee. "See you at lunch, Watson?"

"Not sure. I need to work on that abstract."

I waited for Pascal to leave, then ducked around the corner, where I texted Hernandez, asking for a private interview.

The reply came back immediately: **Of course. 10 a.m. Confirm with Liza.**

I tapped the lock button on my cell and leaned against the wall. This game of spies was proving far too easy. How long before I made a mistake? How long before the FBI or CIA caught up with us?

I tapped a message to Liza to confirm my interview, then headed off to morning rounds.

۹

One week ago, I had reported to Esma Hernandez's office, only to find two government agents waiting for me. They had not outright accused me of any crime, but they had insinuated and implied and asked any number of questions they had no right or reason to ask. And Hernandez had stood by, her only concern about the hospital's reputation.

Today we faced each other with smiles, but I could tell the memory of that interrogation was as fresh with her as it was with me.

"Dr. Watson," she said. "Coffee? Tea?"

"Coffee, please," I said. "If it's no trouble."

Within moments, one of the office minions returned with

a tray with a carafe, two cups, and various containers of sugar and cream. Hernandez politely waited until I had stirred cream into my coffee and drunk a few sips. "Is this about the conference?" she asked.

Had I imagined that flicker of eagerness?

"No, this is a personal matter," I said. "My grandmother has Alzheimer's. Her condition is getting worse. I'd like to take a month's leave, so I can visit and look into proper care for her."

Hernandez nodded. "Not a problem. Of course, you need to attend to your family. How soon do you need to this leave to start?"

"As soon as possible. Friday would be best."

I had been worried she would refuse. Worse, I had worried that she would remind me I had no regular duties, and perhaps I needn't return. But Hernandez merely commented that my absence would present no difficulties, though she hoped I could return before the month was over.

We discussed the details of my absence—whether Chong or Bekker required mentoring during the interim, and if so, who might be the best surgeon to take them on. How the leave affected pay and seniority, not to mention the date for my transition to full-time surgeon.

The dance of politics finished, Hernandez shook my hand and turned me over to her assistant to handle all the electronic forms for my leave of absence. By the time we had finished, and Liza had forwarded copies to my account, I was more than ready to escape into my own office.

♀

Time for the next step. I opened my exclusive signed copy of *Trail of Echoes* to Micha's instruction page. *Press the dots in the margin,* she said. I did.

The ink on the page appeared to shimmer. I stared, breath held, as the three paragraphs of close-written text dissolved into a murky gray blob. The cloud of ink faded back into the paper. A new set of paragraphs had appeared in its place.

By now, you have requested and received a leave of absence. This in turn should deflect any suspicions about your sudden desire to travel south. (Unless, of course, our fine government agents decide to question you more closely.) If at any time you believe our game has been discovered, please take the usual precautions to destroy these instructions.

Way to make a girl feel all warm and cozy, I thought, trying to imagine that moment when FBI agents would take me into custody. Would I have enough warning to press those three dots in the upper right corner? Even if I did, would those same agents simply lock me away and interrogate me with drugs?

First step, do not worry. A difficult task, but I have faith in you.

I snorted. But strangely enough, my anxiety did ease. I read on.

Now, down to business. Call your family in Georgia . . .

What followed was a set of instructions that were just detailed enough, but not so much that I felt overwhelmed. Nothing I couldn't have figured out on my own, but for once I was glad to have a commanding officer in this mission. We were to explain my absence, lay down an electronic trail from DC to Georgia. Arrange for my path to cross Micha's.

While we save the world, I thought with a smile.

The last paragraph included a reminder that more instructions would follow, and I should use the established method and location to retrieve them. Oh, that was clever. Clever but simple. This was like following footprints through a dark and windblown desert, with the prints vanishing behind, while my flashlight could only illuminate a few steps ahead.

I scrolled through my list of contacts until I came to one

for my Aunt Jemele. The phone rang three times, before it clicked over.

"Whatsup?"

A girl's voice, high and breathless. In the background came the clatter of pots. A woman called out, "Tamika! What did I tell you about manners, girl?"

Tamika huffed impatiently, but then she did say, "Watson family residence. May I help you?"

Oh, how those phrases and that accent brought back memories of my own parents, training me and Grace in manners. "Hello, Tamika," I said. "I'd like to talk with Aunt Jemele, please. If she has the time, that is."

Tamika huffed again, and I thought I could hear the sound of her eyes rolling. "Oh, sure. We all gots plenty of time." But then, before her mother scolded again, she quickly added, "I'll fetch her right away. May I ask who's calling?"

"I'm Cousin Janet from up north."

"Oh." Silence. "You."

A world of backstory in that silence.

"Lemme go fetch her."

A babble of voices broke out on the other end of the line. I could make out Tamika's excited announcement about *Cousin Dr. Janet*, and her mother's harried reply about washing up the dishes. Then a soft voice said, "Janet? This is Jemele. What happened? What's wrong?"

I rubbed the bridge of my nose. *This is my own damned fault.*

"Nothing is wrong," I said. "Grace told me about Gramma."

There was a moment of uncomfortable silence before she spoke.

"What I hear is that she told you about Gramma a while back."

That soft voice had taken on an edge. I wanted to tell my aunt I'd spent last year in the army, or the hospital, or trying to piece my life and my body back together. I wanted to tell her about Alton. But that would only be making excuses, and excuses, as my mother said, never made up for anything.

"I'm sorry," I said. "I want to come down for a few days. Maybe go visit those home care services Grace was telling me about. See which one's the best. But only after I talk to you and Gramma."

That provoked a longer silence.

"Maybe you could," she said slowly. "When you thinking to come down?"

"This week?" I said.

Jemele laughed. "Oh, girl, you haven't changed, have you? All don't care until you do, then you want to save the world. Well, fine. Let me know when to expect you. We'll see what we can do."

Our good-byes were short but friendly enough. It was only after I set my cell down that I realized how much my throat hurt.

I'm lying to my family. Never mind it's for the best of reasons. Reasons are like excuses in a better dress.

Enough self-pity. I had two more calls to make.

"Hudson Realty."

Jenna Hudson's voice was cool and remote, as if she'd read the caller ID and was prepared for an unpleasant conversation.

"Jenna, hello," I said. "I have a request. My grandmother down in Georgia needs special care. I want to visit the area to make arrangements for her. Would you consider extending my lease another two months?"

An uncomfortable silence followed, during which I tried to calculate what came next if she refused.

"That's understandable," she said at last.

I didn't mistake that for concern or generosity. But I thanked her politely and she offered best wishes to me and my family.

She would send me an updated lease with the new end date by email, and I was to sign and return it before I left DC.

One last item, the easiest of all.

"Hello, Southeast Airlines?"

I booked the first available flight to Atlanta, Georgia, that Friday. Turns out Southeast was running a special because so many people didn't want to bother with security, never mind the cramped seats and extra fees. Fifty dollars for advance seating. Twenty-five dollars per checked bag. Another twenty-five dollars if I wanted a second carry-on. For an extra hundred dollars, I could sit in the Economy Plus section.

In a fit of extravagance, I chose business class and punched in my credit card number, followed by my passport and driver's license numbers. I clicked the check box that acknowledged I would report two hours early for an interview with the TSA, or I would forfeit any right to rebooking if I missed my flight. After that, navigating the rental car site was simplicity itself.

I flipped Hall's mystery open and reviewed Micha's instructions one last time. In the last hour a new paragraph had materialized.

If you are rereading this page, you know what to do. My advice? Wait another day or two, until you are certain you are ready to proceed.

I decided I wasn't ready to proceed. Not today.

☍

Five P.M. Afternoon rounds brought nothing more challenging than a septic ulcer, aggravated by aspirin and moonshine. Once I returned to my office, I sent off messages to Sydney and Faith Bellaume, canceling my sessions for the next four weeks. Sydney replied with a GIF of balloons, whatever that meant. Faith sent me a cryptic message saying that she trusted my judgment.

Wednesday. A day even emptier than usual. Carter offered to take on my students. Navarette gave me a hug and said she would miss me at rounds, and I better damned not go haring off to another hospital. Pascal said all the right things, but she was clearly distracted. Her daughter, Navarette said, had come down with pneumonia and both mothers were anxious. As for Letova, she was nowhere to be found.

A part of me was relieved. A part wondered if anyone would notice if I never returned.

♀

Thursday night. I vaguely remember eating a carton of Chinese takeout in between packing my carry-on bag and double-checking my to-do list. Tickets, boarding pass, and car reservation downloaded to my cell. Check. Copies printed as a backup. Check. Federal ID, driver's license, and passport. Check. The email from my aunt with exact directions to the farm, since the GPS wasn't reliable. All the rest of my obligations tied off as neatly as a surgeon might tie off a bleeding vein.

I tidied up the kitchen, then poured myself a glass of red wine and read through Micha's letter a second time. I could—*almost*—believe our mission was a simple matter. We would sail across the border, she and I, and make our rendezvous with Sara Holmes, after which I would perform whatever necessary task Sara required of me. Ours would be an effortless victory, because our cause was just, and Micha was gifted with ingenuity.

But life with Sara had taught me to expect danger and complication. Maybe this time I would take a bullet to my head instead of my back. Maybe this time, I would not survive the adventure.

I set the wineglass on the kitchen counter, grabbed my warmest jacket from the closet, and headed down the stairs. The night was cool, the stars bright pinpricks overhead. The sensible part of me was yammering for me to stop this foolishness right now. Sadly, I wasn't listening to Sensible Me. I walked—quickly, but not so quickly someone might get suspicious—until I reached Wisconsin, then I jogged the rest of the way to Thirty-Fourth Street and Adanna Jones's bookstore.

The OPEN sign glowed a soft white. Within, a blurred figure moved from one side of the store toward the register. Before I could second-guess myself, I pushed the door open and stepped inside.

Adanna Jones stood behind the cash register, scanning a dense display of numbers and codes on the screen. As the door swung closed behind me, she glanced up with a polite smile. Immediately her expression turned wary. "Janet."

"Adanna, I—" I gulped down a breath and tried again. "Hello. I—I've come for a good word."

Silence. I desperately wanted to explain. Knew I couldn't, even if I hadn't been constrained by so many secrets. We stared at each other, and I was certain she would order me to leave.

But then her mouth tucked into an unhappy smile. "What's wrong?"

Not exactly a welcome, but better than I hoped.

"I'm leaving DC for a few weeks," I said. "My grandmother is ill. She has Alzheimer's. There's home care services, but . . ." I shook my head, dismissing the rest of my explanation. "Whatever. I'm going to see what I can do."

Her expression eased, just barely. "And you came here for a book to tide you along?"

It was an excuse she offered. I should have said yes. I should have accepted her recommendation, handed over my credit card, laid yet another track for this electronic trail Micha had planned.

I cannot tell you all the truth, but at least I won't lie.

"No. I don't need a book," I said softly. "I came . . . to ask if you would keep me in your thoughts. Please. Nothing more."

Her eyes went wide. Her hands went still above the register's keyboard. So many, many questions in that one glance. As much as I wanted to explain everything, yes, even about Sara and the New Confederacy, I knew I would sound like a madwoman.

Then she leaned across the counter and touched my cheek. "I shall do that. Be well, my friend. Be well."

13

My flight didn't leave until eleven A.M., but regulations stated I had to check in with the front counter by nine A.M. After a quick breakfast, I packed my last few items and left the dirty dishes for Hudson Realty's cleaning service. Glory be, my cab was waiting for me at the curb.

For once, DC traffic cooperated. I reached the Southeast check-in line by eight thirty, and the counter itself by eight fifty-five.

"Name, destination, and ID, please."

"Janet Watson," I said. "Atlanta, Georgia."

I presented my e-ticket, passport, and boarding pass. The clerk glanced over them with a weary expression. "Reason for travel?"

We'd come a long way since the paranoia of the late 2010s but not far enough. Alida Sanches had rolled back the travel bans and other restrictions, but anyone traveling by air had to run a gauntlet of questions. Anyone who had the wrong color, or clothes, or accent, had to go through that and more.

"It's a family matter," I said as patiently as I could manage. "My grandmother is ill. She needs help."

The counter clerk nodded, as if she understood.

"There's just one more thing," I said.

Behind me, I heard a sigh as someone calculated whether they would make their flight after all. *Sorry, not sorry.* I had confirmed with the airline that my device was permitted on board, but I knew better than to trust a phone conversation.

I laid my left arm onto the counter and rolled back my sleeve to expose Lazarus. "I have a medical device," I stated clearly. "This device is both necessary for my profession as a surgeon and permitted under the federal regulations for disabled citizens."

I nearly recited the regulation number and paragraph, but the clerk was clearly not hearing anything I said. "Do you have a medical note?" she said.

"No. It's not required."

She eyed me doubtfully. "I'm not sure. We do require advance notice."

I pointed out on my ticket the notation. "Which I have complied with."

Even so, she continued to frown. "It's a matter for TSA."

I drew a breath, ready to argue. Stopped myself in time. Arguing only made them more suspicious. I gave the clerk a false and cheery smile. "Thank you. I appreciate your concern. I won't take any more of your time."

Her relief was almost embarrassing. She returned my passport and federal ID, tapped the keys to update my boarding pass, and gave me a printed certificate noting I had cooperated with pre-boarding regulations.

On my way to the departure gate, I stopped by a restroom. I hung my bag over the hook inside the stall and extracted my book, and those last instructions, before I launched myself into the impossible. I reviewed the current set once more, then pressed the margin as hard as I could.

The ink faded and reassembled into a new set of paragraphs.

Well done, my friend. Here are your final instructions before we meet again:

- Once you land in Georgia, proceed to your family farm. Make whatever excuses you must but do acquire that list of home services from your aunt.

- If at all possible, arrange to spend the night at your family's house, but if an invitation does not appear, go to the Best Western in Auburn. Avoid the stilted dialog and go with your instincts. Failing that, go with whatever seems easiest.

- Whatever transpires tonight, clothe yourself in the armor of righteousness on the next morn, and continue to the Waffle House outside Montgomery, Alabama.

- And now, if you are certain you wish to continue this adventure, and even if you aren't, take the next step as always. WARNING: Bright lights ahead.

I paused. Considered what madness I had volunteered for. Then, before I lost my nerve, I pressed my thumb against the margin and braced for what came next.

Good thing. The entire page shimmered, so bright I almost dropped the damned book. Before I could catch my breath, the sheet had crumbled into a fine white dust.

Well, that's final.

I wanted to laugh, but my hands were shaking as I shook the ashes into the toilet. At the sink, I scrubbed my right hand clean. The left one, I rubbed gently with a clean towel. By now I was shivering, and my stomach had knotted itself into a tight fist.

No time for drama, however. I hurried to the next stage. Security.

Security had always been a nightmare, but since the Bloody Inauguration, the process had become even more grueling. Most people traveled by train or car or bus these days, but even so, the line snaked out and around to the edge of the nonsecured hall.

Ninety minutes until boarding started. What if I missed my flight?

I sighed, shifted the bag over my shoulder, and shuffled forward with the others.

Eventually I reached the front of the line.

"Next!" The TSA agent signaled me to the ID counter.

I presented my cell with all my electronic paperwork and the printed certificate from the ticketing agent. I shucked off my shoes and loaded a basket with my belongings. I submitted to the pinprick to collect a sample of my DNA, followed by a scan of my thumbprint. A wand swept over my body to detect any dangerous chemicals. The TSA agent paused at Lazarus.

"You have a medical note?" he asked.

"It's not required," I said. "But I did notify the airline in advance."

He shrugged and continued the scan, then waved me forward.

I had another moment of terror when they searched my bag and the agent paused to leaf through the book, but the woman's only comment was that she had never liked the author.

Am I done? Was it really that easy?

No, it was not.

Government regulations stated that racial profiling was illegal. Anything beyond that was the result of random sampling. Random sampling, my ass. So I wasn't surprised when the TSA agent directed me into the quarantine room. Someone didn't like the color of my skin. Someone especially didn't like a black woman with an obviously expensive piece of medical equipment.

The interview started off innocuously, or at least what passed for innocuous these days.

"Ms. Watson," the interviewer said.

I considered the pros and cons of arguing and decided this one was important. "It's Dr. Watson. I work at Georgetown University Hospital."

He nodded. "Are you a U.S. citizen?"

You have all my records. You know my title. You know I'm a citizen.

But I smiled and said yes, I was.

I answered the rest of his questions as calmly as possible. Yes, I was employed in Washington, DC, as a surgeon. No, I had no felonies, nor did I have any connections to terrorist organizations. My degree at Howard University and residency at Georgetown University Hospital didn't matter. My record in the service didn't matter. I was a black woman with a strange device and therefore I was a danger.

My parents had endured the same, that last morning of their lives, before they boarded the plane that took them to Atlanta and to death.

Another agent, a woman this time, joined the first and they ordered me to remove Lazarus. The meshwork of steel alloy over electronics did nothing to reassure them. The man poked at the device with a screwdriver. I wanted to shout at him to be careful, but I knew better than that.

The woman plucked my device from the table and held it up to the glaring lights, as if she could uncover its secrets. "What the hell is this thing anyway?"

I tried to explain, avoiding any mention of electronics or custom programming. I repeated that I was a surgeon, and the device was designed to allow me to continue my work after leaving the service.

"Some people aren't so lucky," she muttered.

Don't I know that?

But I couldn't talk about those who had died. Those who had survived, but with their lives and bodies shattered. If I did, I would not be able to keep my voice soft and calm.

"You say you're a surgeon?"

"I am," I said.

They ran through the same questions the clerk at the counter had. I repeated the information about my position at Georgetown University Hospital, and the reason for my travel to Georgia. I gave them the address and telephone number of the farm, and the same for my sister in Washington State. Eventually they ran out of questions and I was free to continue to the gate.

Oh Christ, oh god. All I wanted to do was huddle in a corner for the next hour, but my flight left in twenty minutes. I fumbled through the steps to reattach Lazarus. Then I snatched up my bag and ran for the gate.

Five minutes past takeoff. The boarding area was empty, but a clerk behind the counter waved me forward. I presented my credentials, skipped down the jet bridge into the airplane itself, where a flight attendant greeted me with a frown. I couldn't blame her. I slid into my seat in the business class section and stowed my carry-on under the seat.

I'm here. I made it.

Our flight departed only twenty minutes past schedule, in spite of my delay. The flight attendants had forgotten or forgiven me, because they all greeted me with the same friendly smiles as they offered to other passengers. I paid for a cup of coffee (hot, strong, and surprisingly good) and a sandwich (cold, soggy, and not-so-surprisingly awful).

Two hours to Atlanta. Less than that. I glanced toward the nearest window. The passenger next to me, a white man in his fifties or thereabouts, muttered under his breath. He was a thickset man, his hair and beard shaved close, which made it look as though he'd been dusted in silver. Even his suit was gray. Businessman in business class, and not at all happy that I'd delayed his flight.

I smiled at him. He flinched and looked away.

So that's how it is.

Briefly, I contemplated hauling out my book. No, I'd had enough mystery for today, considering. I reclined the seat an inch or two and closed my eyes . . .

It was April, a muddy cold April morning with the fog wreathed around our tents. I'd spent ten hours at surgery the day before. The enemy had attacked the border to the south—a useless raid that left hundreds of their dead behind, and hundreds of our own. So many wounded—by IEDs planted in advance of the attack, by rocket launchers, even by bayonets and poison gas. I'd slept as though drugged.

But I'd rolled out of my cot at the first blare from the loudspeakers.

Red alert, red alert! Enemy incoming.

I scrambled into my trousers, still not entirely awake.

Repeat, enemy incoming. This is not a drill. All personnel—

An explosion threw me to the ground. The loudspeaker tower had vanished in a burst of flames and smoke. Only then did I truly take in the warning. I lay there a moment, deafened by the noise, until I came back to myself with a start and a gasp.

"—approaching Atlanta International Airport. Estimated touchdown in fifteen minutes—"

I woke with a gasp. For a heartbeat, I was back in my

nightmare, hearing the staccato rattle of gunfire. Then my vision cleared. I saw the mottled gray seat back in front of me. I had flung myself forward, Lazarus clutched to my chest. My throat felt scraped and raw, as if I had done more than gasp. One of the flight attendants had paused next to me.

I shook my head, willing her to move on.

The loudspeaker went on with its litany of instructions. ". . . Make certain your seat is upright and your belongings are safely stowed under the seat . . ."

My hands, both flesh and metal, were trembling as I adjusted my seat. Only after the flight attendant continued down the aisle did I rub my right hand over my face. My left lay blessedly inert in my lap.

"What the hell is that thing?"

Businessman was eying Lazarus with deep suspicion.

A medal from the war, I wanted to say. I knew better, though. Smile and nod, my mother always said. Doesn't matter what they say to you. Attitude never got anyone anywhere.

I smiled and nodded. "It's a medical experiment."

His mouth dropped open. His face twitched, as though he was working through my words, looking for a reason to complain. But then the flight attendant made her way back up the aisle, collecting any last trash, while the loudspeaker announced our final approach.

We suffered through a bumpy landing, then a delay while the pilots waited for a gate to clear. Atlanta's airport was far busier than DC's, with more flights connecting Europe and Africa to Mexico and South America. It was one reason the terrorists had chosen here and not National or Dulles.

Once we finally could disembark, I followed my fellow passengers through the tube connecting the plane to the gate. There a secondary security check awaited us in case we'd managed to construct a dangerous weapon in the airplane's cramped toilets. Halfway through the wait, I found myself wondering if I could have walked to Atlanta faster.

Eventually, I passed through the body scan, the second DNA test, and another round with TSA as they rummaged through my bag. I had one moment of stark terror, when an agent picked up my Rachel Howzell Hall book and squinted at the title. But he tossed the book back into my bag without doing more than flipping through the pages.

Once again, they pulled me into a separate room for a personal interview, but this side of the flight, the questions were merely tedious. Barely fifteen minutes later, they released me into a maze of gray corridors, with illuminated signs pointing toward the exit and warning me not to turn around.

Most of the other passengers from Flight SX1167 had gone on ahead of me, but crowds from other flights overtook me. I trailed after them automatically, running through the final steps between here and tomorrow morning. My inexpensive rental car. Syncing my cell with the local GPS. Acquiring a paper map as well, since the rural counties didn't have reliable reception.

The interior corridors opened at last to a broad terrace that curved around a vast plaza below. I stopped a moment in surprise. Almost immediately someone bumped into me. An elderly woman, leaning heavily onto her walker. I apologized and stepped off to one side.

Once, just once, I had come through this airport. Not with my parents—we'd traveled by rusted car from Georgia up north. No, I'd come this way once before as a surgeon in the army, on my way home on leave that first year, when it was easier and safer to travel from Illinois to Atlanta by plane, then up north by railroad. Back then, the airport had seemed a bit shabby, in spite of its size.

The terrorists of the New Confederacy had fixed that all right.

Two men with false IDs had infiltrated airport security, bringing with them four suitcases loaded with plastic explosives. They had arrived in a FedEx truck, which the FBI later determined had been stolen. Once inside the airport, they had met with four employees from an airline catering crew. The catering crew had dispersed the suitcases to four points within the central hub of the airport. They were on the point of leaving when the terrorists had triggered the explosion.

Five thousand dead. Two thousand more critically injured. A hundred or more listed missing, because no one could find their remains. Nothing was left of that destruction. No blood, no bodies, not even the remains of the original building.

I breathed, slowly, carefully, steadily, until the panic subsided.

Someday, you must face what happened, Faith Bellaume had told me.

I guess that would be today.

I opened my eyes. The airport that stretched out before me was a glittering modern structure, with a glass ceiling that arced from sky to ground, held together by a cross-work of bright metal frames. Alida Sanches and Congress had dedicated this new building in defiance of the rebels, but all I could think was *Here is where my mother and father died.*

"You lost someone here?"

I blinked back to the present. A black man, dressed in a porter's uniform, had asked the question. No, it wasn't a question. He knew. He had recognized my expression.

"My mother and father," I said. My voice came out as a whisper, thick with tears.

He nodded. He was my age, or a bit older, with broad shoulders and his hair braided close and covered with a cap.

It wasn't just for pity, or for business, that he'd approached me. I recognized that bleak expression.

"You lost someone here, too, didn't you?" I said.

"My brother. His name was Isaac." He sighed, and there was a world of private history in that sigh. Then he shook his head, as though shaking off the grief. "My name's Andrew. If you got a moment before you head on, I want to show you something. A memorial," he added, when I hesitated. "I think you might like it."

He led me down the main escalator, around the tourist information counter, to what looked like a boulder set into the floor. Water cascaded over the rough surface and vanished into a narrow pool. Small plaques engraved with names had been embedded into the rock. I circled around the boulder and found my parents' names. MICHAEL JEFFERSON WATSON. ALICE IFUNANYA WATSON. The plaques overlapped each other, which seemed fitting. I reached out and touched each in turn. Felt the shock of cold water over my fingers.

Maybe I should come back another year. Maybe this is a better pilgrimage than my talks with Mr. Lincoln.

Or maybe there was room enough in my life for both.

I drew back and wiped the tears from my eyes. Andrew had lingered nearby, his attention on a plaque with the name ISAAC THOMPSON.

"Thank you," I breathed.

He smiled. "We got to do for each other, don't you know?"

"That we do," I said.

14

By late afternoon, I had navigated my rental car away from Atlanta's airport and onto Route 85 heading southwest. I'd come into my second wind, and I wanted to drive as fast as the speed limit allowed—faster—but I knew better. This was the South, after all, and while the South wasn't as red as it used to be, all it would take was one bully cop to turn me into a hashtag.

So I kept my foot light on the gas, and put extra distance between me and the car ahead, especially in the choke of traffic that was Atlanta's rush hour. I faithfully used my turn signal. Even when I exited the beltway for 85S, and left the traffic behind, I never let my speed get above 55 mph.

Twenty miles outside the city limits, only a few signs remained of the decades since I'd last visited. The crumbling townships—built from cinder block and false expectations in the late 2010s—were no more. The strip malls and cheap office complexes had managed to survive longer, but with the coming of the New Civil War, these, too, had finally given up. It was like the corridor between DC and Baltimore, the farms and green fields replaced by acres of concrete in that mad rush to build and build. That, too, had turned into a desert of weeds and trash.

I was glad when I finally left the ruins behind for the rural counties beyond. Just outside Molena, I stopped to refill my gas tank and buy a Diet Coke from the station's convenience store. The attendant, an elderly white man, shook his head at my credit card. I stopped myself from sighing just in time and handed over two twenties as a deposit while I filled my own tank. The old man rounded up the charge to the next dollar, then glared at me as if daring me to argue. At least he didn't spit until the screen door closed behind me.

Twenty miles more, thirty. I could almost imagine myself back with my sister and parents, during that long, long ride up north, with our father driving as cautiously as I did now. I drove on while the sun sank into a glorious explosion of color and twilight settled over the land. Every now and then, I consulted the directions from my aunt.

109 to 74. That's Crest Highway. Go down east a couple or so miles, just past Mallory Road, to a dirt road heading east. If you get to Jeff Davis Road, you gone too far.

I nearly missed Mallory Road but saw the rusted street sign just in time. A couple hundred yards past Mallory, I eased my car onto the almost invisible dirt road that wound east and south through cotton fields with their buds just sprouting green. Memories teased at me with snips and snaps of images that almost—but not quite—matched the scene before me. Or maybe this was only the expectation of memory. The brain could be funny like that.

My aunt's directions told me five miles to the next intersection. I turned left, as directed, into an even darker stretch.

Cottonwood trees lined the road. Off to one side, I heard the deep croak of bullfrogs and the peep of birds. Overhead the clouds blocked the stars and the moon. Oh, yes, the land here was beautiful, the night soft and warm and welcoming. But if you weren't a farmer, if you dreamed of a future elsewhere . . .

An old crumbling brick square that called itself a school. No library. The textbooks little more than hand-me-downs from the richer counties. The teachers doing the best they could with the little they had. No wonder Mom and Dad wanted to leave.

At last, I came to an intersection with another, wider dirt road. No street sign. No other indication than the miles recorded by my trip odometer. My GPS gave a hopeful blink before it died again. My aunt's email had seemed damned clear to me the other day, but right now, in the soft damp dark of the Georgia night, I wasn't so sure. I reset the trip odometer, then guided my rental car left into a new set of ruts and hoped for the best.

Almost forty minutes later, with the moon setting over in the west, I pulled into a driveway of gravel and packed dirt. This, *this* I remembered, as if I were suddenly returned to five years old, coming home from the rare treat of a visit to Grandpa Benjamin over in Turner County. The weeds were just as tall, the muddy scent from the creek just as strong. I could even anticipate that final bump before the weeds abruptly stopped and I was faced with a broad expanse of lawn and the old-fashioned farmhouse. The house itself stood just as I remembered it— three stories high, with a wraparound porch and a brick well off to one side. Several barns were just visible beyond the main yard, and I heard a dog yipping excitedly. I'd told myself and Faith Bellaume that I remembered nothing about this place, but I had lied. My blood and my bones remembered. They seemed to vibrate with memories I'd long forgotten.

I turned the engine off and listened to it tick for a moment. Eight twenty. Not that late, even for country hours. The porch was dark, but I could make out dim lights from farther in the house. So maybe I was expecting a welcome committee?

At that I had to laugh. I slung my bag over my shoulder and climbed the two steps to the porch and the front door. No doorbell, of course, so I knocked politely.

Almost at once the door swung open. A skinny girl confronted me, head cocked, eyes narrowed. She wore baggy jeans and a T-shirt with the logo from a video game company. Her hair sprang out in a wild mass of corkscrews. She eyed me and my device with a far-too-knowing expression.

"Are you Tamika?" I said. "I'm your cousin Janet."

"I know that," said Miss Shade.

An older girl, sixteen or seventeen at least, shoved Tamika off to one side. "Cousin Janet. I'm Letitia. Never mind this little pest. Come inside. Let me take that bag for you."

Letitia relieved me of my carry-on and ushered me through an old-fashioned parlor and into the even more old-fashioned kitchen. Memory washed over me like a waterfall, cold and clear. The brick tiles. The broad wooden table in the center of the room, with half a dozen chairs around it. The enormous double sink, the dishes from the evening wash-up stacked in the drainer. The strong smell of soap, leavened by the soft scent of yeast.

Meanwhile, Letitia was explaining how Aunt Jemele was upstairs with her mother, tending to Gramma. I vaguely remembered Letitia's mother, my father's much younger sister. Letitia set my bag next to the table and motioned for me to sit down. "Just wait here a moment. I'll go for Aunt Jemele."

She vanished through another set of doors. From a distance, I heard the noise of many feet trampling, then Letitia shouting, and another voice—a boy's this time—shouting back.

I took a seat at the kitchen table and ran my fingers over its surface. Ancient. Planed smooth by a great-grandfather or an even more ancient great-great-cousin. A few dents here and there, probably owing to an obstreperous cousin. Tamika or someone like her. Might've been me.

I heard the heavy slow tread of footsteps and swiveled around.

A gray-haired woman entered the kitchen. She wore a loose cotton dress and a dark blue scarf over her braids. Her face was seamed from age and weather, her lips were pale against her dark skin, and she moved awkwardly, as if she weren't used to the changes that age and weight had brought. She might have been in her sixties. A bit older than my father would have been, if he had lived.

The woman eased herself into a chair opposite me. "I see you still a curious girl," she said. "I'm your Aunt Jemele. You can stop staring at me now."

I recognized her voice from our last phone conversation. A low and lilting voice, as smooth as molasses. I could just call up a memory of a much younger Jemele, her eyes black and snapping, as she traded jokes with my father.

"Aunt Jemele. I'm sorry to come so late—"

She shrugged. "Don't matter. I know the roads aren't so good."

"That," I agreed. "Besides, I didn't want to drive too fast and get a ticket."

Jemele gave a wheezing laugh. "No, that you don't. Good to see you ain't forgot everything. We'll get you set up here for the night. You must be parched, too." She rapped on the table.

"Young Benjamin! Tamika! I know you both listening behind that door. Get yourselves in here."

The double doors banged open. Young Benjamin and Tamika piled into the kitchen. Both of them kept their expressions meek and dutiful as Jemele told Benjamin to carry his cousin's bag up to the old sewing room, and how Tamika should fetch that plate Jemele had set aside from supper. Both murmured, *Yes, Aunt Jemele. For sure. Doing that right now.* But I saw how they glanced at me with sharp gazes.

Benjamin slung my bag over his shoulder and hurried from the kitchen. Tamika drew a plate of biscuits and gravy from the oven. She set the plate, two glasses, and a pitcher on the table, then ran out the door at her aunt's command.

Jemele herself poured me a tall glass of iced tea, sweet with sugar, just the way I remembered from times and years long ago.

"Mischief, both of them," she said. "Just like their daddy, may he rest in peace. That would be your Uncle T. J. He died a couple years ago. Cancer. That's when Mattie came back home with the children."

Home. As though there could only be one home in the universe.

Aunt Jemele continued to give me the family update while I ate my biscuits and drank the iced tea. News about nieces, nephews, cousins, second cousins, the extended family of in-laws and others less easily categorized. Most of my family had stayed in Georgia, though many of the older grandchildren had moved away, to university, to the cities. To a life far away from a dirt farm.

I wiped my mouth with the napkin and poured myself a second glass of tea before I asked my next and most necessary question.

"How is Gramma doing today?"

Jemele shrugged. "'Bout as well as you might expect."

In other words, not good. Though I knew "not good" could take any number of forms.

"She knows you coming," Jemele added.

"And doesn't like it one bit," I said.

My aunt laughed, a soft, wheezing laugh. "Damn. You got that right. Come on. Finish up that plate and I'll take you to see her."

She took me up the winding stairs at the back of the kitchen, along a dimly lit corridor toward the front of the house. More and more, I recalled walking down this same corridor, to another set of stairs that led to the attic bedroom I shared with Grace and several other cousins. From the thumping overhead, the attic still housed a number of younger cousins, nieces, and nephews.

Jemele stopped in front of a closed door. Gramma's bedroom, my memory supplied. She knocked.

"Mamma? Janet's here to see you, just like you asked."

A pause, then a querulous voice said, "Don't know why you bothered to knock. Tell the girl to come in. And don't you come in either. I don't want you fussing over me."

Jemele shook her head with obvious exasperation. "I'll go see about your room," she said in a low voice. "Just remember she gets tired easy."

Leaving me to face the lion's den. Well, Daniel survived; maybe I would too. I pushed the door open and went into my grandmother's bedroom.

It was as though I'd stepped back in time, a century or more. The old-fashioned oil lamp that gave off a softer light, or so Gramma had always claimed. The enormous rag rug, which Gramma had inherited from her grandmother. The even more ancient wardrobe off to one side. The pale curtains that had once been the purest ivory but had yellowed over time.

An old and musty smell filled the air, layered over the fainter scent of soap and wood polish. My grandmother was sitting up in her bed, a quilt wrapped around her shoulders. She regarded me with a clear and steady gaze. Maybe it wouldn't be so bad after all.

"Hello, Gramma," I said.

She snorted. "You come here awful late, girl. Did you find some trouble along the way, or did trouble find you?"

You a heap of trouble, girl. What you doing teasing your sister like that?

"No trouble at all," I said. "I was just driving careful like."

Another snort. "Come over here. I want to get a better look at you."

She patted a spot next to her. I obeyed and settled onto the edge of the bed.

She had aged. Oh, sure, I had expected changes, especially from what my aunt told me. But the lamplight, that soft and golden and treacherous lamplight, made clear what mere words couldn't. Her hands were sticks, the fingers bent. She was nearly bald. What little hair remained billowed out like a ragged white cloud, too fine to braid. And time had etched a thousand lines over her dark brown face.

Her eyes, however, were bright as she returned my gaze. "You ain't changed one bit, have you? Staring is rude, girl."

"Sorry," I said at once. "It's been so long since . . ."

"Since you got too big and important. Don't go making some mealy-mouthed excuses. Your father—"

She broke off and stared at Lazarus, lying innocently on my lap.

"What fool thing have you done, girl?"

"I signed up for the army, Gramma."

My grandmother shook her head. "Don't see why you done that," she muttered. "Worse than your father, him always thinking he knew what was right. Told him he oughtn't go up north. Selfish boy."

The brightness faded from her eyes. She turned her face away, her lips pressed in a thin firm line and tears tracking over her cheeks. I wanted to wipe the tears away, to tell her I understood, but she jerked her face away while she continued to weep.

A creak in the floorboards sounded just outside the room. Jemele, keeping watch. I was about to stand up and make an excuse to leave when my grandmother murmured something inaudible.

"What was that, Gramma?" I said.

"Don't want to go away. Don't want them to lock me up. I told Jemmie that but she don't listen to me. No one does anymore."

The woman who had ruled our family. I felt a dull ache in my chest. Grief. Pity. She would hate my pity, even now. I kissed her cheek, which she allowed, and stood up from the bed. Her attention had wandered, and she was plucking at the quilt that lay over her lap.

I'm going now, Gramma. But I'll come back. I'll make sure you're looked after.

Jemele was waiting outside. "Don't pay her no mind," she said softly. "She gets caught in the old times. Come on, I'll show you to your room."

She brought me to what had once been my great-grandmother's sewing room, then later a storage room for blankets and quilts, and oddments of furniture, most of them from an earlier century. Most of the oddments remained, and from the looks of it, two or three of the young ones bedded here.

"I'll fetch you a pitcher of water," Jemele told me. "Then I got to get back to your grandmother. You remember where the bathroom is?"

She fetched the water, then left me with the comment that folks got up early, but she'd make sure I had a good breakfast waiting for me. Young Benjamin had set my bag on the bed next to the window. I drank a glass of water, changed into the new set of pajamas I'd bought for the trip, then opened up my bag and laid out my supplies for Lazarus. There wasn't a good level surface anywhere but the floor, but the floor was good enough.

I spread out the towel I'd brought, arranged the wipes and powder and disinfectant. Right before I tapped in the sequence to release my device, I thought I heard soft footsteps outside the door, then whispering.

Cousins. Curious ones.

I resisted the urge to open the door and read them a lecture on privacy. They were kids, and kids would always be curious. Instead, I turned the latch and went back to my preparations for the night. Lazarus went into my bag, which I tucked underneath the bed itself. Then I stretched myself onto the thin mattress, pulled up the quilt that some unknown cousin or aunt had stitched, and stared up into the darkness.

I wish I'd come down sooner.

You were busy. Busy getting shot. Busy patching your life back together.

Even so . . .

Well, you're here now.

I was, but not because I was a dutiful granddaughter. That

would be Grace, who called or wrote letters every week to our aunt.

Grace is a busybody, said my not-so-dutiful self.

True, that. But her character flaws didn't erase mine.

So, I'll just have to keep that promise and come back. I'll have to make sure Gramma gets taken care of.

15

DATE: APRIL 18. *Time: Way too early, what with me getting little or no sleep. Though Micha had given me no orders about my journal, I knew enough to leave it behind with a postscript about buying a new one next month. I was sick unto death of feeding the FBI fake entries. Instead, I'd bought a cheap spiral-bound notebook. These pages weren't the high-tech, touch-and-turn-to-ashes material that Sara had once supplied me with, but they would burn easy enough. Consider this (these?) my last recorded thoughts before we take off into the wild.*

So. Last thoughts and testament.

I dreamed last night. I dreamed of my parents, that last visit before I entered the service. It was night. Rain poured over the windows of their small house; it dripped from the gutters and drummed against the roof. Mom and Pop sat across from me at the kitchen table. Grace had gone home to her husband and daughters, but not until she had made her opinion clear.

I want to serve my country, I said.

You can serve your damned country here, at Georgetown, my father had snapped back.

Hush, my mother had said. You know she's doing exactly what we taught her, even if we don't exactly like it.

Goddamn right we don't like it, my father replied. Then, in a different voice, not angry but close to breaking, Janet, why? What's the real reason you're doing this, girl?

Before my dream self could answer, a great noisy bell woke me. I bolted upright in that hard, narrow bed. For a moment I couldn't remember where I was. A rush of footsteps down the corridor brought me back to the real world. Georgia. The dirt farm. A living therapy session, and like any I'd experienced with Faith Bellaume, so very painful and peculiar.

I set my pen down and regarded the page. Nothing there that hinted at Sara Holmes or Nadine Adler. That would change soon enough, but after the past week of endlessly pretending, I had needed to vent without any second thoughts about who might read my words.

The skin across my forehead felt tight with the promise of a headache. I rubbed the sleep from my eyes and considered the subject of coffee. The window, just visible with dawn, showed a murky gray sky, and from far off came a rumbling that implied rain. By habit I clicked on my cell to check the weather report.

The cell lit up with four bars. When I tapped the weather app, the display flickered a moment before a message popped up. **Thunderstorm warning starting 11 a.m. throughout central and southern Georgia. High winds and possible flooding.**

Time to get packed and moving.

The kitchen was empty when I made my appearance. Just as Jemele had promised, a pot of coffee stood on the stovetop, and a tray of biscuits warmed in the oven. I had settled into my breakfast when Jemele came into the room.

"I see you figured things out," she said.

"I did. Thank you."

She poured herself a cup of coffee and lowered herself into a chair. "So, tell me, Dr. Janet Watson, what you planning to do?"

The look she gave me was shrewd, almost suspicious.

That's my imagination, I told myself.

"You said you had a list of home services," I said. "I thought I'd visit them—yes, I know you did that already, but it's different, with me being a doctor and all. I also wanted to visit the county office for medical assistance."

"We don't need welfare."

I'd heard that same tone from my father, when my mother suggested a government scholarship for me.

"It's not welfare," I said. "It's what we all pay taxes for."

Her only answer was a *hunh.*

"Besides," I went on, "those county offices have records for all the home care outfits. If you have that list of services you contacted, that might save me some time."

"Thought you might say that," my aunt said. She dug a crumpled sheet of paper from her apron pocket. "Here's what I already came up with. Marked what I thought about some."

I scanned the list but didn't recognize any of the names as national chains, which was good. Most of the national chains had nothing in mind but profit, at the government's expense. With single payer, you were guaranteed basic care, but with the conservative politicians fighting every inch of progress, we'd ended up with each state writing its own definition of "basic."

"Any of these offer a home visit plan?" I asked.

Another *hunh* was my answer. "You'd think they would. Some do, but damn, they charge a lot."

Which didn't entirely surprise me. Home services could not bill for meals or linens or any of the other extras that residential homes provided. Fewer charges to the government meant fewer items with a profit margin, so they would hike the prices even more for the services that remained.

I drank another cup of coffee. Eyed the pot on the stove, and wished I'd brought more Advil. "I'll see what I can do. Expect me back in a week. Two at the most."

"And then what?" my aunt demanded. "I thought you was coming down to help out. Looks more like you're running away again."

"I am not—"

I wanted to shout that I was not running away, goddammit. I went to war to serve, not run away. And look where that got me. It took all my strength to keep from pounding the table. I managed to suck down a breath, then another, until my blood stopped pounding and the red gradually faded to the ordinary gray of a rainy morning.

"I'm sorry, Aunt Jemele," I whispered. "I . . . there were times, a time, last year . . ."

"Never you mind," she said just as softly. "I'm sorry too."

We muddled our way through the rest of my breakfast. She cooked me hash browns, a half-dozen fried eggs, and a panful of rashers. I ate everything and drank the rest of the coffee. By the time I'd finished, my nerves had settled. Goddamned family, my father had cursed more than once. But oh, family could be a blessing, too.

After breakfast, I fetched my bag from my room. Jemele walked with me to my rental car. The air felt damp and cool, and overhead the clouds scudded across a muddy gray sky. The farm had changed a great deal in the past couple decades. In the sunlight I could see how much. The old barn had been torn down and replaced. The cornfields had been planted with short dense crops. Peanuts? But balanced against the seeming prosperity was the farmhouse itself, the porch sagging, the pale blue paint cracked and water stained.

I dumped my bag into the trunk and took my leave of my aunt.

She kissed my cheek. "You take care now, hear?"

"That I will. See you in a week or two?"

She smiled. "I guess you will."

Ϙ

Rain fell off and on throughout the morning, but by the time I reached Montgomery, the skies had cleared, and the sun was a hazy white disc overhead. It was warm enough, and humid enough, that I'd turned on the car's AC. *Yet another sign I've been living up north,* I thought.

The Waffle House parking lot was three-quarters full at ten A.M., with half a dozen spots open next to the restaurant itself. Following Micha's instructions, I parked my car at the back of the lot and headed inside with my bag slung over my shoulder.

Inside, the place was hopping. The overworked hostess handed me off to a waiter, who led me back to a booth next to the restrooms. I ordered a serving of grits and redeye gravy and a pot of coffee.

The grits and gravy were delicious. The coffee, hot and strong. Once I finished off my grits, I leaned against the wall with my cup cradled in both hands. From here I had a clear view of the restaurant—the middle-class families with their kids, on a driving vacation to who knows where. More than a few truckers. The locals, farmers mostly, on a break from their Saturday market. No sign of Micha, yet, but I didn't expect her for another hour at least.

Eleven A.M. The waitress took away my empty plate. The customer at the table next to me got up and paid her bill, only to be replaced moments later by an elderly black man. I ordered a second pot of coffee and a hamburger with fries. My stomach was jumping from nerves. One more hour, then I could hand off the spy business to Micha.

I had gone to refill my coffee cup when I heard a familiar voice.

"Janet. So glad you found your way here."

I froze. Micha?

Slowly I turned my head toward the voice. The old man was grinning at me. When he—she—tilted her head, I finally recognized her. Micha's hair was entirely gray and clipped close to her skull. A scar twisted over her cheek, changing the shape of her face and adding deep lines where none had existed before. She wore baggy overalls over a white shirt that had seen better days.

"I didn't recognize you," I said softly. "Did you lose weight?"

Micha laughed soundlessly. "Something like that."

The waitress had returned with her order pad. Micha swiveled around with a brilliant smile. "Oh, honey, you are just in time. I was about to expire from hunger. Lessee. Can I get me a pot of that fine coffee, a short stack, and a plate of hash browns? Oh, and don't forget the hot sauce. It's all that keeps my blood pumping."

Her voice had changed as much as the rest of her. Now it was deep and raspy, with the lilt of the South. I turned back to my hamburger and fries. Micha and I didn't speak again until the waitress returned with Micha's order.

"What comes next?" I murmured.

"We take things slow. Finish off your meal. Take your time. After you pay your bill, make a trip to the restrooms.

You will meet a tall dark stranger who answers to the name Isabelle. Do exactly what she tells you to do. I'll meet up with you in the parking lot."

Orders given a step or two at a time. How much practice did Micha have, handling a newbie spy?

But I followed her instructions exactly, lingering over my excellent hamburger, even though my appetite had vanished. I paid my bill, left a tip, then wandered back to the women's restroom.

A tall black woman waited just inside. Her coloring was a shade or two lighter than mine, but not by much, and she was maybe an inch taller, but she had a heft and weight that resembled mine. I had just enough time to take in all those details before she pulled me inside and locked the door.

"My name is Isabelle," she said. "Take off those clothes." When I hesitated, she made an impatient gesture. "Hurry. We only have a few moments."

Without waiting for me, she stripped down to her underwear. I skinned out of my jacket, T-shirt, and trousers, then changed into the clothes she had discarded—patched and baggy overalls, a long-sleeve T-shirt, and a Rangers baseball cap.

"Give me your cell and the keys to your car," she said. "Is that list inside the car? The one for the medical centers? No? Hand that over too. And your credit card."

I did. "What if my aunt calls?"

"Then she'll get a message saying your voice mail is full. Didn't your friend explain all that?"

She did not. And no, she's not my friend.

"Best if we exchange bags, too," Isabelle said. "No telling who's watching."

She dumped the contents of her bag onto the floor. We had

nearly completed the exchange when the door rattled. "What the hell is going on in there?"

Oh shit.

"Take my bag," Isabelle whispered. "Once you hear me gone, get yourself out the back door. Look for the Ford pickup with the Tennessee license plate G49 77X, Warren County."

She shoved me into the nearest stall, along with her bag, which now contained my belongings. I huddled on the seat while I heard her open the door and explain how the lock must've gotten stuck, and she was sorry if she made any trouble.

There was a muttered exchange. Then, the sound of the outer door swinging open and shut, followed by running water.

I waited another couple moments, then ventured out of the stall. A young white woman stood by the sinks, washing her hands. She shot me a glare. I ducked my head and hastily washed my hands before scurrying out the door.

Isabelle was nowhere in sight. To my left was a metal door, clearly a service entrance. That in turn led me into the parking lot, near the dumpsters.

I found the pickup truck at the far end of the parking lot—a dirty dark blue truck with a bumper sticker for the Democratic Progressive Party, and another for a local baseball team. One of the tires looked to be low on air, and there was enough rust flaking off the doors and the underbelly of the truck that I wondered if we would make it out of the parking lot.

The doors were unlocked, the windows rolled completely open. I slung my bag inside and climbed into the passenger seat. The vinyl seats had cracked sometime in the last millennium, and the stuffing had escaped to the point where I thought I could feel the metal frame. Damn. There was such a thing as too much attention to detail.

"Beautiful truck, don't you think?"

I jumped.

Micha leaned against the driver's side of the truck.

"As long as we don't break down before the next stop-light," I said gruffly.

"We shall not. I promise."

As if to make her a liar, the truck needed two tries before the engine turned over, and even then, it continued to sputter as Micha guided it through the parking lot to the exit. "We've made good time this morning," she said. "I'm thinking four, five hours to the next stop. That should give me plenty of time to explain the situation."

"Oh, has Sara shared more information with you?"

She hesitated, and for once her expression turned anxious. "Yes. But I can't explain here. Let's get away from Montgomery first. We don't want to wait around for any watchers."

That reminder, that someone might have traced Micha from DC to here, that someone might have watched my movements more closely than I realized, was enough to stop my questions.

For now.

16

A few miles outside the city limits, Micha pulled off the highway onto the local roads. We had not left Montgomery entirely behind—beyond the city and its suburbs came the run-down neighborhoods, built from shacks and the remains of strip malls. Micha set a zigzag course through the streets, half of them paved, half dirt, pausing once or twice to check her maps, but also to glance in the rearview mirror.

"Do you really think we'd see them?" I asked.

"What I really think is they'll follow Isabelle if they follow anyone at all. But in case someone decides to ask questions around here later . . . We're two ordinary black folk looking for my great-aunt Mary's address."

She took the next left into a narrow alleyway, where our truck scraped between two brick buildings. Once these had been a garage and an old-fashioned department store, according to the rusted signs. Now the few windows gaped empty and dark, piles of trash blocked the metal service doors, and the bricks looked as though someone had sprayed them with gunfire.

The New Civil War had wounded more than soldiers these past five years. How long before the war ended? How long after that before neighborhoods like this one rebuilt themselves?

The abandoned brick buildings gave way to a series of shacks, which didn't end as much as they collapsed into heaps of rotted wood, lost in a sea of weeds and shoulder-high grass. Micha guided our trunk over the dirt road until we eventually met up with a more official road, such as it was.

"Now?" I said.

Micha gave one last glance around. "Now.

"Our deadline has shifted," she said. "Sara tells me that Our Enemy intends to launch their . . . effort by next week. No, Sara did not explain what that effort might be, nor what caused this sudden change. All I know is that we must get ourselves across the border to a small town, the name of which you don't need to know. There Sara has promised to explain all."

"She didn't say why she needs a surgeon?"

"She did not."

I sucked my teeth. "I don't like it."

"Neither do I, but for different reasons." She shot me a sidelong glance. "Tell me now if you want out. I can drop you back in Montgomery. Isabelle can hand back your car and your cell. You can forget about Sara. Tend to your own family's needs."

Jesus. I hadn't realized how much I wanted just that until she made me the offer. Speaking of Christ and temptation. Oh, Father, won't you take this burden from me?

"You sure know how to push those guilt buttons," I said.

"Learned from the best teachers in the world," Micha replied sweetly.

I scowled and hunched down in my seat. Her offer was

sincere. I could abandon the quest now, this moment. I could return to my life as a respected surgeon at Georgetown University Hospital, with my high-tech device, and reclaim both my career and my sense of self.

The life Sara Holmes had gifted me, back in December.

There was also the small matter of Nadine Adler, who had murdered all those veterans and soldiers with her poisoned drugs, as surely as if she'd injected them herself. The scars on my back, where she'd shot me last October, seemed to draw tight.

"I'm afraid," I said at last.

"You should be. You're a sensible person."

"Then why did I agree in the first place?"

Micha shrugged. "Because you love Sara, just as I do. Because you and she believe in that ridiculous romantic ideal of justice."

At that I did laugh. "So why are you here? You aren't the least bit romantic."

Her gaze remained fixed on the road ahead, but I had the sense she watched me closely. "Perhaps not. But Sara is my favorite cousin. Even if I didn't owe her countless favors . . . But this is going far afield of the question. Do you wish me to call Isabelle?"

"No," I said softly. "I— No, I don't."

"Okay, then."

We drove on through the greening countryside, the fields dotted with trees and the occasional barn, the cows and goats in their pastures, the wreck of one old farmhouse after another, with only a few clusters of brick buildings that marked a prosperous family.

Forget the New Confederacy, my father once said. *We're supposed to be different in these Federal States, they say. We left that old Confederacy behind almost two hundred years ago, they say. My eyes tell me different. I lived down south—the real South, not Wash-ington, DC. Not every black man was poor, not every white man rich, but I saw enough . . .*

Enough that on a Saturday night, he'd drink a beer or two, then rant about the days when he and his brothers and sis-ters had watched Barack Obama on the television for his last State of the Union speech. How they had all yelled and wept because they knew that bad days were to come. Around that time, my mother would herd me and Grace into our bedroom, whispering how we shouldn't pay any mind to what our fa-ther said. It would all be fine.

We stopped for gas at a crossroads between Hanceville and Good Hope. The attendant was an ancient woman, her ruddy brown face tucked and pleated, the epicanthic folds around her eyes sagging with age. She eyed the dirty bills that Micha gave her with deep suspicion, but at least she didn't spit at us. Micha bought a couple bottles of pop and a pack of generic cigarettes before we took off again.

I waited until we got back on the state highway before I spoke again.

"I have a few questions."

"Thought you might."

"Who is Isabelle?"

"A friend."

A very convenient friend, who looked enough like me to take my place. Who had the necessary skills to evade both government agents and others less official, and whatever else a mission like this required.

"Can you trust her?"

"As much as I trust you."

Ouch. Okay, then.

Micha punched the truck's old-fashioned lighter, then ex-tracted one of the cigarettes from the pack and clamped it between her lips. When the lighter popped out, she lit the cig, then jammed the lighter back into its socket and took a long drag. Wreaths of smoke swirled around us both.

I opened the bottle of pop and took a swig. So. We were on our way at last. Everything fine, right? Right? But I wasn't a spy like Sara, or a person of ingenuity like Micha. All I could think of was how many ways our mission could fail.

"Can we make it?" I said softly. "Across the border. To Sara. Tell me the truth, Micha."

For a very long moment, Micha didn't reply. She drove with one hand resting lightly on the steering wheel, the cigarette dangling from her lips and trailing smoke like a dragon's breath. Her expression seemed strangely pensive. I had the strongest urge to tell her, *Never mind, don't tell me the truth, let me believe that everything will come out just fine.*

She took the cig from her mouth and stabbed it into the ashtray.

"I'll make damned sure we do."

Her voice was soft and light, the voice of Micha back in DC. The voice of someone gifted with ingenuity.

Well, okay then. I leaned back, took another swig of pop, and watched the miles unwind.

Later that same day. Huntsville, Alabama.

   Around seven P.M. we pulled off the road at another gas station. Micha bought a pack of cigarettes, then asked for the key to the restroom. I waited in the truck, finishing off the last of my pop. Ten minutes later, she reappeared, and I almost didn't recognize her. She'd gone into that restroom as an elderly man, stoop shouldered and walking as though every joint creaked. The person who climbed into the truck had dropped at least twenty years. The gray and white hair had turned gray and black; the scars and wrinkles had vanished, as though scrubbed away. She still looked old, but definitely brisker.

   Visit the restroom, she said. Then you return the key.

   I was unnerved by how she'd transformed herself. Won't they notice something different about you?

   Micha gave me a funny smile. I doubt it. I'm just moving a bit faster than before. But I do want you to return the key yourself. Just in case.

   I took the opportunity to splash cold water over my face before I returned the key. If that attendant noticed anything except the porn feed on his cell phone, I would have been astonished, but maybe Micha was right.

We traveled the state highway to the outskirts of Huntsville, where Micha took the first exit marked with lodgings. She pulled into the parking lot of one of those sad little motels, the kind that has three single-story sides around the parking lot and a sign reading, $30/DAY, SPECIAL WEEK AND MONTH RATES. Right next door were the usual businesses—liquor store, adult vid shop, and a tiny grocery store.

So, tonight, we are no longer Janet and Micha. We're Alice and Moses Johnson, back from a visit to our great-aunt Mary. I kept my hands stuffed into my jacket pockets to hide Lazarus. Micha paid in cash. She offered a driver's license, which the clerk barely glanced at before he handed over a set of old-fashioned keys.

And not that I'm surprised or anything, but this entry is my last until...

God, I didn't think it would be so hard to write these words.

Deep breaths. Okay. Until we come back.

Until we come back. And we will come back. Me. Micha. Sara.

Sara. I wonder what she has planned for Nadine Adler.

But enough speculation. When we got to our room, Micha took my bag and dumped the contents of it onto the bed. Swiftly and efficiently she sorted through my belongings.

Clothes. Supplies for Lazarus. My mystery novel plus a few others I'd packed. Then her hand dove straight for my new and almost empty journal.

No, she said. Absolutely not. Goddammit, girl. What were you thinking?

I flinched back. I was thinking we'd burn those three or four pages and ditch the notebook.

She gave me a withering look. And what if they be following us right now, sunshine? Setting fire isn't exactly discreet, even in a dump like this one. What if they use some of that fancy CSI on the book and find your DNA? What if they go after Isabelle? Goddamned amateur.

She went on like that for another five minutes, a rant delivered in a soft but stinging voice. When she finished, she lit a cigarette and flipped through the journal's pages before she handed it over to me.

I know what to do, she said. I need to run a few errands right now, but when I get back, we'll get rid of those pages—safely and discreetly—then you'll write a whole new set. Otherwise, folks might get curious about a blank notebook with a few sheets missing. I'll help you with that part.

Micha left me to my own devices (so to speak) to fetch sandwiches and a couple shot bottles. I had explicit permission to write this entry. To get it out of my system, is how she phrased it.

So, let's make this good.

Dear reader, a reader who will never see these words. I'm terrified. All this past week, I thought I was already afraid, but that was just a warm-up. Tomorrow, we cross into Tennessee. Tomorrow night, Micha tells me, we'll meet up with certain friends, who will take us across the border into the New Confederacy.

The same New Confederacy that hates me and mine, whether we're talking about the color of my skin or the gender that I love.

Oh, they claim they love all God's children.

They claim they love the sinner but hate the sin.

But I've watched the news vids and listened to the deeper squirts. I've seen pictures of that strange fruit, which still hangs from trees, even though we elected a black man once. Maybe because we did.

Black people still live over there. Most of them because they can't move away. No money. No car. And it's not like they can take the bus over the border. Same as with Katrina, they're hoping to ride out the storm.

And others . . . others don't leave because whatever the government says, that land is still their home.

17

I was dreaming about Adanna Jones—an all-too-explicit dream—when our alarm clock burst into noise. I jolted awake and grabbed for the clock. My ghost hand plunged through the floor, with the rest of me following. I managed to break my fall with my right arm and landed on my shoulder with a muffled yelp.

I rolled over, cradling my poor abused stump against my chest. I was in a dimly lit room that could've belonged to any run-down motel between Maine and Florida. Two single beds with metal frames. Cheap ugly carpet with stains I didn't care to identify. The unmistakable aroma of chlorine and mold and fried food. Meanwhile the alarm continued to sing the song of its people.

Micha swatted the alarm clock, which gave one last squawk before going silent. She coughed, a deep rasping smoker's cough. "Good morning," she wheezed. "Are we ready to rumble?"

I levered myself up and leaned against the metal frame of the bed. Squinted at the clock. Six A.M. Not as early as I would have guessed. "Give me coffee, and I can do anything," I croaked. "Maybe."

Micha laughed, then coughed again. "Let me take care of that. No, don't you leave the room. Better if no one notices you and your shiny metal friend."

She staggered to her feet and into her clothes from the night before. Twenty minutes later, she returned with four large Styrofoam cups and a bag of hot biscuits with packets of honey. The tiny grocery store had delivered far beyond my expectations. I inhaled the first cup almost without thinking.

Micha broke one of the biscuits in half and spread a honey packet over both pieces. She handed one to me. "First step, we cross into Tennessee. Let's see how that goes and we'll talk about what comes after that."

"Why not tell me now?"

"Because our plans are not fixed."

I stuffed the biscuit into my mouth and chewed while I contemplated her words. "I think," I said, once I'd swallowed, "that's a fancy way of saying you don't know what comes next."

Micha laughed. "You do catch on, girl. Go on and eat those biscuits. I want us across that border by noon."

She made another trip to the grocery store for a second round of coffee while I showered and dressed in jeans and a T-shirt. By the time she returned, I had powdered my stump and reattached Lazarus.

"Should I pack my device instead?" I asked.

"No, no. We can't risk them searching our bags and finding it. And while I have a few hidey holes around the truck, none of them are big enough. I do have a plan, however."

She produced an inflatable cast sleeve, extra large, that covered every inch from my fingers to my stump. Next came a spray can of temporary white hair coloring. For herself, she added clip-on hair extensions and a pair of Coke-bottle glasses. By the time she'd finished, we were two stocky gray-haired women, maybe fifty, maybe sixty years old, with clothes that had seen better days.

We had new names, new IDs, too. She was Eveline and I was Danielle Jackson, two sisters, residents of Tennessee with work permits for Alabama as house cleaners. I recognized the photo as the one from my ID at the VA Medical Center, with the image modified to match my new gray hair.

"Are you sure these IDs will pass?" I said.

"You wound me with your doubt," Micha said. "Behold the encrypted chip, and the watermark, which, by the way, was not as difficult to reproduce as our government agencies would like to believe. Now finish that coffee. We have a date with Tennessee."

Our next fifty miles would be federal highway. In the olden days, back in the early 2000s, the trip from Huntsville, Alabama, to Pulaski, Tennessee, would've taken an hour at the most. That was before our glorious New Civil War.

After the first few terrorist attacks, the states themselves had set up checkpoints. Once the New Confederacy declared war, President Alida Sanches agreed to border checks in certain key states. Anyone crossing from Oklahoma into Tennessee, or Illinois into Ohio, had to produce one of the new federal IDs.

Micha made one unexpected stop a few miles before the border. We pulled off the highway onto a dirt road and parked behind a water cistern. She unscrewed a panel from the driver's-side door, to reveal two metal-lined compartments. My supplies for Lazarus went into the top compartment. A large square vinyl pouch containing cash, Micha's cell, and what looked like another stack of documents and IDs went into the bottom one. A few quick twists of the screwdriver, and the door panel covered everything.

"What if they have a scanner?" I asked.

She grinned. "Special shielding, my friend. Though," she added, "we're obviously in trouble if they decide to dismantle the truck."

So, here we were, half a mile from the border at eleven A.M., and Micha wondering out loud if we should've stopped at that last exit for sandwiches. The air was thick with exhaust fumes, and a headache gripped my skull. I badly wanted another cup of coffee, or, failing that, a bottle of pop.

"Maybe we should turn back. Get those sandwiches first," I said as I rubbed my forehead.

"Not a good idea. They notice things like that," Micha replied mildly. "Don't fret. I'm guessing we'll get through in thirty, forty minutes. We'll take the first exit with a diner. I promise."

Traffic inched forward, and I huddled in my seat, concentrating on the phrase *thirty minutes*. The truck had turned into an oven, hot and sticky and breathless. My scalp itched. My stump ached, as it had not for months, and tiny pinpricks traveled up and down the length of my arm, through flesh that no longer existed. I resisted the urge to tear off the cast.

"Come," Micha said softly. "We're almost to our friendly border guards. Remember that we're in the South. Look humble and cooperative."

The South, yes. I might have lost much of my accent, but I could never forget the South. Because the South was everywhere.

A woman approached our truck, one hand on the Taser at her belt, the other pointing at the far end of rows of inspection stations. She wore the dark blue uniform of a border guard, with patches for rank, state, and the Federal flag. No name tag, of course, not for what had become the new TSA.

"Last lane on the right," she told us. "Number thirty-two."

Micha maneuvered the truck into lane thirty-two. Two fresh-faced young men approached, one on either side. Both of them carried rapid-fire guns.

"Registration, insurance, and driver's license," said guard number one. "And we'll need to see IDs for both of you."

Micha handed over the papers as requested, then waited with hands resting on the steering wheel. Even without prompting, I'd laid my hands on the dashboard. Slowly. No sudden movements.

Guard number one leafed through our documents. He grunted, then nodded to his partner. "Step out of the car, please."

Why? We haven't done anything wrong.

Words I knew better than to speak out loud. Micha and I exited the truck. The inflatable cast made me awkward, and I stumbled, but no one offered to help, for which I was glad.

They patted us down, swiftly and professionally. It could have been worse. No one ordered me to remove the cast. No one decided that *pat down* meant grab my breasts or between my legs. Even so, I had to swallow the rage I felt, when I saw other cars waved through with only a cursory glance at their IDs.

"I'm sorry for the inconvenience," my guard told me. "We had some reports about possible terrorist activity in the area. We're just taking precautions."

"Yes, sir," I said. "I understand." My voice had dropped into the soft drawl of my childhood, slow and careful.

What I understood I couldn't say out loud. Not unless I wanted trouble.

So, I smiled when Guard #1 made a joke about sassy women, and I stood absolutely still while they searched my pockets. But I held my breath every time a hand brushed over my inflatable cast, or their gaze flicked toward the truck itself.

Just when I thought we were done with humiliation, Guard #1 announced he needed to search the contents of the truck. He signaled for us to move over to the side of the road, where his partner stood ready with his weapon, while he unloaded both our bags onto the pavement.

"Standard procedure," the man said as he unzipped my duffel bag.

They didn't find anything, of course. Our bags held clothes, soap, shampoo, hair oil. One bottle of Advil, which Micha explained was for her sister's injured wrist. Half a dozen bottle shots that Micha had bought at the liquor store back in Alabama.

Guard #1 pocketed the bottle shots.

Guard #2 picked up my damned notebook and leafed through it.

I tried to pretend indifference. Failing that, I pretended exhaustion. The latter came more easily. Micha had ripped out the six pages of my own journal entries and soaked them in water until they were soft enough to tear into shreds and flush down the toilet. Then she dictated five new pages of text. One grocery list. A doctor's phone number in Pulaski (which I had no doubt was genuine). A couple scribbled notes about insurance claims for my apparent injury during working hours.

Would anything there withstand a closer look? Or did we just need to get through this next obstacle?

Guard #2 handed the notebook back to me. "Thank you for your cooperation," he said in that toneless voice used by minions of the government.

As if I had a choice. But I kept my expression humble and grateful. "Thank you, sir. Glad to be of help."

Both guards glanced over our tired, dusty truck. I had another tick of panic, before they ordered us to move on.

⚲

Once we cleared the border, Micha made one of her signature quick stops, where she unscrewed the truck's panels, changed one license plate for another, and retrieved her cell phone, before we hurried onward to Pulaski and a roadside shack advertising pork sandwiches. Micha ordered four sandwiches, a double order of fries, and two giant sodas. We sat in the truck in the parking lot to eat, while Micha—reluctantly, I thought—shared our next goal.

"We made it here without any trouble," she said. "That means they don't have a warrant for two black women, no matter what they look like. I'm thinking we should cross over into Mississippi. There's an abandoned logging trail that can take us through what used to be a national forest. We'll meet up with some friends of mine there. They'll handle getting us into the Confederacy."

"You make it sound easy," I said as I licked the barbecue sauce from my fingers.

She lit a cigarette. "Some days it is, other days, not so much. It's really a matter of flexibility."

We drank our soda. I started on a second sandwich. Micha's cell buzzed. She glanced at the incoming number and frowned before she thumbed off the lock.

"Luciano's Bakery," she said. "Can I take your order?"

Whoever it was, they had a lot to say. Ten minutes passed before Micha spoke again.

"Double back," she said in a flat clipped voice. "Use the gambit we talked about, but no tricks, no fancy stuff. If you have *any* trouble, make an exit. Don't argue. Don't delay. Once you hit ground, let me know. I'll handle cleanup."

She thumbed the cell off and slid it back into her pocket.

"What's wrong?" I whispered.

Micha barely glanced at me. "That was Isabelle. Your aunt called and left a voice message not half an hour ago. A stranger came around the farm early this morning, asking about you. Your aunt thought you might want to know."

Oh god.

This had to be the government, come traipsing after my useless self.

Or maybe someone worse.

That was like choosing between a fox and wolf, both of them hungry. Whoever they were might decide my family made a good snack until they tracked me down.

I had to swallow twice to wet my throat enough to speak.

"What's that gambit you were talking about?"

"Better if you don't know." When I opened my mouth to argue, she held up a hand. "Let me rephrase that. It's better for Isabelle if you don't."

"What do we do?" I demanded. "Go home? Try another day?"

"We don't *have* another day," Micha said, and for the first time, I heard the edge of desperation in her voice. "You might. You can step back into your ordinary world without any consequences. But Sara? She has a week before her mission fails."

"So, what *do* we do?" I repeated. "You and I?"

"Oh, that." Her mouth twitched into a bare smile. "We hurry, my friend."

Micha's cell rang a second time, around three P.M., outside Savannah, Tennessee. She thumbed the cell to unlock it and listened. Ten minutes later, she thumbed the phone off and stuffed it into her pocket.

"We have a problem," she said. "A bigger one."

"What happened? What went wrong?"

Micha flipped a hand. "Everything. That stranger who came sniffing after you? They showed up a second time with a government ID. They told your aunt you were a person of interest in certain mysterious deaths at Georgetown University Hospital."

Oh, dear god.

"I thought Isabelle went to ground," I whispered.

"She did. This was my backup agent. She made a second sweep to clean up any loose ends. Tell me about those deaths, please. I need to know what we're dealing with."

I shook my head. It made no sense. I had no clearance at GUH, nothing that would connect me with any patient, living or dead. But I told Micha about the M & M statistics and how the numbers for readmissions had spiked in the past two months.

"I don't understand," I whispered. "I've nothing to do with the patients, and I won't until the CMO grants me full-time status. Besides, we added more safety checks. The numbers went down this past month."

Micha shook her head. "Someone wants to discredit you. But why? Why you and why now?" She tapped her fingers on the steering wheel for a few moments. "Tell me, how did you pass the evening, that last night in DC?"

I said good-bye to Adanna Jones.

"Oh, Christ," I muttered.

Micha came alert at once. "What did you do?"

I asked her to remember me. I asked for a good word before I plunged into danger. Nothing more.

But I refused to believe Adanna had betrayed me to anyone, even by accident.

"Nothing," I said. "Yes, I told a friend about this trip. I said I had family matters to look into. Nothing . . . nothing more."

Micha continued to stare at me, eyes narrowed.

I glared right back. "Don't you look at me that way. I told my CMO the same thing. Dammit, I told Southeast Airlines and the TSA as much."

She sucked her teeth, seemed to consider several different answers, then sighed. "So, so, so. Perhaps what you said or did made no difference. What does matter, my friend, is that we've lost our safe passage across the border. *Someone* has betrayed us. *Someone* has warned my colleagues away from any questionable activities. Which means someone knows, or has guessed, our plans. Let us drive a few miles in silence and consider a different tack."

We cruised along the state route, a careful five miles under the speed limit. Storm clouds had rolled in from the south, blotting out the sun and bringing an early eerie twilight to the afternoon. Micha was a silent shadow next to me. Faceless. Sexless. Only the red dot of her cigarette betrayed any movement as she took another drag, then blew out a cloud of smoke. We had rolled up the windows, leaving a crack for ventilation, and the wind of our passage whistled and roared, like that of a ship driving through high seas.

I wanted to say, *Who betrayed us?*

I wanted to ask, *Will my family be safe?*

But I kept quiet and stared over the rain-drenched fields,

until the storm passed, and a gold and crimson sunset lit the horizon ahead. Without taking her eyes off the road, Micha said, "What you say we get us a good meal up ahead?"

Her voice had slipped into a drawl, slow and easy.

"Sure sounds like a good idea," I replied. I could almost feel my own throat and palate changing shape to match hers.

Six P.M. Selmer, Tennessee. We were two hundred miles from DeWitt in Arkansas, and even longer from the Oklahoma border, but we'd already come across signs of the war. Memphis had been turned into rubble, during the last Confederacy offensive, and while Arkansas had declared for the Union, everyone knew the rebels controlled half the state.

We stopped at the first Waffle House we found. Micha ordered a plate of chili cheese fries, then vanished into the parking lot for twenty minutes, while I picked at our food. She returned before I finished off that first batch, then ordered two hamburgers and another plate of fries. Once the waitress left with our new order, she leaned over the table.

"I made a few calls, left a few messages," she said. "We can slip across the Mississippi border tonight and into Arkansas. We'll meet up with my friends farther down the road."

"Are these definite plans, or maybe ones?" I asked.

"Maybe ones. Fluid, remember?"

We lingered in that Waffle House, drinking pots of coffee and eating more biscuits and gravy than was good for us. I'd forgotten about biscuits down south. Forgotten about the special flour that made them so light, as if we were gobbling down sunshine. Maybe once Sara and I were back in DC, we could order the right flour and make biscuits of our own.

Around six thirty P.M., Micha vanished again to make another phone call or two. Apparently, her friends had agreed to terms and conditions, because when she returned to our booth, she said, "All clear."

Twilight was falling as we reached the Mississippi border. Micha turned onto a muddy road labeled as West Acres Farm. Five miles in, we took a right onto another dirt road, this one without any sign. Micha turned off our headlamps and guided the truck carefully over ruts and puddles. At some point, we had passed into Arkansas. Around three A.M. we reached DeWitt, where we parked behind a Walmart and slept a couple hours before Micha shook me awake.

"Wake up, sunshine," she said. "I want to run a few errands before we head off."

I groaned and rubbed the sleep from my eyes. My face felt sticky, and I wanted nothing more than to find the nearest Comfort Inn, where I could sleep the next ten hours. "Coffee?" I croaked.

"Coffee and breakfast, just as soon as we get to Pine Bluff."

She urged me awake and when that didn't work, she pressed a handful of damp wipes into my right hand. I scrubbed my face with the wipes, then accepted the cup of lukewarm coffee that she had produced from somewhere. We each made a trip into the weeds to relieve ourselves, then cleaned up with more wipes and headed on our way.

Over the course of the morning, Micha stopped by five different ATMs and used a different card at each one, collecting an impressive stack of twenty-dollar bills. A deposit for our new friends, she told me.

At Pine Bluff, we stopped for breakfast and the long-promised coffee. Hot and strong and able to scald the bitter taste from my mouth. Micha waited until halfway through our breakfast before she ducked outside for another phone call.

"Are we okay?" I asked when she came back.

"Yes. No. I don't know yet. They want a couple conditions I'm not happy with. Don't worry. I've already set a few other plans in motion. Fluid, girl, always fluid."

After Little Rock, we meandered along back roads. Stopped twice for gas and a restroom. Bought a truly awful pizza from a roadside truck. Every time we passed a military truck—and that happened more the closer we got to the border—I couldn't help ducking my head and freezing.

On the far side of Hot Springs, Micha pulled into a junk-yard, on a side road off another side road. The truck's clock read ten till midnight. Micha went to work at once, unscrewing the panels on both sides of the truck. We retrieved my supplies for Lazarus, the cache of money, and from a second compartment on the passenger side, several small-caliber handguns. Security measures, Micha called them. Clearly illegal, is what I thought.

"Do you know anything about guns?" Micha said. "Be honest."

"I passed the basic military training," I said. "Enough to hit a slow-moving target. I can't guarantee more."

"Good enough." She handed me the smaller gun. It had a clip loaded and the safety on. "Shoot if you need to. Don't wait for my command."

At her orders, I removed the inflatable cast that had tormented me the past two days and pulled on a pair of leather work gloves. Meanwhile, my companion screwed the door panels back in place. She divided the cash into two bundles and gave one to me before she stuffed the vinyl bag under her shirt.

We'd just finished these preparations when we heard the crunch of tires over gravel. Micha tucked her gun into her pocket. I froze a moment before I did the same.

A dusty white van lurched over the hill and stopped a few feet away. Two men climbed out, both of them blinking in the glare of our headlamps. One black man, one white. Both wore faded overalls, work boots, and OmaHogs baseball caps. They also carried guns.

"Cut the lights," the black man snapped. "Unless you want the *po*lice to stop by and ask a few questions. Mr. Jack won't like that."

"As you wish." Micha switched off the headlamps. Now we only had the moon and the stars to illuminate the clearing. "So, tell me," she said, "what can Mr. Jack do for me and my friend?"

The white man laughed. "Ain't nothing Mr. Jack can't do. You want over the border, right? Easy. What else?"

"Take care of the truck, please. Make certain it's not traceable, however you or Mr. Jack decide to handle that matter. What's most important is, we need to get over the border tonight."

Both men glanced at each other. "Tonight?" the black man said. "Well, okay. That costs more."

The back of my neck prickled at the tone of his voice. Micha, however, seemed undismayed. "Tell me the price. Then I can tell you if it's worth the cost." She spoke as easily as if she were having a chat about the weather.

White man grunted. Black man gave us an easy smile, like a flash of moonlight. "Sure. No problem, ladies."

He pointed his gun at Micha. "The price? Lessee. The price be *all* the pretty cash you're carrying. Credit cards, too. If you got any bank cards, we want those too. Just hand everything over to my friend. Jimmy Ray, you might want to check them for weapons. Don't want any accidents."

My stomach twisted into a sharp knot. This . . . this could not be happening. Micha was the ingenious one. The one Sara trusted to layer plans upon plans in a matter of minutes. Micha, however, had gone still and quiet. No glance toward me. No reassurance a new plan was under way.

Jimmy Ray patted us down, confiscated our guns plus a hunting knife I hadn't realized Micha possessed. Micha handed over her share of the cash and the vinyl pouch. "I gather we won't be making that drive across the border."

"Nah, we are," Jimmy Ray said. "Sam and me, we'd like to meet your friend. Mr. Jack says you can show us the way."

"That won't be necessary," said a familiar voice.

Sara?

Sam dropped to his knees and fired in the direction of the voice. At the same time, Micha drove a kick into Jimmy Ray's kneecap. He doubled over. She snatched up the nearest of our guns and shot him in the face.

I flung myself to the ground and scrabbled underneath the truck. My stomach heaved. I was not dead—not yet—but my left shoulder burned, and the stink of blood filled the air. All I could see was the rebel soldiers, swarming over the medical unit, every one of them armed with knives and machine guns, their eyes blank as they killed and killed.

More bullets riddled the truck. With a gasp, I yanked myself out of the nightmare that had been Alton, Illinois, and dragged myself farther away from the gunfire. I was bleeding, and my head felt light. One of the bullets must have grazed my arm. My ghost arm ached ferociously. My metal arm twitched and shivered.

A thick silence had settled over the junkyard, broken only by my ragged breath and the thunder of my pulse.

Now what?

Micha already had one of our guns. The other lay a few yards away from the truck. I wriggled around the side of the truck, teeth gritted against the burning pain in my shoulder. Jimmy Ray was a dark lump in the center of the clearing. If he still breathed, I couldn't tell.

I stretched out a hand toward the gun.

Immediately, gunfire broke out.

I snatched my hand back and tucked myself behind the

closest wheel. From a short distance away, I heard Micha's laugh. "You're doing fine, my friend," she said softly.

One more bullet punched into the truck. I bit my tongue to keep from crying out.

"Your friend is dead," Sara called from her vantage point above.

Sara. She lived. I wanted to laugh with relief.

"Goddamn you, bitch." That was Sam, evidently alive and furious.

"Damn straight. Are you going to let three bitches take you down?"

More gunfire rang out, this time from all directions. My heart stopped, then stuttered forward. Someone was whimpering. Me, apparently. Farther off, a man cried out piteously. Then a final shot split the night, and all was still.

Oh god. Oh god.

"Sara. So glad you could join us. I was afraid my message went astray."

That was Micha, her voice breathless.

"I came as quickly as I could," Sara replied. "You brought me a surgeon, yes?"

"I did. And if she hasn't expired from terror, she might join us in this most joyous reunion."

I crawled out from underneath the truck and staggered to my feet. My head felt unnaturally light. Blood loss? Pure terror? But I managed to steady myself against the passenger door while I took in the scene.

Jimmy Ray lay dead a few feet before the truck. Sam was nowhere in sight. Micha and Sara still clasped each other by the arms. "My love." Sara turned to me. "You came."

She folded me into a tight embrace. She smelled of gun smoke and sweat and cloves. God, I had not realized how much I missed her. "How did you find us so quickly?"

Sara gave a low throaty chuckle. "Ah, that. Let me introduce you to my own friends. Dane!" she called out. "All clear!"

A flashlight blinked on. I flung a hand over my eyes, half-blinded. I could just make out a tall figure striding toward us. A woman, a black woman, dressed in fatigues and carrying an automatic rifle.

"Dane, these are my friends," Sara said. "My cousin and the surgeon I told you about. My cousin, my friend, this is Dane. As in Great Dane. She's from the Resistance."

18

"Pleased you meet you," Dane said.

Her voice was cool and light, her age impossible to determine. She was at least four inches taller than me, taller even than Sara Holmes, dark as a moonless night and whipcord thin. She gripped my right hand and smiled—a thin sliver of white against her dark brown face.

Dane, as in Great Dane.

"Does everyone in the Resistance have a code name?" I asked.

Dane's grip tightened a fraction. "Maybe. Do you have a problem with that?"

"Ah, no." A breathless laugh escaped me. At some point, my body would recall it was exhausted and wounded, but not yet. "Pleased to meet you, Dane. More than you could possibly imagine."

Her smile widened. "Likewise. Hound tells me you are the key to our mission."

She released my hand. I flexed my fingers and wondered exactly what Sara had said about me.

Now Dane and Micha faced each other. They studied each other warily.

"And what shall we call you?" Dane said. "Puppy? Bunny? Chipmunk?"

Micha's mouth tucked into a smile. "Ferret will do."

"Hmmm. Good choice from what Hound tells me. Ferret you shall be."

They shook hands. Micha tilted her head back, hesitated a moment. "I . . . I believe I remember you, though you went by another name in those days. Aren't you the one who brought Hound back to our family? Twenty years ago, wasn't it?"

"More like twenty-five," Sara said dryly. "To my regret and dismay, not to say Grandmamma'o." She did not specify whether the regret was for the number of years or that she'd returned to her family. "My love," she said to me. "You are looking more pained than usual."

Now I remembered how often I wanted to smack her with a heavy, blunt object. "Oh, don't mind me. Just a matter of a stray bullet. Please don't let me interrupt the reunion."

Micha snorted. Sara rolled her eyes.

Dane herself was grinning. "She bites. And with good reason. Hound, there's a first-aid kit in the glove box. It should have antiseptic and bandages. Will that do for now?" she asked me.

I shrugged. It wasn't as though I could summon a proper medical kit just by wishing. And I'd dealt with less-than-adequate field conditions before. "For now, yes. At some point, I'd like to have antibiotics on hand."

"We can see about that later," Sara said. "Come with me, Doc."

She lit the way with her flashlight through the junkyard, to a section of chain-link fence that had been cut and peeled back. On the other side, almost invisible in the high grass, was a rusted gray Buick with Arkansas plates. She swung the rear door open. "Let's take a look, my friend."

I dropped onto the seat, suddenly dizzy as the adrenaline vanished. Sara held me upright while she extracted me from my jacket. She left me long enough to fetch the first-aid kit and a jug of water.

"No veins nicked," I said. "Otherwise I'd be dead. And they missed Lazarus."

"Who might Lazarus be?"

"My new arm. Risen from the dead. Will it need a new name too?"

I'd begun to babble, whether from exhaustion, or the strain of these past few weeks, or even the relief I was alive. Meanwhile, Sara tended me competently, as though she'd done this many times. She poured water over the wound, then used wipes from the kit to clean away the blood. It was just as I thought, she told me. The bullet had grazed my arm, nothing more. Once she had picked out the cloth fragments—another operation that left me sweating—she covered the wound with gauze and nagged me until I drank from the water jug.

In the meantime, Dane and Micha had transported all our belongings from the truck. "Let's get away from here," Dane said. "Ferret, you drive the truck. I'll make a few calls farther down the road. We can get someone to tie up our loose ends, while we head over the border."

She spoke easily, as though this were an everyday task, but I knew we were ninety miles from the border and less than twenty from the militarized zone. I told myself they'd made the crossing once already. That had to count for something, right?

Sara pressed two pills into my hand and guided them to my mouth. Aspirin, she told me. She stood over me until I'd choked down the pills and finished off the rest of the water jug. Then she eased me onto the backseat and covered me with a blanket. "Sleep well, my love."

I tried to argue, but my tongue felt thick and clumsy. *God-damn you*, I thought. *You drugged me again.*

Not for the first time, not for the last, I thought I heard her whisper.

I woke briefly when the Buick pulled off the road and Micha joined me in the backseat. The skies were dark, except for a sprinkling of stars. Two signs were just visible in the red glow of the Buick's brake lights. Mile marker 63. A larger one that read Y CITY 27 MILES, LAST EXIT FOR CIVILIANS. Micha settled next to me, and I fell back to sleep.

Another stop, another brief waking. Still night, but the skies now a dark blue along the horizon. The engine hissed softly. Dane leaned against the car, talking on her cell. Micha snored faintly next to me. Sara was a featureless silhouette against the dashboard lights.

"Wake, wake, my love. For we must fly."

I flinched and grabbed hold of the hand on my arm. My fingers locked, hard. Sara waited, still and silent, until the fog cleared from my brain. Slowly I unlocked my fingers and le-vered myself upright. We were parked on the side of a dirt road, in the middle of a forest. The air had a clean fresh scent, of pine needles and damp earth.

"Sorry," I muttered.

"We all have our little habits," she said lightly.

Only Sara would call my panic a habit. I rubbed the sleep from my eyes. "Where are we?"

"In a maze of twisty passages all alike. Drink. Take a piss.

Beware the dwarf with an axe. Or if you need a more precise answer, we are in the middle of what was a national forest, may she rest in peace. But no more questions. Drink. Arise. We can eat as we walk."

Sara handed me a thermos. Coffee, from the smell of it.

The coffee was cold and stale and strong. I drank it down, along with two aspirin—genuine ones this time. By now Micha was awake and grumbling and gulping down her own coffee. Dane and Sara stood off a distance, heads close. Both wore baggy trousers in a camouflage pattern. Sara's elegant locs were covered by a brown scarf. In the sunlight, I could see the thin sharp lines, more pronounced than ever, around her eyes and mouth.

I stumbled into the brush to relieve myself. From above, a blue jay called out a warning; another farther off replied. The closest jay took off in a flurry of noise and feathers, its shrill cry echoing between the trees.

Christ. Might as well send up a signal flare to the enemy.

Leaves rustled off to my left. My breath froze. Images of soldiers with machine guns, charging over open muddy ground, flickered across my mind's eye. I dropped to my knees, expecting any moment to feel the bullets ripping through my flesh.

Silence settled over the land. No gunfire. No explosions. No soldiers. Just the intermittent birdsong of early morning, and from farther off, the murmur of conversation between my companions.

I expelled a breath. Reached hard for my quiet place. Panic, hah, what a fucking inadequate word. Yes, I'd expected to be afraid. Yes, I knew—thought I knew—all the implications a journey across the border had for me and my not-quite-healed self. No matter that we were miles away from the border. Alton had been well away from the border too.

Eventually my pulse slowed. I cycled through the drills Faith Bellaume had taught me. Drills aren't magical, she'd told me more than once. But sometimes they're all we have.

When I returned to the car, Sara and the others had already unpacked the Buick and divided everything into four backpacks. Dane handed out sandwiches of stale white bread, grilled sausage, and mustard. "Thirty miles to the end of the rainbow," she said. "We eat as we march. Are you up to that, Doc?"

I nodded. "I am."

She studied me with an assessing gaze, as if to say, *Are you going to be our weak link?* And if I were, I had no doubt she would leave me behind, this instant, no matter what Sara Holmes said.

But I must have passed inspection, because Dane nodded briskly. "Well, then. Let's go."

We ate as we hiked through the woods. It was late spring down here. Up in DC, the cherry blossoms would be in full bloom. Congress would be bickering about budget cuts and concessions between progressives and conservatives, while the progressives would be bickering about what it meant to be a true progressive. Back on the farm in Georgia, my older cousins would be plowing the fields, or milking the cows, or weeding the garden, while Aunt Jemele tended to my grandmother.

I had lied to them—Jemele, Gramma, my sister. I had promised to get proper care for our grandmother. Never mind my noble reasons. Never mind how the FBI had shattered those plans. None of that would do my grandmother any good.

Later. Once I come back. I'll make those lies into the truth.

As the hours unwound, the sun climbed higher, and the air grew thick and hot. Every so often, we stopped to rest our feet and share a drink from the water jug, or to relieve ourselves away from the trail. My scalp itched with sweat, and I'd lost track of the miles and the hours. All I knew was that we were still in Arkansas. We had to be, or we would've met up with soldiers by now.

At the thought of soldiers, I had to choke back a cry. Dane glanced in my direction. I shrugged and smiled. Dane failed to look convinced, but then Sara asked her about the possibility of a storm moving in, and the moment passed.

Around noon, judging by the sun, Dane called another, longer halt. This time, Sara built a small fire from deadfall and wood shavings, while Dane turned off the trail and vanished into the woods. A short while later, she returned with two plastic gallon jugs of water and a cloth bag. Dirt and bits of moss and bark clung to the bag, which made me think they'd buried this cache on the way to rescue us.

"Lunch, my friends," she announced. "Eat, drink, and be merry."

"For tomorrow we die?" Micha asked.

"Only if I lose my temper with you, my dear Ferret," Dane replied easily.

She unpacked the bag, which contained a jar of instant coffee, a tin pot, and cold beef sandwiches wrapped in wax paper. Sara measured water and coffee into the tin pot, then set the pot onto the fire to boil while we ate our sandwiches. My feet had barely stopped aching before Dane gave the order to break camp and start walking. We buried the remains of the fire, packed up our trash, and set off through the woods to our next destination.

"And how are you, my love?" Sara asked me.

She'd slipped back to my side and spoke in a soft voice.

"Well enough," I replied. "I'll want antibiotics, just to make sure, but I won't be losing the rest of my arm any time soon. How much longer?"

"Two miles to our next goalpost," Dane said, as if she'd been a part of our conversation all along.

I bit back any reply. Sara merely shook her head and fell back to talk to her cousin. Soon after that, the trail died out, and the ground underfoot was covered by dead leaves. The sun hung overhead in a faint white haze. We trudged onward through the underbrush until Dane lifted a hand.

Micha and Sara halted at once. I bent over, trying to catch my breath. The forest stretched off for miles in all directions, a blanket of oak trees with the occasional island of pines, the land rolling up toward ridges, then dropping away. My legs ached, my feet ached, my stump felt warm to the touch.

"Are we there yet?" Micha croaked.

Oh, good. Glad to see I'm not the only one.

"For some definition of *there*, yes," Dane said. "Hound, I need your help."

She and Sara dug into the loose dirt until they had uncovered two rope handles. Together, on the count of three, they heaved, and a mass of dirt and roots swung upward to reveal a brick-lined tunnel. A series of handholds led down into the darkness.

"You didn't tell me it was gym day," I said dryly. The handholds looked sturdy enough—they were clearly manufactured, either resin or heavy-duty plastic, and bolted into the side of the wall—but I wasn't sure my hands, flesh or metal, could keep a grip after today.

"You worry too much," Sara said. "You always have."

"She plays to her strengths," Micha added. "Or so I've noticed. Doc, why don't you go between me and Hound? We'll make sure you don't fall."

But we made it to the bottom without any trouble. Dane was the last down, and she closed the makeshift hatch after her. Sara clicked her flashlight on. We were standing in a small chamber, maybe five by six. The floor and the walls were packed dirt, reinforced with bricks and wooden beams. The air smelled of damp earth and a musty scent of small rodents. A narrow tunnel led off into the dark. It couldn't have been more than five feet high.

I wondered if there were insects. Or spiders.

Let's just leave that happy thought behind.

This was the Jenson Railroad Tunnel, Dane told us. Dug in the 1880s for smuggling and extended by the Resistance in 2018 when "things took a turn for the worse," as she phrased it. A friend would be waiting for us on the other side. And yes, there were insects and there were spiders.

The tunnel was too low for us to walk, even hunched over. Instead, we crawled on our hands and knees over dirt and broken rocks. Every half hour or so, we took a break to drink a couple swallows of water and to rest our knees and arms. I tried to imagine how fast Sara and Dane must have crawled to reach us in time. Then I tried to imagine slaves using a tunnel like this to escape the South. Except we were crawling *into* the New Confederacy.

At the midway point, we took a longer break. We drank our fill of water, ate strips of beef jerky that Dane produced from a pocket, and a handful of chocolate squares. I even managed a short nap.

"How is your arm?" Sara asked me when I woke.

I'd almost forgotten, which was a good sign. "Fine so far, but I'll need—"

"—antibiotics and a surgical kit. Yes, yes, I know. I am not so far from remembering our last conversation. We'll get you both once we reach our safe house. I promise. Are you done with the water bottle? Yes? Let's get going."

Onward, onward, until my joints creaked with every movement and I'd forgotten the feel of sunlight on my skin.

I counted one, or maybe two, more stops. Then a truly uncomfortable interval when the cold and damp of underground had seeped into my bones.

At last, we reached the end of the tunnel. Here thick vertical posts lined the walls of a muddy chamber. More posts framed the entryway into that chamber, with iron chains looped around them. A few good tugs, and the whole section would collapse. Someone had planned this, in case of an emergency, someone who expected the worst.

Not Sara, though. This came from years and decades of experience.

A sturdy metal ladder brought us up to the surface. Dane exited first. When she gave the signal, Micha followed, with me and Sara after her.

I staggered and caught hold of the nearest tree—a skinny sapling that barely took my weight. We stood in pine forest, on the banks of a noisy creek. The sun had set hours ago; a new moon hung low in the sky. The air smelled of rain and crushed pine needles. It could have been Arkansas, or Tennessee, or even Georgia.

And then I saw him. A white man in a Confederate uniform. He sat on a flat rock, across the creek, with a fishing pole wedged into a crevice, and a rifle resting in his lap.

I choked and spun around. Sara caught me by my arm. "Stop. Coyote's a friend, Doc."

Coyote scrambled to his feet and waved. He looked about fifty or so. His pale face was a mass of freckles, his hair was shaved close, and the dark gray uniform he wore carried a corporal's badge above the Confederate flag. Friend or not, the sight of that damned flag made me ill.

Dane and the man exchanged hand signals. I had the impression that we were very close to the front. I found myself gulping down breath after breath, until Sara laid a hand on my shoulder. She touched a finger to her lips, then to mine, and mouthed the words *My love.*

I am not your love.

But I *was* her friend, and by now I understood what she meant by that endearment.

We swept dirt and leaves over the cover to the tunnel, then forded the creek to join our new friend, who had gathered up his fishing gear and gun. With Coyote in the lead, we climbed the low ridge beyond the creek. On the other side, the ground slanted down to a one-lane gravel road, the kind you might find running through farmland, or leading to a spot where the fishing was good.

A military cargo truck was parked in a pull-out—an ancient Mercedes-Benz with a fresh coat of camouflage pattern and a dull green canvas cargo cover. Even though I knew this belonged to the Resistance, my gut shivered. Coyote continued down to the road and stowed his fishing gear in the back of the truck, taking his time about it. He scanned the road in both directions, then gave us the thumbs-up.

We jogged across the road and tumbled into the rear of the truck, squeezing past several enormous steel drums labeled HAZARDOUS MATERIALS. There was just enough room between the barrels and the cab for us to lie down on our backs. Our friend laid our backpacks on top of us, then covered us with a tarp that smelled strongly of grease and a sharper, chemical scent.

I swallowed against the painful knot in my throat. I felt trapped, like a rabbit in a hutch. On either side of me, Sara and Micha breathed steadily. I tried to imitate them, to reach for that quiet, safe place—

—the rattle of machine guns cut the silence. Not dreams. Not nightmares. I bolted upright, gasping and struggling against the suffocating tarp. Sara grasped my arm and hauled me back down.

"Got a problem back there?" our friend called back.

"Nothing we can't handle," Sara replied.

Coyote grumbled something about how we better handle it, or we wouldn't make it past the first checkpoint. But he started up the truck and we lurched onto the gravel road. Another burst of gunfire echoed from a different direction. Then an explosion? Dear god, we weren't close to the front. We were in the middle of it.

I stuffed my metal fist into my mouth. This, this was worse than the panic I'd felt before. This was a terror that bit deep and cold into my bones.

Be still, be brave. We can make it.

Words I'd spoken to my patients, in that muddy ditch in Alton. If only I could believe myself as well as they had believed me.

Sara reached a hand to clasp my shoulder. "Seventy miles," she whispered. "Three hours. We can make it."

"Hush, both of you," Dane whispered.

We hushed. My world narrowed down to this truck, to this breath, to Sara's warm hand against my shoulder. Seventy miles, she'd said. I knew thoughts and wishes couldn't make a difference, but right now, I wished myself at that safe house Sara had mentioned. I wished myself back on the dirt farm.

I wished I were back in DC, walking into Rainbow Books to see Adanna Jones.

I had dozed off when the truck stopped abruptly, and a harsh light poured through the window dividing the cab from the trailer. Sara's hand tightened over my shoulder—an unnecessary warning.

"ID and password," said a young man.

One of the checkpoints, then.

I listened, hardly daring to breathe, while Coyote handed over whatever papers and ID were required. He sounded weary, like a man who been on the road too many hours. To the young man's demand about a destination, our friend replied that he was transporting a load of phosgene to Big Cedar.

All the spit vanished from my mouth.

Oh god, oh god, oh god. Fucking phosgene.

Phosgene was a pesticide. It was also a handy poison in warfare if you didn't mind breaking the Geneva Conventions.

Apparently, the young man at the checkpoint had a similar reaction. He cursed, then barked out orders for the truck to keep moving.

"Pretty good tactic, to scare the enemy," Sara whispered.

I wanted to agree but I was too terrified to speak.

♀

Two more stops. Two more demands for ID and password. The truck picked up speed when we turned onto a paved road. I'd long ago lost track of the hours. I was exhausted, but I could not sleep.

The truck took an abrupt turn onto rough ground. We stopped. I heard a woman's voice close by. "All clear."

Dane crawled between the barrels and vaulted from the truck. "Everybody out," she said. "Ferret, hand me those backpacks. Someone help Doc find her feet."

Micha and Sara unloaded our packs, then me. I stood there, blinking. We were in the middle of a rolling wheat field, which looked silvery in the faint moonlight. Off to one side, an oil derrick dipped and rose. A road sign said, ROUTE 144; another said, CLOUDY, OK.

Our friend pulled back onto the road and headed off into the night. Dane was hugging another woman close. "Raven," she said. "I am so damned glad to see you."

"You should be," Raven said, but she was grinning too. "Going off to rescue kittens and puppies. You," she said to me. "You better be worth it."

"She will be," Sara said. "If you must torment her, wait until we get under cover."

"Gonna take a while for that," Raven said. "What with the patrols on all the main roads."

Dane went still and alert. "Any trouble?"

"No more than usual. But the rats are nervous."

"They should be," Dane muttered.

She and Raven chivvied us into yet another car. Our packs went into the trunk. Dane and Raven took the front seats, while Micha, Sara, and I crowded into the back. Raven handed us each a folder with work papers, stamped with a 2-D barcode. According to the human-readable text, we were part of the late-night cleaning crew at a nearby factory.

Papers, just like back in the days before the first Civil War.

"They get all antsy about black folk near the border," Raven said. "Think we might be up to trouble. Imagine that."

The others laughed quietly. I tucked Lazarus under my other arm and pretended to sleep. My thoughts bounced back to the old Civil War. To patrollers who hunted runaway slaves.

> *Run, run, de patter-roller catch you*
> *Run, run, it's almost day*
> *Run, run, de patter-roller catch you*
> *Run, run, and try to get away*

The old rhyme echoed around my brain as we drove through the night. Maybe we were lucky. Maybe Raven had timed our arrival just right. Because there were no more checkpoints, no patrols, official or otherwise, demanding to see our papers.

I was barely awake when Raven pulled into a parking lot and shut off the car's headlights. It was silent, except for the engine ticking. Dane and Raven waited a moment before they stepped out of the car. Even though they were invisible in the dark, I knew they carried guns and they were surveying our surroundings for any witnesses. Soldiers, in a different kind of war.

Raven opened the rear door. "Inside," she whispered. "Now. Don't worry about your bags."

I staggered out of the car, with Micha close behind. The parking lot was nothing more than a square of concrete, broken and crumbled, with weeds growing between the cracks. On the other side of a plastic barrier stood a low dark building with a yellow neon sign. HONEYDEW INN, ROOMS RENTED BY HOUR, DAY, OR WEEK.

"Come, my love," Sara said. "Almost home."

She guided me over the plastic barrier and through an archway. Two anonymous rectangles faced an equally anonymous parking lot, this one lighted by a single fluorescent lamp. All the windows were dark, and the air smelled faintly of cigarettes and beer.

Raven had hurried ahead to the far end of the parking lot, but Dane paused next to a door. I barely had time to register the keys in her hand before she swung the door open and Sara pushed me into a dark room.

I stumbled and fell face-first onto a bed. Oh god, that was lovely. The blankets smelled of fresh soap, and the mattress was thin but blessedly soft. My entire body ached, as though I'd spent the past three days in surgery, and my ghost arm kept arguing with Lazarus. All I wanted to do was plunge into sleep.

Two women were whispering. Then another voice, also a woman, ordered them to shut up. She—at least I believed it was the same person—drew the blankets over my shoulders. Her fingers massaged my neck, easing the knots from my muscles, then gently exploring my left arm, the cuff where metal met flesh.

She tapped the controls. Someone—Sara, this time—protested. The woman cut her off with a sharp word. Then with a few more taps, the suction released its grip, and Lazarus fell away to be caught by my anonymous caretaker.

"She will sleep better so," the woman said.

19

I slept—a drunken, dreamless sleep that lasted the rest of the night, and into the next afternoon. When I finally woke, and only because a faint golden light insisted, I had no idea where I was. I stretched, one of those long lazy stretches where you twist your body as if it's a Mobius strip. The muscles in my legs and shoulders complained, but not as much as they should have . . .

That's when memory snapped into life—the confrontation with Sam and Jimmy Ray. Dane and Sara to the rescue. The miles upon miles of hiking through a forest. Our endless ride in the back of that truck in the company of hazardous chemicals. Sara and her friends smuggling me and Micha across the border.

I rolled over onto my back. The mattress underneath me was thin and hard. Above me was another mattress just like it, supported by a couple wooden slats.

"Good afternoon, Doc."

In panic, I heaved myself upright, and nearly toppled over

when I tried to catch hold of the bunk bed supports with my ghost arm.

A young woman sat on the bunk bed next to mine, reading a book. She wore canvas overalls and a faded gray T-shirt. Her straight black hair was pulled back into a ponytail, and freckles dotted her nose, almost invisible against her brown skin. She seemed amused.

"Where am I?" I croaked.

"In a safe place. How are you feeling?"

I pressed one hand against my eyes. "I've felt better. Where are . . ." I couldn't remember Sara's or Micha's code name. "Where are the others?"

"Elsewhere. Are you hungry? Thirsty?"

I ran my tongue over my lips, which felt gummy. Now I recognized the woman's voice. She was the one who had insisted on removing Lazarus.

"Let's go with all of the above."

She smiled, this time with more compassion than amusement, and laid aside her book. "Then I shall fetch you something to eat and drink. Stay away from the window, please. If anyone should knock, do not answer, even if you believe you recognize their voice. Most definitely do not open the door."

With that comforting list of instructions, she exited the room. The door swung shut with a loud click.

Out of curiosity, I levered myself to my feet, my joints creaking and my muscles making their own opinions known, and tried the door handle. It didn't budge.

Huh. So, all that talk about not opening the door was nonsense. Was I a prisoner, then, or a valued guest?

Maybe a little of both.

I leaned against the door and surveyed my prison—excuse me, safe house. The room was larger than average, but otherwise it looked much like any other you'd find where the motel did their best business with transient workers. Three bunk beds took up most of the floor space. Besides the exit door, there were two more doors, one of them blocked by the beds, the other leading to the bathroom, I guessed. A dirty window, half covered with newspaper, grudgingly admitted the late afternoon sunlight. The air smelled of disinfectant and soap. My caretaker and guardian had left the window open a crack, and I heard a dog barking without much enthusiasm. *You and me both.*

The lock clicked open. I jumped away from the door, and the other woman slipped inside, juggling a thermos, a paper sack, and a roll of paper towels in her arms. She took in my presence by the door, but her only reaction was a quirk of her mouth.

She swung the door shut with one elbow and handed me the thermos.

"My apologies," she said. "We have no table or chairs."

"Nor fine linen and a wine list," I replied.

That provoked a laugh. "Indeed. And I'm afraid the food isn't much, but you'll get a proper dinner later."

The thermos contained black coffee; the sack contained a fried chicken sandwich wrapped in tinfoil, plus a container of grits and redeye gravy. My caretaker laid out my meal on my bed, along with several paper towels. The coffee was bitter, but it served to wash the scum from my mouth and wake me up. The fried chicken sandwich, on the other hand, was delicious, even if it was cold. I ate it down to the crumbs and licked my fingers. The grits would be hard to manage without a second hand, but at least I no longer felt groggy and starved.

"Better?" the woman asked. She had locked the door with the interior bolt and remained by the window while I ate.

"Thank you," I said. "Much better. Um, what should I call you?"

"Kite will do."

As in the bird, swift and deadly. I decided the name was a warning, so I didn't press her for an explanation for the locked door, or where exactly Sara and Micha had gone. Were they in a different room in this same motel? And what about dear Lazarus?

Even so, my face must have given away my thoughts because Kite smiled. "Your bag and your device are under your bed if you need them. The bathroom is over there." She indicated the other door.

I scouted the bathroom first. It was tiny but clean, with a toilet, sink, and shower stall crammed into a five-by-five square. Not suitable for tending to my stump, but more than good enough for everything else. I rinsed out my mouth with a handful of water, then splashed more water over my face. Once I felt truly awake, I took an inventory of myself.

Joints sore. Muscles aching from unaccustomed effort. Nothing surprising, considering the miles we'd spent crawling through that damned tunnel. The bullet graze, at least, showed the best signs. The wound had scabbed over—dear god, it itched—and my stump was in far better shape than I expected, after three days of outright neglect. But I couldn't put that off any longer.

Kite had returned to her bunk and her novel. When I came back into the main room, she glanced up, a questioning look.

"I'll do," I said.

"I'm glad to hear that. It would be an unfortunate waste of everyone's time otherwise. Do you need help with your device?"

I bit back my first irritated reply. "No, thank you. I can manage."

I wrestled my bag and my device out from under the bed with my one arm, then laid out my supplies on the blanket.

We weren't talking a sterile operating surface, but at least these were genuine field conditions. Kite had thoughtfully left the roll of paper towels on my bunk, and I used those to create a work surface. The antiseptic pads and the powder took longer, but I worried my way through that as well. At last I lay on my bunk, panting, with Lazarus attached.

Meanwhile, Kite continued to read her novel, seemingly indifferent to me. I could just make out the title and the author's name. Courtney Milan, *The Suffragette Scandal*. One of my mother's favorite books. *Only time I ever cried about thimbles,* she told me. *All those people like to say romance is nothing special. We all need something to take us through the bad times. We all need books where there's a happy ending.*

Maybe once I got back to DC, I'd look up these books myself.

"When do you expect the others?" I asked.

"No more than two hours."

I had no cell or watch, and I noted the room had no clock. Well, then.

"Do you have another book?" I asked.

"Alas, no."

I flung myself back onto my bed. Raised my arm and observed the glitter of brass and steel. Felt a shiver of electricity, like a shiver of life, run down the length of my arm from flesh to metal.

Time for drills, I thought.

I flexed my left hand. Lazarus obeyed without the least hesitation. Ten times for each drill, Sydney had told me that first day. Keep at it until you stop thinking about each movement.

Ain't no such thing as a magical cure, I thought, *but there is such a thing as progress.*

I moved on to the keyboard exercise, running each finger

in turn over my imaginary keyboard. A melody worked best, but I was no musician. Instead, I pretended I was Sara, playing her favorite piece, *Appassionata*.

Chord by thundering chord, the melody in my imagination rose upward like a host of angels.

At sunset, a loud rap sounded at the door.

Kite slid the paperback under her pillow and materialized next to the door, a gun in one hand. When I started up from my bed, she gestured sharply for me to stand back. I subsided onto the mattress and considered what weapons might be at hand.

To my great relief, Dane barked out, "Goddammit, what the hell you doing in there? I've had a piss-poor day, and all I want to do is take a quick lie-down."

Apparently, that was the secret code phrase, because Kite grinned and flipped the bolt open. Dane pushed through the door, followed by three other women. Dane and Sara each carried a bag of groceries. Raven had a bag slung over one shoulder. The third I didn't recognize at all until she spoke.

"Doc," said Micha. "I see you finally woke up."

When I'd first encountered Micha face-to-face, back in DC, I'd thought her a stocky woman in her fifties, square built and plain. In Georgia, she'd transformed herself into an elderly man, then a woman of uncertain age with gray hair and callused hands. Now she was a woman in her late thirties or early forties, lean and angular, her hair a soft brown halo around her unlined face.

"Where is Owl?" Kite demanded.

"Scouting," Dane replied. She tossed a manila envelope to me. "Welcome to your new identity, Doc. Please read and memorize."

The envelope contained two sets of IDs. One was a small plastic card with an embedded chip for one Callie Mae Johnson, citizen of Oklahoma and the NCR. The other was a stamped and dated permit that allowed the same Callie Mae Johnson to travel between Cloudy, Oklahoma, and the Sooner State Machine Parts factory, her place of employment, during curfew. The photo on the plastic card was close enough to mine. I wasn't so sure about the bio-identity data stored in the chip, but if Micha had anything to do with this, the data would match my own DNA and fingerprints.

"Congratulations," Dane said. "You are now officially part of the cleaning crew."

"Excellent," I said. "How's the pay?"

"Top of the line," Sara told me. "Considering. Eat, while we give you the long-promised explanation."

Dinner consisted of biscuits, red beans and rice, and barbecued pork ribs. We had more paper towels for napkins and several cans of Sprite and Diet Coke. As I ate, Sara launched into her explanation.

"Adler," she said. "Nadine Adler, youngest sister in that very successful trio who founded Adler Industries and Livvy Pharmaceuticals. The official story claims Nadine died after a shoot-out with government officials, after that incident involving veterans from the New Civil War. But Adler did not die. She used the delay by my superiors to escape from New Jersey and smuggle herself into the headquarters for Adler Industries, where she had an enormous sum of cash stored in a safe in her office. She took that and fled across the border. Costa Rica, my chief said. I said otherwise. An obsession, you called it," she said softly. "Turns out my obsession is fed by instinct."

"I still don't understand," I said. "Adler sold those drugs to both sides. The New Confederacy lost as many, maybe even more soldiers than we did. They can't be happy with her."

"They did," Dane said. "And they're not. And by *they*, I mean both the government and any number of ordinary folks. *They* want those peace talks just as much as the Federal States do. Too many dead. Cities and farms destroyed or abandoned. I doubt the New Confederacy would've lasted this long without help from outside."

The Russians, I thought. Or the Chinese. Possibly both, each working for their own reasons to keep the United States divided and unstable.

"So why here?" I said quietly. "Why not Costa Rica after all?"

"I don't know," Sara said. "My guess is that she couldn't risk traveling so far under a false identity. Better to hide with the enemy until the search for her died down. And it did." She blew out a breath. "I went to my chief, the day after the Bloody Inauguration. He agreed there might be a connection. A week later, the decision came from on high not to pursue the matter. I waited," Sara continued. "Then I had my data back."

Rose Adler had salvaged the main holdings for Adler Industries, she went on, but the government had shut down Livvy and indicted the four chief officers, plus the head of research. The rest of the employees had been released with a warning to remain in the DC area for the trials.

"Most had found new jobs," Sara went on. "Even with the scandal. I tracked them all down. All except one. That one person being a biochemist named Dr. Salmah Sa'id, last sighted on December 10, when she entered her bank to make a withdrawal. That same day, she paid her rent in advance through May, and arranged to have her mail held, both paper and electronic transactions. I checked the airlines and Amtrak, but no one matching her description purchased a ticket or made reservations."

Vanished. Just like Katherine Calloway.

My mouth went dry. I took a swig of soda.

"That is when Hound made contact with us," Dane said. "She asked if we'd noticed any unusual activity since November." She laughed. "There's always something unusual going on in these parts. Some of that is our fault. Some . . . is because of a group named the Brotherhood of Redemption. They don't want any peace talks. They don't want any compromise with the Federal States. For them, it's all or nothing.

"Speaking of which . . . Even before Hound sent her message, we knew the Brotherhood had acquired an abandoned factory here in Cloudy—that was back in July. They bought used equipment, hired workers to fill a day shift, all of this under a shell company. And they did manufacture machine parts, which probably helped fund their other activities. So, we kept a watch, noticed a fair amount of traffic at night, as well as day."

"Which means," Sara said, "that when Nadine Adler turned up, asking for refuge in exchange for her services, the Brotherhood was ready. My data sources told me about the patterns of money and equipment, which confirmed Dane's observations. I went to my chief again. He agreed I had enough evidence, but *his* chief decided the matter belonged to the CIA. That's when—"

Once again, her fingers knotted together, and she drew a deep breath before she continued. "Our beloved government sent an undercover agent to investigate. He was betrayed and executed. That is when I decided to take over the mission."

What a typical Sara understatement.

"We had already infiltrated the cleaning crew by February," Dane said. "That's how we discovered the laboratory behind the main factory floor. Ignorant motherfuckers thought because we were black, we had to be stupid as well. At first, we suspected they were working on new explosives—another Bloody Inauguration—but then Hound showed up with her own theory about the missing biochemist."

"I couldn't risk showing my face," Sara said. "Not with Adler so often on site. However, Dane smuggled a written message from me. A read-and-destroy message. I offered her federal immunity if she would testify about Nadine Adler and the Brotherhood. Three days went by before she answered. *I will do it. But they have my sister. You must rescue her as well. And she has need of a surgeon.*"

I growled in frustration. "That's . . . very vague."

"She's frightened," Dane said. "She could barely bring herself to talk to me."

"But I need more information," I said. "What kind of surgery? What surgical tools will I need?"

"That is why you will ask her tonight," Sara said.

20

Eight forty-five P.M. Time for the Sugar Sweet Cleaning Crew to set out for work.

Raven had mustered up a uniform that nearly fit me. The ugly brown coveralls, made out of cheap synthetic material, itched like hell, but my rubber-soled shoes were durable and sturdy. I tucked my hair underneath the regulation head wrap and pulled on my industrial gloves. The gloves were thick enough that Lazarus's metal joints were not visible.

Sara and Micha, I noticed, wore black boots, dark cotton jerseys, and loose camouflage pants. Almost military, and definitely nothing like a Sugar Sweet uniform.

"You aren't joining us?" I asked.

Sara checked over a handgun before she tucked it into a pocket holster. "Too risky," she said. Her gaze roved over the array of weapons Kite had produced from the blocked-off closet. With a pleased growl, she selected a knife and eyed the blade. The knife evidently passed inspection, because she slid that into a wrist sheath on her left arm.

"Besides," Micha said. "We need to do some of our own

scouting. No offense to the local experts." She and Raven exchanged edged smiles, which were not entirely hostile, but also not entirely friendly.

Huh. Maybe a bit of competition going on there?

Dane peeked through the window. "Our friends are here. Hound, you and Ferret wait until true dark before you do any scouting. I mean that, hear? Keep to the back roads, and don't give no sass to anyone, black or white. Doc, Hound says Adler won't recognize you. Just in case, I want you to be the dumbest, quietest woman in our crew. Just scrub and mop and follow orders. Think you can do that?"

"Sure can," I mumbled. "Don't like scrubbing any toilets, though."

Dane's mouth quirked in a smile. "Close enough, sunshine. Though you might wanna practice your accent on the ride over. Let's go."

Sara and Micha departed with Kite in a red pickup truck. Dane, Raven, and I joined the rest of the crew in the same rusted Buick from the day before. The driver was Owl, a lean white woman whose wispy brown hair was streaked with gray. The other two women, one white and one black, shrugged when I asked their code names.

"Don't fret," Owl said. "We just like to be careful."

She eased the car out of the motel parking lot and headed west. Cloudy, Oklahoma, was a nothing little settlement, founded in the early twentieth century and known for not having anything to know about it. *Nothing* and *little* sure did sum up the town. Cloudy had no real main street, just a state highway running through the center. Besides the motel, the town included the usual collection of gas station, church, and all-purpose grocery store. Coulda been any small town, this side or that of the border. Coulda been Georgia.

Except, except, all kinds of differences, dontcha know.

Twilight was fading into dark by the time we reached the factory, which sat atop a small rise, surrounded by wetlands and fields of shoulder-high grass. Once, there'd been farms and a town here as well, like a village outside a medieval fortress. Well, the fortress had fallen during the war, the peasants had fled, and the village no longer existed except for a few broken walls.

Bright lights atop the factory illuminated the parking lot and the front of the building, which appeared to be in good shape, but here and there were signs of bullets and fire. The barbarians had done some damage.

We parked off the road, in the weeds, and followed a dirt track to the employee entrance. A guard with an AK-47 leaned against the wall. He looked bored.

Owl presented her ID. He scanned it with a handheld device. The other white woman followed after her, with barely a blip in the guard's attention. He did take more care with Raven and Dane, but clearly, he recognized them. When I offered my own ID, he paused and squinted at the credentials.

"You're new," he said.

"Yessir," I replied. "I come here to my cousin Billie looking for work—"

I shut myself up before I could babble myself into trouble. Dane had paused by the doorway, pretending to adjust the laces for her boots. Beyond that, Owl and Raven hovered. I didn't know what the three of them might do if the guard objected to my credentials.

The guard studied me for a long moment. His eyes were pale blue. His brown hair was cropped short and plastered against his skull. He looked young, and I wondered why he wasn't serving at the front.

He glanced over my ID a second time, then shrugged. "Go on, then."

Dane nodded and beckoned me inside. "What the man said. Come on, Callie Mae. We don't have time for you to laze about."

We loaded up three trolleys with mops and cleaning supplies from a closet, then advanced to the factory floor. Rows of CNC machines occupied half the open space, with bright yellow stripes marking off the stations from the aisles. On the far side of the building I spotted the wide doors for the loading dock. Running down this side were a couple glass-walled offices, a break room, and of course the restrooms.

It all looked so ordinary—except for the second armed security guard patrolling on the catwalk overhead, and an unmarked door near the loading dock doors, with what looked like an ID access pad, leading into another section of the building.

Oh, yes. That would be where we find Dr. Sa'id.

"Missy, Charlene." Owl rapped out the names. "Y'all start on the shop floor. Billie, Callie Mae, you take care of those two offices."

"Lemme guess," Raven said. "That means I gotta clean those damned bathrooms. Again."

"You and me together," Owl said. "Can't say any fairer than that."

"Maybe I could," Raven grumbled. But she dutifully followed after Owl, dragging one of the trolleys after her. Missy and Charlene headed onto the main floor with the second trolley. Dane took charge of the third and chivvied me over to the closest office, as if I were a not-very-bright child. "I hope to God you know somethin' about mopping and dusting and such," she muttered. "Unless Gramma lied about that."

"Course I do," I muttered back at her. "Didn't I already tell you, I done cleaned plenty of motel rooms when I was a kid?"

I sniffed, as if annoyed.

Dane gave me a side-eye, as if to say, *Don't overdo it.*

We both bowed our heads, both acting annoyed for the white men and their cameras. Missy and Charlene were already hard at work, sweeping dust and metal shavings from the factory floor. Dane headed into the first office with me following after.

Both offices swept and cleaned, and none too fast. After we finished, we reported back to Owl, who looked us over with that same suspicious gaze I'd come to expect since I was eight years old and finished my chores too soon.

"Sure you all done?" Owl said.

"Sure I'm sure," Dane said. "We don't dawdle like *some* folk."

Owl rolled her eyes. "Well, then I guess you get a treat. You and Callie Mae go on and do those rooms in the back."

She signaled to the guard on the catwalk, who nodded and pulled out a cell. A couple minutes later, a third security guard came in through the employee entrance.

Three guards for one factory. Scratch that, three guards I can see. And all of them armed with rapid-fire assault weapons.

My skin crawled with dread. Ours was a mission impossible. How could we even talk with Sa'id, never mind rescue her from this prison?

The guard sauntered through the yellow-lined aisles, to the unmarked door. He slid a plain white card through a reader slot, and the door clicked open. Then he handed a second card, this one with a metallic strip, to Dane.

"You know the drill," he said.

Dane ducked her head. "Yes, sir. I know. Don't even try to go into that office. Don't go into that laboratory." She drew the last word out in a drawl. "Just stick to the kitchen and those bathrooms. Oh, and remember to sweep the hallway this time."

"And don't forget to give me the card back "

"Course I will, sir."

"The new girl is your responsibility. She makes trouble, you get trouble. Understand?"

"Yes, sir. I understand, sir."

It was so odd to watch Dane play meek and deferential. She even managed to appear smaller in the face of this armed white man. A code switch of body, as well as speech. I felt the hot bubble of rage inside my chest, but I swallowed that rage and bent my head to the white man.

One day, my rage whispered, *we won't be so biddable.*

But not here, not tonight.

Dane tucked the card into her uniform pocket, and we guided the trolley through the door and into a large windowless cube, with one door opposite us and a light fixture overhead. Dane had warned me about the security cameras and audio pickup in this section. No doubt the light fixture doubled as another means of surveillance.

The door behind us closed. Seconds later, the other one opened—like an air lock, though whether the air lock operated automatically, or whether the security guard had to activate it, I couldn't tell.

Our new door opened into a corridor running the width of the factory. Recessed lamps overhead lit the moment we entered. More cameras? Definitely high tech. Someone had spent a great deal of money on this section. I wondered if that would be the Brotherhood, or Adler, or a very wealthy entity who saw a benefit in what took place here.

The door from the air lock clicked shut, leaving us in this bright blank corridor. I tentatively tried the handle. Locked, of course. There was an ID pad with a card reader on this side as well. Hmmm.

So, nobody gets in or out without being authorized.

"Stop playing wi' things," Dane grumbled, for all the world sounding like an older cousin scolding her not-so-bright younger cousin. She pointed to a door at our end of the corridor, which had a palm-print ID panel and a card reader. "That be the office. Man says don't go in there, so we don't. Only the boss lady goes in there. Our business be through that other one. Come on, girl, and stop gawking. We got lots of work ahead of us."

We guided the trolley to the door at the opposite end of the corridor, which Dane's card unlocked. "Fancy card," she said quietly as we continued through. "Man told us that first day all about it. How it don't work except nights. How it don't unlock *this* door unless all the others be locked. Goddamned card even *counts* how many times we use it."

"Huh," I said with my best impression of gawking. "That *is* fancy."

Dane's expression told me I wasn't doing nearly as good a job pretending as I'd thought. With a great sigh, she jerked the trolley through the door and swung it around with a practiced air. I followed into what turned out to be a combination kitchen and break room.

Like everything else on this side of the factory, the kitchen was outfitted with all the items you'd expect—stove, sink, dishwasher, coffeemaker, refrigerator. Everything you'd need to cook meals or prepare a quick snack. Everything bright and gleaming and new.

But not nearly as bright and new as the laboratory, visible through a large window on our left. Though I knew little enough about biochemistry, I sucked in a breath of astonishment at the expensive equipment in that room. Racks of jewel-bright reagents. A dozen different workstations with microscopes, analytical scales, and other devices I couldn't begin to guess at. Opposite the kitchen, another window overlooked the lab. That would be the forbidden office.

In the center of the laboratory, two women stood on opposite sides of a cluttered worktable. I stopped and stared, unable to help myself.

I recognized Adler at once. Here was the woman who had shot me in the back, last October. Here was the woman who had murdered all those soldiers and veterans. All those photos from the newsfeeds had burned themselves into my memory. Publicity stills, with Adler dressed in a corporate suit, her hair clipped close. Young and ambitious and confident.

Nadine Adler today barely resembled those photos. The past six months had aged her a decade at least. She was older, thinner, more anxious, her pale brown skin drawn taut over her bones. And though her hair was neatly clipped, it had furrows as though she'd spent the past six months raking her fingers through it. *Good*, I thought.

The other woman could only be our biochemist, Dr. Salmah Sa'id. Sa'id was clearly a much older woman, her silvery hair tucked behind her ears. She was of middle height, but still half a dozen inches taller than Adler. They stood on opposite sides of a worktable, Adler with both hands flat and leaning forward, while Sa'id gestured emphatically. The thick glass muted their voices, but clearly this was not a friendly discussion.

"Don't stare," Dane said in a low voice. "Boss lady in there? She don't like that. If she sees you dawdling, she's gonna get unhappy. We don't want that." In a softer, worried tone, she added, "She ain't almost never here at night. Musta come inside while we was cleaning up those offices."

We set to work, scrubbing down the table and counters, all the while conscious Adler could see us if she glanced in our direction. If she did, she would see two minions, contract labor assigned the dirty and undesirable tasks. Dane was a known quantity, as far as Adler was concerned. I was the new girl, and therefore suspect, but Adler had never caught a glimpse of my face during that almost deadly confrontation last October.

At least, I hoped that was true.

We had progressed to sweeping the floors when Adler exited the lab into the kitchen. Her gaze swept over us and she paused. My pulse thrummed faster, and it took all my will to keep my head bent. The moment passed, and Adler slapped her palm against the ID pad. The door hissed open and she vanished into the outer corridor.

"Whew, boss lady gone for the day," Dane said with obvious satisfaction.

"How you know that?" I said.

She nodded in the direction of the office window. "She sees us, but we see her. Always good to know when the boss lady's about."

"Ain't that the truth."

We finished sweeping. Dane emptied the garbage can. I filled the mop's canister with cleaning fluid and began scrubbing the floor. Several moments later, Sa'id came into the kitchen and fixed herself a cup of tea from the supplies on the counter. She paid no attention to us, and we kept our attention on our work.

Cameras, I told myself. But damned if I hadn't glimpsed a moment of tension in her eyes when she spotted me.

We finished up with the kitchen, leaving Sa'id to her tea, and continued through a short passageway into a larger space that included the showers, locker rooms, and toilets. Another door, also without a lock, stood at the far end. Was that where the lab employees lived? Or were they permitted to go home, while Sa'id and her sister remained here?

Three toilets. Two urinals. A single shower stall. Half a dozen lockers. Not a big staff, then, wherever they lived.

Dane pointed me toward the toilets, while she set to scrubbing the sinks. We worked slowly and steadily. After about fifteen minutes, Sa'id marched into the room and locked herself in the nearest toilet. Not one I'd already cleaned; thank god for small favors.

Dane wrung out her rags and flung them into a bucket on the trolley. Then she picked up a can of air freshener and knocked it against the side of the toilet stall.

"Hush," Sa'id said sharply.

"You told me there weren't any cameras in here," Dane said.

"There aren't. At least that I've discovered. I just . . ."

She broke off with a sob. Terrified. Not that I could blame her.

Dane and I waited for her to recover. At the same time, we couldn't dither around forever in these back rooms. I made a sign to Dane, who nodded.

"You're afraid," I said. "I understand. I'm afraid too."

A moment of uncomfortable silence followed this.

"You're the surgeon?"

No, girl, I just like pretending, all so I can put myself in danger.

"Who else would I be?" I said crisply. "And I have a few questions for you."

I could almost hear her eyes go wide. Perhaps she had never encountered someone with more salt than her. After the previous two weeks of dodging the FBI, the CIA, and the New Confederacy, I had more salt than the Aral Sea.

"Very well," she said. "Ask your questions."

I didn't answer right away. I squirted cleaning foam over the toilet, then wiped down the surfaces. Next to me, I heard Sa'id breathing harshly and felt a twinge of regret. I didn't want to punish her. I only wanted her to *see* me, to see the Resistance who had risked so much for even this brief conversation.

"You wanted a surgeon for your sister," I said. "What kind of operation does she need?"

Now it was her turn to hesitate. "The whole mess is my fault. I should have left that goddamned company months ago. But no, I told myself, I was making important discoveries. Important." She spat on the floor. "I knew better, I just didn't want to go through another round of applications for visas."

I could understand that. I made an encouraging noise.

"Besides"—Her breath hissed out—"I had my own lab and my own budget. I was going to invent the perfect medical device to combine scheduled doses with internal monitoring, one that could be dissolved by remote control."

I'd read about such work in the medical journals. Such a device would reduce the number of invasive surgeries, which itself could increase the speed and likelihood of recovery.

"Then came disaster. Livvy shut down. Everyone detained for questioning. All my work confiscated by the investigators." She spoke faster now, as if she had released a flood tide of memories. "I'd begun a search for a new job when those terrorists, that Brotherhood, sent me a message. They had taken my sister hostage. They had robbed my laboratory of my work. They even had my latest experimental model. They said . . ."

Her voice failed. I bit my lip, wanting to shout at her to hurry up. I thought I could hear the minutes and seconds racing past. Any moment, a guard might wonder why we took so long at our work. Any moment, the security system might do the same.

Dane waited silently, patiently, for her to continue.

"They claimed they had implanted one of my own devices into Kalila. If I refused to work for them, she would die. I . . . I was afraid. I said I would."

"What is in this particular packet?"

"Poison. Snake venom. From a black mamba."

Oh. God. Yes. My skin shivered.

"Where is the packet located?" I asked, keeping my voice neutral. "And does your sister have any allergies? Latex? Antibiotics?"

"No allergies. Just below her rib cage. Right side, immediately under the skin. I could remove the damned thing myself with a razor blade, but they warned me that if I tried, they would execute her in front of me. And if my sister and I did escape, they would trigger the packet to dissolve."

Thus losing their hold over her, but tonight was not the moment to point this out.

"Doc here can take care of that," Dane said. "We will rescue you and your sister both. I promise."

"But you don't understand. Adler—she's the dangerous one. She's the one who told the Brotherhood about my sister. She's the one who told me exactly how Kalila would die if I did not follow orders. And she's the one who planned out the Bloody Inauguration. A trial run, she called it. I was supposed to design the packets to release the poison. Her pet surgeons in Washington, DC, would implant the packets and monitor the outcome. I knew what she wanted, even if she didn't say it. Monsters, all of them—"

I leaned against the wall of the toilet stall, fighting against a wave of dizziness. I could still see the bloody and broken bodies in the streets. And Adler had simply used them for a fucking experiment.

"Do you know what she intends?" Dane was asking. "And why the sudden change in plans?"

"Assassination. A senator. I don't know his name. He was scheduled for a stent implant in June. Adler was excited because the implant meant a drug implant and a remote monitoring unit. Then a few days ago, Adler got word the senator had rescheduled his operation to next week. He wanted more recovery time before the peace negotiations."

I sucked in my breath. *Oh, dear Christ, this can't be possible.* But all the pieces fit together—A senator. A stent that could deliver drugs at regular intervals, coupled with remote monitoring. I didn't want to know the answer, but I had to ask.

"Which hospital?"

"She didn't say, but I can guess. Georgetown. Georgetown University Hospital."

Of course. Georgetown was the favored choice for senators and high-ranking government officials. Georgetown had the best surgeons. We even had our new standard procedure to insert medical packets before we discharged patients in high-risk categories.

Could the traitor possibly be Hernandez?

My thoughts skittered away from that possibility.

The consequences were all too clear, however. If a senior senator were assassinated, especially one who favored negotiations between the Federal States and the New Confederacy, that would destabilize both governments. Especially if that death could be laid at the New Confederacy's door.

But . . . But . . . My brain yammered at me about the many holes in this explanation. How had a tiny fringe group like the Brotherhood managed to create this extra-secure facility in just a few months? Or was this part of a much older, much bigger plan?

Let's table that question for later. Back to Sa'id and her sister Kalila, and the mystery of Georgetown.

"Did Adler tell you which surgeons were the traitors?"

Sa'id made an impatient noise. "No. I only know what I overheard that one time. And Georgetown is but one player in the game, as she calls it. She has friends, several friends in very high places."

"But who—"

"No more time. I need to get back."

Sa'id flushed the toilet and marched out of the stall. She made a show of washing her hands before she hurried through the kitchen and back into the lab. Cameras or no cameras, I knew enough not to detain her. Dane herself continued to mop.

"Should we try again?" I asked. "Tell her when to expect a rescue?"

Dane shrugged. "Maybe better if it's a surprise."

Maybe. Maybe not, as Joseph said.

We finished our assigned work in the showers and toilets. Back in the lab, Dr. Sa'id was bent over a microscope. The office window was a dark blue blank. Nothing unusual, nothing outside the ordinary. Dane did a quick tally on her task list, then nodded for us to exit back to the factory.

Her card admitted us into the outer corridor. We had just maneuvered the trolley around when Nadine Adler came storming out of the air lock room.

She stopped and stared directly into my face.

I gulped and ducked my head. Next to me, Dane went still.

After a very long moment, Adler continued into her office. I closed my eyes and breathed a prayer to God, who was sometimes my god after all.

Had we betrayed ourselves?

We'd find out tomorrow night.

21

Back in the motel room. Ten of us crowded onto the bunk beds or sitting cross-legged on the scuffed linoleum floor. Kite had drawn the shades and turned the overhead light to its dimmest setting. Midnight was long past, but we were all too keyed up to care. On our blessedly uneventful return from the factory, we'd found Micha and Sara studying an out-size tablet with hi-res maps of the area. Kite had handed out several more tablets to Dane and the rest of us.

"Nice tech," I said to her when I got mine. "Did you go shopping last night?"

Kite shrugged.

Fine. I guess we're still keeping secrets from each other.

I settled onto a bed and pretended to study the maps on my tablet, but my uncooperative brain kept veering back to that moment when Nadine Adler had stared straight into my eyes. *Don't worry,* Dane had told me. *She always looks that angry.*

Meanwhile Micha and Raven had started an argument over the technical capabilities of certain rapid-fire guns, and Owl was adding her own commentary.

Sara cleared her throat. Everyone went quiet.

"We launch the rescue tomorrow," she said. "Yes, tomorrow," she said when Owl started to protest. "I know it's sooner than we first planned, but our dear friends have obviously moved their own schedule up."

Dane was nodding. "I wish we could make our move tonight. Those rats are more nervous than I'd have expected." When Micha raised her eyebrows in question, Dane told her, "Adler was there. A very unhappy Adler. We . . . had a bit of an encounter."

"Doc," Sara said in that soft rough voice of hers. "What have you done?"

"Nothing," Dane told her. "Just . . . she noticed us. How much, I can't say."

"All the more reason to act quickly."

Sara tapped her fingers over the tablet, making the display flicker through a dozen images. "So. A few changes to the plan you and I discussed," she said to Dane. "I'd meant for Doc to stay outside the factory, away from the explosions, but after last night, it might look suspicious. Raven, you join the outside crew, while Doc goes inside." To me, she said, "Do try to keep out of trouble, my love."

Micha snorted. Raven eyed me with a speculative glance.

"We are not loves," I stated clearly.

"Oh, no," Micha said. "Your love owns a bookstore back in DC."

"She— Oh, never mind."

"Children, children, please," Sara said. "Here is a rough draft of our plan. Same crew, minus Raven, who has called in sick. Owl, you will slip on the wet floor, say, half an hour into the shift. Alas, you shall be unable to continue and must beg leave to wait for the others in your car. Don't be too dramatic. Plausible is our goal."

"The things I do for a good cause," Owl said under her breath.

Sara flicked her gaze toward Owl. "We all make sacrifices, my dear. Moving on. The crew is now shorthanded and possibly less organized without their supervisor."

Dane's smile was brief and edged. "Indeed. We cannot hope to work as diligently without our overseer."

We all laughed softly, including Owl.

"At ten fifteen," Sara went on, "Ferret and Raven shall create a major distraction at the loading dock, and several smaller ones scattered about the grounds. Once we've drawn the guards away, the outside brigade shall penetrate the factory and arm our comrades inside."

"Meanwhile," Dane said, "Doc and I will extract Sa'id and her sister, join the rest of you, and make our grand escape. Obviously, this means we need to evacuate our people and equipment from the area. Kite, please make arrangements for that. One van with a clean record and driver will do . . . say, our Coyote. We also want a reliable off-road truck with a cargo cover—one with military camouflage would be lovely—and new papers for everyone."

Kite noted all these items on her tablet. She didn't appear overwhelmed by the assignment.

"How much time will you need for the operation?" Sara asked me.

I made a rapid calculation. "Based on what Sa'id told me . . . Half an hour max, including prep and closing the patient."

Dane sucked her teeth. "Tricky. We intend to take out all the guards, but we can't guarantee that we won't have pursuit."

"It is what it is," Sara said. "Ferret, Raven? Can you provide us with enough gunpower for that kind of situation? It will be noisy," she told Dane. "But then, we won't be exactly quiet when we make our assault."

I could see that Dane was unhappy, but she didn't argue.

"We'll work things out," Micha said. "Raven knows a few reliable suppliers. But we need a few more details before we go shopping. And what about the small matter of crossing the border? Are the nice boys and girls of the Federal Army going to shoot first and ask questions later? Or will they just shoot first, then shoot again?"

"We have to take that risk," Sara said.

"We do not," Micha insisted.

Dane made a hushing noise. "We have more details to work out. We know that. Hound, Ferret, Raven. Let's go next door. Doc, we need a complete list of medicine, equipment, whatever you need. Don't second-guess yourself. Pretend the Lord's Own Supply Clerk can grant your every wish."

Kite locked the door behind them, then settled back onto her bed and fiddled with her tablet. Working out the evacuation, I guessed. Owl and the other women bunked down for the night, like good soldiers who trusted their commanders to make the right decisions.

The motel walls were thin enough I could hear the conversation next door, the tone if not the words themselves. Conversation, my ass. Micha had launched into a tirade, which Dane attempted to mediate. Once, Sara laughed. Once, I heard a thump, as though Micha had punched the wall.

I sighed and tapped my tablet. The detailed map evaporated in a cloud of pixels, leaving a blank screen. *Some desktop,* I thought.

"Tap again," Kite said softly.

I tapped again. The "desktop" jiggled, then resolved

into a different color, with half a dozen of the usual icons at the bottom. I tapped open the text editor with an empty document.

Okay, Lord's Own Supply Clerk, let's get rolling.

Appendectomy Kit, I wrote. Those should be fairly common, and they'd include most of the surgical instruments I'd need. *Make sure the kit is labeled ultrasonic cleaned.*

Emergency Surgical Kit came next. There'd be an overlap with the appendectomy kit, but my time in the army told me that redundancy was never a bad thing. The surgical kit would have needles, sutures, bandages, and antibiotic gel, among other useful items.

Medicine. That was where I truly did need the Lord's Supply Clerk. I had no idea what the laws in the New Confederacy were. But if I could have whatever I desired . . .

Sedatives, to calm the patient. Diazepam or lorazepam would do.

Lidocaine, to block the pain. Which meant a sterile syringe and needle combo. Make that a box of combos.

Oral and liquid antibiotics. Even though Sa'id claimed her sister had no allergies, I didn't want to take chances. Amoxicillin, clindamycin, sulfamethoxazole. And as long as we were wishing, an SAIMR polyvalent antivenom kit.

Then there was the matter of scrubbing up. Strict procedure would have had me sterilize Lazarus with an electron-beam unit, and even better, a handheld device for emergency work, but such a device didn't exist yet, and even the Lord's Own Supply Clerk could not whistle up a future technology. I'd have to trust to the gloves to protect my patient.

One box of surgical sterile gloves. Neoprene.

I wrote down all the medications and supplies I could imagine I needed and then some. But was it enough? I chewed on my thumb as I considered how much would or could go wrong with my patient.

I want a trained surgical nurse. I want an anesthesiologist. Oh, hell, I want a sterile surgical theater and full staff, not this twenty-some-minute panicked field operation.

But heaven's supply clerk could only do so much. *It is what it is,* Sara had said.

I gave up second-guessing myself, saved the document, and tapped the screen to close the app. Pixels whirled around like snowflakes before dissolving into the familiar blank screen. Very slick tech, indeed. I was tempted to tap the screen a second time to see what other goodies the tablet contained.

"Don't mess around with it," Kite said. "It's programmed to wipe clean if you don't have the right access."

And evidently, I did not. I handed the tablet over to Kite and stretched.

"You should get some sleep," she said. She nodded at the other women, all of them deeply asleep or making a damn good show of it. I rubbed my hands over my face. Lazarus's metal skin felt nearly as warm and damp as my hand of flesh. Was it my imagination or this Oklahoma spring night?

The voices from next door were barely audible. Softer and more deliberate. Good. Maybe now they'd settled down to working out those details.

"I need some air," I said.

Kite made a soft noise of doubt, but after a moment's consideration, she unlocked the door.

Outside a breeze lifted the sweat from my skin. I breathed in the night air, air laden with the sweet scent of wildflowers, of grass crushed underfoot, and a drift of exhaust fumes. The moon had set hours ago, leaving behind a scattering of stars. Cloudy, Oklahoma, lay invisible, without even a neon sign from the motel or gas station to break the darkness. From a distance came the faint creaking of frogs, the ripple of a creek, all the soft, soothing voices of the night.

Sara had not once questioned my ability to perform this surgery. Nor had anyone else, not really. They, all of them, took for granted that I could do the job.

As if I were a genuine surgeon, with two good hands.

I held up Lazarus and studied my left hand. A faint gleam from the starlight flowed over the bright metal mesh, somewhat less bright since Georgia. Tomorrow I'd have to go over the electronics and connection points, test the response times on the micro-movement setting.

I curled Lazarus into a fist, then uncurled each finger one by one. The simplest drill, the first one Sydney taught me. Repeat three times, each round faster than the last. Next, the piano-key drills, which had driven Sara to distraction when I practiced on the electronic keyboard, now silent as I played upon keys of air and imagination.

Halfway through the drill, a door opened behind me. Quietly, so that I felt its movement rather than heard it. Micha and Raven emerged first. Both looked weary, and Micha had a faintly distracted air, as though she were calculating logistics. Kite admitted them after Raven scratched on the door.

A few moments later, Sara and Dane exited the room.

"Can't sleep, Doc?" Dane said.

I shrugged.

"I could mix you a special drink," Sara offered.

"Thank you, but no," I replied.

She chuckled. "My heart, it is stricken, that you do not trust me."

"Perhaps I should do a spot of surgery on your heart, then."

"Hound, stop it," Dane said. "I won't have you upsetting my people. Go to bed. I want to spend a few moments outside with Doc, enjoying the fresh air." When Sara cast a doubtful eye at her, Dane made shooing motions. Sara stifled a laugh, but I noticed she did as Dane asked, a thing I'd thought impossible.

Quiet settled over the motel parking lot. Dane leaned against the wall next to me and took a small bottle from her jacket pocket. "Care for a taste of Oklahoma's finest?"

I accepted the bottle shot and unscrewed the cap. Powerful fumes rose straight up my nose, making my eyes water. "Phew. What is that stuff? Homebrew?"

Dane laughed softly. "Local brewery. Part of the disguise." She extracted a second bottle and drank the shot in one gulp. Even watching made my throat burn. I took a tentative sip. Choked back a cough and tried again. That second sip went down more easily than the first.

"It's the grit that gives it flavor," Dane said. "You get used to it."

She was quiet another few moments as we both watched the night sky. I tried a third sip. Considered briefly the possibility that Dane meant to drug me to sleep, much as Sara had done last autumn. No, not her style. She was the conscientious commander, checking on all her troops.

"So, tell me, Doc. Where did you meet Hound?"

Her voice was liquid, soft, and low. I knew better than to mistake its softness for friendliness. Very carefully, I chose my words. "We met back in DC. A friend introduced us."

"Heh." She laughed. "Are they still your friend?"

My gut untangled itself. "He is. What about you? How did you meet Sara?"

A long silence followed, while I wished I could recall that slip of the tongue.

Dane pulled out another bottle shot and took a meditative sip. "Don't worry. I knew that detail before." She paused, then went on, "Maybe it's best you know. Not the deep dark secrets but the others . . . Yes, let's do this."

We both took a swallow. Dane wiped her mouth. "We go back a ways, Sara and I," she said. "Went to university together. Her an NYC kid with parents too rich to know any better. Me, a kid off the cornfields of Kansas. She was an obnoxious little shit in those days, but so was I."

She took another swig from her bottle.

"Anyway," she went on. "We ranted about politics. We marched in the streets. We did all the ordinary stuff. Nothing worked, not for long. I wanted to give up, but Sara said no, no way. We were the guardians of the future, she told me. I told her that God had not appointed her the Hound of Justice."

Ah, yes. I could picture such a conversation.

We both drank.

"Eventually," Dane said, "we wore ourselves out with all the legal means. We attempted the very illegal and lost. I don't want to go into what we did, what we tried to do. All I can say is that we weren't squeaky-clean kids, for damn sure. But the white judges and juries of this land, Confederates and Federals, have already judged us as terrorists, no matter what we do."

Dane finished off her bottle shot, produced two more. Though I didn't want any more, I took the bottle, not wanting to interrupt the flow of her talk.

"I won't say we were right or wrong," Dane said softly. "But I can say that Sara . . . lost part of herself one day. I don't like to remember that day myself. A few months after that, Ferret came to collect her. The family would see that she had proper care, she said. And maybe they were right, because a few years after that, Hound applied to the FBI and ended up with one of their shadow units. She chose to change the world one way. I chose to join the Resistance. I can't say either of us was wrong."

Wasn't much I could say myself. We all took different roads, hoping to reach that selfsame destination.

"Thank you," I said softly.

"Thought you should know," she answered. "Here, give me that bottle. Go get yourself to sleep."

Smart advice from a smart commander. I handed over the bottle and scratched at the door. As I slid inside, I saw Dane outside, still studying the skies.

❦

By the time I woke up—very late—everyone except Kite had vanished from the motel room. Kite herself hunched over her tablet, clearly absorbed in her assigned tasks. Even though I'd made no sound, she said, "Coffee in the thermos. Biscuits and honey in the bag next to it."

"Has anyone ever told you that you are one unnerving woman?" I said as I levered myself upright and searched around for the promised coffee.

A brief smile lightened her expression. "Frequently."

Oh, I see. A mischievous nerd, are we?

I managed to pour a cup of coffee without scalding myself and drank that down while the sleep drained from my body. A second cup and a biscuit followed, me taking my time, because I knew the day would stretch out long enough without any help. Besides, someone had found the best biscuit maker in all of Oklahoma, and I wanted to do justice to their art.

Sara reappeared an hour later, just as I was running through my drills with Lazarus. "What's the word?" she asked Kite.

"We have the van and two cars," Kite said. "Still working on that off-road vehicle, but I have a few leads. Should have that tied up before three P.M. What's the matter?" she asked with a twinkle in her eye. "Don't you trust me?"

Oh, burn. Yes. I was right. She is a wicked nerd.

Sara bit back a reply and, like a cat, pretended her true goal was a cup of coffee. This was a Sara I had never seen before—openly nervous, uncertain. It had to be because she was not the field agent in charge. These were Dane's people, and they answered to her.

"How is our friend?" Sara said next, nodding at Lazarus.

"Awake and lively," I said. "Which is more than I can say."

"I did offer to drug you last night."

"Which I deeply appreciate. However, a nap this afternoon will do just as well."

I went back to my drills. Kite continued to concentrate on her work. Eventually, Sara asked for and received a tablet. She called up the detailed maps of the area once more and studied them. Around noon, Dane returned with bags of sandwiches. Kite fetched more coffee and cups from her secret source. Micha and Raven made their return soon after that, each carrying two grocery bags overflowing with bags of potato chips.

They unpacked the chips and laid out the various other supplies hidden underneath.

"We found everything on your list," Raven said to me. "Emergency kits, antibiotics. Surgical gloves. By god, we even found the antivenom, though we had to go all the way to Ardmore. Check these over and let me know if anything is missing."

"What about our explosives?" Dane asked.

"Found. Bought. Buried," Micha said. "Just as you ordered."

"What explosives?" I said.

"For our distraction," Sara said. "Remember?"

"Don't worry about it," Raven added.

I lifted my eyebrows and stared at them both. Micha choked back a laugh. "I told you," she murmured to Raven, who offered a wry smile in return.

"Comrades," Dane said. "We have a great deal to accomplish before tonight. Kite? Update, please."

"All vehicles acquired," Kite said. "Skunk and her crew are heading down to help with the evacuation. Our man Coyote will drive the van. Skunk wants to know if you need a driver for crossing the border."

"We're still talking about that," Dane said. "What about our new papers?"

"Inked and with the standard courier."

"Good work. Raven, give us the munitions report."

Raven rattled off a series of makes and numbers, which I guess corresponded to guns and explosives. Whatever they were, both Dane and Sara nodded with satisfaction.

"I got us some extra treats," Raven added. She extracted a plastic bag filled with clear pellets from the medical supplies on the bed. "Sleeping gas pellets. Fired with an air gun, they explode on impact. Our supplier gave us breath masks to go along with them."

"Oh, very good," Dane murmured. "Very, *very* good. Thank you."

The rest of the afternoon was spent double-checking our plans. Raven and Micha had acquired all that I needed for the operation, and then some. Owl and the other women returned by four P.M. We ate an early dinner of rice and beans. At Dane's orders, we took a brief catnap.

Seven P.M. All of us awake and gathered around Dane for our final briefing.

"We start off the same as every other night," she said. "Owl, you tell our guards that Raven called in sick. It won't be the first time, so they won't care. Around nine thirty, you take your tumble. Waste as much time as you can, then limp outside. Everyone else? Dawdle as much as you can, but don't get the guards worked up. We want them stupid and careless."

"Won't be hard," one of the nameless women muttered.

"Don't count on it," Dane said. "Besides, those stupid people have guns. So. At ten fifteen, Doc and I will ask the guard for the ID into the lab. The rest of you, make any excuse you can to work *away* from the loading dock. Raven and Ferret here will set explosives to break that door wide open. They'll come pouring in, shoot the guards, and hand out weapons."

"What about the sister?" I asked. "Do we know where they've locked her up?"

"West side," Micha said. "Hound and I measured out the factory foot by foot. We have an acetylene torch to cut through any interior doors. If necessary, we also have low-impact explosives."

Right. No chance anything could go wrong there.

But from everyone's grim faces, I could tell they were not taking anything for granted. We ate a second light meal, more from determination than anything else. Owl and Raven went outside for a smoke. Dane leaned against the wall, eyes closed, resting and not resting. Only Kite seemed unaffected, though with her, it was hard to tell.

Around quarter to nine, the regular cleaning crew, minus Raven, loaded up into the rusted Buick and headed over the back roads to Sooner State Machine Parts. Within the hour, Kite and her friends would have all the equipment loaded into Coyote's van and would head to wherever and whoever needed the Resistance next. Meanwhile, Sara, Micha, and Raven drove off in one of the newly acquired cars.

We were quiet, all of us in the Buick, driving through the soft April night. The car's tires thumped over the dusty road.

A chorus of frogs sang from the nearby creek. From far away came the bark of a night heron, the throaty call of the owl. My nerves had settled, and I felt calm and centered, the same as before a difficult operation.

The calm vanished when we pulled off the dirt road and into the factory parking lot.

Dane stared fiercely at the military-style jeeps and the small battered Porsche. "I should have expected that."

"Expected what?" I said.

"Adler. That's her car. And I bet my mama's earrings we'll find extra guards on duty tonight."

Owl had pulled the Buick to a stop well away from the other vehicles. "Now what, Captain? Do we cancel the operation? Try again after the rats settle down?"

"We can't." Dane's frustration bubbled over into her voice. "Adler's going to launch the first assassination next week." She sighed. "Fine. Let's start the show."

We unloaded our unhappy selves and queued up at the door. Our friend the security guard examined each of our badges with a great deal more care than he had the night before. "Where's Ruby?" he asked.

"Sick," Owl told him. "She ate somethin' bad."

"You mean she got drunk," the guard muttered. "Ain't the first time." He waved Owl inside and held his hand out for my ID. "What about you? You sick, too, girl?"

"Me? Oh, no, sir. I'm not sick."

He squinted at me, and I had to tell myself to breathe, act normal, ain't nobody doing anything wrong here, officer. Apparently, I passed inspection, because he gave a loud sigh and ordered me inside.

We collected our trolleys and our cleaning supplies from the closet, all of us pretending not to see the two extra guards

patrolling on the catwalk overhead. Owl and the other three
women headed to the side of the factory next to the hidden
laboratory, where they spread out with brooms for a first pass
over the floor. Dane and I set to work in the offices. We took
our time, but not so much that the guards would notice.

Almost nine thirty. The floor crew finished sweeping and
took out their mops. Dane and I cleaned one office and had
emptied the office wastepaper baskets in the second when
Owl tripped and landed on her knees with a yelp that echoed
throughout the factory. Everyone from the Sugar Sweet Cleaning Crew gathered around her, fussing and arguing until one
of the guards showed up. He helped Owl to her feet and was
listening to her tearful complaint that she'd busted her knee
and couldn't walk no more when the door to the lab swung
open and Nadine Adler marched over to us.

"Do we have a problem?" she said crisply.

"No, ma'am, no," Chad-the-guard said hurriedly. "One of
the girls had an accident."

Adler surveyed the group with narrowed eyes. Her face
was gray with fatigue, her eyes rimmed with red, and her
hair was matted and tangled. I tried to tell myself that her
gaze had not lingered on my face. "No more accidents, you
hear? I can always hire a smarter crew. You," she said to Owl,
"will have your pay docked for carelessness."

She vanished into the back rooms, while Chad-the-guard
helped Owl limp across the floor to a bench. The rest of us
stared at each other, muttering, until he returned and shouted
at us to get back to work.

Only nine forty-five, and Adler on the alert. The floor crew
were steadily working their way to the corner opposite the
loading dock. Dane and I muddled through our chores, with
far more accidents and bumbling than usual. Even so, we

could only delay so much without being obvious, so it was only ten past the hour when we presented ourselves to Chad for our card key to the back rooms.

"Ain't you supposed to do those bathrooms?" he asked.

"Miss Bonnie didn't say nothing about that," Dane said. "She told us, do those offices, then the back rooms. Maybe Missy over there can move her ass."

Chad soon found out Missy didn't want nothing to do with those nasty bathrooms any more than we did. The three of us wasted another few minutes arguing before he gave up and handed us the temp ID card, while Missy stomped back to her mop and pail, muttering dark threats about the ride home.

Ten thirteen. Dane slid the card through the reader. The lock snicked open. I grabbed the handle at the front of the trolley and yanked the trolley at an angle over the threshold, making the wheels jam.

"Goddamn you, Callie Mae," Dane shouted at me. "Can't you do nothing right?"

She hauled the trolley back onto the factory floor, still cursing at me, while Chad stood off to one side, muttering about these dumb-ass black girls. All I could think about was that Raven and Micha had better launch their attack soon.

A round of gunfire echoed outside from the direction of the loading dock. Chad swung around into a crouch with his gun in hand. Dane didn't wait. She hooked her foot around his ankle and slammed his head against the floor. She took his gun, shot him through the neck, and had his ID card in hand within a few moments.

Not a moment too soon. The guards on the catwalk aimed a spray of bullets in our direction. Dane dove for the floor and scuttled inside after me. We heard the dull boom of explosions outside, then the outer door slid closed.

"That was close," Dane breathed.

"Understatement of the fucking year." My voice came out as a croak.

She released a puff of laughter. "Oh, my dear Doc. You doing a damn sight better than I would've thought. If you want a career with us, you got one." She laid a hand on my arm and I flinched. "Just kidding," she said softly. "You do fine up there in DC. But oh glory, the door is opening. Let's find us our biochemist."

The air lock's second door slid open just as the office door opposite did the same.

Nadine Adler stood in the entryway, a cell phone in hand. For a moment, we stood face-to-face, both of us frozen. Then Adler punched a number into her cell. "Emergency. Repeat, emergency—"

Without stopping to think, I drove my right fist into her gut. Adler folded over, the cell still clutched in her hand. Dane shoved me to one side and grabbed Adler by the arm and with a quick twist, had Adler facedown on the floor. "Get the door," she barked at me.

I flung myself at the office door and caught it just in time. Adler was cursing and doing her best to break free. Dane pressed her gun into the woman's neck. Her eyes were bright with anger. "I wish I could shoot you now," she growled. "Lucky for you, my friend wants you for evidence."

Another burst of gunfire sounded, this one closer, then Raven called out, "Dane. Goddamn you. Open up."

I grabbed a book from Adler's desk and wedged the office door open. Dane handed me Chad's card, which I slid through the slot. The panel blinked red. Fuck. We couldn't open the outer door until the inner one closed, and I had no idea if we'd run through our count for the night.

Meanwhile, Raven was still pounding at the outer door.

"Gimme a minute," Dane called out. "Check our friend's

pockets," she said to me. "Oh no, none of that, do you hear?" she said to Adler, who was kicking and squirming, in spite of the gun.

"Goddamned n—"

Dane smacked the back of Adler's head. "Tsk, tsk," she said. "Such a limited vocabulary. Doc, ignore her. Raven sounds a bit impatient."

Adler's pockets yielded several old-fashioned keys, the electronic fob to her Porsche, and . . . yes, victory! A security card with a pattern of flat metallic dots scattered over its surface—another high-tech item that made me wonder about who had financed this operation.

I slid the card through the reader. The door clicked open, and Raven, wearing an air filter mask, stepped through with a .45 ACP in one hand, and several more weapons slung from a gun belt. She eyed Adler on the ground and the AK-15 in Dane's hand. "Guess you didn't need me after all."

"I shall always need you," Dane said. "Give Doc a gun and help me with our friend."

Raven produced what looked like police-issue speed cuffs and a hobble strap. In spite of Dane's pressing her knee between Adler's shoulders, Adler continued to curse and struggle. "Fuck you, fuck—"

I shoved Dane to one side and grabbed a handful of Adler's shirt. With a growl, I rolled Adler onto her back and leaned in close until she couldn't look anywhere but my face. "Fuck *you*," I said. "You murdered my friend. You murdered my patients."

Her face went still with shock. And confusion. As if she'd never before considered the dead. I wanted to kill her with my own hands. Saúl. Belinda Díaz. They'd been nothing except nameless obstacles to her. I wanted to shout at her until she acknowledged what she'd done. Except she never would understand, she never would care.

I felt a gentle touch on my arm.

"Later," Dane murmured in my ear. "We'll have our revenge. Doc, can you hear me?"

I drew a shaky breath. I'd almost lost myself there. Dane waited another moment before she nodded to Raven. Raven snapped the cuffs over Adler's wrists. Dane sat on Adler's legs and looped the strap around her ankles. At last, Adler was bound and hobbled.

Dane retrieved Adler's cell and stuffed it into her pocket. "Go get Kalila," she said to Raven. "Doc and I will fetch Dr. Sa'id and drag this one outside."

Another dull boom echoed through the corridor. "Goddamn that Ferret," Raven said. "Having herself fun without me. I best get back out there."

She readjusted her air mask and exited through the outer door. Dane and I gagged Adler and shoved her into her office entryway as a life-size doorstop. Adler never stopped fighting us, but by the time we finished, she could barely move.

Leaving our hostage for later, we hurried down the corridor and through the next door into the kitchen—where we ran smack-dab into another crisis.

Tables and chairs scattered about. Garbage all over the floor. The door to the lab swinging on its hinges. Two men were attempting to drag a furious and disheveled Sa'id toward the back rooms. The moment we entered, one of them spun around with gun in hand. Dane dropped to one knee and shot him before he could take aim. The other yanked Sa'id against his chest and snatched up a knife.

My pulse stuttered to a halt.

"Stop," he shouted. "Or she dies."

Sa'id's face paled. Her lips moved, as though in prayer.

Dane sighed. "Such drama."

The man grinned and pressed his blade against Sa'id's neck—hard enough for a trickle of blood. I started forward, but Dane laid a hand on my arm. Sa'id went limp and the two staggered backward. Before the man could recover his balance, she stamped down—hard—on his instep and broke free.

No sooner than her target was clear, Dane fired twice in quick succession, and the man dropped to the floor. Dane lurched to her feet. "Dr. Sa'id. Time to go."

Sa'id stared down at the two dead men with a wild-eyed look. Dane had to repeat herself before the woman heard. "What about my sister?"

"My friends are getting her out now. Come."

"Not yet." She knelt by the man who still clutched the knife in his dead hand and searched through his pockets, unfazed by the blood.

Dane hissed in frustration. "Dr. Sa'id, we don't have time—"

"And I am telling you we must take the time. We need to take everything from the lab's safe—the venom, all my lab notes, the packets I've already created—or Adler will have her victory. Ah, here it is—"

Sa'id plucked a black disc from the dead man's pocket and ran into the lab. She slid the disc through the reader slot of a cabinet, flung the door open, and emptied its contents onto a nearby worktable, her hands moving swiftly and surely. Dozens of vials packed in insulating foam. Thumb drives. Several bound notebooks. And a small box that she stared at with a strange and furious expression.

"These are the ones," she said in a low voice. "The ones she meant to use next week."

"Right," Dane said. "Let's get Adler and—oh shit."

I followed the direction of her horrified gaze and swore. Nadine Adler had broken free of the hobble strap and now stood over her desk, her hands still bound behind her back. She grinned at us over her gag, then smashed her forehead onto her desk. A siren wailed.

Fuck, fuck, fuck.

Overused word of the day. We tumbled all of Sa'id's things into a plastic garbage bag and made a hasty exit from the lab and into the corridor. Adler's office door was shut. Dane rattled the handle. "It's locked. Give me her card."

I handed it over, but the reader only blinked red. "Emergency override," Dane growled. "Damn it. We have to leave without her."

"But the remote trigger," Sa'id cried out.

"Unless she can work it while she's handcuffed, she won't be setting it off any time soon. But it does mean we best get going. Fast."

Outside on the factory floor, the shoot-out was over. Six guards lay dead in pools of blood, while two more made wet gasping noises. Missy sat on the floor, cradling her left arm. Her shirtsleeve was blood soaked, and her freckles stood out against her pale face.

"How many casualties?" Dane demanded.

"One," Charlene said. "Only . . . Just one. Over there."

She pointed to the loading dock, to a still body that lay as if flung to one side. I abandoned Missy for the moment and started toward the body (and oh, yes, I knew the sight and stillness of death), but Dane shoved me back.

"Who is it?" I whispered.

"Owl," Charlene replied softly. "Sniper got her."

Owl lay in a pool of blood. Even at this distance I could see how the bullets had torn her throat open. Dane's breath hitched. She walked slowly, stiffly, toward Owl, as though every movement brought great pain. Then she bent down and gathered her friend into her arms. Without a word, she strode through the gaping holes of the loading dock doors.

Ain't no one left behind in this army of the Resistance.

Dr. Sa'id followed after Dane. Charlene and I helped Missy to her feet. "It's nothing," she mumbled. "Just a flesh wound."

Charlene gave a breathless laugh. "Now I know you'll be fine. Won't she, Doc?"

"Absolutely," I said. "She's not even—"

Not even mostly dead, but I couldn't make a joke, not with Owl's blood turning dark and sticky on the floor. My adrenaline was crashing down around me, leaving me shaking and close to tears. Charlene laid a hand on my shoulder. "You done fine, Doc. Let's get with the others now, hear?"

Outside, someone had extinguished the factory's exterior lights. Mist was rising from the nearby wetlands, and the siren was only a muted whine. Tight-beam flashlights sparked and glinted through the mist, and by their light, I could make out a rusted, dented van with a white man in the driver's seat, and on the other side of the Buick, an honest-to-god military truck. Charlene helped Missy over to the van. I headed toward the truck, where I found Salmah Sa'id, the bag with her lab notes clutched to her chest, arguing with Raven.

"For the one hundredth time," Raven said. "Please get into this truck."

"No. I will not go without my sister. I—"

Sa'id broke off her argument with a cry. The next moment she had dropped her bag and was tearing over the parking lot, toward three women emerging from the fog.

"Kalila!"

The sisters buried themselves in a tight embrace. Both were sobbing and laughing and kissing each other's cheeks.

Micha and Sara strolled over to Raven to catch up on the news. Micha glanced around, eyebrows raised. "We appear to be missing one guest."

Dane joined us. Her eyes were red rimmed, as though she'd been weeping. "Goddamned woman locked herself in her office," she said. "My fault. Hound—"

"Hush," Sara said. "We can trade blame later, if you like. Right now, let's get out before reinforcements show up. Dr. Sa'id?" She gently touched Sa'id's arm. "Come, we have very little time as you know."

Sa'id detached herself from her sister, who appeared dazed at her sudden rescue, and led her to the truck. Raven deposited the bag at her feet, then headed toward the van. I got into the back of our escape vehicle with the sisters. Benches with safety harnesses lined both sides, and the front of the cargo area was stuffed with crates and boxes.

Micha took the wheel, with Sara next to her. "Medical kit at your feet," Micha called to me. "More supplies in the crates for later."

A plastic cooler at my feet contained the drugs I would need for the surgery. I found the sedatives and gave Kalila Sa'id two tablets, which she swallowed dry. Meanwhile, Micha had eased the truck over the gravel parking lot to the driveway. The others had split between the van and a second car, leaving the Buick behind. Before she jumped into the van, Raven lobbed a small object at the Buick.

A dull boom rolled through the air, and the sky lit up with flames.

"I wish we could've bombed that factory," Sara muttered.

"No time and you know that," Micha replied. "Safety belts fastened, please. Ready? Takeoff in one, two, three . . ."

With a jolt, the truck leaped forward. Sa'id gave a yelp, and my teeth clicked together. Micha didn't even slow down. We were bouncing around on our seats, in spite of those safety belts.

"How is everyone doing back there?" she called out.

"Oh, just spiffy," I said. "Drive faster, why don't you?"

Micha laughed. Sa'id had recovered some of her salt, because now she launched into a tirade about how we had promised to remove the poison from her sister. There was no telling, she said, when the Brotherhood would answer Adler's alarm and trigger the packet from afar.

"Goddammit, we *know* that," Sara snapped. "But we need to put some distance between us and that factory. Settle *down*, lady."

Our biochemist settled down, but with an audible huff that said she wasn't satisfied. Kalila leaned her head against her sister's shoulder and whispered in Arabic. I didn't need to translate the words to know they were still anxious, still uncertain about their rescuers.

Yeah, what if those nasties had taken Grace captive, and I'd been forced into treason? I might not be so mellow neither.

My heart squeezed tight at the thought. *Give a drop of mercy*, Reverend Francis had told us. *One day, you might need a drop yourself.* Maybe the old gospel had it right.

Without warning, Micha swung the truck into a hard left, leaving the road and the other two vehicles. The next half hour felt like a never-ending nightmare as we bounced and swerved over the uneven ground. The cargo was hot and airless and reeked of tobacco. Grass whipped against the truck's sides. We had no headlights, just a sliver of moon and the stars. Where had Kite found this truck?

By whatever criteria Micha used—map or mileage or simply instinct—she finally judged we were far enough from the factory. "Good enough," she said. "Let's get to work. Everyone out of the truck."

Within moments, Micha had spread a plastic sheet over the floor of the cargo area, and Sara had unpacked the crate with my surgical instruments. That, it seemed, would be my operating table. The truck's overhead light was bright enough, and the floor of the cargo area made a steady surface, but these were not the most ideal conditions.

Understatement of the year, trademark pending.

Even so, better than Alton, Illinois.

"What else do you need?" Micha asked.

"A nurse," I said. "Dr. Sa'id. I want you to assist."

"Of course."

Sara and Micha took up guard outside the truck with two AK-15s.

"Take off your shirt and lie down," I told Kalila. "Head pointing to the driver's-side door, please."

Sa'id and I climbed into the back. Micha's clever foresight had provided me with a canister of hot water and disinfectant soap. Sa'id and I both donned masks. At my direction, she scrubbed her hands and forearms thoroughly, while I scrubbed just my right hand and arm. Even though my nerves were yammering at me to hurry, hurry, I waited through five more minutes to let the disinfectant work. Then we pulled on our surgical gloves.

"We don't have a suction unit," I told Sa'id. "But when I call for it, you'll swab away the blood with these sterile gauze pads."

She nodded, her eyes dark and wide over her mask.

I laid out my instruments, naming them as I did. Scalpel. Forceps. Needle with sutures threaded. Needle driver. Then I filled two syringes each with the 1 percent lidocaine solutions. My hands both trembled, and I was reviewing all my drills under my breath. This was a simple operation, I reminded myself.

The packet made a slight bulge directly below the eighth rib. I wiped down the incision site with antiseptic swabs. Injected the first dose next to the site, taking care to avoid the packet itself.

"Four minutes," I told the sisters. "Then we test for numbness."

Those four minutes felt longer than the thirty we'd taken to drive here. Without a clock I had to count the time. When I reached my best guess, I gently probed the site with my scalpel. Kalila moaned. Immediately I stopped. "You need another dose?"

"Yes, but don't wait any longer. I want that . . . that *thing* out of my body."

Right. She'd lived with that threat for almost six months.

I gave her a second injection, then, working as quickly as I dared, I made a subcostal incision parallel to her rib cage and just below the packet itself. "Swab," I said. Sa'id wiped away the blood welling up from the cut. Luckily there wouldn't be much, not with such a shallow incision.

Now I gently worked my fingers into the incision and around the edge of the packet. As I started to ease it from my patient, I felt a faint resistance and immediately stopped.

What the hell?

Very cautiously, I explored with my right hand, trusting more to my human nerves than my electronic ones.

A small rectangle. Two point five millimeters by five millimeters according to Lazarus's readout. Standard size for a medical implant these days. Not that you needed much space for a dose of mamba venom. I proceeded with even more caution, until I'd worked my way around to the opposite side, where my fingers encountered a thick filament, attached to the packet and continuing deeper into the chest cavity.

Shit, shit, shit.

Kalila stirred uneasily. Salmah Sa'id whispered to her soothingly in Arabic, but her eyes were fixed on me. Location, location, where did that filament lead? It wasn't simply a left-over suture from the original operation.

I closed my eyes and thought hard. Of course, Adler would not rely on a single, simple threat to keep her biochemist in line. (Though god knows, black mamba poison was hardly simple.) No. Adler had a twisty brain. That much I'd seen. She had to be the one behind all those interlocking safeguards for the laboratory. So. What was that filament connected to? The abdominal aorta was a good candidate—Kalila would bleed out in seconds if it ruptured.

But that made no sense. A careless surgeon might have attempted to remove the packet without noticing the fila-ment, but Adler must have planned for *all* possible paths.

My head hurts.

"Why did you stop?" Sa'id's voice was thin and edged with panic.

I leaned toward her and whispered. "A complication. There's a . . . you might call it a string. Connected to the packet and something else, deeper underneath her ribs. I could cut the string and investigate later, once we're across the border and in a hospital. But . . ."

"But you suspect we cannot."

"Exactly. I'm going to give your sister a stronger dose of anesthesia. I'll remove the packet, then see where that string leads."

"Doc." That was Micha. "What's the status?"

"Almost ready to close up," I lied.

I snipped the filament and oh so carefully removed the packet. "Ziplock bag, please."

Sa'id extracted one from our supply crate. I dropped the packet into the bag, and at my order, she sealed it and stowed it in the crate.

Now I reviewed the vials of anesthesia. Filled a syringe with another dose of the lidocaine. We were skirting close to the maximum dose, but I didn't want my patient to make any sudden movements.

While we waited for the lidocaine to take effect, I stripped off my surgical gloves. I wasn't sure what we'd find, but my instincts told me that I'd need Lazarus's micro-surgical programming. I flicked the control panel open and tapped in the necessary sequence. Maybe it was my imagination, but an electric buzz seemed to ripple down my arm, both ghost and metal, as Lazarus responded to the commands.

Once more I scrubbed my right hand and arm, then pulled on a fresh pair of gloves.

"Retractor," I said. "Keep that incision open, please."

I might need to cut deeper, but I wanted a line of direction for that filament.

I probed the incision and located the filament. Nothing, nothing. I picked up my scalpel with Lazarus and slid the blade along the filament millimeter by millimeter. Blood welled up. Without my asking, Sa'id held the retractor open with one hand and wiped away the blood with more gauze.

More exploration. The electric buzz along my ghost arm turned into a fierce bright burning sensation. Dammit. Sydney had never warned me about such a reaction. Maybe I was special.

I was sweating, and not just from the warm humid night.

"Doc?" Sa'id whispered.

"Give me a minute."

Except we had very few minutes to spare. I breathed through my nose and willed my ghost arm to behave. Nothing doing, said ghost arm. *Right. Then it's time to bite down and finish the operation anyway.*

More blood. More gauze. More of my wishing I had a real operating theater with all the instruments and devices that came with it.

And then, my fingers brushed against a noticeable lump, directly under the ninth rib. I froze. Oh, dear god. Of course. She implanted two packets, one to trigger the next, in case anyone got careless. And if we left this one alone, she could still trigger it from a distance.

Taking up my scalpel, I cut slowly and cautiously around the new packet, aiming up directly into the chest cavity. My left arm felt like a strange double entity, the ghost arm consumed by imaginary flames, Lazarus edging closer to the packet, each movement precise.

My fingers closed around packet number two. For a horrible moment, I wondered if Adler had connected yet a third packet, but I soon determined that wasn't so. I drew the packet out of my patient. "Gauze," I croaked. "Then a ziplock."

Sa'id hadn't bothered to wait. She packed gauze into the incision, then dumped the second packet in its own ziplock next to the first one. By now that strange doubled sensation had died away, though my instincts still yammered at me to hurry, hurry, hurry before the enemy overran the border, and didn't I hear that warning siren?

I took up the needle with its thread of suture. Focused on its bright sharp point. Just a moment, because we truly did need to hurry. But this wasn't Alton. This was Cloudy, Oklahoma, or close enough for government purposes. And this time, *this time*, I would have my damned victory.

I stitched the wound closed. Washed the skin with antiseptic. Checked the patient's stats. Blood pressure high. Pulse rapid. Both within normal for the situation. If Nadine Adler had any more tricks to throw at us, they weren't evident.

"Doc, what the hell are you doing in there?" Micha's voice was hardly more than a whisper.

"All done," I said. "Patient is doing well."

"Good, because we're about to get company."

Methodical switched places with *in a tearing hurry*. I covered Kalila with a blanket and dumped all my instruments into the crate. Micha already had the engine running.

Sara climbed into the back of the truck. Her eyes widened at all the bloody gauze, but she only said, "Dr. Sa'id, you ride up front next to Ferret. I'm taking the rear guard."

Sa'id scrambled out of the truck, then into the front seat. Sara doused the overhead lights and pulled the tailgate shut. "Make yourself steady," she told me. "We have a rough ride ahead of us. Ferret, let's go!"

She braced herself into a corner, weapon ready. I grabbed the backseat and a handy tie-down bolt. Micha floored the gas pedal. The truck jumped forward and we took off.

Just in time, because I heard the roar of an engine in the distance. How the hell had they tracked us?

"Please tell me those are kids out late with Daddy's ATV," I said.

"That *would* be lovely," Sara agreed. "By the way—"

The truck took a hard bounce, and Kalila Sa'id gave a muffled cry. Sara went silent as I hurriedly checked the sutures. No bleeding, but obviously the lidocaine was wearing off.

"What happened with the operation?" Sara continued, once I was done.

"A surprise gift from Adler," I said. "Not one packet, but two, connected."

"Ah. Then it's possible . . ."

We burst out of the grass, onto a paved road. Micha swung the truck hard to the right. The truck swerved, fishtailing into the grass, then Micha gunned the engine and we took off down what looked like a state highway.

"How far to the border?" I called out.

"Sixty miles, maybe seventy," Micha shouted back. "Not exactly sure where we are right now. Sara? Any idea?"

"Absolutely. About ten steps ahead of the goddamned enemy."

As if God were listening to our inanities, headlights flashed behind us. That would be our pursuers, making the same wild turn as we had.

"One vehicle," Sara observed. "Not so bad."

She laid her AK-15 to one side, plucked a small round object from one of the cargo nets. With a flick of her thumb, she released the safety pin, then took aim and threw.

Smoke and fire exploded on the road. The truck swerved. Missed, dammit. But Sara had already launched a second grenade. The truck regained the highway just as the grenade exploded. Headlights spun over and over, then came to rest.

"Yes! Oh, dammit, no! Ferret, stop, stop now."

A figure, illuminated by the flames, staggered out of the other truck.

"Adler," Sara breathed.

Oh god. It can't be.

Abruptly the world appeared to slow. I remember crawling toward the rear of our truck and staring at that lone survivor of the wreck. A burst of fire illuminated the scene. Adler faced forward, unsteady on her feet. Her face was masked in blood. She held one arm at an awkward angle. The other cradled a rifle.

Micha had slowed our truck and glanced over her shoulder. "Shit."

She gunned the engine—just in time. Bullets ricocheted off the side of our truck. Sara snatched up her AK-15 and fired back. More bullets sprayed the truck. Swearing, Sara loosed another round at the same moment Adler did.

Adler spun around in the spray of blood. She dropped to her knees and toppled over.

I was about to cheer, when Sara dropped her gun and tumbled out of the truck.

"Stop! Stop!" I screamed.

Micha jammed on the brakes and ran to the back of the truck. She was cursing under her breath. "No time," she breathed. "We have to make the border and soon or—" Her voice broke on a sob. "Sa'id, you take the wheel. Keep driving."

"But—"

"Don't argue. Now go!"

She grabbed her gun and vanished into the night.

22

I snatched up a flashlight and aimed it down the highway. The beam caught Micha's silhouette—a blurred shadow running toward the spot where Sara had fallen from our truck. Not far beyond that, a faint red glow marked Adler's burning vehicle. My imagination supplied any number of bodies scattered about. There might even have been an armed survivor or two.

"Micha!" I called out.

Micha never slowed. Damn, that woman could run. I had sucked in my breath to shout again when her shadow ducked to the ground, then vanished. I frantically swept the flashlight beam around, but the fog had grown thicker and even the distant flames were dying down.

Swearing softly to myself, I spun around on my heels. Salmah Sa'id was still in the passenger seat, her head bowed, her hands clasped together, as though imploring the gods to intervene. I wanted to smack her into action. At the same time, I was damned close to collapsing into tears myself.

My first duty, however, was to my patient.

Kalila Sa'id's pulse beat far too fast, and her skin felt

clammy to my touch. Shock. On the positive side, her stitches had held, and the liquid seeping out was clear. All signs and symptoms good, considering.

But we still had a helluva way to go. I rummaged through the medicine chest, found the vial of diazepam. Filled another of my syringes, swiped the injection site with an alcohol pad, and injected my patient with a 10 ml dose.

Kalila sucked in a breath at the needle's prick but didn't jerk away. "What happened? Why did we stop?"

"Nothing to worry about," I told her. "We just had to check a few directions."

Her eyes narrowed. I smiled back at her and cradled her hand in mine while I counted her pulse. Before I'd reached the count of fifty, her pulse slowed, her eyelids drifted closed.

"Will she live?" Salmah Sa'id said softly.

"She will. But only if we get our tails out of here. You heard Micha—Ferret. Get your sorry ass over to that driver's seat and step on the gas."

That jerked Sa'id out of her pity party and into action. She climbed into the driver's seat and switched on the headlights. Finding the keys and turning over the ignition took a few more tries. My breath trickled out when the engine roared back into life.

She floored the pedal and we shot down the highway. Sixty, seventy miles to the border itself. But how to cross that thrice-damned military zone? We were three women of color. We didn't have a white man like Coyote to smuggle us through the military checkpoints. We could only hope this road led through a hole in their network, and right now, I'd run out of hope.

An ancient road sign flashed past. DE QUEEN, ARKANSAS, 70 MI. STATE BORDER, 48 MI. The New Confederacy must've fallen down with highway repairs because we were bumping and jumping over ruts and potholes. Just as well I'd sedated my patient. Salmah Sa'id wasn't about to slow down and I didn't want her to. Better to die fighting.

All of a sudden, a bright glare cut through the fog and the night.

A steady thump, thump, thump of helicopter blades. The roar of engines. The dust swirling over the highway. A short sharp image of Alton, Illinois, flashes through my mind. But this time we are behind the enemy lines.

I sucked down a breath, brought myself back to here and now. Helicopters. Three of them, including one large transport helicopter. Had Adler called up *more* backup before the crash? Or were these military?

The lights overhead swung around as one of the smaller copters swooped over our truck. Sa'id momentarily lost control, then jammed the gas pedal.

A voice boomed out from a loudspeaker. "Micha, goddamn you. Slow the fuck down. You wanted backup, you better damn well stop playing chicken . . ."

Oh, Christ in heaven. It's her friends.

"Stop," I shouted. "Stop, goddammit!"

Sa'id slammed her foot onto the brake. Our truck swerved into the grass. I braced myself and my patient just in time, though my right arm felt nearly wrenched from its socket. Lazarus . . . Lazarus had become a dead weight, no trace of that ghostly limb nor any electrical nerves.

The first two helicopters landed on the highway in front of us, the other neatly behind, and their lights winked off. A dozen personnel swarmed out from the transport copter, all of them armed. Several others disembarked from what looked like a medevac—one of the larger ones.

"These are friends?" Sa'id said softly.

"According to some definition," I replied.

Sa'id snorted. I couldn't say she was wrong.

One person emerged from the mass of shadowy figures and into view of our headlights. A woman, a stocky black woman of middle height. The others in her company spread out, military fashion. Not Adler's people, but still dangerous.

Moving slowly, cautiously, I unlocked the hatch and exited the truck. The woman at the head of this operation flicked a light over me, then back to our truck.

"Where is Micha?" she said in a low, rough voice. "Where is my sister?"

I swallowed against the sudden dryness in my throat. "Gone."

The light flashed back, full into my face. "Dead?"

Her voice was flat and cold. Not—as I had learned after weeks with Micha, months with Sara—without emotion.

"Gone," I repeated. "I don't know where. Sara . . ."

"Do not talk to me about Sara. She has enough to answer for." The flashlight flicked over the truck. Shadows masked her face, but I heard the woman's sigh. "I see. Yes, that is a complication. You have those two women at least?"

I nodded. I didn't trust myself to speak calmly.

Micha's sister gave a shout over her shoulder. Two men with a stretcher hurried over to the truck, where they swiftly and professionally transferred Kalila Sa'id from the backseat, then jogged back to the medevac. Salmah Sa'id ran behind, her bag of notes and other evidence tucked under one arm.

I started to follow, but Micha's sister intercepted me. "We have our own medical attendants on board. You, come with me."

"But what about—"

"Save your questions for later. We've got to evacuate before someone notices all the noise."

I wasn't about to argue with an angry woman with a gun, so when another woman took my arm, I allowed myself to be escorted to the transport copter. When I fumbled with the safety harness, they took over, adjusted the straps, and clipped the buckle. My stump ached ferociously. Lazarus responded to my commands, but the sense of disconnection persisted.

Lights from all the helicopters switched on. The medevac with Sa'id and her sister lifted off first, circled around once, then zoomed eastward. Ours was next, and as we rose into the air, the copter's lights cast a wide circle over the highway and surrounding fields. I pressed my face against the window, the straps cutting into my shoulder. Down below, our truck jerked into motion, back onto the road. Just like Dane and her people, this company would leave no evidence behind.

Without warning, exhaustion dropped on me like a fifty-ton weight. I covered my face with my hands and wept.

♀

No one spoke to me throughout the flight. Good thing. I could barely string two words together, and those would be *fuck everything.*

Eventually I ran out of tears, if not grief. I wiped my face with the back of my hand, which still smelled faintly of disinfectant. *Oh, Sara, Sara, my love. I truly believed you were invincible.*

But Sara had died, shot by Nadine Adler. And Micha . . . Micha had vanished into the night, deep in enemy territory.

At least my patient had survived. At least we'd rescued Salmah and Kalila Sa'id from Adler and the New Confederacy. How to complete the rest of Sara's mission . . .

I'll think about that tomorrow.

Less than half an hour later, the medevac copter swung around, its searchlights flashing. Down below, landing lights appeared in the middle of the endless dark.

The medevac dropped down to the helipad. All I could see were black dots streaming from the copter to the edge of the pad as the medics unloaded my patient and rushed off . . . hopefully to a surgical facility. Once the medevac took off, our transport copter made its descent. The crew disembarked with weapons in hand. Hostile territory? Or standard procedure? Micha's sister had already vanished who knew where. One of the crew helped me out of my harness and onto the ground, steadying me with a hand when my knees buckled.

"Dr. Watson. Would you come with me?"

I blinked, adjusted my gaze to a lower level. A girl dressed in a brightly colored wrap came toward me. She might have been Tamika's age, or a bit older. She smiled.

"Please," she said. "Grandmamma would like to talk with you."

She took my hand and led me over the lawn. By the lights of the helipad, I could make out an enormous building in the distance, and a wall of trees that enclosed this clearing. The air was cool, ripe with the scent of crushed grass and moldering leaves, filled with the whispering of branches stirred by a breeze.

The building turned out to be a brick mansion, faced with a column-lined portico. Thick curtains blocked the windows, but light leaked out around the edges. My escort climbed the steps and opened the heavy wooden doors. "This way," she said.

I was too numb and exhausted to demand an explanation, so I followed her into the mansion, to the vast entryway with its two staircases winding upward, and a crystal chandelier casting a faint glow over the whole impossible scene.

We turned left through an archway into a formal parlor. Style: 1850s. Ivory ceiling moldings. Windows that had never seen an energy audit. Except . . . those family portraits were of black women and men. And the tapestries and rugs used patterns from West Africa and not the old Confederacy. Hmmmm.

"Dr. Watson, welcome. I am Ekene Nkiru. Sara's grandmother."

In front of me, in a padded chair next to the fireplace, an ancient woman stared at me with bright black eyes. Sara's grandmother. It didn't surprise me to see the array of screens at her side, nor the gleam of silver implants at her temples. With a word, she dismissed the girl, then tilted her hand toward another chair. At her gesture, the screens went blank and retracted into the floor. I stood there, glaring.

Her mouth tucked into a smile. "Micha was right about you."

Right? Right? My vision blurred into a red haze.

"Goddamn you," I whispered. "Goddamn you to hell. You, *you* abandoned your granddaughter. *You* left her to die in Oklahoma. Micha, too. What kind of family demands a debt from their children?"

The terror and fury of these past three weeks poured out of me. Loud. Angry. Both hands clenched into fists. Ekene Nkiru watched with that same dispassionate gaze, unmoved by my rage.

At last my fury wound down. I stood there panting and trembling.

"Sit," the old woman said firmly.

I sat.

Nkiru touched a keypad on the arm of her chair. A boy

hurried into the parlor with a tray of breadfruit, wine, and cups. I noted in passing that he carried a Taser tucked into his sash. He poured two cups of palm wine and served us before he backed out of the room.

Ekene Nkiru drank from her cup, then continued to study its contents. Her face was thin, cut into sharp angles, but with the lines softened by loose skin. A dark, implacable face, which reminded me of Sara. Her eyes, though bright, were rimmed with red, and I had the impression she had only recently left off weeping.

"She was my favorite grandchild," she said at last. "My Sara."

My breath caught at the tears in her voice.

"We owe you—I owe you a great debt," she continued. "You have been a great friend to both my granddaughters. You have given trust for trust, faith for faith. I have never worried about Micha, but Sara . . . My Sara doesn't have many friends. She can be difficult, as you know."

In spite of everything, I had to choke back a laugh. "Family trait?"

Ekene Nkiru offered a bland smile. "You might say so. But." And here she leaned forward. "Let us discuss the matter for which you risked your life, and for which Sara lost hers."

Together, over breadfruit and wine, she laid out her plans. First, the matter of Kalila Sa'id. Nkiru's own private team of physicians would take over her medical care. Micha had forwarded the essential details. My own observations would be welcome.

Thank you for your confidence. So happy to oblige.

But I stifled any comments. What mattered was Sara's mission.

Which Ekene Nkiru had not forgotten. The family, she told me, would arrange for Dr. Salmah Sa'id to meet with trusted officials in the Federal States. Ekene Nkiru herself guaranteed these officials would launch a thorough investigation.

"As for you," she said. "You will stay with us for a time. I need a few weeks to untangle these affairs."

She leaned forward, took both my hands within hers. Her skin felt cool and paper dry. "I am forever in your debt. I and the family both. When you return to Washington, you will find your name cleared. You have my promise on this."

23

MAY 13. *Hello, Journal.*

I stared at those four words as if a stranger had written them.

Perhaps I was a stranger to the me-of-today. I remembered—as if through a glass, darkly—another Janet Watson who wrote a never-ending stream of bitter-bright commentary on her life. Oh, sure, my journals had some dark entries, especially after Alton, Illinois. But today . . . today the thought of recording anything from the past few weeks left me weeping.

I wiped the tears from my face.

No, dammit. I will not lose this part of me as well.

So. Start again.

MAY 13. *My first journal entry since the night Micha confiscated my notebook. To be sure, Ekene Nkiru ordered a stack of new journals for me, together with all the expensive inks I could use in a lifetime. That I ignored her*

*gifts, and spent my days staring out the window, was likely
a factor in her decision to send me home.*

Home. Let's think about that word a moment.

Moment over. More tissues used to dry my tears.

*Here I am, back in Georgia on the dirt farm, with a
cheap notebook and a ballpoint pen. Ekene Nkiru did not
exaggerate when she promised to protect me and mine.
Two bodyguards drove me to the Nashville airport, an
hour's drive from wherever the secret family fortress lay.
One left with the car. The other, a slim and deadly-looking
young woman, took charge of our luggage and negotiated
our way through check-in. She stayed at my side through
the flight and took the wheel of the rental car. I would
have been terrified at the implications if I were thinking
clearly.*

*It wasn't until we reached the driveway to my
grandmother's farm that my bodyguard spoke to me. "Take
the wheel. Drive to the house. They're expecting you."*

*"And you?" I said. "How will you get back to
civilization?"*

"I won't. I'm to guard you until I get word it's safe."

Safe. What a funny word. I will never be safe again.

I took another emotion break. Breathed slowly until my
thoughts cleared. *Grief and rage are twins,* Faith Bellaume once
told me. Dear Faith, who seemed to have an aphorism for
every facet of depression. Well, and, she was right. Maybe we
could talk honestly once I returned to DC.

My ghost arm shivered. The rest of me went still. I'd not
allowed myself to think of DC until this moment. Maybe it
was a sign. Maybe it was just a thought.

I took up my pen to finish my entry.

My bodyguard handed me a familiar-looking device. It wasn't the same one Sara had given me last year, but close enough for government work. Use this if you need to contact me, she said. It's programmed to recognize your voice.

I accepted the device, and as she vanished into the brush and cottonwoods, I took over the wheel and continued down the driveway to the farmhouse. One more rusted truck had joined the others. The chickens were squabbling in the yard. Four P.M. it was, on a late April afternoon. I parked the car, slung my bag over my shoulder, knocked at the front door. An extra-long moment passed with no answer. I had just enough time to believe Ekene Nkiru had lied to me, that the FBI or some other nefarious operation had carted off my family, before Aunt Jemele flung the door open.

"You," she breathed. Then, "We been expecting you."

And that was that. I spent most of the last two weeks sleeping and hiding from other humans. Jemele left me alone for the most part. She or Tamika or Letitia brought me meals and took away my clothes for laundering. If they listened to my weeping in the night, they never said anything. Eventually, I came out of the room, to sit in the sunlight or listen to Benjamin practice for Sunday choir. Then came a phone call came from Atlanta HHC, one of the premier service companies in the state. For a modest fee, they could supply a home visitation specialist three times a week, plus daily visits from a registered nurse. The modest fee would be paid through a government grant.

All the loose ends tied up, just as Sara would have liked

I threw the damned pen across the room and tried to tear out the pages from my notebook, but Lazarus locked with fingers outstretched and, no matter how hard I pounded my hand against the bed, refused to obey. I gave up, cradling my left arm close to my chest, and wept.

Damn you, Sara Holmes. Damn you, Micha.

"Janet?" Aunt Jemele knocked at the door. "You okay?"

No, I am not. And you know it.

Aunt Jemele had asked no questions since I turned up with my bag and an attitude. She had not hovered over me, exactly, but it was clear that she knew all was not right, and that I wasn't willing or able to tell her more.

"Dinner at five o'clock," she said. "Gramma says she's coming downstairs."

The APRN assigned by the HHC had conducted a thorough physical exam, followed by a day at the county hospital for neurological tests. The result was a prescription for medication that might, possibly, reverse the worst effects of Alzheimer's. All because Ekene Nkiru had vowed that she owed a debt to me and my family.

One of these days, I need to earn a reward that has nothing to do with people dying.

I drank down the glass of water next to my bed. "I'll come down," I promised.

Jemele swung the door open and eyed me doubtfully. "Still working on that paper?"

I shrugged. "Not right now. Maybe tomorrow."

That provoked a snort. "Girl. Stop fussing around. Write the damned thing, or not. But don't go singing about how you is okay when we both know you ain't."

At that I had to laugh. "Fine. I'll come down for dinner, Aunt Jemele. And . . . And thank you."

"Don't never mind, child. You still part of the family."

She left me to my lonesome self and my journal.

I decided I was sick of bleeding my emotions all over the page. I tossed my journal aside, then took up my tablet. Only three P.M., plenty of time before dinner. Maybe I should take another stab at that proposal.

I called up the document labeled *Possible Maybe Ideas for that Goddamned Conference*. So far, I'd jotted down twelve different titles and no content.

Medicine and . . .

Surgery and . . .

Ethics and . . .

All these were bullshit feel-good titles. I was done feeling good. Maybe it was time for honesty.

Without giving myself a chance to second-guess, I cleared the document and typed, *The Politics of Medicine.*

Whew. Talk about honest. That topic went far beyond honest into reckless. Hernandez would never approve anything with *politics* in the title, no matter how hard she played the political game.

Fuck it. I don't care.

An hour later, I had the bare bones of a presentation. I scanned through the text, a thousand words guaranteed to destroy my career, or make me famous. Maybe both. What would Hernandez say? *Could* she say anything? The deadline was midnight tomorrow.

I tweaked a few words, rearranged a few phrases. Sucked on my teeth.

"Jaaaaaanet! Whatcha doin'?"

Tamika pounded at my bedroom door.

"Holy shit, girl. Ain't you got no manners?"

Tamika took that as an invitation and flung the door open. "Betty had her kittens. You said you wanted to see them."

Her hair was sticking out in corkscrews and her grin was brighter than the moon. The girl had told me a few days ago that she wanted to design video games. Aunt Mattie wasn't sure they had the money. I'd spent some time wondering if

Ekene Nkiru's promise extended to my cousins. Then I'd decided, *Why not,* and sent a message to my nameless guard to forward on. I was still waiting on a reply.

"Maybe I do," I told Tamika. "But maybe I need to finish off this paper."

Tamika huffed. "Better not take too long."

She banged the door shut with all the impatience of a fourteen-year-old.

I laughed, as I'd thought I could not, until laughter gave way to tears. *Bless her heart, dear Lord, and bless it in all the best ways.*

I scanned over the text of my proposal and decided it was as done as could be. I hit *Send* and followed Tamika down the stairs.

24

May 30. A bright sunny day in Washington, DC. The cherry blossoms had scattered their petals over the Mall. The air felt more like midsummer than late spring, with a hint of August's coming heat, but here in 2809 Q Street, the air conditioner hummed, and the sweat evaporated from my skin.

I set my right thumb to the apartment's bio-identity pad. The security light flickered green, the lock clicked open. *I am not ready for this.*

I took a firm grip on my bag and walked into apartment 2B.

And stopped, sucker punched by memory.

Oh god, this lovely refuge, this gift of beauty and peace, which had not changed one whit since April. The exquisite marble archway, the scent of wood polish, the whiff of roses and wildflowers drifting up from the garden and through the latticed windows. I remembered . . .

I remembered the moment when Jenna Hudson opened the door and welcomed me inside. (For some definition of *welcome*.) I remembered—fuck, what a stupid memory—how astonished I'd been by all the closets. And then the moment when Sara Holmes smiled at me and said, *It's not as expensive as you think.*

I blew out a breath and continued along the interior corridor toward my bedroom.

More memories stirred up, like dust motes in the sun. Sara's bedroom, now entirely empty, without even a bed or her piano. The so-called astonishing closets, which stared down at me with blank eyes. My own bedroom looked unchanged, or near enough. My books remained in the bookshelves cataloged by my own idiosyncratic system. Someone had made my bed with fresh linens, however, and mail covered the table next to the window.

I dumped my bag on the bed and kicked off my shoes. Wandered past the windows, where I deliberately paid no attention to the stranger in the alleyway. That would be my own personal bodyguard, who had taken over my car on the drive to the airport, then accompanied me back to Dulles. Even when she'd dropped out of sight, I had the subtle persistent sense of others, that invisible perimeter guard, which didn't vanish even after I closed the doors to 2809 Q.

They will guard you until we know you are safe, Ekene Nkiru had promised me.

Odd how I found that not the least bit comforting.

Reluctantly, I returned to my desk. Hudson Realty had faithfully collected my mail, as requested, and left it in half a dozen neat piles. Most bills and receipts came through email or payment feeds, but enough paper receipts still showed up, mixed in with local political flyers and cheap ads from car dealers. The result wasn't exactly towering, but daunting enough. I poured myself a double shot of whiskey, courtesy of a last-minute purchase at Dulles airport, then settled down to business.

Paper receipt for my student loan. File. Credit card offer of dubious origin. Toss. Three, count them, three flyers from a "local neighborhood association" asking me to support their "quality initiative." Oh, golly. That sounds like we got us a new dog whistle. Toss, toss, and toss. What's this?

Three oversize manila envelopes addressed to *Occupant*, and each with a sticker reading, *Complimentary Sample Issue*. Huh. What kind of mailing list had I landed on?

An eclectic one, apparently. The first envelope yielded a copy of *Essence* magazine, the February issue, complete with a glossy cover. The second contained a recent copy of *National Review* and a letter offering me a discount if I subscribed to Vintage Publications before the end of the month.

One of these is not like the other, I thought as I opened the third envelope. *And what will we find here? A copy of the* Wall Street Journal?

Almost. The third envelope contained a copy of the *Washington Post,* printed on clean bright paper, clearly not the usual newsfeed printer garbage. I smoothed out the front page and nearly fainted in shock.

MAY 31. SIX SENATORS INDICTED
IN CONSPIRACY CHARGES.

That's tomorrow.

Very casually, aware that my every move was recorded, I glanced at the metered mail stamp on the envelope. May 29. Yesterday. Someone had obtained a very early copy. Or someone had created this issue especially for me.

Micha? If she had survived. If—

I rifled through the pages and pretended to scan the articles, but it took me another few moments before the words made sense.

May 31. Rumors swirl around Adler Industries and its primary research branch, Livvy Pharmaceuticals, recently

implicated in a scandal involving illicit drug testing of Federal soldiers.

Not exactly what happened, but close enough.

Ex-CEO Nadine Adler, once believed killed in a shoot-out with federal agents, has been reported as a coconspirator with extremist faction the Brotherhood of Redemption in January's Bloody Inauguration, which resulted in dozens being killed and hundreds more critically injured. According to unnamed government sources, the attack was merely a prelude to an assassination plot involving key members of Congress.

For a moment I had to close my eyes and breathe steadily, never mind what the cameras saw. Ekene Nkiru had not lied. She had brought Dr. Salmah Sa'id safely to DC, to people in authority who could hear her testimony and see that justice was done. Sara's death was not in vain.

But oh, Sara, is it enough?

I wanted nothing more than to take a long nap, to hide from the world and my memories, but I continued to read, knowing that these pages had been smuggled into this apartment to give me . . . closure of sorts. Several more paragraphs detailed the conspiracy, the formal denunciation by the New Confederacy government, and the intimation that Nadine Adler had died at the hands of the Brotherhood when she had failed to deliver the promised revolution.

Then came the meat of the article.

Attorney General Jeremy Wade announced a special counsel to investigate possible corruption charges in the Senate, FBI, and CIA. Special Counsel Robert White has collected

a number of talented and experienced legal minds to assist
with his investigation. To this date, the DOJ has brought
indictments against six ranking senators and two key in-
telligence officials. Charges include conspiracy against the
government, to destabilize the Federal States in advance
of the proposed peace talks with the New Confederacy.
The chief witness for the prosecution is Dr. Salmah Sa'id, a
former employee of Livvy Pharmaceuticals, who provided
evidence connecting the events of the Bloody Inauguration
to Adler and the Brotherhood.

No surprises there. Even so, I was not prepared for the
final paragraph.

... The most shocking surprise came when the special pros-
ecutor charged two surgeons from Georgetown University
Hospital with murder and attempted murder as part of that
same conspiracy. Agents took Dr. Allison Carter into custody late Monday night. Carter, who has been held without
bail, admitted to holding more than one conversation with
several members of the medical community who were sym-
pathetic to the Confederate cause. One of those named was
Dr. Nina Letova, a resident at Georgetown University Hospital. Dr. Letova was discovered dead in her apartment by law
enforcement officials. Her death has been ruled a suicide.

The newspaper slipped out of my fingers and slithered
onto the floor. *Pick it up,* my brain told me. *Act naturally. Remember the cameras . . .*

Fuck the FBI and their cameras. Fuck Ekene Nkiru. And
fuck the goddamned Brotherhood and whoever was pouring
money into their cause.

I had believed all the danger to be across the border. But

while I lay comfortable in my grandmother's house, writing those fine words about medicine and politics, my friend Nina had taken her own life.

By now I was weeping. *Why, oh why? Why did you do such a thing?*

Because I knew exactly what she had done. She had operated on victims of the bombing, on children brought in for emergency procedures, and she had deliberately inserted poisonous packets while pretending to honor her oath to her patients.

I wanted—desperately—to believe that Carter had blackmailed her. That she felt she had no choice. Except she wasn't someone bound by impossible conditions. Not her, not a qualified surgeon at a well-respected hospital. Though the *Post* didn't mention names, I knew the patients. She had wept after each one. She had gone on to murder more.

Sara was dead, but I could honestly mourn her, my friend, the Hound of Justice.

Not Nina. Maybe later, I could separate the woman who once cared so deeply about her patients from the woman who inserted those deadly packets.

Or not. I'll think about that later. I'm too angry right now.

I wiped more tears from my eyes.

I had believed—dear god, how hard I had believed—back in April, when Micha first told me about our mission, that we would free Sa'id and save the world.

We had. Oh, sure, we were still a nation divided. We were still faced with a hole in the heart of our country, in spirit as well as territory. And Donnovan wasn't the glorious light of liberty so many of us wanted. But in the end, we had stopped Nadine Adler. We had saved the Federal States from chaos.

I just had not known how much our victory would cost.

25

Another day, another surgery.

"Ready to close," I said. "Checklist, please."

RN Patwary counted off the sponges and instruments on the tray by name, her voice clear in spite of the surgical mask. RN Tayac followed up with his own count. All their numbers matched each other and the original. No discrepancies, then. Good.

"Suture and needle, first phase."

Patwary had the threaded needle ready, of course. I'd observed her work before. She was steady and competent, and not afraid to state an opinion. Considering her thirty years of experience, I was glad about that.

Layer by layer, each one needing a different pattern, a different kind of suture, I stitched the incision closed. Gunshot wounds were tricky, especially ones requiring the spleen removed and part of the small intestine sliced and reconnected. In spite of all the restrictions on guns and other weapons, DC had seen an uptick in illegal firearm injuries these past few months.

The Brotherhood?

Or, in spite of their protestations, the New Confederacy?

Useless speculation at this point. I focused my attention on my patient, a forty-year-old white male named Joshua Zimmerman. My left and right hands moved with my every thought, as though both were connected by nerves and muscle, and not one by electrodes and wires. Lazarus . . .

Gone were the strange sensations I'd experienced in Oklahoma. Sydney had examined Lazarus thoroughly when I described the deadness, the heaviness. (Though I left out any mention of how I'd felt immersed in flames.) Possible electric overload, she'd said. She'd gone over and recalibrated every node, every sensor.

Though I'd stopped thinking of my left arm as a thing apart, the name still sounded right to me, even more than before. We had both truly come back to life.

Surgery done. Patient closed.

I glanced toward the stats board. All vital signs good, considering. The next few hours would tell.

"Take him to Recovery," I said.

Patwary and Tayac handed Zimmerman over to the orderlies. I blew out a deep breath and rotated my shoulders. Five hours, mostly because of the damage to the intestines.

Chong and Bekker stood off to one side of the OR. Up in the tiny observation booth, Sydney was tapping furiously on her keyboard, no doubt making notes for our next drill session. She gave me a quick thumbs-up, which I returned. Sydney had warned me, back when Hernandez first reinstated me as a surgeon, that Hernandez had ordered her to monitor my surgeries. Just a precaution, Sydney had added.

Precaution my fat ass.

In truth, I had not cared. My true test had taken place weeks ago, in the fields of Oklahoma.

Outside the OR, I peeled off my surgical costume and

changed into fresh scrubs. Chong had that *I've got questions* expression that promised a vigorous debate about surgical techniques. However, a world of electronic forms and documentation awaited me, including extra treats from the DC police force. I told Chong to meet me after our shift, then headed up the stairs to my office.

I was halfway there when my cell chimed for an incoming message.

Please come to my office ASAP. EHernandez.

Oh Christ. I exited the stairwell at the next landing and took the elevator to the fourth floor. As I hurried down the corridor to Hernandez's office, a part of me was ranting under my breath, about how I had fulfilled every goddamned requirement, and several more beyond that, and why on God's green earth were you hounding me like this, woman?

Hernandez's executive assistant was at her desk. She greeted me with a cheery smile. "Dr. Hernandez is expecting you. Go right in, please."

Nothing in her tone or expression came across as ominous. I managed a smile in return and went through the doors.

Hernandez noted my entrance with the barest of nods. "Good news," she said. "The ICCC contacted me this morning. They'd like you to present an extended version of your synopsis at the conference. I wanted to give you the good news in person."

She paused. Protocol said I ought to thank her profusely for her encouragement, but Hernandez was studying me with a frown.

"Is something wrong?" I said.

Hernandez shook her head. "No, I . . . That is, I was wrong. Then I was almost wrong again, except you helped me avoid that by submitting your extract directly to the conference. I would have recommended a different topic. Something politically safer." Her mouth tucked into a wry smile at the word *politically*.

Ah, yes. Hospital gossip said President Donnovan had dropped Hernandez's name from the list of potential candidates for the HHS position. Gossip also said the search for two more surgeons to replace Carter and Letova had stalled. Too many potential candidates didn't want to connect their names and careers to a hospital in the news for all the wrong reasons. Navarette in particular believed the board might pressure Hernandez to resign.

"Thank you," I said at last. "I appreciate your kind words."

"Thank *you*," Hernandez said. "I'll forward you the info packet for the conference, as well as the guidelines for your presentation. You'll need to submit your completed paper by August fifteenth . . ."

We reviewed my schedule for the next month. Hernandez asked about Chong and Bekker, and whether I would take on another student or two. Neither of us mentioned Carter's trial, nor Nina's suicide.

Carter blackmailed her, Navarette had told me. *Her brother owed money. He started running drugs for his dealer. Carter said she would turn him over to the police if Nina didn't cooperate. Though how Carter ever found out about the drugs, I don't know.*

Because the Brotherhood made it their business to find out. Because someone else, some other larger, more powerful organization, wanted the Brotherhood to succeed. But I hadn't told Navarette my suspicions, because talking about the Brotherhood meant talking about the New Confederacy and Nadine Adler, subjects both too secret and too painful.

⚲

The promised info packet waited in my message queue, along with the raw video and diagnostic records from Zimmerman's operation. Avoiding the inevitable forms work, I clicked open the info packet and skimmed the requirements for presentations. *Speaker slots are limited to thirty minutes, including Q & A. Requests for audiovisual equipment must be submitted with the final text of your presentation.* Yeah, yeah, yeah.

I was already making mental notes on how and where to expand my abstract when I came to the section about hotels and meals. No need for a hotel, with my living in the city. And the breakfast/lunch package looked truly awful, not to mention expensive. Then a paragraph near the end caught my attention:

First Night Banquet, Seven-Course meal created by Master Chef Sophie Santini. Tickets $200/guest. Each conference speaker receives two tickets for themselves and a guest. RSVP by July 1.

Huh. That was a major perk. Even I had heard of Master Chef Santini.

Sara would love this dinner. Exquisite food and exquisite snark.

My breath caught. The next moment I was weeping silently.

Goddammit. I thought I'd run out of tears weeks ago. Apparently not. Grief kept catching me up with memories of Sara—Sara plucking herbs from her miniature garden as she cooked. Sara with her feet on the coffee table, smoking a clove cigarette and expounding on politics, literature, or music. Sara running her fingers over the keyboard of her piano. Sara, the imp of mischief, eyeing me with glee over a cup of coffee after she'd driven me into exasperation.

Live, my love. Live and laugh.

The memory came to me in Sara's voice and for a moment my throat squeezed shut.

Easy for you to say, I thought. Then laughed painfully. But what if . . . What if I dared to survive, as Faith Bellaume once said in response to my rage and grief? What if I dared to live a life whole?

I pulled out my cell and tapped the number I had tried to forget and could not. Adanna Jones answered within the first ring.

"Hello, Rainbow Books . . . Oh. It's you."

Her voice was quick and breathy. Impossible to read anything from that.

I took a deep breath and jumped into my fate. "Hi," I said. "I just wanted—I mean—Are you busy September fifteenth?"

Now she laughed, though more like a laugh of relief. "I have no idea. Why?"

"I'm giving a presentation at a medical conference. In September. There's a banquet the first night. Master Chef Santini, very fancy. And . . . I wondered if you would like to go."

She didn't answer at first, and I felt a weight of questions in that silence.

"I'm sorry," I said in a rush. "I shouldn't have bothered you—"

"No, wait! Janet, please." She breathed an audible sigh. "Oh, Janet. I'm sorry. It's just you surprised me. Thank you. I would like to go to this banquet." Then in a softer voice, "I missed you."

"I missed you, too. And . . . Oh god, I need someone to write better dialogue for me."

Adanna laughed again, a low and easy laugh that seemed to ripple through my body. "Hey, girl," she said. "You sound like you need a night out. Are you free tonight? I know where a good band is playing."

The auditorium of the Washington Hilton stretched out before me, all dark velvet and sumptuous chairs. Lights illuminated the steps winding around both sides of the hall, picking out the blue and silver in the carpet. Ordinary members of the conference occupied the central section. Honored visitors watched from balconies on either side of the podium. The first row had been reserved for speakers and their guests.

I glanced at the digital clock next to the speaker's stand. With a tap on the podium's holo-keyboard, I brought up the last page and paragraphs of my speech. I'd written six different versions of this section. Esma Hernandez had argued for a kinder, gentler conclusion. I had refused.

Adanna Jones sat in the front row, among the other guests and next to my own empty chair. Her gaze met mine, and she gave me that small and secretive smile I had come to know these past few weeks.

I took a deep breath, felt a flutter beneath my ribs, and continued.

"Politics," I said, "in short, isn't just a section in the feeds and squirts. It's not just a topic for conversation. It's woven through every facet of our lives, including medicine. Politics drives our decisions about which diseases to research, which ones aren't important. It determines where we allocate our time, our doctors, and our funding.

"It decides who lives, and who dies."

I paused, just long enough to take a deep breath.

"We will never have enough money, or people, or time. But we have compassion. We have our oath to our patients. That is the politics we should serve. Thank you."

The auditorium went silent as the audience digested my words, and while I considered the wisdom in calling out the medical establishment. Then, Adanna Jones began to clap. Another person, farther in the back, joined in, the scattered applause gradually building up to echo throughout the hall.

By the time the room had quieted, the speaker's clock had ticked to zero. The speakers' coordinator signaled me to leave the podium. "If you are available tomorrow," she said, "I'd like to schedule a Q & A session with you and a few other panelists."

"Of course," I replied distractedly. "Text me later with the time."

Three more people interrupted me on my way back to my seat, asking if I would consider speaking at their conference or association. I handed over my business card and accepted theirs, simply to get them out of my way. At long last I regained my seat next to Adanna and collapsed with a sigh.

"Well done, *ma brave*," she murmured.

She clasped my hand in hers. I pressed my forehead against hers, then attempted to give my attention to the next speaker.

But God and the heavens weren't done with dealing me challenges, apparently. As Adanna and I headed toward the banquet hall after the last presentation, a familiar voice called out to me.

"Janet, Janet!"

Angela Gray emerged from the crowd.

Oh god. Not here. Not now.

My once beloved paused a few feet away. A part of me registered the many small and subtle changes. Her face thinner, sharper, as if the years had etched away the softness. Her hair with a sheen of gold and braided in an intricate pattern. Very sleek, very professional.

"Hello, Angela," I managed to say.

I noticed another woman—shorter, rounder, her hair cascading in soft curls—hovering behind Angela and felt another pinch in my gut as I recognized her face from the wedding announcement in Howard University's alumni newsletter. This was Maggie, Angela's wife.

Our conversation, such as it was, sputtered and died.

Adanna came to my rescue and held out a hand. "So pleased to meet you," she said. "I'm Adanna Jones, Janet's friend. She's told me a great deal about you."

Angela blinked, then her mouth quirked into a smile, and once more I saw the old Angela. "Oh dear. Yes. I can imagine that."

They shook hands. All very polite, very professional. Angela introduced Maggie, then she turned to me. "Janet, I goddamn loved your speech. You gave a badly needed shakeup to this conference. And I hope . . . I hope you keeping kicking butt as hard at Georgetown as you did at Howard."

Code words for *I'm sorry I hurt you. Please don't be angry with me.*

Except that wasn't fair. I'd volunteered for the service without even talking to Angela about my decision. I had run away from her gifts for years, until I finally, truly ran away from her. Angela had simply recognized the truth sooner than I did.

I held out my hands, clasped both her hers in mine. "Thank you," I said softly. "I expect you to do the same."

The banquet was glorious. Afterward, there was dancing.

Later, much later, Adanna and I walked along the brick sidewalks of Georgetown, through the warm September night. A breeze, soft and damp, washed over my face, and the sidewalks gleamed, wet from the morning's rain. The air was filled with the scents of damp earth, of moldering leaves, and of Adanna's spicy perfume.

We came to 2809 Q Street. All the windows were dark. If anyone watched us, two black women in this very upscale neighborhood, I saw no sign of it. Even so, there were other watchers.

"I would like to invite you up to my apartment," I said. "But the neighbors . . ."

"Nosey, are they?" she asked.

I considered the recording devices inside the apartment, still active as far as I knew. The watchers on the outside, those from the FBI or CIA, as well as the perimeter guard Sara's grandmother had insisted on. "That's one way to put it."

"Oh?"

We'd come to that moment again. All those unspoken questions she had about that night I appeared in her bookshop, so obviously distressed, about the headlines in the newsfeeds, about Sara's absence—those had hovered, palpable, at the edge of our conversations these past few weeks.

I took both her hands in mine. "I will never lie to you," I said. "But I cannot answer all your questions. I can't even tell you why. Those secrets are not mine to give away."

She tilted her head. "I won't say I understand, but . . . I do believe you."

Live. Live and love.

I leaned forward and brushed my lips against hers. She gave a throaty chuckle, then wrapped her arms around me and pulled me into a deeper kiss. Later, later, when I signed the papers on my new apartment, the one newly painted to my specifications and with none of those goddamned miniblinds, then we would do far more than kiss.

Eventually we ran out of air. Adanna pulled back, kissed me lightly. "I should get home, Dr. Watson."

"Let me walk you to the Metro stop."

Onward through the starlit night. One last kiss. A date made for tomorrow once the conference ended.

Back to 2809 Q, up the stairs, and into 2B.

I touched the light switch in the entryway. Breathed in the scent of wood polish. Caught a whiff of roses.

Sara's favorite perfume. Perhaps memory is that strong.

But then I saw the enormous porcelain vase on the parlor's coffee table. A vase stuffed so full of roses that they overflowed onto the table. Roses so dark a red that they were almost black, and their scent drenched the air. My nerves lit with apprehension.

I cautiously circled the table. Saw a white square tucked among the petals.

Congratulations, said the gold script on the envelope. Another gift from Adanna? Not likely. Adanna had already had a bouquet of white roses delivered to my office earlier that day. Never mind that she had no way to get into the building, much less this apartment. I opened the envelope and extracted the stiff white card.

To Dr. Watson, Best wishes in all your endeavors.

No signature, no name. Not Adanna. Not Angela. Who would leave such a mysterious message for me? And how did they get into my apartment?

There could be only one person . . .

Hardly daring to hope, I ran my fingertips over the card and found the faint bumps on the back of it. I pressed hard.

My love, my friend. I cannot apologize for my silence, so I shall not. I can only tell you that I am with friends, doing good deeds in parts unknown. Some of those deeds are even permitted. Thank you for your courage and your honor. Will write again when I have news. —Hound

I released my breath and realized I was trembling.

Sara. Sara alive. And Micha, too, because who else could

infiltrate this building and this apartment in spite of all the watchers.

The ink shimmered, re-formed into a new message.

PRESS ME, IDIOT.

Right. No use leaving evidence lying around.

I pressed the upper right corner of the card to disappear Sara's message. Then I tucked a rose in my hair and headed for my bed and dreams of Adanna Jones.

ACKNOWLEDGMENTS

Writing a novel can be a lonely business. You sit (figuratively) alone in your head and dream up people who don't exist. You wrestle with plot knots and character motivations. You research medical terms, or languages, or the phase of the moon on a certain date. You lie awake at night wondering if you forgot some key detail, or worse, got that detail wrong.

But then, you also have friends who help you along the way. Many, many thanks to . . .

Tempest Bradford and Nisi Shawl, and their workshops about Writing the Other.

Delia Sherman, Heather Rose Jones, and Paul Weimer, for your sharp-eyed commentary.

My editor, Amber Oliver, for her on-point suggestions that made my story stronger and better.

Aja Pollock, whose copy edits and queries saved me from all kinds of embarrassing mistakes.

Chris McGrath, for creating yet another brilliant cover

that is true to the story and to my characters. Have I mentioned recently how much I love your work?

Caro Perny, publicist extraordinaire, and the rest of the team at Harper Voyager, for all their hard work in turning my manuscript into a real book, then making sure people knew about it.

And not the least, to my son and husband for all your support.

Insights,
Interviews
& More . . .

About the author

About the book

Read on

Meet Claire O'Dell

Rob Bernobich

CLAIRE O'DELL grew up in the suburbs of Washington, DC, in the years of the Vietnam War and the Watergate scandal. She attended high school just a few miles from the house where Mary Surratt once lived and where John Wilkes Booth conspired to kill Lincoln. All this might explain why she spent so much time in the history and political science departments at college. Claire currently lives in Manchester, Connecticut, with her family and two idiosyncratic cats.

On Writing
Janet Watson

THE SEEDS for this book came from an
online discussion of fan fiction. I had
never tried writing fan fiction before,
but I've always loved the Sherlock
Holmes stories. I've read a few stories
that showed different takes on Watson
and Holmes, and of course I knew about
Sherlock and *Elementary*. But one thing
bothered me. Holmes was always a
man. I thought, what if Holmes were a
woman? What if they both were? And
why did either one have to be white?
And then I had the image of Watson
returning home from a war.

Her whole life has crashed. She's
weary and bitter and suffering badly
from PTSD. But she isn't going to give
up, dammit. That's when I had to write
her story. The book took me several
drafts and eight months to write, mostly
on the weekends. (I work full-time as
a web developer.) I chose Washington,
DC, for the location of the book because
I grew up in the suburbs, not far from
Suitland, Maryland, where Janet grew
up, and my high school was half a mile
from the house where Mary Surratt once
lived, and where John Wilkes Booth
died. Janet's story is one of politics and
race because of where I grew up. It's one
of gender because of who I am. ∾

An Excerpt from
A Study in Honor

"Captain? Dr. Watson? Is that you?"

A lean and knobby black man limped toward me and reached out a hand. I flinched back, still tangled up in my earlier panic.

His smile flickered upward and then faded at my silence. "Do you remember me?" he said.

His face was a study in brown, crisscrossed with old scars. His hair was a grizzled gray and covered his skull in patches. It was the combination of the limp and the scars that reminded me who he was. Jacob. Corporal Jacob Bell. He had transferred to our medical unit and served as my assistant before taking a disability discharge.

"I remember," I said. "I'm sorry—"

"It doesn't matter, Captain. I understand."

To be sure, he would. He had been captured by the enemy and tortured. He had escaped on his own, but some things you could never leave behind.

"How you doing these days?" I said.

"Good enough, Captain. Busy. Not nearly as busy as I was in the service, though." He paused, and I could see the many, many questions he wanted to ask.

"I know a tasty diner," he said at last. "I'm hungry. Are you?"

To my surprise, I was.

I nodded. "Lead on, Corporal."

His tasty diner was a restaurant in the U Street corridor that specialized in Greek dishes. We ordered an enormous plate of feta cheese and hot peppers to share, then a second one of baked phyllo stuffed with roasted lamb and spinach. There were hot tea, cold water, and an abundance of food of the kind and quality I had dreamed about in Illinois. For a while I could do nothing but eat. Jacob did not trouble me. He understood the need to devour food when we had the opportunity. Eventually, however, we both slowed and I could take in my surroundings and my companion. I refilled my water glass. Jacob poured tea for us both.

"You surprised me," I told him. "Popping up like a rabbit the way you did. What happened to going back home to Maine?"

His hesitation was brief but said a lot. "Times be hard, Captain. You know how it goes. The job they were holding for me went to someone else. And . . . other things were harder. Anyway, I ended up in DC. The VA found me a job in the medical center. Orderly. It's not my first choice, but they added a student loan for a local tech college to sweeten things. I go to classes there afternoons and evenings. You?"

"I do well enough," I said. "It's early days, but . . ." With an effort, I expelled a breath and found I could almost smile. "I need money. I want to stay in the city a few months or so. They said they might find me a new arm."

Jacob simply nodded. "Might be. Could be."

Neither of us mentioned the waiting lists, or the cuts in funding that made those waiting lists even longer. ▸

An Excerpt from *A Study in Honor*
(continued)

We fell silent over the remains of our lunchtime feast. The waitress brought us a second pot of tea and our bill, with the murmured addendum that we need not rush. We didn't. I was grateful for this chance meeting with an old friend. Jacob too seemed glad for the unhurried meal and the conversation that followed.

"You want a job," he said eventually. "And a better place than that hostel."

I had described my room to him—a bit too vividly, no doubt.

"The problem is money," I said.

"It always is. But maybe I can help. I know someone . . ." He glanced around. "Not sure if she's right for you, though."

"She?"

He shrugged. "A friend of mine. She's not service, but she's not so bad."

I waited, knowing there was more.

"She's . . . particular about things," he went on. "Some might call her difficult, but she has her good points, too. I happen to know she's looking for a partner to split rent on some rooms."

My throat went dry with a sudden and all-too-familiar panic. A stranger. Someone to witness my nightmares, to stare at my missing arm while pretending not to. It was difficult enough in the hostel.

Jacob was watching me with that same kindly smile I remembered from our time in the service, on the days when blood and death became too much for me to bear. A smile that spoke of understanding and not pity.

"You can always say no," he said.

"That I could." My voice came out shakier than I liked. "When do you think I could meet her?"

"Today, if you like. I know where to find her on Saturdays."

No, no, that was much too soon. I needed time—

The panic rushed back, stronger than before. I shut my eyes and gripped the edge of my seat. Usually I could pinpoint the cause. The bang of a car engine that recalled the explosions of war. The touch of a stranger, which yanked me back to that struggle with enemy soldiers as I tried to save my patients. This . . . this was less easy to identify. So I breathed deeply and steadily until the panic subsided.

When I opened my eyes, Jacob appeared to be studying the bill.

"Let's go," I whispered.

He paid the bill over my protests. I retaliated with a generous tip.

"You say you know where to find her?" I asked once we had exited the diner.

"Always. Or, always when she's in the city."

"Then she has rooms now. What happened? Did she secretly murder her former roommate?"

Jacob laughed softly and shook his head. "Not that I've ever heard. No, she lived with friends who had a house in Alexandria. A temporary thing, she said. But then her friends took jobs on the West Coast, and Sara wanted to stay in DC. She found a new set of rooms. They cost more than she likes to pay, but ▶

she's decided she has to have this apartment and no other. As I said, she's particular."

"Sara." I repeated the name to myself. "Sara what?"

"Holmes. We met last year. In a movie theater, if you can believe that. She kept cursing up and down about the soundtrack. Which I can tell you was awful, but still. Making that kind of ruckus does no good. I told her to take her noisy self to see the manager, or if she couldn't do that, she ought to buy me a drink. She bought me a drink, then argued with me the whole time."

I laughed. "But you like her."

He smiled back, somewhat ruefully. "As much as she lets me, yes. We talk now and then. Now and then, she buys me a drink. For old times' sake, she says. She knows a fair bit about the service, for all that she's never served." He indicated the crosswalk, where the pedestrian signal blinked green. "Let's turn here. Less traffic this way."

"Where are we going?"

"National Gallery. She likes to spend her Saturdays there, when she can."

We followed R Street east a few blocks, then turned south again onto Ninth, avoiding the tide of Labor Day weekend tourists and the high-security zone around the White House. Drones passed by overhead, marking the outlying borders of that zone. They were thicker in the air than before—a precaution against those latest threats from the New

Confederates? Or more of the same from those days when ISIS and al-Qaeda sent their suicide bombers to our shores, when right-wing protesters from within our own country turned violent and presidents could not rely on their own security details?

On the ground, the telephone poles carried signs for the upcoming election. Posters for Jeb Foley and Roy Donnovan were plastered over those of their old opponents from the primaries. Another businessman turned politician, running on the Independent ticket. There were even a few digital signs for the Communist Party, which some prankster had rewired to read Ellison, Obama, and Booker. Two months and a couple days until the vote. I had hardly thought about the elections before now. War and surgery had consumed all my thoughts. Then came the invasion and my own personal combat to regain myself. Foley and his conservative friends were easy to reject. They hated me and mine, and only a couple of steps separated them from the New Confederacy, as far as I could see. Donnovan . . . was a more difficult pill to swallow. A white man, a straight white man with a history of voting the Centrist Party line, with one or two progressive causes he favored. I understood why Sanches had taken him for her VP, but as president?

At Constitution, we turned back east to the main entrance to the National Gallery. Every spring my teachers had organized a trip to the Mall to see the cherry blossoms. Every autumn, my parents had insisted on a visit to ▶

the Museum of Natural History or the
Museum of African Art. If Grace and I
were extra well behaved, they added the
Air and Space Museum to the list.

I miss them. I wish . . .

I wished I'd had the prescience to take
a break after the all-consuming years of
medical school and my residency. But
there were so few doctors and so many
casualties. As the war continued into
Sanches's second term and Congress
debated whether to undo civil rights
for all those people who'd been told
they were less than equal because of the
color of their skin or gender they loved,
just to placate the New Confederacy, I
told myself that it was my duty to serve.
There would be time enough after my
tour of duty ended.

Then came a letter from the State
Department, informing me of what I
already knew from the newsfeeds—
that my parents had died along with
hundreds of others when terrorists
from the New Confederacy bombed
the Atlanta airport. Then a letter
from my grandmother, insisting I quit
the military, as if she could rule the
government as she had once ruled our
family. The even more formal letter
from my sister's lawyer, dividing our
inheritance.

And then, and then . . .

And then came the bloody dawn, with
thousands of rebel soldiers overrunning
the front lines. The frantic broadcasts
from the camp radio tower, broken off

with the first explosion, and the even more frantic hours that followed as I and the other surgeons attempted to carry our patients to safety.

***

We climbed the broad steps to the National Gallery's marble portico and into the rotunda with its black tiled floor and the fountain of silver-veined stone. Cool air fell over me like rainwater as we passed through wide corridors to a staircase leading down to the lower level. After that came a series of smaller rooms with paintings from the twentieth century, then a longer gallery dedicated to works by French and Belgian masters. At last we arrived in a small chamber anchored by two marble statues in opposite corners, and a grand sweep of canvas against the far wall.

Dalí's *Sacrament of the Last Supper*.

I was no Christian, not these days. But, oh, those luminous colors. The images upon images. The small trickeries my teachers had pointed out that added layers of story to the most obvious and outermost one. It almost didn't matter that the Son of Man, a child of Israel and the King of the Jews, was portrayed as a pale-skinned man with yellow hair.

Fuck it, I'm lying. It *did* matter, the same way it rankled when people— mostly white people—stared when I said I was a doctor, a surgeon, and a veteran of the wars. But I could still look beyond the unthinking bigotry of this particular artist, and the assumptions of his age, to the moment he portrayed, when Christ drank the wine and spoke of his body ▶

An Excerpt from *A Study in Honor*
(continued)

and his blood. I shivered and passed a hand over my eyes.

Only then did I notice a woman standing in the corner.

She was tall and lean. Her complexion was the darkest brown I had ever seen, the angles of her face were sharp enough to cut, and she wore her hair in locs, arranged in a careless, complicated fashion wound around her head, then plaited and pinned, so they fell in a thick cascade down her back. The cant of her cheekbones, the almost imperceptible folds next to her eyes, spoke of East Asia, or certain nations in Africa. Of a world outside my own.

And she was wealthy. I could tell by the clothes she wore. Loose trousers cut in the latest fashion, and a thin sleeveless shirt made from an ivory cloth, gleaming bright as sunlight and shot through with gold threads. A few pearls were visible among her locs.

Holmes's expression was contained, but I had the distinct impression she was amused. "Bell," she said, her voice rough and low. "What have you brought me?"

"A friend," Jacob said. "Sara Holmes, my friend Dr. Janet Watson. Shake hands, Sara. I know you can."

Sara laughed, a laugh that matched her voice. We closed the distance between us, then both of us hesitated. I sensed a Rubicon before me, an array of choices wise or foolish. Gaius Julius Caesar had made his own choice in that matter and died. Or perhaps I was being fanciful.

Then Holmes reached out to me with a hand covered in lace. "You've come from the war in Oklahoma," she said, and clasped my hand in hers.

My pulse jumped. Of course, I told myself, she would see my metal arm and recognize that I was a wounded vet.

"Hardly a difficult guess," I said. "Unless you stopped reading the newsfeeds."

Sill holding my hand, she regarded me with an amused expression. "True. I don't need this"—here she lifted her other hand, also gloved, and twisted it around—"to make that deduction."

Light glittered off the metallic lace, changing the pale gold to threads of silver. Even in the muddy fields of Alton, we'd heard about this newest offering in network connectivity. I spotted the tiny earbuds that confirmed my guess, and just behind them, the small black discs that implied permanent implants. If she could afford this kind of advanced technology, why did she need someone to share the rent?

"You like my toys?" Holmes said.

My stomach lurched. Not so much at her words, but the attitude behind them. I knew the likes of her from medical school—rich and privileged and mocking those beneath them.

"No," I replied evenly. "I do not like them."

Now she was smiling. "I'm not surprised, Dr. Watson. But my toys tell me you graduated second in your class at Howard University. You finished your residency with honors. And you had three offers within the week, all very good ▶

positions as a surgeon. You even had a lover, with lucrative offers of her own in the city. Yet you decided to enlist in the army."

I was sweating, but I knew the cause this time.

"I joined because I wished to," I said. "And I am not afraid of your toys."

She regarded me with wide bright eyes, eyes the color of a midnight sky, flecked with molten copper. "Maybe not. But you are afraid, nevertheless. You have been, since long before the New Civil War and the Shame of Alton. That missing arm terrifies you, Dr. Watson. But not as much as the terror you felt that you could never truly succeed, even with the best arm in the world."

I tried to draw a breath and found no air to fill my lungs. Dimly, I heard Jacob Bell scolding Holmes, but I could not get my throat and tongue to cooperate. A hand clasped my arm. I felt something brush against my leg. Abruptly I broke away and ran back through the corridor. Someone—Jacob—called after me. I rounded a corner into a nest of smaller exhibit rooms, then went to the stairs leading up.

But I could not face the city streets and all those strangers. Not yet. I ducked through to another hall and found a marble bench where I could sit and gather my shreds of courage. To my relief, the hall was empty. I bent over double, arms clasped around my knees, waiting for the thundering in my skull to die down. From a distance came the echo of voices—tourists arguing over their next stop. Then a set of footsteps, as sharp as nails on the tiled floor, approached the nearby entryway. I waited, sick and apprehensive, but no one entered. No one spoke to me.

The footsteps retreated. Gradually the quiet returned. Much more gradually, my pulse slowed and I found my breath again.

God. Dear goddamned God with your so-called love that does not include me or mine. What the everlasting fuck were you thinking to bring me and her together?

God was a trickster, my father used to say. If so, then Sara Holmes could be its manifestation, cruel and capricious.

The image of Holmes as God's trickster called up laughter, however weak. I rubbed my hand over my face. Poor Jacob, the unwilling witness to that scene. I would have to track him down later and apologize. Not here in the museum, though. Not where Sara Holmes might still be lurking. Best to leave now before I encountered her again.

As I pushed myself to my feet, an unfamiliar weight bumped against my leg. What the hell? I scrambled away, but the thing bumped me again, dragging at one of my pockets. Then I remembered that scuffle, the hand clasping my arm, the brush against my trousers. *Holmes, goddamn it.*

As if it could hear my thoughts, the thing burst into a loud staccato buzz. Swearing under my breath, I fumbled inside the pocket. My hand closed ▶

over a small flat rectangle that vibrated angrily. A cell phone?

I extracted the device, which immediately stopped vibrating. The thing was the size of an old-fashioned playing card and almost as thin. Made from some kind of silvery metal that felt warm to my touch. It continued to buzz, but more quietly. I ran my thumb over its surface, then along the edges. No buttons, recessed or otherwise. Then I remembered reading about the new voice-activated screens. "Holmes," I said. "Is that you?"

The buzzing stopped. The center of the object transformed from silver to black. Amber text flowed over its surface.

I am sorry. I have the bad habit of showing off, as Jacob will confirm. However, my tendencies do not excuse the hurt I've caused.

The address is 2809 Q Street NW. Your better judgment will no doubt send you back to your hostel room, there to seek quarters less troubling. If by chance you decide to meet the challenge, however, I've instructed the rental agency to send a representative to meet us at 3 p.m. Whatever you choose, I would suggest you take the job with the VA Medical Center.

Regards and Regrets, Sara Holmes

I choked back a laugh, then rubbed my hand over my face, which felt numb from the lingering rage. Difficult, Jacob had called her. Impossible was more like it. However genuine the apology, I could foresee more episodes like this one if we lived in the same apartment.

The text dissolved into a new message: **Are you afraid?**

"Damn you," I whispered. "Damn you to hell, Sara Holmes." ❧

Discover great authors, exclusive offers, and more at hc.com.